KT-119-789

HIS UNTIL MIDNIGHT

REESE RYAN

THE RIVAL'S HEIR

JOSS WOOD

MIX

Paper from
responsible sources

FSC

FSC C007454

This book is produced from independently certified FSC™
paper to ensure responsible forest management.

For more information visit: www.harpercollins.co.uk/green

Printed and bound in Spain
by CPI, Barcelona

MILLS & BOON

All rights reserved including the right of reproduction in whole or in part in any form. This edition is published by arrangement with Harlequin Books S.A.

This is a work of fiction. Names, characters, places, locations and incidents are purely fictional and bear no relationship to any real life individuals, living or dead, or to any actual places, business establishments, locations, events or incidents. Any resemblance is entirely coincidental.

This book is sold subject to the condition that it shall not, by way of trade or otherwise, be lent, resold, hired out or otherwise circulated without the prior consent of the publisher in any form of binding or cover other than that in which it is published and without a similar condition including this condition being imposed on the subsequent purchaser.

® and ™ are trademarks owned and used by the trademark owner and/or its licensee. Trademarks marked with ® are registered with the United Kingdom Patent Office and/or the Office for Harmonisation in the Internal Market and in other countries.

First Published in Great Britain 2018
by Mills & Boon, an imprint of HarperCollinsPublishers,
1 London Bridge Street, London, SE1 9GF

His Until Midnight © 2018 Harlequin Books S.A.
The Rival's Heir © 2018 Joss Wood

Special thanks and acknowledgement are given to Reese Ryan for her contribution to the Texas Cattleman's Club: Bachelor Auction series.

ISBN: 978-0-263-93629-2

1218

MORAY COUNCIL
LIBRARIES &
INFO.SERVICES

20 45 68 24

Askews & Holts	
RF	

HIS UNTIL MIDNIGHT

REESE RYAN

To Johnathan Royal, Stephanie Perkins,
Jennifer Copeland, Denise Stokes, Sharon Blount,
Stephanie Douglas-Quick and all of the amazing
readers in the Reese Ryan VIP Readers Lounge
on Facebook. Seriously, y'all rock!
I appreciate your readership, engagement,
enthusiasm and continued support.
Thank you to each and every one of you!

To my infinitely patient and ever-insightful editor,
Charles Griemsman, thank you for all you do.

One

Tessa Noble stared at the configuration of high and low balls scattered on the billiard table.

"I'm completely screwed," she muttered, sizing up her next move. After a particularly bad break and distracted play, she was losing badly.

But how on earth could she be expected to concentrate on billiards when her best friend Ryan Bateman was wearing a fitted performance T-shirt that highlighted every single pectoral muscle and his impressive biceps. He could have, at the very least, worn a shirt that fit, instead of one that was a size too small, as a way to purposely enhance his muscles. And the view when he bent over the table in a pair of broken-in jeans that hugged his firm ass like they were made for it…

How in the hell was she expected to play her best?

"You're not screwed," Ryan said in a deep, husky

voice that was as soothing as a warm bath. Three parts sex-in-a-glass and one part confidence out the wazoo.

Tessa's cheeks heated, inexplicably. Like she was a middle schooler giggling over double entendres and sexual innuendo.

"Maybe not, but you'd sure as hell like to be screwed by your best friend over there," Gail Walker whispered in her ear before taking another sip of her beer.

Tessa elbowed her friend in the ribs, and the woman giggled, nearly shooting beer out of her nose.

Gail, always a little too direct, lacked a filter after a second drink.

Tessa walked around the billiard table, pool cue in hand, assessing her options again while her opponent huffed restlessly. Finally, she shook her head and sighed. "You obviously see something I don't, because I don't see a single makeable shot."

Ryan sidled closer, his movements reminiscent of a powerful jungle cat stalking prey. His green eyes gleamed even in the dim light of the bar.

"You're underestimating yourself, Tess," Ryan murmured. "Just shut out all the noise, all the doubts, and focus."

She studied the table again, tugging her lower lip between her teeth, before turning back to him. "Ryan, I clearly don't have a shot."

"Go for the four ball." He nodded toward the purple ball wedged between two of her opponent's balls.

Tessa sucked in a deep breath and gripped the pool cue with one hand. She pressed her other hand to the table, formed a bridge and positioned the stick between her thumb and forefinger, gliding it back and forth.

But the shot just wasn't there.

"I can't make this shot." She turned to look at him. "Maybe you could, but I can't."

"That's because you're too tight, and your stance is all wrong." Ryan studied her for a moment, then placed his hands on either side of her waist and shifted her a few inches. "Now you're lined up with the ball. That should give you a better sight line."

Tessa's eyes drifted closed momentarily as she tried to focus on the four ball, rather than the lingering heat from Ryan's hands. Or his nearness as he hovered over her.

She opened them again and slid the cue back and forth between her fingers, deliberating the position and pace of her shot.

"Wait." Ryan leaned over beside her. He slipped an arm around her waist and gripped the stick a few inches above where she clenched it. He stared straight ahead at the ball, his face inches from hers. "Loosen your grip on the cue. This is a finesse shot, so don't try to muscle it. Just take it easy and smack the cue ball right in the center, and you've got this. Okay?"

"Okay." Tessa nodded, staring at the center of the white ball. She released a long breath, pulled back the cue and hit the cue ball dead in the center, nice and easy.

The cue ball connected with the four ball with a smack. The purple ball rolled toward the corner pocket and slowed, teetering on the edge. But it had just enough momentum to carry it over into the pocket.

"Yes!" Tessa squealed, smacking Ryan's raised palm to give him a high five. "You're amazing. You actually talked me through it."

"You did all the work. I was just your cheering section." He winked in that way that made her tummy flutter.

"Well, thank you." She smiled. "I appreciate it."

"What are best friends for?" He shrugged, picking up his beer and taking a sip from the bottle.

"Thought I was playing Tess," Roy Jensen grumbled. "Nobody said anything about y'all tag-teaming me."

"Oh, quit complaining, you old coot." Tessa stared down her opponent. "I always turn a blind eye when you ask for spelling help when we're playing Scrabble."

Roy's cheeks tinged pink, and he mumbled under his breath as Tessa moved around the table, deciding which shot to take next. She moved toward the blue two ball.

"Hey, Ryan." Lana, the way-too-friendly barmaid, sidled up next to him, her chest thrust forward and a smile as wide as the Rio Grande spread across her face. "Thought you might want another beer."

"Why thank you, kindly." Ryan tipped an imaginary hat and returned the grin as he accepted the bottle.

Tessa clenched her jaw, a burning sensation in her chest. She turned to her friend, whispering so neither Lana nor Ryan could hear her.

"Why doesn't she just take his head and smash it between the surgically enhanced boobs her ex-boyfriend gave her as a consolation prize? It'd be a lot easier for both of them."

"Watch it there, girl. You're beginning to sound an awful lot like a jealous girlfriend." Gail could barely contain her grin.

"There's nothing to be jealous of. Ryan and I are just friends. You know that."

"*Best* friends," her friend pointed out, as she studied Ryan flirting with Lana. "But let's face it. You're two insanely attractive people. Are you really going to try and convince me that neither of you has ever considered—"

"We haven't." Tessa took her shot, missing badly. It was a shot she should've hit, even without Ryan's help. But she was too busy eavesdropping on his conversation with Lana.

"Well, for a person who doesn't have any romantic interest in her best friend, you seem particularly interested in whether or not he's flirting with the big-boobed barmaid." Gail shrugged when Tessa gave her the stink eye. "What? You know it's true."

Tessa scowled at her friend's words and the fact that Roy was taking advantage of her distraction. He easily sank one ball, then another. With no more striped balls left on the table, Roy had a clear shot at the eight ball.

He should be able to make that shot blindfolded.

"Well?" Gail prodded her.

"I'm not jealous of Lana. I just think Ryan could do better. That he *should* do better than to fall for the calculated ploy of a woman who has dollar signs in her eyes. Probably angling for butt implants this time."

Gail giggled. "And why would he want a fake ass when he was mere inches from the real deal?" She nodded toward Tessa's behind, a smirk on her face.

Tessa was fully aware that she'd inherited her generous curves from her mother. She was just as clear about Ryan Bateman's obliviousness to them. To him, she was simply one of the guys. But then again, the comfy jeans and plaid button-down shirts that filled her closet didn't do much to highlight her assets.

Hadn't that been the reason she'd chosen such a utilitarian wardrobe in the first place?

"Dammit!" Roy banged his pool cue on the wooden floor, drawing their attention to him. He'd scratched on the eight ball.

Tessa grinned. "I won."

"Because I scratched." Roy's tone made it clear that he felt winning by default was nothing to be proud of.

"A win's a win, Jensen." She wriggled her fingers, her palm open. "Pay up."

"You won? Way to go, Tess. I told you that you had this game in the bag." Ryan, suddenly beside her, wrapped a big, muscular arm around her shoulder and pulled her into a half hug.

"Well, at least one of us believed in me." Tessa counted the four wrinkled five-dollar bills Roy stuffed in her palm begrudgingly.

"Always have, always will." He beamed at her and took another swig of his beer.

Tessa tried to ignore the warmth in her chest that filtered down her spine and fanned into areas she didn't want to acknowledge.

Because they were friends. And friends didn't get all…whatever it was she was feeling…over one another. Not even when they looked and smelled good enough to eat.

Tessa Noble always smelled like citrus and sunshine. Reminded him of warm summer picnics at the lake. Ryan couldn't peel an orange or slice a lemon without thinking of her and smiling.

There was no reason for his arm to still be wrapped

around her shoulder other than the sense of comfort he derived from being this close to her.

"Take your hands off my sister, Bateman." Tessa's brother Tripp's expression was stony as he entered the bar. As if he was about five minutes away from kicking Ryan's ass.

"Tessa just beat your man, Roy, here." Ryan didn't move. Nor did he acknowledge Tripp's veiled threat.

The three of them had been friends forever, though it was Tessa who was his best friend. According to their parents, their friendship was born the moment they first met. Their bond had only gotten stronger over the years. Still, he'd had to assure Tripp on more than one occasion that his relationship with Tess was purely platonic.

Relationships weren't his gift. He'd made peace with that, particularly since the dissolution of his engagement to Sabrina Calhoun little more than a year ago. Tripp had made it clear, in a joking-not-joking manner, that despite their longtime friendship, he'd punch his lights out if Ryan ever hurt his sister.

He couldn't blame the guy. Tess definitely deserved better.

"Way to go, Tess." A wide grin spread across Tripp's face. He gave his sister a fist bump, followed by a simulated explosion.

The Nobles' signature celebratory handshake.

"Thanks, Tripp." Tessa casually stepped away from him.

Ryan drank his beer, captivated by her delectable scent which still lingered in the air around him.

"You look particularly proud of yourself today, big brother." Tessa raised an eyebrow, her arms folded.

The move inadvertently framed and lifted Tessa's rather impressive breasts. Another feature he tried hard, as her best friend, to not notice. But then again, he was a guy, with guy parts and a guy brain.

Ryan quickly shifted his gaze to Tripp's. "You still pumped about being a bachelor in the Texas Cattleman's Club charity auction?"

Tripp grinned like a prize hog in the county fair, his light brown eyes—identical to his sister's—twinkling merrily. "Alexis Slade says I'll fetch a mint."

"Hmm…" Ryan grinned. "Tess, what do you think your brother here will command on the auction block?"

"Oh, I'd say four maybe even five…dollars." Tessa, Ryan, Gail and Roy laughed hysterically, much to Tripp's chagrin.

Tripp folded his arms over his chest. "I see you all have jokes tonight."

"You know we're just kidding." Ryan, who had called next, picked up a pool cue as Roy gathered the balls and racked them. "After all, I'm the one who suggested you to Alexis."

"And I may never forgive you for creating this monster." Tessa scowled at Ryan playfully.

"My bad, I wasn't thinking." He chuckled.

"What I want to know is why on earth you didn't volunteer yourself?" Gail asked. "You're a moderately good-looking guy, if you like that sort of thing." She laughed.

She was teasing him, not flirting. Though with Gail it was often hard to tell.

Ryan shrugged. "I'm not interested in parading across the stage for a bunch of desperate women to bid on, like I'm a side of beef." He glanced apologetically at his friend, Tripp. "No offense, man."

"None taken." Tripp grinned proudly, poking a thumb into his chest. "This 'side of beef' is chomping at the bit to be taken for a spin by one of the lovely ladies."

Tessa elbowed Ryan in the gut, and an involuntary "oomph" sound escaped. "Watch it, Bateman. We aren't *desperate*. We're civic-minded women whose only interest is the betterment of our community."

There was silence for a beat before Tessa and Gail dissolved into laughter.

Tessa was utterly adorable, giggling like a schoolgirl. The sound—rooted in his earliest memories of her—instantly conjured a smile that began deep down in his gut.

He studied her briefly. Her curly, dark brown hair was pulled into a low ponytail and her smooth, golden brown skin practically glowed. She was wearing her typical winter attire: a long-sleeved plaid shirt, jeans which hid her curvy frame rather than highlighting it, and the newest addition to her ever-growing sneaker collection.

"You're a brave man." Ryan shifted his attention to Tripp as he leaned down and lined his stick up with the cue ball. He drew it back and forth between his forefinger and thumb. "If these two are any indication—" he nodded toward Tess and Gail "—those women at the auction are gonna eat you alive."

"One can only hope." Tripp wriggled his brows and held up his beer, one corner of his mouth curled in a smirk.

Ryan shook his head, then struck the white cue ball

hard. He relished the loud cracking sound that indicated a solid break. The cue ball smashed through the triangular formation of colorful balls, and they rolled or spun across the table. A high and a low ball dropped into the pockets.

"Your choice." Ryan nodded toward Tessa.

"Low." Hardly a surprise. Tessa always chose low balls whenever she had first choice. She walked around the table, her sneakers squeaking against the floor, as she sized up her first shot.

"You know I'm only teasing you, Tripp. I think it's pretty brave of you to put yourself out there like that. I'd be mortified by the thought of anyone bidding on me." She leaned over the table, her sights on the blue two ball before glancing up at her brother momentarily. "In fact, I'm proud of you. The money you'll help raise for the Pancreatic Cancer Research Foundation will do a world of good."

She made her shot and sank the ball before lining up for the next one.

"Would you bid on a bachelor?" Ryan leaned against his stick, awaiting his turn.

He realized that Tess was attending the bachelor auction, but the possibility that she'd be bidding on one of them hadn't occurred to him until just now. And the prospect of his best friend going on a date with some guy whose company she'd paid for didn't sit well with him.

The protective instinct that had his hackles up was perfectly natural. He, Tripp and Tessa had had each others' backs since they were kids. They weren't just friends, they were family. Though Tess was less like a little sister and more like a really hot distant cousin, three times removed.

"Of course, I'm bidding on a bachelor." She sank another ball, then paced around the table and shrugged. "That's kind of the point of the entire evening."

"Doesn't mean you have to. After all, not every woman attending will be bidding on a bachelor," Ryan reminded her.

"They will be if they aren't married or engaged," Gail said resolutely, folding her arms and cocking an eyebrow his way. "Why, Ryan Bateman, sounds to me like you're jealous."

"Don't be ridiculous." His cheeks heated as he returned his gaze to the table. "I'm just looking out for my best friend. She shouldn't be pressured to participate in something that makes her feel uncomfortable."

Tessa was sweet, smart, funny, and a hell of a lot of fun to hang out with. But she wasn't the kind of woman he envisioned with a paddle in her hand, bidding on men as if she were purchasing steers at auction.

"Doesn't sound like Tess, to me. That's all I'm saying." He realized he sounded defensive.

"*Good*. It's about time I do something unexpected. I'm too predictable...too boring." Tessa cursed under her breath when she missed her shot.

"Also known as consistent and reliable," Ryan interjected.

Things were good the way they were. He liked that Tessa followed a routine he could count on. His best friend's need for order balanced out his spontaneity.

"I know, but lately I've been feeling... I don't know...stifled. Like I need to take some risks in my personal life. Stop playing it so safe all the time." She sighed in response to his wide-eyed, slack-jawed stare. "Relax, Rye. It's not like I'm paying for a male escort."

"I believe they prefer the term *gigolo*," Gail, always helpful, interjected, then took another sip of her drink.

Ryan narrowed his gaze at Gail, which only made the woman laugh hysterically. He shifted his attention back to Tessa, who'd just missed her shot.

"Who will you be bidding on?"

Tessa shrugged. "I don't know. No one in particular in mind, just yet. The programs go out in a few days. Maybe I'll decide then. Or… I don't know…maybe I'll wait and see who tickles my fancy when I get there."

"Who *tickles your fancy*?" Ryan repeated the words incredulously. His grip on the pool cue tightened.

He didn't like the sound of that at all.

Two

Tessa followed the sound of moaning down the hall and around the corner to her brother's room.

"Tripp? Are you all right?" She tapped lightly on his partially opened bedroom door.

"No!" The word was punctuated by another moan, followed by, "I feel like I'm dying."

Tessa hurried inside his room, her senses quickly assailed by a pungent scent which she followed to his bathroom. He was hugging the porcelain throne and looking a little green.

"Did you go out drinking last night?"

"No. I think it's the tuna sandwich I got from the gas station late last night on my way back in from Dallas."

"How many times have I told you? Gas station food after midnight? No *bueno*." She stood with her hands on her hips, looking down at her brother who looked like he might erupt again at any minute.

Austin Charles Noble III loved food almost as much as he loved his family. And usually he had a stomach like a tank. Impervious to just about anything. So whatever he'd eaten had to have been pretty bad.

"I'm taking you to Urgent Care."

"No, I just want to go to bed. If I can sleep it off for a few hours, I'm sure I'll be fine." He forced a smile, then immediately clutched his belly and cringed. "I'll be good as new for the bachelor auction."

"Shit. The bachelor auction." Tess repeated the words. It was the next night. And as green at the gills as Tripp looked, there was little chance he'd be ready to be paraded on stage in front of a crowd of eager women by then. The way he looked now, he probably wouldn't fetch more than five dollars and a bottle of ipecac at auction.

"Here, let me help you back to bed." She leaned down, allowing her brother to drape his arm around her and get enough leverage to climb to his feet on unsteady legs. Once he was safely in bed again, she gathered the remains of the tainted tuna sandwich, an empty bottle of beer, and a few other items.

She set an empty garbage can with a squirt of soap and about an inch of water beside his bed.

"Use this, if you need to." She indicated the garbage can. "I'm going to get you some ginger ale and some Gatorade. But if you get worse, I'm taking you to the doctor. Mom and Dad wouldn't be too happy with me if I let their baby boy die of food poisoning while they were away on vacation."

"Well, I am Mom's favorite, so…" He offered a weak smile as he invoked the argument they often teased each other about. "And don't worry about the auction,

I'll be fine. I'm a warrior, sis. Nothing is going to come between me and—" Suddenly he bolted out of bed, ran to the bathroom and slammed the door behind him.

Tessa shook her head. "You're staying right here in bed today and tomorrow, 'warrior.' I'll get Roy and the guys to take care of the projects that were on your list today. And I'll find a replacement for you in the auction. Alexis will understand."

Tripp mumbled his thanks through the bathroom door, and she set off to take care of everything she had promised him.

Tessa had been nursing her brother back to health and handling her duties at the ranch, as well as some of his. And she'd been trying all day to get in touch with Ryan.

Despite his reluctance to get involved in the auction, he was the most logical choice as Tripp's replacement. She was sure she could convince him it was a worthy cause. Maybe stroke his ego and tell him there would be a feeding frenzy for a hot stud like him.

A statement she planned to make in jest, but that she feared also had a bit of truth to it. Tessa gritted her teeth imagining Lana, and a whole host of other women in town who often flirted with Ryan, bidding on him like he was a prize steer.

Maybe getting Ryan to step in as Tripp's replacement in the auction wasn't such a good idea after all. She paced the floor, scrolling through a list of names of other possible options in her head.

Most of the eligible men that came to mind were already participating, or they'd already turned Alexis and Rachel down, from what Tessa had heard.

She stopped abruptly mid-stride, an idea brewing in her head that made her both excited and feel like she was going to toss her lunch at the same time.

"Do something that scares you every single day." She repeated the words under her breath that she'd recently posted on the wall of her office. It was a quote from Eleanor Roosevelt. Advice she'd promised herself that she would take to heart from here on out.

Tessa glanced at herself in the mirror. Her thick hair was divided into two plaits, and a Stetson was pushed down on her head, her eyes barely visible. She was the textbook definition of Plain Jane. Not because she wasn't attractive, but because she put zero effort into looking like a desirable woman rather than one of the ranch hands.

She sighed, her fingers trembling slightly. There was a good chance that Alexis and Rachel would veto her idea for Tripp's replacement. But at least she would ask.

Tessa pulled her cell phone out of her back pocket and scrolled through her contacts for Alexis Slade's number. Her palms were damp as she initiated the call. Pressing the phone to her ear, she counted the rings, a small part of her hoping that Alexis didn't answer. That would give her time to rethink her rash decision. Maybe save herself some embarrassment when Alexis rejected the idea.

"Hey, Tess. How are you?" Alexis's warm, cheerful voice rang through the line.

"I'm good. Tripp? Not so much. I think he has food poisoning." The words stumbled out of her mouth.

"Oh my God! That's terrible. Poor Tripp. Is he going to be okay?"

"I'm keeping an eye on him, but I'm sure he'll be

fine in a few days. I just don't think he's going to recover in time to do the bachelor auction."

"We'll miss having him in the lineup, but of course we understand. His health is the most important thing." The concern was evident in Alexis's voice. "Tell him that we hope he's feeling better soon. And if the auction goes well, maybe we'll do this again next year. I'll save a spot in the lineup for him then."

"Do you have anyone in mind for a replacement?" Tessa paced the floor.

"Not really. We've pretty much tapped out our list of possibilities. Unless you can get Ryan to change his mind?" She sounded hopeful.

"I considered that, and I've been trying to reach him all day. But just now, I came up with another idea." She paused, hoping that Alexis would stop her. Tell her that they didn't need anyone else. When the woman didn't respond, she continued. "I was thinking that I might replace my brother in the lineup." She rushed the words out before she could chicken out. "I know that this is a bachelor auction, not a bachelorette—"

"Yes!" Alexis squealed, as if it were the best idea she'd heard all day. "OMG, I think that's an absolutely fabulous idea. We'll provide something for the fellas, too. Oh, Tessa, this is brilliant. I love it."

"Are you sure? I mean, I like the idea of doing something completely unexpected, but maybe we should see what Rachel thinks." Her heart hammered in her chest.

She'd done something bold, something different, by offering to take Tripp's place. But now, the thought of actually walking that stage and praying to God that someone…anyone…would bid on her was giving her heart palpitations.

"That's a good idea, but I know she's going to agree with me. Hold on."

"Oh, you're calling her now?" Tessa said to the empty room as she paced the floor.

Rachel Kincaid was a marketing genius and an old college friend of Alexis's. She'd come to Royal as a young widow and the mother to an adorable little girl named Ellie. And she'd fallen in love with one of the most eligible bachelors in all of Texas, oil tycoon Matt Galloway.

"Okay, Rachel's on the line," Alexis announced a moment later. "And I brought her up to speed."

"You weren't kidding about doing something unexpected." There was a hint of awe in Rachel's voice. "Good for you, Tess."

"Thanks, Rachel." She swallowed hard. "But do you think it's a good idea? I mean, the programs have already been printed, and no one knows that there's going to be a bachelorette in the auction. What if no one bids on me? I don't want to cause any embarrassment to the club or create negative publicity for the event."

"Honey, the bachelors who aren't in the auction are going to go crazy when they discover there's a beautiful lady to bid on," Rachel said confidently.

"We'll put the word out that there's going to be a big surprise, just for the fellas. I can email everyone on our mailing list. It will only take me a few minutes to put the email together and send it out," Alexis said.

"Y'all are sure we can pull this off?" Tess asked one last time. "I swear I won't be offended if you think we can't. I rather you tell me now than to let me get up there and make a fool of myself."

"It's going to be awesome," Alexis reassured her.

"But I'm sensing hesitation. Are you second-guessing your decision? Because you shouldn't. It's a good one."

Tessa grabbed a spoon and the pint of her favorite Neapolitan ice cream hidden in the back of the freezer. She sat at the kitchen island and sighed, rubbing her palm on her jeans again. She shook her head, casting another glance in the mirror. "It's just that… I'm not the glamorous type, that's for sure."

"You're gorgeous, girl. And if you're concerned… hey, why don't we give you a whole beauty makeover for the event?" Rachel said excitedly. "It'll be fun and it gives me another excuse to buy makeup."

"That's a fantastic idea, Rachel!" Alexis chimed in. "Not that you need it," she added. "But maybe it'll make you feel more comfortable."

"Okay, yeah. That sounds great. I'd like that." Tessa nodded, feeling slightly better. "I was gonna take tomorrow off anyway. Give myself plenty of time to get ready. But I'm sure you both have a million things to do. I don't want to distract you from preparing for the auction, just to babysit me."

"Alexis is the queen of organization. She's got everything under control. Plus, we have a terrific crew of volunteers," Rachel piped in. "They won't miss us for a few hours. I promise, everything will be fine."

"Have you considered what date you're offering?"

"Date?" Tessa hadn't thought that far in advance. "I'm not sure. I guess…let me think about that. I'll have an answer for you by tomorrow. Is that all right?"

"That's fine. Just let me know first thing in the morning," Alexis said.

"I'll make a few appointments for the makeover

and I'll text you both all the details." Rachel's voice brimmed with excitement.

"Then I guess that's everything," Tessa said, more to herself than her friends. "I'll see you both tomorrow."

She hung up the phone, took a deep breath, and shoveled a spoonful of Neapolitan ice cream into her mouth.

There was no turning back now.

Three

Ryan patted the warm neck of his horse, Phantom, and dismounted, handing the majestic animal off to Ned, one of his ranch hands. He gave the horse's haunches one final pat as the older man led him away to a stall.

Ryan wiped his sweaty forehead with the back of his hand. He was tired, dirty and in desperate need of a shower.

He'd been out on the ranch and the surrounding area since the crack of dawn, looking for several steer that had made their great escape through a break in the fence. While his men repaired the fence, he and another hand tracked down the cattle and drove them back to the ranch.

He'd been in such a hurry to get after the cattle, he'd left his phone at home. Hopefully, his parents hadn't called, worried that he wasn't answering because he'd burned down the whole damn place.

He grumbled to himself, "You nearly burn the barn down as a kid, and they never let you forget it."

Then again, his parents and Tess and Tripp's seemed to be enjoying themselves on their cruise. Their calls had become far less frequent.

Who knows? Maybe both couples would decide it was finally time to retire, give up ranch life, and pass the torch to the next generation. Something he, Tessa and Tripp had been advocating for the past few years. They were ready to take on the responsibility.

When he'd been engaged to Sabrina, his parents had planned to retire to their beach house in Galveston and leave management of the ranch to him. Despite the fact that they hadn't much liked his intended. Not because Sabrina was a bad person. But he and Sabrina were like fire and ice. The moments that were good could be really good. But the moments that weren't had resulted in tense arguments and angry sex.

His mother, in particular, hadn't been convinced Sabrina was the girl for him. She'd been right.

A few months before their wedding, Sabrina had called it off. She just couldn't see herself as a ranch wife. Nor was she willing to sacrifice her well-earned figure to start "popping out babies" to carry on the Bateman name.

He appreciated that she'd had the decency to tell him to his face, well in advance, rather than abandoning him at the altar as Shelby Arthur had done when she'd decided she couldn't marry Jared Goodman.

At least she'd spared him *that* humiliation.

Besides, there was a part of him that realized the truth of what she'd said. Maybe some part of him had always understood that he'd asked her to marry him because it felt like the right thing to do.

He'd been with Sabrina longer than he'd stayed in any relationship. For over a year. So when she'd hinted that she didn't want to waste her time in a relationship that wasn't going anywhere, he'd popped the question.

Neither he nor Sabrina were the type who bought into the fairy tale of romance. They understood that relationships were an exchange. A series of transactions, sustained over time. Which was why he believed they were a good fit. But they'd both ignored an essential point. They were just too different.

He loved everything about ranch life, and Sabrina was a city girl, through and through.

The truth was that he'd been relieved when Sabrina had canceled the wedding. As if he could breathe, nice, deep, easy breaths, for the first time in months. Still, his parents called off their plans to retire.

Maybe this trip would convince them that he and the Bateman Ranch would be just fine without them.

Ryan stretched and groaned. His muscles, taut from riding in the saddle a good portion of the day, protested as he made his way across the yard toward the house.

Helene Dennis, their longtime house manager, threw open the door and greeted him. "There you are. You look an unholy mess. Take off those boots and don't get my kitchen floor all dirty. I just mopped."

Sometimes he wondered if Helene worked for him or if he worked for her. Still, he loved the older woman. She was family.

"All right, all right." He toed off his boots and kicked them in the corner, patting his arms and legs to dislodge any dust from his clothing before entering the house. "Just don't shoot."

Helene playfully punched his arm. "Were you able to round up all of the animals that got loose?"

"Every one of them." Yawning, he kneaded a stubborn kink in his back. "Fence is fixed, too."

"Good. Dinner will be ready in about a half an hour. Go ahead and hop in the shower. Oh, and call Tess when you get the chance."

"Why?" His chest tightened. "Everything okay over at the Noble Spur?"

"Don't worry." She gave him a knowing smile that made his cheeks fill with heat. "She's fine, but her brother is ill. Tess is pretty sure it's food poisoning. She's been trying to reach you all day."

"I was in such a hurry to get out of here this morning, I forgot my phone."

"I know." She chuckled softly "I found it in the covers when I made your bed this morning. It's on your nightstand."

Managing a tired smile for the woman he loved almost as much as his own mother, he leaned in and kissed her cheek. "Thanks, Helene. I'll be down for dinner as soon as I can."

Ryan dried his hair from the shower and wrapped the towel around his waist. The hot water had felt good sluicing over his tired, aching muscles. So he'd taken a longer shower than he'd intended. And though he was hungry, he was tempted to collapse into bed and forgo dinner.

Sighing wearily, he sat on the bed and picked up his phone to call Tess.

She answered in a couple of rings. "Hey, Rye. How'd it go? Were you able to find all the steer you lost?"

Helene had evidently told her where he was and why he hadn't been answering his cell phone.

"Yes, we got them all back and the fence is fixed." He groaned as he reached out to pick up his watch and put it back on. "How's Tripp? Helene said he got food poisoning."

"Wow, you sound like you've been ridden hard and put away wet." She laughed. "And yes, my brother's penchant for late night snacks from suspect eateries finally caught up with him. He looks and feels like hell, but otherwise he's recovering."

"Will he be okay for the auction tomorrow?"

"No." She said the word a little too quickly, then paused a little too long. "He thinks he'll be fine to go through with it, but I'm chalking that up to illness-induced delusion."

"Did you tell Alexis she's a man down?"

"I did." There was another unusual pause. Like there was something she wanted to say but was hesitant.

Ryan thought for a moment as he rummaged through his drawers for something to put on.

"Ahh…" He dragged his fingers through his damp hair. "Of course. She wants to know if I'll take Tripp's place."

Tessa didn't respond right away. "Actually, that's why I was trying so hard to reach you. I thought I might be able to convince you to take Tripp's place…since it's for such a good cause. But when I couldn't reach you, I came up with another option."

"Which is?" It was like pulling teeth to get Tess to just spit it out. He couldn't imagine why that would be…unless he wasn't going to like what she had to say. Uneasiness tightened his gut. "So this other option… are you going to tell me, or should I come over and you can act it out in charades?"

"Smart-ass." She huffed. "No charades necessary. *I'm* the other option. I decided to take Tripp's place in the auction."

"You do know that it's women who will be bidding in this auction, right?" Ryan switched to speakerphone, tossed his phone on the bed, then stepped into his briefs. "Anything you need to tell me, Tess?"

"I'm going to give you a pass because I know you're tired," she groused. "And we've already considered that. If you check your in-box, you'll see that Alexis sent out an email informing all attendees and everyone else on the mailing list that there is going to be a surprise at the end of the auction, just for the gents."

"Oh."

It was the only thing that Ryan could think to say as the realization struck him in the gut like a bull running at full speed. A few days ago, he'd been discomfited by the idea of his friend bidding on one man. Now, there would be who knows how many guys angling for a night with her.

"You sure about this?" He stepped into a pair of well-worn jeans and zipped and buttoned them. "This just doesn't seem much like you."

"That's exactly why I'm doing it." Her voice was shaky. "It'll be good for me to venture outside of my comfort zone."

He donned a long-sleeved T-shirt, neither of them speaking for a moment.

Ryan rubbed his chin and sank on to his mattress.

He slipped on a pair of socks. "Look, I know I said I didn't want to do it, but with Tripp being sick and all, how about I make an exception?"

"You think this is a really bad idea, don't you?" She choked out the words, her feelings obviously hurt.

"No, that's not what I'm saying at all." The last thing he wanted to do was upset his best friend. He ran a hand through his hair. "I'm just saying that it's really last minute. And because of that, it might take people by surprise, that's all."

"I thought of that, too. Alexis and Rachel are positive they can drum up enough interest. But I thought that…just to be safe…it'd be good to have an ace up my sleeve."

"What kind of an ace?"

"I'm going to give you the money to bid on me, in case no one else does. I know it'll still look pretty pathetic if my best friend is the only person who bids on me, but that's a hell of a lot better than hearing crickets when they call my name."

"You want me to bid on you?" He repeated the words. Not that he hadn't heard or understood her the first time. He was just processing the idea. Him bidding on his best friend. The two of them going out on a date…

"Yes, but it'll be my money. And there's no need for us to actually go on the date. I mean, we can just hang out like usual or something, but it doesn't have to be a big deal."

"Sure, I'll do it. But you don't need to put up the money. I'm happy to make the donation myself."

His leg bounced. Despite what his friend believed, Ryan doubted that he'd be the only man there willing to bid on Tessa Noble during her bachelorette auction.

"Thanks, Ryan. I appreciate this." She sounded relieved. "And remember, you'll only need to bid on me if no one else does. If nothing else, your bid might prompt someone else to get into the spirit."

"Got it," he said gruffly. "You can count on me."

"I know. Thanks again, Rye." He could hear the smile in her sweet voice.

"Hey, since Tripp won't be able to make it…why don't we ride in together?"

"Actually, I'm going straight to the auction from… somewhere else. But I'll catch a ride with a friend, so we can ride home together. How's that?"

"Sounds good." He couldn't help the twinge of disappointment he felt at only getting to ride home with her. "I guess I'll see you there."

"I'll be the one with the price tag on her head." Tessa forced a laugh. "Get some rest, Rye. And take some pain meds. Otherwise, your arm'll be too sore to lift the auction paddle."

Her soft laughter was the last thing he heard before the line went dead. Before he could say good-night.

Ryan released a long sigh and slid his feet into his slippers. He didn't like the idea of Tess putting herself on the auction block for every letch in town to leer at. But she was a grown woman who was capable of making her own decisions.

Regardless of how much he disagreed with them.

Besides, he wasn't quite sure what it was that made him feel more uneasy. Tess being bid on by other men, or the idea that he might be the man who won her at the end of the night.

Four

Tessa had never been plucked, primped and prodded this much in her entire life.

She'd been waxed in places she didn't even want to think about and had some kind of wrap that promised to tighten her curves. And the thick head of curls she adored had been straightened and hung in tousled waves around her shoulders. Now Milan Valez, a professional makeup artist, was applying her makeup.

"I thought we were going with a natural look," Tess objected when the woman opened yet another product and started to apply what had to be a third or fourth layer of goop to her face.

"This *is* the natural look." The woman rolled her eyes. "If I had a dime for every client who doesn't realize that what they're calling the natural look is actually a full face." The woman sighed, but her expression softened as she directed Tess to turn her head. "You're a beautiful woman with gorgeous skin. If you're not a makeup wearer, I know it feels like a lot. But I'm just using a few tricks to enhance your natural beauty. We'll make those beautiful eyes pop, bring a little drama to these pouty lips, and highlight your incredible cheekbones. I promise you won't look too heavily made up. Just trust me."

Tessa released a quiet sigh and nodded. "I trust you."

"Good. Now just sit back and relax. Your friends should be here shortly. They're going to be very pleased, and I think you will, too." The woman smiled. "Now look up."

Tessa complied as Milan applied liner beneath her eyes. "You sure I can't have a little peek?"

"Your friends made me promise. No peeking. And you agreed." She lifted Tess's chin. "Don't worry, honey, you won't have to wait much longer."

"Tessa? Oh my God, you look...incredible." Rachel entered the salon a few minutes later and clapped a hand over her mouth. "I can hardly believe it's you."

Alexis nearly slammed into the back of Rachel, who'd made an abrupt stop. She started to complain, but when she saw Tessa, her mouth gaped open, too.

"Tess, you look...stunning. Not that you aren't always beautiful, but...wow. Just wow."

"You two are making me seriously self-conscious right now." Tessa kept her focus on Milan.

"Don't be," the woman said emphatically. "Remember what we talked about. I've only enhanced what was already there."

Tessa inhaled deeply and nodded. She ignored the butterflies in her stomach in response to the broad grins and looks of amazement on Alexis's and Rachel's faces.

"There, all done." Milan sat back proudly and grinned. "Honey, you look absolutely beautiful. Ready to see for yourself?"

"Please." Even as Tessa said it, her hands were trembling, and a knot tightened in her stomach. How could something as simple as looking in the mirror be so fraught with anxiety? It only proved she wasn't cut out for this whole glamour-girl thing.

Milan slowly turned the chair around and Alexis and Rachel came over to stand closer, both of them bouncing excitedly.

Tessa closed her eyes, took a deep breath and then opened them.

"Oh my God." She leaned closer to the mirror. "I can hardly believe that's me." She sifted her fingers through the dark, silky waves with toffee-colored highlights. "I mean, it looks like me, just…more glamourous."

"I know, isn't it incredible? You're going to be the star of the evening. We need to keep you hidden until you walk across the stage. Really take everyone by surprise." Rachel grinned in the mirror from behind her.

"Oh, that's a brilliant idea, Rachel," Alexis agreed. "It'll have more impact."

"This is only the beginning." Rachel's grin widened. "Just wait until they get a load of your outfit tonight. Every man in that room's jaw will hit the floor."

Tessa took another deep breath, then exhaled as she stared at herself in the mirror. Between her makeover and the daring outfit she'd chosen, there was no way Ryan, or anyone else, would take her for one of the boys.

Her heart raced and her belly fluttered as she anticipated his reaction. She couldn't wait to see the look of
surprise on Ryan's face.

Ryan entered the beautiful gardens where The Great
Royal Bachelor Auction was being held. Alexis Slade,
James Harris and the rest of the committee had gone
out of their way to create a festive and beautiful setting
for the event. Fragrant wreaths and sprigs of greenery
were strung from the pergolas. Two towering trees decorated with gorgeous ornaments dominated the area.
Poinsettias, elegant red bows and white lights decorated the space, giving it a glowing, ethereal feel. The
garden managed to be both romantic and festive. The
kind of setting that almost made you regret not having
someone to share the night with.

He sipped his Jack and Coke and glanced around the
vicinity. Everyone who was anyone was in attendance.
He made his way through the room, mingling with
Carter Mackenzie and Shelby Arthur, Matt Galloway
and Rachel Kincaid, Austin and Brooke Bradshaw, and
all of the other members of the club who'd turned out
for the event. Several of the bachelors moved around
the space, drumming up anticipation for the auction
and doing their best to encourage a bidding frenzy.

But Tessa was nowhere to be found. Had she
changed her mind? He was looking forward to hanging out with her tonight, but he'd understand if she'd
gotten cold feet. Hell, there was a part of him that was
relieved to think that maybe she'd bailed.

Then again, Tess had said she'd be coming from
somewhere else. So maybe she was just running late.

He resisted the urge to pull out his cell phone and

find out exactly where she was. For once in his life, he'd be patient. Even if it killed him.

"Ryan, it's good to see you." James Harris, president of the Texas Cattleman's Club, shook his hand. "I hate that we couldn't convince you to be one of our bachelor's tonight, but I'm glad you joined us just the same."

"Didn't see your name on the list of bachelors either." Ryan smirked, and both men laughed.

"Touché." James took a gulp of his drink and Ryan did the same.

"Looks like y'all are doing just fine without me." Ryan gestured to the space. "I wouldn't have ever imagined this place could look this good."

"Alexis Slade outdid herself with this whole romantic winter wonderland vibe." James's eyes trailed around the space. "To be honest, I wasn't sure exactly how her vision would come together, but she's delivered in spades. I'm glad we gave her free rein to execute it as she saw fit."

"Judging from everyone here's reaction, you've got a hit on your hands." Ryan raised his glass before finishing the last of his drink.

"Let's just hope it motivates everyone to dig deep in their pockets tonight." James patted Ryan on the back. "I'd better go chat with Rose Clayton." He nodded toward the older woman, who looked stunning in her gown. The touch of gray hair at her temples gleamed in the light. "But I'll see you around."

"You bet." Ryan nodded toward the man as he traversed the space and greeted Rose.

"Ryan, how are you?" Gail Walker took a sip of her drink and grinned. "You look particularly handsome tonight. But I see Alexis still wasn't able to talk you into joining the list of eligible bachelors."

"Not my thing, but looks like they've got plenty of studs on the schedule for you to choose from." Ryan sat his empty glass on a nearby tray. "And you clean up pretty well yourself."

"Thanks." She smoothed a hand over the skirt of her jewel-tone green dress. "But I've got my eye on one bachelor in particular." Her eyes shone with mischief. "And I'm prepared to do whatever it takes to get him."

"Well, I certainly wouldn't want to be the woman who has to run up against you." Ryan chuckled. "Good luck."

"Thanks, Ryan. See you around." Gail made her way through the crowd, mingling with other guests.

Ryan accepted a napkin and a few petite quiches from a server passing by. Ignoring the anticipation that made his heart beat a little faster as he considered the prospect of bidding on his friend.

Tessa paced the space that served as the bachelors' green room. Everyone else had spent most of the night mingling. They came to the green room once the start of the auction drew closer. But she'd been stuck here the entire evening, biding her time until she was scheduled to make her grand entrance.

"Tessa Noble? God, you look…incredible." Daniel Clayton shoved a hand in his pocket. "But what are you doing here? Wait…are you the surprise?"

"Guilty." Her cheeks warmed as she bit into another quiche.

She tried her best not to ruin the makeup that Milan had so painstakingly applied. The woman had assured her that she could eat and drink without the lipstick fading or feathering. But Tess still found herself being extra careful.

"Everyone will definitely be surprised," he said, then added, "Not that you don't look good normally."

"It's okay, Daniel. I get it." She mumbled around a mouth full of quiche. "It was a surprise to me, too."

He chuckled, running a hand through his jet-black hair. "You must be tired of people telling you how different you look. How did Tripp and Ryan react?"

"Neither of them has seen me yet." She balled up her napkin and tossed it in the trash. "I'm a little nervous about their reaction."

"Don't be," Daniel said assuredly. "I can't imagine a man alive could find fault with the way you look tonight." He smiled, then scrubbed a hand across his forehead. "Or any night...of course."

They both laughed.

"Well, thank you." She relaxed a little. "You already know why I feel like a fish out of water. But why do you look so out of sorts tonight?"

He exhaled heavily, the frown returning to his face. "For one thing, I'd rather not be in the lineup. I'm doing this at my grandmother's insistence."

"Ms. Rose seems like a perfectly reasonable woman to me. And she loves you like crazy. I'm pretty sure if you'd turned her down she would've gotten over it fairly quickly."

"Maybe." He shrugged. "But the truth is that I owe my grandmother so much. Don't know where I would've ended up if it wasn't for her. Makes it hard to say no." A shadow of sadness passed over his handsome face, tugging at Tessa's heart.

Daniel had been raised by Rose Clayton after his own mother dumped him on her. It made Tessa's heart ache for him. She couldn't imagine the pain Daniel must feel at being abandoned by a woman who preferred drugs and booze to her own son.

"Of course." Tess nodded, regretting her earlier flippant words. She hadn't considered the special relationship that Daniel had with his grandmother and how grateful he must be to her. "I wasn't thinking."

They were both quiet for a moment, when she remembered his earlier words.

"You said 'for one thing.' What's the other reason you didn't want to do this?"

The pained look on Daniel's face carved deep lines in his forehead and between his brows. He drained the glass of whiskey in his hand.

"It's nothing," he said in a dismissive tone that made it clear that they wouldn't be discussing it any further.

She was digging herself deeper into a hole with every question she asked of Daniel tonight. Better for her to move on. She wished him luck and made her way over to the buffet table.

"Hey, Tessa." Lloyd Richardson put another slider on his small plate. "Wow, you look pretty amazing."

"Thanks, Lloyd." She decided against the slider and put some carrots and a cherry tomato on her plate instead.

There wasn't much room to spare in her fitted pantsuit. She wore a jacket over the sleeveless garment to hide the large cutout that revealed most of her back. That had been one idea of Rachel's for which she'd been grateful.

"Hey, you must be plum sick of people saying that

to you by now." Lloyd seemed to recognize the discomfort she felt at all of the additional attention she'd been getting.

Tess gave him a grateful smile. No wonder her friend Gail Walker had a crush on Lloyd. He was handsome, sweet and almost a little shy. Which was probably why he hadn't made a move on Gail, since he certainly seemed interested in her.

"Okay, bachelors and bachelorette." Alexis acknowledged Tess with a slight smile. "The proceedings will begin in about ten minutes. So finish eating, take a quick bathroom break, whatever you need to do so you'll be ready to go on when your number is called."

Alexis had her serious, drill sergeant face on. Something Tessa knew firsthand that a woman needed to adopt when she was responsible for managing a crew of men—be they ranchers or ranch hands.

Still, there was something in her eyes. Had she been crying?

Before she could approach Alexis and ask if she was all right, she noticed the look Alexis and Daniel Clayton exchanged. It was brief, but meaningful. Chock full of pain.

Could Alexis be the other reason Daniel hadn't wanted to be in the bachelor auction? But from the look of things, whatever was going on between them certainly wasn't sunshine and roses.

Tessa caught up with Alexis as she grabbed the door handle.

"Alexis." Tessa lowered her voice as she studied her friend's face. "Is everything okay? You look like you've been—"

"I'm fine." Alexis swiped at the corner of one eye,

her gaze cast downward. "I just… I'm fine." She forced a smile, finally raising her eyes to meet Tessa's. "You're going to kill them tonight. Just wait until you come out of that jacket. We're going to have to scrape everyone's jaws off the floor." She patted Tess's shoulder. "I'd tell you good luck, but something tells me that you aren't going to need it tonight."

With that, Alexis dipped out of the green room and was gone.

When Tess turned around, Daniel was standing there, staring after the other woman. He quickly turned away, busying himself with grabbing a bottle of water from the table.

There was definitely something going on with the two of them. And if there was, Tessa could understand why they wouldn't want to make their relationship public. Daniel's grandmother, Rose Clayton, and Alexis's grandfather, Gus Slade, once an item, had been feuding for years.

In recent months, they seemed to at least have found the civility to be decent toward one another. Most likely for the sake of everyone around them. Still, there was no love lost between those two families.

"Looks like Royal has its very own Romeo and Juliet," she muttered under her breath.

Tess took her seat, her hands trembling slightly and butterflies fluttering in her stomach. She closed her eyes, imagining how Ryan would react to seeing her out there on that stage.

Five

Ryan hung back at the bar as the bachelor auction wound down. There were just a couple more bachelors on the list, then Tess would be up.

He gulped the glass of water with lemon he was drinking. He'd talked to just about everyone here. But with neither Tripp nor Tess to hang out with, he'd been ready to leave nearly an hour ago.

Then again, his discomfort had little to do with him going stag for the night and everything to do with the fact that his best friend would be trotted out onto the stage and bid on. His gaze shifted around the garden at the unattached men in attendance. Most of them were members of the Texas Cattleman's Club. Some of them second, third or even fourth generation. All of them were good people, as far as he knew. So why was he assessing them all suspiciously? Wondering which of them would bid on his best friend.

The next bachelor, Lloyd Richardson, was called onto the stage and Alexis read his bio. Women were chomping at the bit to bid on the guy. Including Gail Walker. She'd started with a low, reasonable bid. But four or five other women were countering her bids as quickly as she was making them.

First the bid was in the hundreds, then the thousands. Suddenly, Steena Goodman, a wealthy older woman whose husband had been active in the club for many years before his death, stood and placed her final bid. Fifty-thousand dollars.

Ryan nearly coughed. What was it about this guy that had everyone up in arms?

Steena's bid was much higher than the previous bid of nine thousand dollars. The competing bidders pouted, acknowledging their defeat.

But not Gail. She looked angry and hurt. She stared Steena down, her arms folded and breathing heavily.

Alexis glanced back and forth at the two women for a moment. When Rachel nudged her, she cleared her throat and resumed her duties as auctioneer. "Going once, going twice—"

"One hundred thousand dollars." Gail stared at Steena, as if daring her to outbid her.

The older woman huffed and put her paddle down on the table, conceding the bid.

"Oh my God! One hundred thousand dollars." Alexis began the sentence nearly shrieking but ended with an implied question mark.

Probably because she was wondering the same thing he was.

Where in the hell did Gail Walker get that kind of cash?

Alexis declared Gail the winner of the bid at one hundred thousand dollars.

The woman squealed and ran up on stage. She wrapped her arms around Lloyd's neck and pulled him down for a hot, steamy kiss. Then she grabbed his hand and dragged him off the stage and through the doors that led from the garden back into the main building.

Ryan leaned against the bar, still shocked by Gail's outrageous bid. He sighed. Just one more bachelor, Daniel Clayton. Then Tess was up.

"That was certainly unexpected." Gus Slade ordered a beer from the bar. "Had no idea she was sitting on that kind of disposable cash."

"Neither did I, but I guess we all have our little secrets."

The older man grimaced, as if he'd taken exception to Ryan's words. Which only made Ryan wonder what secrets the old man might be hiding.

"Yes, well, I s'pose that's true." Gus nodded, then walked away.

Ryan turned his attention back to the stage just in time to see Daniel Clayton being whisked away excitedly by an overeager bidder.

There was a noticeable lull as Alexis watched the woman escort Daniel away. Rachel placed a hand on her cohost's back as she took the microphone from Alexis and thanked her for putting on a great event and being an incredible auctioneer.

Alexis seemed to recover from the momentarily stunned look she'd had seconds earlier. She nodded toward Rachel and then to the crowd which clapped appreciatively.

"This has been an amazing night, and thanks to

your generosity, ladies, and to the generosity of our bachelors, we've already exceeded our fund-raising goal for tonight. So thank you all for that. Give yourselves a big hand."

Rachel clapped a hand against the inside of her wrist as the rest of the audience clapped, hooted and shouted.

"But we're not done yet. It's time for the surprise you gents have been waiting for this evening. Fellas, please welcome our lone bachelorette, Miss Tessa Noble."

Ryan pulled out his phone. He'd promised Tripp that he'd record his sister's big debut.

There was a collective gasp in the room as Tessa stepped out onto the stage. Ryan moved away from the bar, so he could get a better view of his friend.

His jaw dropped, and his phone nearly clattered to the ground.

"Tess?" Ryan choked out the word, then silently cursed himself, realizing his stunned reaction would end up on the video. He snapped his gaping mouth shut as he watched her strut across the stage in a glamorous red pantsuit that seemed to be designed for the express purpose of highlighting her killer curves.

Damn, she's fine.

He wasn't an idiot. Nor was he blind. So he wasn't oblivious to the fact that his best friend also happened to be an extremely beautiful woman. And despite her tomboy wardrobe, he was fully aware of the hot body buried beneath relaxed fit clothing. But today…those curves had come out to play.

As if she was a professional runway model, Tess pranced to the end of the stage in strappy, glittery heels, put one hand on her hip and cocked it to the side. She seemed buoyed by the crowd's raucous reaction.

First there was the collective gasp, followed by a chorus of Oh my Gods. Now the crowd was whooping and shouting.

A slow grin spread across her lips, painted a deep, flirtatious shade of red that made him desperate to taste them. She turned and walked back toward where Rachel stood, revealing a large, heart-shaped cutout that exposed the warm brown skin of her open back. A large bow was tied behind her graceful neck.

Tessa Noble was one gift he'd give just about anything to unwrap.

She was incredibly sexy with a fiercely confident demeanor that only made him hunger for her more.

Ryan surveyed the crowd. He obviously wasn't the only man in the room drooling over Tessa 2.0. He stared at the large group of men who were wide-eyed, slack-jawed and obviously titillated by the woman on stage.

Tessa's concerns that no one would bid on her were obviously misplaced. There were even a couple of women who seemed to be drooling over her.

Ryan's heart thudded. Suddenly, there wasn't enough air in the tented, outdoor space. He grabbed his auction paddle and crept closer to the stage.

Rachel read Tessa's bio aloud, as Alexis had done with the bachelors who'd gone before her. Tessa stood tall with her back arched and one hand on her hip. She held her head high as she scanned the room.

Was she looking for him?

Ryan's cheeks flushed with heat. A dozen emotions percolated in his chest, like some strange, volatile mixture, as he studied his friend on stage. Initially, he wanted to rush the stage and drape his jacket over her shoulders. Block the other men's lurid stares. Then there was his own guttural reaction to seeing Tess this way. He wanted to devour her. Kiss every inch of the warm, brown skin on her back. Glide his hands over her luscious bottom. Taste those pouty lips.

He swallowed hard, conscious of his rapid breathing. He hoped the video wasn't picking that up, too.

Rachel had moved on from Tessa's bio to describing her date. "For the lucky gentleman with the winning bid, your very special outing with this most lovely lady will be every man's fantasy come true. Your football-themed date will begin with seats on the fifty-yard line to watch America's team play football against their division rivals. Plus, you'll enjoy a special tailgating meal before the game at a restaurant right there in the stadium. Afterward, you'll share an elegant steak dinner at a premium steak house."

"Shit." Ryan cringed, realizing that, too, would be captured on the video.

There was already a stampede of overly eager men ready to take Tessa up on her offer. Now she'd gone and raised the stakes.

Just great.

Ryan huffed, his free hand clenched in a fist at his side, as her words reverberated through him.

You're only supposed to bid if no one else does.

Suddenly, Tessa's gaze met his, and her entire face lit up in a broad smile that made her even more beautiful. A feat he wouldn't have thought possible.

His heart expanded in his chest as he returned her smile and gave her a little nod.

Tess stood taller. As if his smile had lifted her. Made her even more confident.

And why shouldn't she be? She'd commanded the attention of every man in the room, single or not. Had all the women in the crowd enviously whispering among themselves.

"All right, gentlemen, get your paddles ready, because it's your turn to bid on our lovely bachelorette." Rachel grinned proudly.

He'd bet anything she was behind Tessa's incredible makeover. Ryan didn't know if he wanted to thank her or blame her for messing up a good thing. Back when no one else in town realized what a diamond his Tess was.

He shook his head. *Get it together, Bateman. She doesn't belong to you.*

"Shall we open the bidding at five-hundred dollars?" Rachel asked the crowd.

"A thousand dollars." Clem Davidson, a man his father's age, said.

"Fifteen hundred," Bo Davis countered. He was younger than Clem, but still much older than Tess.

Ryan clenched the paddle in his hand so tightly he thought it might snap in two as several of the men bid furiously for Tess. His heart thumped. Beads of sweat formed over his brow and trickled down his back as his gaze and the camera's shifted from the crowd of enthusiastic bidders to Tessa's shocked expression and then back again.

"Ten thousand bucks." Clem held his paddle high and looked around the room, as if daring anyone else to bid against him. He'd bid fifteen hundred dollars more than Bo's last bid.

Bo grimaced, but then nodded to Clem in concession.

"Twelve thousand dollars." It nearly came as a surprise to Ryan that the voice was his own.

Clem scowled. "Thirteen thousand."

"Fifteen thousand." Now Ryan's voice was the one that was indignant as he stared the older man down.

Clem narrowed his gaze at Ryan, his jaw clenched. He started to raise his paddle, but then his expression softened. Head cocked to the side, he furrowed his brows for a moment. Suddenly, he nodded to Ryan and put his paddle back down at his side.

"Fifteen thousand dollars going once. Fifteen thousand dollars going twice." Rachel looked around the room, excitedly. "Sold! Ryan Bateman, you may claim your bachelorette."

Ryan froze for a moment as everyone in the room looked at him, clapping and cheering. Many of them with knowing smiles. He cleared his throat, ended the recording and slowly made his way toward the stage and toward his friend who regarded him with utter confusion.

He stuffed his phone into his pocket, gave Tess an awkward hug and pressed a gentle kiss to her cheek for the sake of the crowd.

They all cheered, and he escorted Tess off the stage. Then Rachel and Alexis wrapped up the auction.

"Oh my God, what did you just do?" Tessa whispered loudly enough for him to hear her over all the noise.

"Can't rightly say I know," he responded, not looking at her, but fully aware of his hand on her waist, his thumb resting on the soft skin of her back. Electricity sparked in his fingertips. Trailed up his arm.

"I appreciate what you did, Rye. It was a very generous donation. But I thought we agreed you would only bid if no one else did." Tessa folded her arms as she stared at him, searching his face for an answer.

"I know, and I was following the plan, I was. But I just couldn't let you go home with a guy like Clem."

Tessa stared up into his green eyes, her own eyes widening in response. Ryan Bateman was her oldest and closest friend. She knew just about everything there was to know about him. But the man standing before her was a mystery.

He'd gone beyond his usual protectiveness of her and had landed squarely into possessive territory. To be honest, it was kind of a turn-on. Which was problematic. Because Rye was her best friend. Emphasis on *friend*.

She folded her arms over her chest, suddenly self-conscious about whether the tightening of her nipples was visible through the thin material.

"And what, exactly, is it that you have against Clem?"

Ryan shook his head. "Nothing really." He seemed dazed, maybe even a little confused himself. "I just didn't want you to go out with him. He's too old for you."

"That's ageist." She narrowed her gaze.

It was true that she'd certainly never considered Clem Davidson as anything other than a nice older man. Still, it wasn't right for Ryan to single him out because of his age. It was a football date. Plain and simple. There would be no sex. With anyone.

"Clem isn't that much older than us, you know. Ten or fifteen years, tops." She relaxed her arms and ran her fingers through the silky waves that she still hadn't gotten accustomed to.

Ryan seemed to tense at the movement. He clenched his hand at his side, then nodded. "You're right on both counts. But what's done is done." He shrugged.

"What if it had been Bo instead? Would you have outbid him, too?"

"Yes." He seemed to regret his response, or at least the conviction with which he'd uttered the word. "I mean…yes," he said again.

"You just laid down fifteen grand for me," Tess said as they approached the bar. "The least I can do is buy you a drink."

She patted her hips, then remembered that her money and credit cards were in her purse backstage.

"Never mind. I've got it. Besides, I'm already running a tab." Ryan ordered a Jack and Coke for himself and one for her, which she turned down, requesting club soda with lime instead. "You…uh…you look pretty incredible."

"Thanks." She tried to sound grateful for the compliment, but when everyone fawned over how good she looked tonight, all she heard was the implication that her everyday look was a hot mess.

Her tomboy wardrobe had been a conscious choice, beginning back in grade school. She'd developed early. Saw how it had changed the other kids' perception of her. With the exception of Ryan, the boys she'd been friends with were suddenly more fascinated with her budding breasts than anything she had to say. And they'd come up with countless ways to cop an "accidental" feel.

Several of the girls were jealous of her newfound

figure and the resulting attention from the boys. They'd said hateful things to her and started blatantly false rumors about her, which only brought more unwanted attention from the boys.

Tess had recognized, even then, that the problem was theirs, not hers. That they were immature and stupid. Still, it didn't stop the things they'd said from hurting.

She'd been too embarrassed to tell Tripp or Ryan, who were a few grades ahead of her. And she was worried that Ryan's temper would get him in serious trouble. She hadn't told her parents, either. They would've come to her school, caused a scene and made her even more of a social pariah.

So she'd worn bulky sweaters, loose jeans and flannel shirts that masked her curves and made her feel invisible.

After a while, she'd gotten comfortable in her wardrobe. Made it her own. Until it felt like her daily armor.

Wearing a seductive red pantsuit, with her entire back exposed and every curve she owned on display, made her feel as vulnerable as if she'd traipsed across the stage naked.

But she was glad she'd done it. That she'd reclaimed a little of herself.

The bartender brought their drinks and Ryan stuffed a few dollars into the tip jar before taking a generous gulp of his drink.

"So, is this your new look?" An awkward smile lit Ryan's eyes. "'Cause it's gonna be mighty hard for you to rope a steer in that getup."

"Shut it, Rye." She pointed a finger at him, and they both laughed.

When they finally recovered from their laughter, she took his glass from his hand and took a sip of his drink. His eyes darkened as he watched her, his jaw tensing again.

"Not bad. Maybe I will have one." She handed it back to him.

Without taking his eyes off of her, Ryan signaled for the bartender to bring a Jack and Coke for her, too. There was something in his stare. A hunger she hadn't seen before.

She often longed for Ryan to see her as more than just "one of the boys." Now that it seemed he was finally seeing her that way, it was unsettling. His heated stare made her skin prickle with awareness.

The prospect of Ryan being as attracted to her as she was to him quickened her pulse and sent a shock of warmth through her body. But just as quickly, she thought of how her relationship with the boys in school had changed once they saw her differently.

That wasn't something she ever wanted to happen between her and Ryan. She could deal with her eternal, unrequited crush, but she couldn't deal with losing his friendship.

She cleared her throat, and it seemed to break them both from the spell they'd both fallen under.

They were just caught up in emotions induced by the incredibly romantic setting, the fact that she looked like someone wholly different than her everyday self, and the adrenaline they'd both felt during the auction. Assigning it meaning…that would be a grave mistake. One that would leave one or both of them sorely disappointed once the bubble of illusion burst.

"So…since it's just us, we don't need to go out on a

date. Because that would be…you know…weird. But, I'm totally down for hanging out. And seats on the fifty-yard line…so…yay."

"That's what I was really after." Ryan smirked, sipping his drink. "You could've been wearing a brown potato sack, and I still would've bid on those tickets. It's like the whole damned date had my name written all over it." His eyes widened with realization. "Wait… you did tailor it just for me, didn't you?"

Tessa's cheeks heated. She took a deep sip of her drink and returned it to the bar, waving a hand dismissively.

"Don't get ahead of yourself, partner. I simply used your tastes as a point of reference. After all, you, Tripp and my dad are the only men that I've been spending any significant time with these days. I figured if you'd like it, the bidders would, too."

"Hmm…" Ryan took another sip of his drink, almost sounding disappointed. "Makes sense, I guess."

"I'm glad you get it. Alexis and Rachel thought it was the least romantic thing they could imagine. They tried to talk me into something else. Something grander and more flowery."

"Which neither of us would've enjoyed." Ryan nodded. "And the makeover… I assume that was Rachel's idea, too."

"Both Alexis and Rachel came up with that one. Alexis got PURE to donate a spa day and the makeover, so it didn't cost me anything." Tessa tucked her hair behind her ear and studied her friend's face. "You don't like it?"

"No, of course I do. I love it. You look…incredible.

You really do. Your parents are going to flip when they see this." He patted the phone in his pocket.

"You recorded it? Oh no." Part of her was eager to see the video. Another part of her cringed at the idea of watching herself prance across that stage using the catwalk techniques she'd studied online.

But no matter how silly she might feel right now, she was glad she'd successfully worked her magic on the crowd.

The opening chords of one of her favorite old boy band songs drew her attention to the stage where the band was playing.

"Oh my God, I love that song." Tessa laughed, sipping the last of her drink and then setting the glass on the bar. "Do you remember what a crush I had on these guys?"

Rye chuckled, regarding her warmly over the rim of his glass as he finished off his drink, too. "I remember you playing this song on repeat incessantly."

"That CD was my favorite possession. I still can't believe I lost it."

Ryan lowered his gaze, his chin dipping. He tapped a finger on the bar before raising his eyes to hers again and taking her hand. "I need to make a little confession."

"You rat!" She poked him in the chest. "You did something to my CD, didn't you?"

A guilty smirk curled the edges of his mouth. "Tripp and I couldn't take it anymore. We might've trampled the thing with a horse or two, then dumped it."

"You two are awful." She realized that she'd gone a little overboard in her obsession with the group. But trampling the album with a horse? That was harsh.

"If I'm being honest, I've always felt incredibly

guilty about my role in the whole sordid affair." Ryan placed his large, warm hand on her shoulder. The tiny white lights that decorated the space were reflected in his green eyes. "Let me make it up to you."

"And just how do you plan to do that?" Tessa folded her arms, cocking a brow.

He pulled out his phone, swiped through a few screens. "First of all, I just ordered you another copy of that album—CD and digital."

She laughed. "You didn't need to do that, Rye."

"I did, and I feel much better now. Not just because it was wrong of us to take away something you loved so much. Because I hated having that secret between us all these years. You're the one person in the world I can tell just about anything. So it feels pretty damn good to finally clear my conscience." He dropped his hand from her shoulder.

"All right." She forced a smile, trying her best to hide her disappointment at the loss of his touch. "And what's the second thing?"

He held his large, open palm out to her. "It seems I've bought myself a date for the night. Care to dance?"

"You want to dance to this sappy, boy band song that you've always hated?"

He grabbed her hand and led her to the dance floor. "Then I guess there's one more confession I need to make… I've always kind of liked this song. I just didn't want your brother to think I'd gone soft."

Tessa laughed as she joined her best friend on the dance floor.

Six

Gus Slade watched as Tessa Noble and Ryan Bateman entered the dance floor, both of them laughing merrily. Gus shook his head. Ryan was one of the prospects he'd considered as a good match for his granddaughter Alexis. Only it was clear that Ryan and Tess were hung up on each other, even if the self-proclaimed "best friends" weren't prepared to admit it to themselves.

It was no wonder Ryan's brief engagement to that wannabe supermodel he'd met in the city didn't last long enough for the two of them to make it to the altar.

Encouraging Alexis to start something with the Bateman boy would only result in heartache for his granddaughter once Ryan and Tess finally recognized the attraction flickering between them.

He'd experienced that kind of hurt and pain in his life when the woman he'd once loved, whom he thought truly loved him, had suddenly turned against him, shutting him out of her life.

It was something he'd never truly gotten over. Despite a long and happy marriage that lasted until the death of his dear wife.

Gus glanced over at Rose Clayton, his chest tightening. Even after all these years, the woman was still gorgeous. Just a hint of gray was visible at her temples. The rest of her hair was the same dark brown it was when she was a girl. She wore it in a stylish, modern cut that befit a mature woman. Yet, anyone who didn't know her could easily mistake her for a much younger woman.

And after all these years, Rose Clayton still turned heads, including his. The woman managed to stay as slim now as she had been back when she was a young girl. Yet, there was nothing weak or frail about Rose Clayton.

Her every move, her every expression, exuded a quiet confidence that folks around Royal had always respected. And tonight, he had to admit that she looked simply magnificent.

Gus glanced around the tented garden area again. The space looked glorious. Better than he could ever have imagined when the club first decided to undertake a major renovation of this space and a few other areas of the club, which had been in operation since the 1920s.

Alexis had headed up the committee that put on the auction. And his granddaughter had truly outdone herself.

Gus searched the crowd for Alexis. Her duties as

Mistress of Ceremony appeared to be over for the night. Still, he couldn't locate her anywhere.

Gus walked toward the main building. Perhaps she was in the office or one of the other interior spaces. But as he looked through the glass pane, he could see Alexis inside, hemmed up by Daniel Clayton. From the looks of it, they were arguing.

Fists clenched at his sides, Gus willed himself to stay where he was rather than rushing inside and demanding that Daniel leave his granddaughter alone. If he did that, then Alexis would defend the boy.

That would defeat the purpose of the elaborate plan he and Rose Clayton had concocted to keep their grandkids apart.

So he'd wait there. Monitor the situation without interfering. He didn't want his granddaughter marrying any kin to Rose Clayton. Especially a boy with a mother like Stephanie Clayton. A heavy drinker who'd been in and out of trouble her whole life. A woman who couldn't be bothered to raise her own boy. Instead, she'd dumped him off on Rose who'd raised Daniel as if he was her own son.

From where he stood, it appeared that Daniel was pleading with Alexis. But she shoved his hand away when he tried to touch her arm.

Gus smirked, glad to see that someone besides him was getting the sharp end of that fierce stubborn streak she'd inherited from him.

Suddenly, his granddaughter threw her arms up and said something to Daniel that he obviously didn't like. Then she turned and headed his way.

Gus moved away from the door and around the corner to the bar as quickly and quietly as he could. He waited for her to pass by.

"Alexis!" Gus grabbed hold of her elbow as she hurried past him. He chuckled good-naturedly. "Where's the fire, darlin'?"

She didn't laugh. In fact, the poor thing looked dazed, like a wounded bird that had fallen out of the nest before it was time.

"Sorry, I didn't see you, Grandad." Her eyes didn't meet his. Instead, she looked toward the office where she was headed. "I'm sorry I don't have time to talk right now. I need to deal with a major problem."

"Alexis, honey, what is it? Is everything all right?"

"It will be, I'm sure. I just really need to take care of this now, okay?" Her voice trembled, seemed close to breaking.

"I wanted to tell you how proud I am of you. Tonight was magnificent and you've raised so much money for pancreatic cancer research. Your grandmother would be so very proud of you."

Alexis suddenly raised her gaze to his, the corners of her eyes wet with tears. Rather than the intended effect of comforting her, his words seemed to cause her distress.

"Alexis, what's wrong?" Gus pleaded with his darling girl. The pain in her blue eyes, rimmed with tears, tore at his heart. "Whatever it is, you can talk to me."

Before she could answer, Daniel Clayton passed by. He and Alexis exchanged a long, painful look. Then Daniel dropped his gaze and continued to the other side of the room.

"Alexis, darlin', what's going on?"

The tears spilled from her eyes. Alexis sucked in a deep breath and sniffled.

"It's nothing I can't handle, Grandad." She wiped away the tears with brusque swipes of her hand and shook her head. "Thank you for everything you said. I appreciate it. Really. But I need to take care of this issue. I'll see you back at home later, okay?"

Alexis pressed a soft kiss to his whiskered cheek. Then she hurried off toward the clubhouse offices.

Gus sighed, leaning against the bar. He dropped on to the stool, tapped the bar to get the bartender's attention, and ordered a glass of whiskey, neat. He gripped the hard, cold glass without moving it to his lips.

Their little plan was a partial success. Neither he nor Rose had been able to match their grandchildren up with an eligible mate. Yet, they'd done exactly what they'd set out to do. They'd driven a wedge between Daniel and Alexis.

So why didn't he feel good about what they'd done?

Because their grandkids were absolutely miserable.

What kind of grandfather could rejoice in the heartbreak of a beautiful girl like Alexis?

"Hello, Gus." Rose had sidled up beside him, and ordered a white wine spritzer. "The kids didn't look too happy with each other just now."

"That's an understatement, if ever I've heard one." He gripped his glass and gulped from it. "They're in downright misery."

"Is it that bad?" She glanced over at him momentarily, studying his pained look, before accepting her glass of wine and taking a sip.

"Honestly? I think it's even worse." He scrubbed a hand down his jaw. "I feel like a heel for causing baby girl so much pain. And despite all our machinations, neither of us has found a suitable mate for our respective grandchildren."

She nodded sagely. Pain dimmed the light in her gray eyes. And for a moment, the shadow that passed over her lovely face made her look closer to her actual years.

"I'm sorry that they're both hurting. But it's better that they have their hearts broken now than to have it happen down the road, when they're both more invested in the relationship." She glanced at him squarely. "We've both known that pain. It's a feeling that never leaves you. We're both living proof of that."

"I guess we are." Gus nodded, taking another sip of his whiskey. "But maybe there's something we hadn't considered." He turned around, his back to the bar.

"And what's that?" She turned on her bar stool, too, studying the crowd.

"Daniel and Alexis share our last names, but that doesn't make them us. And it doesn't mean they're doomed to our fates."

Rose didn't respond as she watched her grandson Daniel being fawned over by the woman who'd bought him at auction. He looked about as pleased by the woman's attentions as a man getting a root canal without anesthesia.

"We did what was in their best interests. The right thing isn't always the easiest thing. I know they're hurting now, but when they each find the person they were meant to be with, they'll be thankful this happened."

Rose paid for her drink and turned to walk away.

"Rose."

She halted, glancing over her shoulder without looking directly at him.

"What if the two of them were meant to be together? Will they be grateful we interfered then?"

A heavy sigh escaped her red lips, and she gathered her shawl around her before leaving.

His eyes trailed the woman as she walked away in a glimmering green dress. The dress was long, but form-fitting. And despite her age, Rose was as tantalizing in that dress as a cool drink of water on a hot summer day.

After all these years he still had a thing for Rose Clayton. What if it was the same for Daniel and Alexis?

He ordered another whiskey, neat, hoping to God that he and Rose hadn't made a grave mistake they'd both regret.

Seven

Ryan twirled Tessa on the dance floor and then drew her back into his arms as they danced to one of his favorite upbeat country songs. Everyone around them seemed to be singing along with the lyrics which were both funny and slightly irreverent.

Tessa turned her back to him, threw her hands up, and wiggled her full hips as she sang loudly.

His attention was drawn to the sway of those sexy hips keeping time to the music. Fortunately, her dancing was much more impressive than her singing. Something his anatomy responded to, even if he didn't want it to. Particularly not while they were in the middle of a crowded dance floor.

Ryan swallowed hard and tried to shove away the rogue thoughts trying to commandeer his good sense. He and Tessa were just two friends enjoying their night together. Having a good time.

Nothing to see here, folks.

"Everything okay?" Tessa had turned around, her beautiful brown eyes focused on him and a frown tugging down the corners of her mouth.

"Yeah, of course." He forced a smile. "I was just... thinking...that's all." He started to dance again, his movements forced and rigid.

Tessa regarded him strangely, but before she could probe further, Alexis appeared beside them looking flustered. Her eyes were red, and it looked like she'd been crying.

"Alexis, is something wrong?" Tessa turned to her friend and squeezed her hand.

"I'm afraid so. I've been looking everywhere for you two. Would you mind meeting with James and me in the office as soon as possible?" Alexis leaned in, so they could both hear her over the blaring music.

"Of course, we will." Tessa gave the woman's hand another assuring squeeze. "Just lead the way."

Alexis made her way through the crowd with Tessa and Ryan following closely behind.

Ryan bit back his disappointment at the interruption. If the distress Alexis appeared to be experiencing was any indication, the situation was one level below the barn being on fire. Which triggered a burning in his gut.

Whatever Alexis and James wanted with the two of them, he was pretty sure neither of them was going to like it.

"Tessa, Ryan, please, have a seat." James Harris, president of the Texas Cattleman's Club, gestured to the chairs on the other side of the large mahogany desk in his office.

After such a successful night, he and Alexis looked incredibly grim. The knot that had already formed in her gut tightened.

She and Ryan sat in the chairs James indicated while Alexis sat on the sofa along one wall.

"Something is obviously wrong." Ryan crossed one ankle over his knee. "What is it, James?"

The other man hesitated a moment before speaking. When he did, the words he uttered came out in an anguished growl.

"There was a problem with one of the bids. A *big* problem."

"Gail." Tessa and Ryan said her name simultaneously.

"How does something like this happen?" Ryan asked after James had filled them both in. "Can anyone just walk in off the street and bid a bogus hundred K?"

James grimaced.

Tessa felt badly for him. James hadn't been president of the Texas Cattleman's Club for very long. She could only imagine how he must be feeling. He'd been riding high after putting on what was likely the most successful fund-raiser in the club's history. But now he was saddled with one of the biggest faux pas in the club's history.

"It's a charity auction. We take folks at their word when they make a bid," James replied calmly, then sighed. "Still, I don't like that this happened on my watch, and I'll do everything I can to remedy the situation."

Tessa's heart broke for the man. She didn't know James particularly well, but she'd heard the tragic story about what had happened to his brother and his sister-in-law. They'd died in an accident, leaving behind their orphaned son, who was little more than a year old, to be raised by James.

He was a nice enough guy, but he didn't seem the daddy type. Still, he was obviously doing the best he could to juggle all the balls he had in the air.

Tessa groaned, her hand pressed to her forehead. "I knew Gail had a thing for Lloyd Richardson, but I honestly never imagined she'd do something so reckless and impulsive."

"No one thinks you knew anything about it, Tess. That's not why we asked you here," Alexis assured her.

"Then why are we here?" Ryan's voice was cautious as he studied the other man.

"Because we have another dilemma that could compound the first problem." James heaved a sigh as he sat back in his chair, his hands steepled over his abdomen. "And we could really use your help to head it off."

"Was there another bid that someone can't make good on?" Ryan asked.

"No, but there is a reporter here, whom I invited." Alexis cringed as she stood. "He's intrigued by that one-hundred thousand dollar bid, and he wants to interview Gail and Lloyd."

"Damn. I see your dilemma." Ryan groaned sympathetically. "Instead of getting good press about all of the money the club did raise, all anyone will be talking about is Gail and her bogus bid."

"It gets even worse," Alexis said. She blew out a frustrated breath as she shook her head, her blond locks flipping over her shoulder. "We can't find hide nor hair of either Gail or Lloyd. It's like the two of them simply vanished."

Ryan shook his head. "Wow. That's pretty messed up."

"What is it that you want Ryan and me to do?" Tessa looked at James and then Alexis.

"The reporter was also very intrigued by everyone's reaction to you and all the drama of how Ryan beat out Clem and Bo's bids." A faint smile flickered on Alexis's mouth. "So we suggested that he follow the two of you on your little date."

"What?"

Panic suddenly seized Tessa's chest. It was one thing to play dress up and strut on the stage here at the club. Surrounded mostly by people she'd known her entire life. It was another to be followed by a reporter who was going to put the information out there for the entire world to see.

"We hadn't really intended to go on a date," Tessa said. "Ryan and I were just going to hang out together and have fun at the game. Grab a bite to eat at his favorite restaurant. Nothing worthy of reporting on."

"I know." There was an apology in Alexis's voice. "Which is why I need to ask another big favor..."

"You want us to go on a real date after all." Ryan looked from Alexis to James.

"Going out with a beautiful woman like Tess here, who also just happens to be your best friend...not the worst thing in the world that could happen to a guy." James forced a smile.

"Only...well, I know that the date you'd planned is the perfect kind of day for hanging with the guys." Alexis directed her attention toward Tess. "But this needs to feel like a big, romantic gesture. Something worthy of a big write-up for the event and for our club."

"I d-don't know, Alexis," Tessa stuttered, her heart

racing. "I'm not sure how comfortable either of us would feel having a reporter follow us around all day."

"We'll do it," Ryan said suddenly. Decisively. "For the club, of course." He cleared his throat and gave Tess a reassuring nod. "And don't worry, I know exactly what to do. I'll make sure we give him the big, romantic fantasy he's looking for."

"I'm supposed to be the one who takes you out on a date," Tess objected. "That's how this whole thing works."

"Then it'll make for an even grander gesture when I surprise you by sweeping you off your feet."

He gave her that mischievous half smile that had enticed her into countless adventures. From searching for frogs when they were kids to parasailing in Mexico as an adult. After all these years, she still hadn't grown immune to its charm.

"Fine." Tessa sighed. "We'll do it. Just tell him we'll need a day or two to finalize the arrangements."

"Thank you!" Alexis hugged them both. "We're so grateful to you both for doing this."

"You're saving our asses here and the club's reputation." James looked noticeably relieved, though his eyebrows were still furrowed. "I can't thank you enough. And you won't be the only ones on the hot seat. Rose Clayton persuaded her grandson Daniel to give the reporter an additional positive feature related to the auction."

Alexis frowned at the mention of Daniel's name, but then she quickly recovered.

"And about that bid of Gail's...no one outside this room, besides Gail and Lloyd, of course, knows the situation." James frowned again. "We'd like to keep it that way until we figure out how we're going to resolve this. So please, don't whisper a word of this to anyone."

"Least of all the reporter," Alexis added, emphatically.

Tessa and Ryan agreed. Then Alexis introduced them to the reporter, Greg Halstead. After Greg gathered some preliminary information for the piece, Ryan insisted that he be the one to exchange contact information with Greg so they could coordinate him accompanying them on their date.

Every time Greg repeated the word *date*, shivers ran down Tessa's spine.

The only thing worse than having a thing for her best friend was being shanghaied into going on a fake date with him. But she was doing this for the club that meant so much to her, her family and the community of Royal.

Alexis had worked so hard to garner positive publicity for the club. And she'd raised awareness of the need to fund research for a cure for pancreatic cancer—the disease that had killed Alexis Slade's dear grandmother. Tess wouldn't allow all of her friend's hard work to be squandered because of Gail's selfish decision. Not if she could do something to prevent it.

Maybe she hadn't been aware of what Gail had planned to do tonight. But she'd been the one who'd invited Gail to tonight's affair. Tess couldn't help feeling obligated to do what she could to rectify the matter.

Even if it meant torturing herself by going on a pretend date that would feel very real to her. No matter how much she tried to deny it.

Eight

Ryan and Tessa finally headed home in his truck after what felt like an incredibly long night.

He couldn't remember the last time he and Tessa had danced together or laughed as much as they had that evening. But that was *before* James and Alexis had asked them to go on an actual date. Since then, things felt…different.

First, they'd politely endured the awkward interview with that reporter, Greg Halstead. Then they'd gone about the rest of the evening dancing and mingling with fellow club members and their guests. But there was a strange vibe between them. Obviously, Tessa felt it, too.

Why else would she be rambling on, as she often did when she was nervous.

Then again, lost in his own thoughts, he hadn't been very good company. Ryan drummed his fingers on the steering wheel during an awkward moment of silence.

"This date…it isn't going to make things weird between us, is it?" Tess asked finally, as if she'd been inside his head all along.

One of the hazards of a friendship with someone who knew him too well.

He forced a chuckle. "C'mon, Tess. We've been best buds too long to let a fake date shake us." His eyes searched hers briefly before returning to the road. "Our friendship could withstand anything."

Anything except getting romantically involved. Which is why they hadn't and wouldn't.

"Promise?" She seemed desperate for reassurance on the matter. Not surprising. A part of him needed it, too.

"On my life." This time, there was no hesitation. There were a lot of things in this world he could do without. Tessa Noble's friendship wasn't one of them.

Tessa nodded, releasing an audible sigh of relief. She turned to look out the window at the beautiful ranches that marked the road home.

His emphatic statement seemed to alleviate the anxiety they'd both been feeling. Still, his thoughts kept returning to their date the following weekend. The contemplative look on Tess's face, indicated that hers did, too.

He changed the subject, eager to talk about anything else. "What's up with your girl bidding a hundred K she didn't have?"

"I don't know." Tess seemed genuinely baffled by Gail's behavior.

Tessa and Gail certainly weren't as close as he and

Tess were. But lately, at her mother's urging, Tessa had tried to build stronger friendships with other women in town.

She and Gail had met when Tessa had used the woman's fledgling grocery delivery business. They'd hit it off and started hanging out occasionally.

He understood why Tess liked Gail. She was bold and a little irreverent. All of the things that Tess was not. But Ryan hadn't cared much for her. There was something about that woman he didn't quite trust. But now wasn't the time for I told you so's. Tessa obviously felt badly enough about being the person who'd invited Gail to the charity auction.

"I knew she had a lightweight crush on Lloyd Richardson," Tessa continued. "Who doesn't? But I certainly didn't think her capable of doing something this crazy and impulsive."

"Seems there was a lot of that going around," Ryan muttered under his breath.

"Speaking of that impulsiveness that seemed to be going around…" Tessa laughed, and Ryan chuckled, too.

He'd obviously uttered the words more to himself than to her. Still, she'd heard them, and they provided the perfect opening for what she'd been struggling to say all night.

"Thank you again for doing this, Rye. You made a very generous donation. And though you did the complete opposite of what I asked you to do—" they both laughed again "—I was a little…no, I was a *lot* nervous about going out with either Clem or Bo in such a high pressure situation, so thank you."

"Anything for you, Tess Noble." His voice was deep and warm. The emotion behind his words genuine. Something she knew from their history, not just as theory.

When they were in college, Ryan had climbed into his battered truck, and driven nearly two thousand miles to her campus in Sacramento after a particularly bad breakup with a guy who'd been an all-around dick. He'd dumped her for someone else a few days before Valentine's Day, so Ryan made a point of taking her to the Valentine's Day party. Then he kissed her in front of everyone—including her ex.

The kiss had taken her breath away. And left her wanting another taste ever since.

Tessa shook off the memory and focused on the here and now. Ryan had been uncharacteristically quiet during the ride home. He'd let her chatter on, offering a grunt of agreement or dissension here or there. Otherwise, he seemed deep in thought.

"And you're sure I can't pay you back at least some of what you bid on me?" Tessa asked as he slowed down before turning into the driveway of the Noble Spur, her family's ranch. "Especially since you're commandeering the planning of our date."

"Oh, we're still gonna use those tickets on the fifty-yard line, for sure," he clarified. "And there's no way I'm leaving Dallas without my favorite steak dinner. I'm just going to add some flourishes here and there. Nothing too fancy. But you'll enjoy the night. I promise." He winked.

Why did that small gesture send waves of electricity down her spine and make her acutely aware of her nipples prickling with heat beneath the jacket she'd put on to ward against the chilly night air?

"Well, thank you again," she said as he shifted his tricked out Ford Super Duty F-350 Platinum into Park. Ryan was a simple guy who didn't sweat the details—except when it came to his truck.

"You're welcome." Ryan lightly gripped her elbow when she reached for the door. "Allow me. Wouldn't want you to ruin that fancy outfit of yours."

He hopped out of the truck and came around to her side. He opened the door and took her hand.

It wasn't the first time Ryan had helped her out of his vehicle. But something about this time felt different. There was something in his intense green eyes. Something he wouldn't allow himself to say. Rare for a man who normally said just about anything that popped into his head.

When she stepped down onto the truck's side rail, Ryan released her hand. He gripped her waist and lifted her to the ground in a single deft move.

Tessa gasped in surprise, bracing her hands on his strong shoulders. His eyes scanned her once more. As if he still couldn't believe it was really her in the sexiest, most feminine item of clothing she'd ever owned.

Heat radiated off his large body, shielding her from the chilliness of the night air and making her aware of how little space there was between them.

For a moment, the vision of Ryan's lips crashing down on hers as he pinned her body against the truck flashed through her brain. It wasn't an unfamiliar image. But, given their positions and the way he was looking at her right now, it felt a little too real.

Tessa took short, shallow breaths, her chest heaving.

She needed to get away from Ryan Bateman before she did something stupid. Like lift on to her toes and press a hot, wet kiss to those sensual lips.

She needed to get inside and go to her room. The proper place to have ridiculously inappropriate thoughts about her best friend. With her battery-operated boyfriend buried in the nightstand drawer on standby, just in case she needed to take the edge off.

But walking away was a difficult thing to do when his mouth was mere inches from hers. And she trembled with the desire to touch him. To taste his mouth again. To trace the ridge behind the fly of his black dress pants.

"Good night." She tossed the words over her shoulder as she turned and headed toward the house as quickly as her feet would carry her in those high-heeled silver sandals.

"Tessa." His unusually gruff voice stopped her dead in her tracks.

She didn't turn back to look at him. Instead, she glanced just over her shoulder. A sign that he had her full attention, even if her eyes didn't meet his. "Yes?"

"I'm calling an audible on our date this weekend." Ryan invoked one of his favorite football terms.

"A last-minute change?" Tessa turned slightly, her curiosity piqued.

She'd planned the perfect weekend for Ryan Bateman. What could she possibly have missed?

"I'll pick you up on Friday afternoon, around 3:00 p.m. Pack a bag for the weekend. And don't forget that jumpsuit."

"We're spending the entire weekend in Dallas?" She turned to face him fully, stunned by the hungry look on his face. When he nodded his confirmation, Tessa focused on slowing her breath as she watched the cloud her warm breath made in the air. "Why? And since when do you care what I wear?"

"Because I promised Alexis I'd make this date a big, grand gesture that would keep the reporter preoccupied and off the topic of our missing bachelor and his hundred-thousand-dollar bidder." His words were matter of fact, signaling none of the raw, primal heat she'd seen in his eyes a moment ago.

He shut the passenger door and walked around to the driver's side. "It doesn't have to be that same outfit. It's just that you looked mighty pretty tonight. Neither of us gets much of a chance to dress up. Thought it'd be nice if we took advantage of this weekend to do that." He shrugged, as if it were the most normal request in the world.

This coming from a man who'd once stripped out of his tuxedo in the car on the way home from a mutual friend's out-of-town wedding. He'd insisted he couldn't stand to be in that tuxedo a moment longer.

"Fine." Tessa shrugged, too. If it was no big deal to Ryan, then it was no big deal to her either. "I'll pack a couple of dresses and skirts. Maybe I'll wear the dress I'd originally picked out for tonight. Before I volunteered to be in the auction."

After all that waxing, she should show her baby smooth legs off every chance she got. Who knew when she'd put herself through that kind of torture again?

"Sounds like you got some packing to do." A restrained smirk lit Ryan's eyes. He nodded toward the house. "Better get inside before you freeze out here."

"'Night, Ryan." Tessa turned up the path to the

house, without waiting for his response, and let herself in, closing the door behind her. The slam of the heavy truck door, followed by the crunch of gravel, indicated that Ryan was turning his vehicle around in the drive and heading home to the Bateman Ranch next door.

Tessa released a long sigh, her back pressed to the door.

She'd just agreed to spend the weekend in Dallas with her best friend. Seventy-two hours of pretending she didn't secretly lust after Ryan Bateman. Several of which would be documented by a reporter known for going after gossip.

Piece of cake. Piece of pie.

Nine

"Tessa, your chariot is here," Tripp called to her upstairs. "Hurry up, you're not gonna believe this."

Tripp was definitely back to his old self. It was both a blessing and a curse, because he hadn't stopped needling her and Ryan about their date ever since.

She inhaled deeply, then slowly released the breath as she stared at herself in the mirror one last time.

It's just a weekend trip with a friend. Ryan and I have done this at least a dozen times before. No big deal.

Tessa lifted her bag on to her shoulder, then made her way downstairs and out front where Tripp was handing her overnight suitcase off to Ryan.

Her eyes widened as she walked closer, studying the sleek black sedan with expensive black rims.

"Is that a black on black Maybach?"

"It is." Ryan took the bag from her and loaded it into the trunk of the Mercedes Maybach before closing it and opening the passenger door. He gestured for her to get inside. "You've always said you wanted to know what it was like to ride in one of these things, so—"

"You didn't go out and buy this, did you?" Panic filled her chest. Ryan wasn't extravagant or impulsive. And he'd already laid out a substantial chunk of change as a favor to her.

"No, of course not. You know a mud-caked pickup truck is more my style." He leaned in and lowered his voice, so only she could hear his next words. "But I'm supposed to be going for the entire illusion here, remember? And Tess…"

"Yes?" She inhaled his clean, fresh scent, her heart racing slightly from his nearness and the intimacy of his tone.

"Smile for the camera." Ryan nodded toward Greg Halstead who waved and snapped photographs of the two of them in front of the vehicle.

Tess deepened her smile, and she and Ryan stood together, his arm wrapped around her as the man clicked photos for the paper.

When Greg had gotten enough images, he shook their hands and said he'd meet them at the hotel later and at the restaurant tomorrow night to get a few more photos.

"Which hotel? And which restaurant?" Tessa turned to Ryan.

A genuine smile lit his green eyes and they sparkled in the afternoon sunlight. "If I tell you, it won't be a surprise, now will it?"

"Smart-ass." She folded her arms and shook her

head. Ryan knew she liked surprises about as much as she liked diamondback rattlesnakes. Maybe even a little less.

"There anything I should know about you two?" Tripp stepped closer after the reporter was gone. Arms folded over his chest, his gaze shifted from Ryan to her and then back again.

"You can take the protective big brother shtick down a notch," she teased. "I already explained everything to you. We're doing this for the club, and for Alexis."

She flashed her I'm-your-little-sister-and-you-love-me-no-matter-what smile. It broke him. As it had for as long as she could remember.

The edge of his mouth tugged upward in a reluctant grin. He opened his arms and hugged her goodbye before giving Ryan a one-arm bro hug and whispering something to him that she couldn't hear.

Ryan's expression remained neutral, but he nodded and patted her brother on the shoulder.

"We'd better get going." Ryan helped her into the buttery, black leather seat that seemed to give her a warm hug. Then he closed her door and climbed into the driver's seat.

"God, this car is beautiful," she said as he pulled away from the house. "If you didn't buy it, whose is it?

"Borrowed it from a friend." He pulled on to the street more carefully than he did when he was driving his truck. "The guy collects cars the way other folks collect stamps or Depression-era glass. Most of the cars he wouldn't let anyone breathe on, let alone touch. But he owed me a favor."

Tessa sank back against the seat and ran her hand along the smooth, soft leather.

"Manners would dictate that I tell you that you shouldn't have, but if I'm being honest, all I can think is, Where have you been all my life?" They both chuckled. "You think I can have a saddle made out of this leather?"

"For the right price, you can get just about anything." A wide smile lit his face.

Tessa sighed. She was content. Relaxed. And Ryan seemed to be, too. There was no reason this weekend needed to be tense and awkward.

"So, what did my brother say to you when he gave you that weird bro hug goodbye?"

The muscles in Ryan's jaw tensed and his brows furrowed. He kept his gaze on the road ahead. "This thing has an incredible sound system. I already synced it to my phone. Go ahead and play something. Your choice. Just no more '80s boy bands. I heard enough of those at the charity auction last week."

Tessa smirked. "You could've just told me it was none of my business what Tripp said."

His wide smile returned, though he didn't look at her. "I thought I just did."

They both laughed, and Tessa smiled to herself. Their weekend was going to be fun. Just like every other road trip they'd ever taken together. Things would only be uncomfortable between them if she made them that way.

Ryan, Tessa and Greg Halstead headed up the stone stairs that led to the bungalow of a fancy, art-themed boutique hotel that he'd reserved. The place was an easy drive from the football stadium.

Tessa had marveled at the hotel's main building and

mused about the expense. But she was as excited as a little kid in a candy store, eager to see what was on the other side of that door. Greg requested to go in first, so he could set up his shot of Tessa stepping inside the room.

When he signaled that he was ready, Ryan inserted the key card into the lock and removed it quickly. Once the green light flashed, he opened the door for her.

Tessa's jaw dropped, and she covered her mouth with both hands, genuinely stunned by the elegant beauty of the contemporary bungalow.

"So…what do you think?" He couldn't shake the nervousness he felt. The genuine need to impress her was not his typical MO. So what was going on? Maybe it was the fact that her impression would be recorded for posterity.

"It's incredible, Ryan. I don't know what to say." Her voice trembled with emotion. When she glanced up at him, her eyes were shiny. She wiped quickly at the corners of her eyes. "I'm being silly, I know."

"No, you're not." He kissed her cheek. "That's exactly the reaction I was hoping for."

Ryan stepped closer and lowered his voice. "I want this to be a special weekend for you, Tess. What you did last week at the charity auction was brave, and I'm proud of you. I want this weekend to be everything the fearless woman who strutted across that stage last Saturday night deserves."

His eyes met hers for a moment and his chest filled with warmth.

"Thanks, Rye. This place is amazing. I really appreciate everything you've done." A soft smile curled the edges of her mouth, filling him with the overwhelming desire to lean down and kiss her the way he had at that Valentine's Day party in college.

He stepped back and cleared his throat, indicating that she should step inside.

Tessa went from room to room of the two-bedroom, two-bath hotel suite, complete with two balconies. One connected to each bedroom. There was even a small kitchen island, a full-size refrigerator and a stove. The open living room boasted a ridiculously large television mounted to the wall and a fireplace in both that space and the master bedroom, which he insisted that she take. But Tessa, who could be just as stubborn as he was, wouldn't hear of it. She directed the bellman to take her things to the slightly smaller bedroom, which was just as beautiful as its counterpart.

"I think I have all the pictures I need." Greg gathered up his camera bag and his laptop. "I'll work on the article tonight and select the best photos among the ones I've taken so far. I'll meet you guys at the restaurant tomorrow at six-thirty to capture a few more shots."

"Sounds good." Ryan said goodbye to Greg and closed the door behind him, glad the man was finally gone. Something about a reporter hanging around, angling for a juicy story, felt like a million ants crawling all over his skin.

He sank on to the sofa, shrugged his boots off, and put his feet up on the coffee table. It'd been a short drive from Royal to Dallas, but mentally, he was exhausted.

Partly from making last-minute arrangements for their trip. Partly from the effort of reminding himself that no matter how much it felt like it, this wasn't a real date. They were both just playing their parts. Making the TCC look good and diverting attention from the debacle of Gail's bid.

"Hey." Tess emerged from her bedroom where she'd gone to put her things away. "Is Greg gone?"

"He left a few minutes ago. Said to tell you goodbye."

"Thank goodness." She heaved a sigh and plopped down on the sofa beside him. "I mean, he's a nice guy and everything. It just feels so... I don't know..."

"Creepy? Invasive? Weird?" he offered. "Take your pick."

"All of the above." Tessa laughed, then leaned forward, her gaze locked on to the large bouquet of flowers in a glass vase on the table beside his feet.

"I thought these were just part of the room." She removed the small envelope with her name on it and slid her finger beneath the flap, prying it open. "These are for me?"

"I hope you like them. They're—"

"Peonies. My favorite flower." She leaned forward and inhaled the flowers that resembled clouds dyed shades of light and dark pink. "They're beautiful, Ryan. Thank you. You thought of everything, didn't you?" Her voice trailed and her gaze softened.

"I meant it when I said you deserve a really special weekend. I even asked them to stock the freezer with your favorite brand of Neapolitan ice cream."

"Seriously?" She was only wearing a hint of lip gloss in a nude shade of pink and a little eyeshadow and mascara. But she was as beautiful as he'd ever seen her. Even more so than the night of the auction when she'd worn a heavy layer of makeup that had covered her creamy brown skin. Sunlight filtered into the room, making her light brown eyes appear almost golden. "What more could I possibly ask for?"

His eyes were locked on her sensual lips. When he finally tore his gaze away from them, Tess seemed disappointed. As if she'd expected him to lean in and kiss her.

"I like the dress, by the way."

"Really?" She stood, looking down at the heather-gray dress and the tan calf-high boots topped by knee socks. The cuff of the socks hovered just above the top of the boot, drawing his eye there and leading it up the side of her thigh where her smooth skin disappeared beneath the hem of her dress.

His body stiffened in response to her curvy silhouette and her summery citrus scent.

Fucking knee socks. *Seriously*? Tess was *killing* him.

For a moment he wondered if she was teasing him on purpose. Reminding him of the things he couldn't have with her. The red-hot desires that would never be satisfied.

Tess seemed completely oblivious to her effect on him as she regarded the little gray dress.

Yet, all he could think of was how much he'd like to see that gray fabric pooled on the floor beside his bed.

Ryan groaned inside. This was going to be the longest seventy-two hours of his life.

Ten

"Is that a bottle of champagne?" Tessa pointed to a bottle chilling in an ice bucket on the sideboard along the wall.

She could use something cold to tamp down the heat rising in her belly under Ryan's intense stare. It also wouldn't be a bad idea to create some space between them. Enough to get her head together and stop fantasizing about what it would feel like to kiss her best friend again.

"Even better." Ryan flashed a sexy, half grin. "It's imported Italian Moscato d'Asti. I asked them to chill a bottle for us."

Her favorite. Too bad this wasn't a real date, because Ryan had ticked every box of what her fantasy date would look like.

"Saving it for something special?"

"Just you." He winked, climbing to his feet. "Why don't we make a toast to kick our weekend off?"

Tessa relaxed a little as she followed him over to the ice bucket, still maintaining some distance between them.

Ryan opened the bottle with a loud pop and poured each of them a glass of the sparkling white wine. He handed her one.

She accepted, gratefully, and joined him in holding up her glass.

"To an unforgettable weekend." A soft smile curved the edges of his mouth.

"Cheers." Tessa ignored the beading of her nipples and the tingling that trailed down her spine and sparked a fire low in her belly. She took a deep sip.

"Very good." Tessa fought back her speculation about how much better it would taste on Ryan's lips.

Ryan returned to the sofa. He finished his glass of moscato in short order and set it on the table beside the sofa.

Tessa sat beside him, finishing the remainder of her drink and contemplating another. She decided against it, setting it on the table in front of them.

She turned to her friend. God, he was handsome. His green eyes brooding and intense. His shaggy brown hair living in that space between perfectly groomed and purposely messy. The ever-present five o'clock shadow crawling over his clenched jaw.

"Thanks, Rye." She needed to quell the thoughts in her head. "This is all so amazing and incredibly thoughtful. I know this fantasy date isn't real, but you went out of your way to make it feel that way, and I appreciate it."

Tessa leaned in to kiss his stubbled cheek. Something she'd done a dozen times before. But Ryan turned his head, likely surprised by her sudden approach, and her lips met his.

She'd been right. The moscato did taste better enmeshed with the flavor of Ryan's firm, sensual lips.

It was an accidental kiss. So why had she leaned in and continued to kiss him, rather than withdrawing and apologizing? And why hadn't Ryan pulled back either?

Tessa's eyes slowly drifted closed, and she slipped her fingers into the short hair at the nape of Ryan's neck. Pulled his face closer to hers.

She parted her lips, and Ryan accepted the unspoken invitation, sliding his tongue between her lips and taking control. The kiss had gradually moved from a sweet, inadvertent, closed-mouth affair to an intense meshing of lips, teeth and tongues. Ryan moved his hands to her back, tugging her closer.

Tessa sighed softly in response to the hot, demanding kiss that obliterated the memory of that unexpected one nearly a decade ago. Truly kissing Ryan Bateman was everything she'd imagined it to be.

And she wanted more.

They'd gone this far. Had let down the invisible wall between them. There was nothing holding them back now.

Tessa inhaled deeply before shifting to her knees and straddling Ryan's lap. He groaned. A sexy sound that was an undeniable mixture of pain and pleasure. Of intense wanting. Evident from the ridge beneath his zipper.

As he deepened their kiss, his large hand splayed against her low back, his hardness met the soft, warm space between her thighs, sending a shiver up her spine. Her nipples ached with an intensity she hadn't experienced before. She wanted his hands and lips on her naked flesh. She wanted to shed the clothing that prevented skin-to-skin contact.

She wanted…sex. With Ryan. Right now.

Sex.

It wasn't as if she'd forgotten how the whole process worked. Obviously. But it'd been a while since she'd been with anyone. More than a few years. One of the hazards of living in a town small enough that there was three degrees or less of separation between any man she met and her father or brother.

Would Ryan be disappointed?

Tessa suddenly went stiff, her eyes blinking.

"Don't," he whispered between hungry kisses along her jaw and throat that left her wanting and breathless, despite the insecurities that had taken over her brain.

Tess frowned. "Don't do what?"

Maybe she didn't have Ryan Bateman's vast sexual experience, but she was pretty sure she knew how to kiss. At least she hadn't had any complaints.

Until now.

"Have you changed your mind about this?"

"No." She forced her eyes to meet his, regardless of how unnerved she was by his intense stare and his determination to make her own up to what she wanted. "Not even a little."

The edge of his mouth curved in a criminally sexy smirk. "Then for once in your life, Tess, stop over-thinking everything. Stop compiling a list in your head of all the reasons we shouldn't do this." He kissed her again, his warm lips pressed to hers and his large hands gliding down her back and gripping her bottom as he pulled her firmly against him.

A soft gasp escaped her mouth at the sensation of his hard length pressed against her sensitive flesh. Ryan swept his tongue between her parted lips, tangling it with hers as he wrapped his arms around her.

Their kiss grew increasingly urgent. Hungry. Desperate. His kiss made her question whether she'd ever *really* been kissed before. Made her skin tingle with a desire so intense she physically ached with a need for him.

A need for Ryan's kiss. His touch. The warmth of his naked skin pressed against hers. The feel of him inside her.

Hands shaking and the sound of her own heartbeat filling her ears, Tessa pulled her mouth from his. She grabbed the hem of her dress and raised it. His eyes were locked with hers, both of them breathing heavily, as she lifted the fabric.

Ryan helped her tug the dress over her head and he tossed it on to the floor. He studied her lacy, gray bra and the cleavage spilling out of it.

Her cheeks flamed, and her heart raced. Ryan leaned in and planted slow, warm kisses on her shoulder. He swept her hair aside and trailed kisses up her neck.

"God, you're beautiful, Tess." His voice was a low growl that sent tremors through her. He glided a callused hand down her back and rested it on her hip. "I think it's pretty obvious how much I want you. But I need to know that you're sure about this."

"I am." She traced his rough jaw with her palm. Glided a thumb across his lips, naturally a deep shade of red that made them even more enticing. Then she crashed her lips against his as she held his face in her hands.

He claimed her mouth with a greedy, primal kiss that strung her body tight as a bow, desperate for the release that only he could provide.

She wanted him. More than she could ever remember wanting anything. The steely rod pressed against the slick, aching spot between her thighs indicated his genuine desire for her. Yet, he seemed hesitant. As if he were holding back. Something Ryan Bateman, one of the most confident men she'd ever known, wasn't prone to do.

Tess reached behind her and did the thing Ryan seemed reluctant to. She released the hooks on her bra, slid the straps down her shoulders and tossed it away.

He splayed one hand against her back. The other glided up and down her side before his thumb grazed the side of her breast. Once, twice, then again. As if testing her.

Finally, he grazed her hardened nipple with his open palm, and she sucked in a sharp breath.

His eyes met hers with a look that fell somewhere between asking and pleading.

Tessa swallowed hard, her cheeks and chest flushed with heat. She nodded, her hands trembling as she braced them on his wide shoulders.

When Ryan's lips met her skin again, she didn't fight the overwhelming feelings that flooded her senses, like a long, hard rain causing the creek to exceed its banks. She leaned into them. Allowed them to wash over her. Enjoyed the thing she'd fantasized about for so long.

Tessa gasped as Ryan cupped her bottom and pulled her against his hardened length. As if he was as desperate for her as she was for him. He kissed her neck, her shoulders, her collarbone. Then he dropped tender, delicate kisses on her breasts.

Tessa ran her fingers through his soft hair. When he raised his eyes to hers, she leaned down, whispering in his ear.

"Ryan, take me to bed. Now."

Before she lost her nerve. Before he lost his.

Ryan carried her to his bed, laid her down and settled between her thighs. He trailed slow, hot kisses down her neck and chest as he palmed her breast with his large, work-roughened hand. He sucked the beaded tip into his warm mouth. Grazed it with his teeth. Lathed it with his tongue.

She shuddered in response to the tantalizing sensation that shot from her nipple straight to her sex. Her skin flamed beneath Ryan's touch, and her breath came in quick little bursts. He nuzzled her neck, one large hand skimming down her thigh and hooking behind her knee. As he rocked against the space between her thighs, Tessa whimpered at the delicious torture of his steely length grinding against her needy clit.

"That's it, Tess." Ryan trailed kisses along her jaw. "Relax. Let go. You know I'd never do anything to hurt you." His stubble scraped the sensitive skin of her cheek as he whispered roughly in her ear.

She did know that. She trusted Ryan with her life. With her deepest secrets. With her body. Ryan was sweet and charming and well-meaning, but her friend could sometimes be a bull in the china shop.

Would he ride roughshod over her heart, even if he didn't mean to?

Tessa gazed up at him, her lips parting as she took

in his incredibly handsome form. She yanked his shirt from the back of his pants and slid her hands against his warm skin. Gently grazed his back with her nails. She had the fleeting desire to mark him as hers. So that any other woman who saw him would know he belonged to her and no one else.

Ryan moved beside her, and she immediately missed his weight and the feel of him pressed against her most sensitive flesh. He kissed her harder as he slid a hand up her thigh and then cupped the space between her legs that throbbed in anticipation of his touch.

Tessa tensed, sucking in a deep breath as he glided his fingertips back and forth over the drenched panel of fabric shielding her sex. He tugged the material aside and plunged two fingers inside her.

"God, you're wet, Tess." The words vibrated against her throat, where he branded her skin with scorching hot kisses that made her weak with want. He kissed his way down her chest and gently scraped her sensitive nipple with his teeth before swirling his tongue around the sensitive flesh.

Tessa quivered as the space between her thighs ached with need. She wanted to feel him inside her. To be with Ryan in the way she'd always imagined.

But this wasn't a dream; it was real. And their actions would have real-world consequences.

"You're doing it again. That head thing," he muttered in between little nips and licks. His eyes glinted in the light filtering through the bedroom window. "Cut it out."

God, he knew her too well. And after tonight, he would know every single inch of her body. If she had her way.

Eleven

Ryan couldn't get over how beautiful Tessa was as she lay beside him whimpering with pleasure. Lips parted, back arched and her eyelashes fluttering, she was everything he'd imagined and more.

He halted his action just long enough to encourage her to lift her hips, allowing him to drag the lacy material down her legs, over her boots, and off. Returning his attention to her full breasts, he sucked and licked one of the pebbled, brown peaks he'd occasionally glimpsed the outline of through the thin, tank tops she sometimes wore during summer. He'd spent more time than he dared admit speculating about what her breasts looked like and how her skin would taste.

Now he knew. And he desperately wanted to know everything about her body. What turned her on? What would send her spiraling over the edge, his name on her lips?

He eagerly anticipated solving those mysteries, too.

Ryan inserted his fingers inside her again, adding a third finger to her tight, slick channel. Allowed her body to stretch and accommodate the additional digit.

He and Tess had made it a point not to delve too deeply into each other's sex lives. Still, they'd shared enough for him to know he wouldn't be her first or even her second. She was just a little tense, and perhaps a lot nervous. And she needed to relax.

Her channel stretched and relaxed around his fingers as he moved to her other nipple and gave it the same treatment he'd given the first. He resumed the movement of his hand, his fingers gliding in and out of her. Then he stroked the slick bundle of nerves with his thumb.

Tessa's undeniable gasp of pleasure indicated her approval.

The slow, small circles he made with his thumb got wider, eliciting a growing chorus of curses and moans. Her grip on his hair tightened, and she moved her hips in rhythm with his hand.

She was slowly coming undone, and he was grateful to be the reason for it. Ryan wet his lips with a sweep of his tongue, eager to taste her there. But he wanted to take his time. Make this last for both of them.

He kissed Tessa's belly and slipped his other hand between her legs, massaging her clit as he curved the fingers inside her.

"Oh god, oh god, oh god, Ryan. Right there, right there," Tess pleaded when he hit the right spot.

He gladly obliged her request, both hands moving with precision until he'd taken Tess to the edge. She'd called his name, again and again, as she dug the heels of her boots into the mattress and her body stiffened.

Watching his best friend tumble into bliss was a thing of beauty. Being the one who'd brought her such intense ecstasy was an incredible gift. It was easily the most meaningful sexual experience he'd ever had, and he was still fully clothed.

Ryan lay down, gathering Tess to him and wrapping her in his arms, her head tucked under his chin. He flipped the cover over her, so she'd stay warm.

They were both silent. Tessa's chest heaved as she slowly came down from the orgasm he'd given her.

When the silence lingered on for seconds that turned to minutes, but felt like hours, Ryan couldn't take it.

"Tess, look, I—"

"You're still dressed." She raised her head, her eyes meeting his. Her playful smile eased the tension they'd both been feeling. "And I'm not quite sure why."

The laugh they shared felt good. A bit of normalcy in a situation that was anything but normal between them.

He planted a lingering kiss on her sweet lips.

"I can fix that." He sat up and tugged his shirt over his head and tossed it on to the floor unceremoniously.

"Keep going." She indicated his pants with a wave of her hand.

"Bold and bossy." He laughed. "Who is this woman and what did she do with my best friend?"

She frowned slightly, as if what he'd said had hurt her feelings.

"Hey." He cradled her face in one hand. "You know that's not a criticism, right? I like seeing this side of you."

"Usually when a man calls a woman bossy, it's code for bitchy." Her eyes didn't quite meet his.

Ryan wanted to kick himself. He'd only been teasing when he'd used the word bossy, but he hadn't been thinking. He understood how loaded that term was to Tess. She'd hated that her mother and grandmother had constantly warned her that no ranch man would want a bossy bride.

"I should've said assertive," he clarified. "Which is what I've always encouraged you to be."

She nodded, seemingly satisfied with his explanation. A warm smile slid across her gorgeous face and lit her light brown eyes. "Then I'd like to assert that you're still clothed, and I don't appreciate it, seeing as I'm not."

"Yes, ma'am." He winked as he stood and removed his pants.

Tessa gently sank her teeth into her lower lip as she studied the bulge in his boxer briefs. Which only made him harder.

He rubbed the back of his neck and chuckled. "Now I guess I know how the fellas felt on stage at the auction."

"Hmm…" The humming sound Tess made seemed to vibrate in his chest and other parts of his body. Specifically, the part she was staring at right now.

Tess removed her boots and kneeled on the bed in front of him, her brown eyes studying him. The levity had faded from her expression, replaced by a heated gaze that made his cock twitch.

She looped her arms around his neck and pulled his mouth down toward hers. Angling her head, she kissed him hard, her fingers slipping into his hair and her naked breasts smashed against his hard chest.

If this was a dream, he didn't want to wake up.

Ryan wrapped his arms around Tess, needing her body pressed firmly against his. He splayed one hand against the smooth, soft skin of her back. The other squeezed the generous bottom he'd always quietly admired. Hauling her tight against him, he grew painfully hard with the need to be inside her.

He claimed her mouth, his tongue gliding against hers, his anticipation rising. He'd fantasized about making love to Tess long before that kiss they'd shared in college.

He'd wanted to make love to her that night. Or at the very least make out with her in his truck. But he'd promised Tripp he wouldn't ever look at Tess that way.

A promise he'd broken long before tonight, despite his best efforts.

Ryan pushed thoughts of his ill-advised pledge to Tripp and the consequences of breaking it from his mind.

Right now, it was just him and Tess. The only thing that mattered in this moment was what the two of them wanted. What they needed from each other.

Ryan pulled away, just long enough to rummage in his luggage for the condoms he kept in his bag.

He said a silent prayer, thankful there was one full strip left. He tossed it on the nightstand and stripped out of his underwear.

Suddenly she seemed shy again as his eyes roved every inch of her gorgeous body.

He placed his hands on her hips, pulling her close to him and pressing his forehead to hers.

"God, you're beautiful, Tess." He knew he sounded like a broken record. But he was struck by how breathtaking she was and by the fact that she'd trusted him with something as precious as her body.

"You're making me feel self-conscious." A deep blush stained Tess's cheeks and spread through her chest.

"Don't be." He cradled her cheek, hoping to put her at ease. "That's not my intention. I just…" He sighed, giving up on trying to articulate what he was feeling.

One-night stands, even the occasional relationship… those were easy. But with Tess, everything felt weightier. More significant. Definitely more complicated. He couldn't afford to fuck this up. Because not having Tess as his friend wasn't an option. Still, he wanted her.

"Ryan, it's okay." She wrapped her arms around him. "I'm nervous about this, too. But I know that I want to be with you tonight. It's what I've wanted for a long time, and I don't want to fight it anymore."

He shifted his gaze to hers. A small sigh of relief escaped his mouth.

Tess understood exactly what he was feeling. They could do this. Be together like this. Satisfy their craving for each other without ruining their friendship.

He captured her mouth in a bruising kiss, and they both tumbled on to the mattress. Hands groping. Tongues searching. Hearts racing.

He grabbed one of the foil packets and ripped it open, sheathing himself as quickly as he could.

He guided himself to her slick entrance, circling his hips so his pelvis rubbed against her hardened clit. Tessa gasped, then whimpered with pleasure each time he ground his hips against her again. She writhed against him, increasing the delicious friction against the tight bundle of nerves.

Ryan gripped the base of his cock and pressed its head to her entrance. He inched inside, and Tess whimpered softly. She dug her fingers into his hips, her eyes meeting his as he slid the rest of the way home. Until he was nestled as deeply inside her as the laws of physics would allow.

When he was fully seated, her slick, heated flesh surrounding him, an involuntary growl escaped his mouth at the delicious feel of this woman who was all softness and curves. Sweetness and beauty. His friend and his lover.

His gaze met hers as he hovered above her and moved inside her. His voice rasping, he whispered to her. Told her how incredible she made him feel.

Then, lifting her legs, he hooked them over his shoulders as he leaned over her, his weight on his hands as he moved.

She gasped, her eyes widening at the sensation of him going deep and hitting bottom due to the sudden shift in position.

"Ryan... I...oh... God." Tessa squeezed her eyes shut.

"C'mon, Tess." He arched his back as he shifted his hips forward, beads of sweat forming on his brow and trickling down his back. "Just let go. Don't think. Just feel."

Her breath came in quick pants, and she dug her nails in his biceps. Suddenly, her mouth formed a little *O* and her eyes opened wide. The unmistakable expression of pure satisfaction that overtook her as she called his name was one of the most beautiful things he'd ever seen. Something he wanted to see again and again.

Her flesh throbbed and pulsed around him, bringing

him to his peak. He tensed, shuddering as he cursed and called her name.

Ryan collapsed on to the bed beside her, both of them breathing hard and staring at the ceiling overhead for a few moments.

Finally, she draped an arm over his abdomen and rested her head on his shoulder.

He kissed the top of her head, pulled the covers over them, and slipped an arm around her. He lay there, still and quiet, fighting his natural tendency to slip out into the night. His usual MO after a one-night stand. Only he couldn't do that. Partly because it was Tess. Partly because what he'd felt between them was something he couldn't quite name, and he wanted to feel it again.

Ryan propped an arm beneath his head and stared at the ceiling as Tessa's soft breathing indicated she'd fallen asleep.

Intimacy.

That was the elusive word he'd been searching for all night. The thing he'd felt when his eyes had met hers as he'd roared, buried deep inside her. He'd sounded ridiculous. Like a wounded animal, in pain. Needing someone to save him.

Ryan scrubbed a hand down his face, one arm still wrapped around his best friend. Whom he'd made love to. The woman who knew him better than anyone in the world.

And now they knew each other in a way they'd never allowed themselves to before. A way that made him feel raw and exposed, like a live wire.

While making love to Tess, he'd felt a surge of power as he'd teased her gorgeous body and coaxed her over the edge. Watched her free-fall into ecstasy, her body trembling.

But as her inner walls pulsed, pulling him over the cliff after her, he'd felt something completely foreign and yet vaguely familiar. It was a thing he couldn't name. Or maybe he hadn't wanted to.

Then when he'd startled awake, his arm slightly numb from being wedged beneath her, the answer was on his tongue.

Intimacy.

How was it that he'd managed to have gratifying sex with women without ever experiencing this heightened level of intimacy? Not even with his ex—the woman he'd planned to marry.

He and Sabrina had known each other. What the other wanted for breakfast. Each other's preferred drinks. They'd even known each other's bodies. *Well.* And yet he'd never experienced this depth of connection. Of truly being known by someone who could practically finish his sentences. Not because Tessa was so like him, but because she understood him in a way no one else did.

Ryan swallowed the hard lump clogging his throat and swiped the backs of his fingers over his damp brow.

Why is it suddenly so goddamned hot in here?

He blew out a long, slow breath. Tried to slow the rhythm of his heart, suddenly beating like a drum.

What the hell had he just done?

He'd satisfied the curiosity that had been simmering just below the surface of his friendship with Tessa. The desire to know her intimately. To know how it would feel to have her soft curves pressed against him as he'd surged inside her.

Now he knew what it was like for their bodies to move together. As if they were a single being. How it made his pulse race like a freight train as she called his name in a sweet, husky voice he'd never heard her use before. The delicious burn of her nails gently scraping his back as she wrapped her legs around him and pulled him in deeper.

And how it felt as she'd throbbed and pulsed around his heated flesh until he could no longer hold back his release.

Now, all he could think about was feeling all of those things again. Watching her shed the inhibitions that had held her back at first. Taking her a little further.

But Tessa was his best friend, and a very good friend's sister. He'd crossed the line. Broken a promise and taken them to a place they could never venture back from. After last night, he couldn't see her and not want her. Would never forget the taste and feel of her.

So what now?

Tess was sweet and sensitive. Warm and thoughtful. She deserved more than being friends with benefits. She deserved a man as kind and loving as she was.

Was he even capable of being that kind of man?

His family was nothing like the Nobles. Hank and Loretta Bateman weren't the doting parents that kissed injured knees and cheered effort. They believed in tough love, hard lessons and that failure wasn't to be tolerated by anyone with the last name Bateman.

Ryan knew unequivocally that his parents loved him, but he was twenty-nine years old and could never recall hearing either of them say the words explicitly.

He'd taken the same approach in his relationships.

It was how he was built, all he'd ever known. But Tess could never be happy in a relationship like that.

Ryan sucked in another deep breath and released it quietly. He gently kissed the top of her head and screwed his eyes shut. Allowed himself to surrender to the sleep that had eluded him until now.

They'd figure it all out in the morning. After he'd gotten some much-needed sleep. He always thought better with a clear head and a full stomach.

Twelve

Tessa's eyes fluttered opened. She blinked against the rays of light peeking through the hotel room curtain and rubbed the sleep from her eyes with her fist. Her leg was entwined with Ryan's, and one of her arms was buried beneath him.

She groaned, pressing a hand to her mouth to prevent a curse from erupting from her lips. She'd made love with her best friend. Had fallen asleep with him. She peeked beneath the covers, her mouth falling open.

Naked. Both of them.

Tessa snapped her mouth shut and eased the cover back down. Though it didn't exactly lie flat. Not with Ryan Bateman sporting a textbook definition of morning wood.

She sank her teeth into her lower lip and groaned internally. Her nipples hardened, and the space between her thighs grew incredibly wet. Heat filled her cheeks.

She'd been with Ryan in the most intimate way imaginable. And it had been…incredible. Better than anything she'd imagined. And she'd imagined it more than she cared to admit.

Ryan had been intense, passionate and completely unselfish. He seemed to get off on pleasing her. Had evoked reactions from her body she hadn't believed it capable of. And the higher he'd taken her, the more desperate she became to shatter the mask of control that gripped his handsome face.

Tessa drew her knees to her chest and took slow, deep breaths. Willed her hands to stop shaking. Tried to tap into the brain cells that had taken a siesta the moment she'd pressed her lips to Ryan's.

Yes, sex between them had been phenomenal. But the friendship they shared for more than two decades— that was something she honestly couldn't do without.

She needed some space, so she could clear her head and make better decisions than she had last night. Last night she'd allowed her stupid crush on her best friend to run wild. She'd bought into the Cinderella fantasy. Lock, stock and barrel.

What did she think would happen next? That he'd suddenly realize she was in love with him? Maybe even realize he was in love with her, too?

Not in this lifetime or the next.

She simply wasn't that lucky. Ryan had always considered her a friend. His best friend, but nothing more. A few hours together naked between the sheets wouldn't change that.

Besides, as her mother often reminded her, tigers don't change their stripes.

How many times had Ryan said it? *Sex is just sex.* A way to have a little fun and let off a little steam. Why would she expect him to feel differently just because it was her?

Her pent-up feelings for Ryan were her issue, not his.

Tessa's face burned with an intense heat, as if she was standing too close to a fire. Waking up naked with her best friend was awkward, but they could laugh it off. Blame it on the alcohol, like Jamie Foxx. Chalk it up to them both getting too carried away in the moment. But if she told him how she really felt about him, and he rejected her...

Tessa sighed. The only thing worse than secretly lusting after her best friend was having had him, knowing just how good things could be, and then being patently rejected. She'd never recover from that. Would never be able to look him in the face and pretend everything was okay.

And if, by some chance, Ryan was open to trying to turn this into something more, he'd eventually get bored with their relationship. As he had with every relationship he'd been in before. They'd risk destroying their friendship.

It wasn't worth the risk.

Tessa wiped away tears that stung the corners of her eyes. She quietly climbed out of bed, in search of her clothing.

She cursed under her breath as she retrieved her panties—the only clothing she'd been wearing when they entered the bedroom. Tessa pulled them on and grabbed Ryan's shirt from the floor. She slipped it on and buttoned a few of the middle buttons. She glanced back at his handsome form as he slept soundly, hoping everything between them would be all right.

Tessa slowly turned the doorknob and the door creaked open.

Damn.

Wasn't oiling door hinges part of the planned maintenance for a place like this? Did they not realize the necessity of silent hinges in the event a hotel guest needed a quiet escape after making a questionable decision with her best friend the night before?

Still, as soundly as Ryan was sleeping, odds were, he hadn't heard it.

"Tess?" Ryan called from behind her in that sexy, sleep-roughened voice that made her squirm.

Every. Damn. Time.

She sucked in a deep breath, forced a nonchalant smile and turned around. "Yes?"

"Where are you going?"

He'd propped himself up in bed on one elbow as he rubbed his eyes and squinted against the light. His brown hair stood all over his head in the hottest damn case of bed head she'd ever witnessed. And his bottle-green eyes glinted in the sunlight.

Trying to escape before you woke up. Isn't it obvious?

Tessa jerked a thumb over her shoulder. "I was about to hop into the shower, and I didn't want to wake you."

"Perfect." He sat up and threw off the covers. "We can shower together." A devilish smile curled his red lips. "I know how you feel about conserving water."

"You want to shower…together? The two of us?" She pointed to herself and then to him.

"Why? Were you thinking of inviting someone else?"

"Smart-ass." Her cheeks burned with heat. Ryan was in rare form. "You know what I meant."

"Yes, I do." He stalked toward her naked, at more than half-mast now. Looking like walking, talking sex-on-a-stick promising unicorn orgasms.

Ryan looped his arms around her waist and pressed her back against the wall. He leaned down and nuzzled her neck.

Tessa's beaded nipples rubbed against his chest through the fabric of the shirt she was wearing. Her belly fluttered, and her knees trembled. Her chest rose and fell with heavy, labored breaths. As if Ryan was sucking all the oxygen from the room, making it harder for her to breathe.

"C'mon, Tess." He trailed kisses along her shoulder as he slipped the shirt from it. "Don't make this weird. It's just us."

She raised her eyes to his, her heart racing. "It's already weird *because* it's just us."

"Good point." He gave her a cocky half smile and a micro nod. "Then we definitely need to do something to alleviate the weirdness."

"And *how* exactly are we going to do—" Tess squealed as Ryan suddenly lifted her and heaved her over his shoulder. He carried her, kicking and wiggling, into the master bathroom and turned on the water.

"Ryan Bateman, don't you dare even think about it," Tessa called over her shoulder, kicking her feet and holding on to Ryan's back for dear life.

He wouldn't drop her. She had every confidence of that. Still…

"You're going to ruin my hair."

"I like your curls better. In fact, I felt a little cheated that I didn't get to run my fingers through them. I always wanted to do that."

Something about his statement stopped her objections cold. Made visions dance in her head of them together in the shower with Ryan doing just that.

"Okay. Just put me down."

Ryan smacked her bottom lightly before setting her down, her body sliding down his. Seeming to rev them both up as steam surrounded them.

She slowly undid the three buttons of Ryan's shirt and made a show of sliding the fabric down one shoulder, then the other.

His green eyes darkened. His chest rose and fell heavily as his gaze met hers again after he'd followed the garment's descent to the floor.

Ryan hooked his thumbs into the sides of her panties and tugged her closer, dropping another kiss on her neck. He gently sank his teeth into her delicate flesh, nibbling the skin there as he glided her underwear over the swell of her bottom and down her hips.

She stepped out of them and into the shower. Pressed her back against the cool tiles. A striking contrast to the warm water. Ryan stepped into the shower, too, closing the glass door behind him and covering her mouth with his.

Tessa lay on her back, her hair wound in one of Ryan's clean, cotton T-shirts. He'd washed her hair and taken great delight in running a soapy loofah over every inch of her body.

Then he'd set her on the shower bench and dropped to his knees. He'd used the removable shower head as a makeshift sex toy. Had used it to bring her to climax twice. Then showed her just how amazing he could be with his tongue.

When he'd pressed the front of her body to the wall, lifted one of her legs, and taken her from behind, Tessa honestly hadn't thought it would be possible for her to get there again.

She was wrong.

She came hard, her body tightening and convulsing, and his did the same soon afterward.

They'd gone through their morning routines, brushing their teeth side by side, wrapped in towels from their shower together. Ryan ordered room service, and they ate breakfast in bed, catching the last half of a holiday comedy that was admittedly a pretty crappy movie overall. Still, it never failed to make the two of them laugh hysterically.

When the movie ended, Ryan had clicked off the television and kissed her. A kiss that slowly stoked the fire low in her belly all over again. Made her nipples tingle and the space between her thighs ache for him.

She lay staring up at Ryan, his hair still damp from the shower. Clearly hell-bent on using every single condom in that strip before the morning ended, he'd sheathed himself and entered her again.

Her eyes had fluttered closed at the delicious fullness as Ryan eased inside her. His movements were slow, deliberate, controlled.

None of those words described the Ryan Bateman

she knew. The man she'd been best friends with since they were both still in possession of their baby teeth.

Ryan was impatient. Tenacious. Persistent. He wanted everything five minutes ago. But the man who hovered over her now, his piercing green eyes boring into her soul and grasping her heart, was in no hurry. He seemed to relish the torturously delicious pleasure he was giving her with his slow, languid movements.

He was laser-focused. His brows furrowed, and his forehead beaded with sweat. The sudden swivel of his hips took her by surprise, and she whimpered with pleasure, her lips parting.

Ryan leaned down and pressed his mouth to hers, slipping his tongue inside and caressing her tongue.

Tessa got lost in his kiss. Let him rock them both into a sweet bliss that left her feeling like she was floating on a cloud.

She held on to him as he arched his back, his muscles straining as his own orgasm overtook him. Allowed herself to savor the warmth that encircled her sated body.

Then, gathering her to his chest, he removed her makeshift T-shirt turban and ran his fingers through her damp, curly hair.

She'd never felt more cherished or been more satisfied in her life. Yet, when the weekend ended, it would be the equivalent of the clock striking twelve for Cinderella. The dream would be over, her carriage would turn back into a pumpkin, and she'd be the same old Tessa Noble whom Ryan only considered a friend.

She inhaled his scent. Leather and cedar with a hint of patchouli. A scent she'd bought him for Christmas three years ago. Ryan had been wearing it ever since.

Tess was never sure if he wore it because he truly liked it or because he'd wanted to make her happy.

Now she wondered the same thing about what'd happened between them this weekend. He'd tailored the entire weekend to her. Had seemed determined to see to it that she felt special, pampered.

Had she been the recipient of a pity fuck?

The possibility of Ryan sleeping with her out of a sense of charity made her heart ache.

She tried not to think of what would happen when the weekend ended. To simply enjoy the moment between them here and now.

Tessa was his until "midnight." Then the magic of their weekend together would be over, and it would be time for them to return to the real world.

Thirteen

Ryan studied Tessa as she gathered her beauty products and stowed them back into her travel bag in preparation for checkout. They'd had an incredible weekend together. With the exception of the time they spent politely posing for the reporter at dinner and waxing poetic about their friendship, they'd spent most of the weekend just a few feet away in Ryan's bed.

But this morning Tessa had seemed withdrawn. Before he'd even awakened, she'd gotten out of bed, packed her luggage, laid out what she planned to wear to the football game, and showered.

Tessa opened a tube of makeup.

"You're wearing makeup to the game?" He stepped behind her in the mirror.

"Photos before the game." She gave his reflection a cursory glance. "Otherwise, I'd just keep it simple. Lip gloss, a little eye shadow. Mascara."

She went back to silently pulling items out of her makeup bag and lining them up on the counter.

"Tess, did I do something wrong? You seem really… I don't know…distant this morning."

A pained look crimped her features, and she sank her teeth into her lower lip before turning to face him. She heaved a sigh, and though she looked in his direction, she was clearly looking past him.

"Look, Rye, this weekend has been amazing. But I think it's in the best interest of our friendship if we go back to the way things were. Forget this weekend ever happened." She shifted her gaze to his. "I honestly feel that it's the only way our friendship survives this."

"Why?"

His question reeked of quiet desperation, but he could care less. The past two days had been the best days of his life. He thought they had been for her, too. So her request hit him like a sucker punch to the gut, knocking the wind out of him.

She took the shower cap off her head, releasing the long, silky hair she'd straightened with a blow-dryer attachment before they'd met Greg at the restaurant for dinner the night before.

"Because the girl you were attracted to on that stage isn't who I am. I can't maintain all of this." She indicated the makeup on the counter and her straightened hair. "It's exhausting. More importantly, it isn't me. Not really."

"You think all of this is what I'm attracted to? That I can't see…that I haven't always seen you?"

"You never kissed me before, not seriously," she added before he could mention that kiss in college. "And we certainly never…" She gestured toward the bed, as if she was unable to bring herself to say the words or look at the place where he'd laid her bare and tasted every inch of her warm brown skin.

"To be fair, you kissed me." Ryan stepped closer.

She tensed, but then lifted her chin defiantly, meeting his gaze again. The rapid rise and fall of her chest, indicated that she was taking shallow breaths. But she didn't step away from him. For which he was grateful.

"You know what I mean," she said through a frustrated little pout. "You never showed any romantic interest in me before the auction. So why are you interested now? Is it because someone else showed interest in me?"

"Why would you think that?" His voice was low and gruff. Pained.

Her accusation struck him like an openhanded slap to the face. It was something his mother had often said to him as a child. That he was only interested in his old toys when she wanted to give them to someone else.

Was that what he was doing with Tess?

"Because if I had a relationship…a life of my own, then I wouldn't be a phone call away whenever you needed me." Her voice broke slightly, and she swiped at the corners of her eyes. "Or maybe it's a competitive thing. I don't know. All I know is that you haven't made a move before now. So what changed?"

The hurt in her eyes and in the tremor of her voice felt like a jagged knife piercing his chest.

She was right. He was a selfish bastard. Too much of a coward to explore his attraction to her. Too afraid of how it might change their relationship.

"I… I…" His throat tightened, and his mouth felt dry as he sought the right words. But Tessa was his best friend, and they'd always shot straight with each other. "Sex, I could get anywhere." He forced his gaze to meet hers. Gauged her reaction. "But what we have… I don't have that with anyone else, Tess. I didn't want to take a chance on losing you. Couldn't risk screwing up our friendship like I've screwed up every relationship I've ever been in."

She dropped her gaze, absently dragging her fingers through her hair and tugging it over one shoulder. Tess was obviously processing his words. Weighing them on her internal bullshit meter.

"So why risk it now? What's changed?" She wrapped her arms around her middle. Something she did to comfort herself.

"I don't know." He whispered the words, his eyes not meeting hers.

It was a lie.

Tess was right. He'd been prompted to action by his fear of losing her. He'd been desperate to stake his claim on Tess. Wipe thoughts of any other man from her brain.

In the past, she had flirted with the occasional guy. Even dated a few. But none of them seemed to pose any real threat to what they shared. But when she'd stood on that stage as the sexiest goddamn woman in the entire room with men falling all over themselves to spend a few hours with her…suddenly everything was different. For the first time in his life, the threat of losing his best friend to someone else suddenly became very real. And he couldn't imagine his life without her in it.

Brain on autopilot, he'd gone into caveman mode. Determined to win the bid, short of putting up the whole damn ranch in order to win her.

Tessa stared at him, her pointed gaze demanding further explanation.

"It felt like the time was right. Like Fate stepped in and gave us a nudge."

"You're full of shit, Ryan Bateman." She smacked her lips and narrowed her gaze. Arms folded over her chest, she shifted to a defensive stance. "You don't believe in Fate. 'Our lives are what we make of them.' That's what you've always said."

"I'm man enough to admit when I'm wrong. Or at least open-minded enough to explore the possibility."

She turned to walk away, but he grasped her fingertips with his. A move that was more of a plea than a demand. Still, she halted and glanced over her shoulder in his direction.

"Tess, why are you so dead set against giving this a chance?"

"Because I'm afraid of losing you, too." Her voice was a guttural whisper.

He tightened his grip on her hand and tugged her closer, forcing her eyes to meet his. "You're not going to lose me, Tess. I swear, I'm not going anywhere."

"Maybe not, but we both know your MO when it comes to relationships. You rush into them, feverish and excited. But after a while you get bored, and you're ready to move on." She frowned, a pained look furrowing her brow. "What happens then, Ryan? What happens once you've pulled me in deep and then you decide you just want to go back to being friends?" She shook her head vehemently. "I honestly don't think I could handle that."

Ryan's jaw clenched. He wanted to object. Promise to never hurt her. But hadn't he hurt every woman he'd ever been with except the one woman who'd walked away from him?

It was the reason Tripp had made him promise to leave his sister alone. Because, though they were friends, he didn't deem him good enough for his sister. Didn't trust that he wouldn't hurt her.

Tessa obviously shared Tripp's concern.

Ryan wished he could promise Tess he wouldn't break her heart. But their polar opposite approaches to relationships made it seem inevitable.

He kept his relationships casual. A means of mutual satisfaction. Because he believed in fairy-tale love and romance about as much as he believed in Big Foot and the Loch Ness Monster.

Tess, on the other hand, was holding out for the man who would sweep her off her feet. For a relationship like the one her parents shared. She didn't understand that Chuck and Tina Noble were the exception, rather than the rule.

Yet, despite knowing all the reasons he and Tess should walk away from this, he couldn't let her go.

Tessa's frown deepened as his silent response to her objection echoed off the walls in the elegant, tiled bathroom.

"This weekend has been amazing. You made me feel like Cinderella at the ball. But we've got the game this afternoon, then we're heading back home. The clock is about to strike midnight, and it's time for me to turn back into a pumpkin."

"You realize that you've just taken the place of the Maybach in this scenario." He couldn't help the smirk that tightened the edges of his mouth.

Some of the tension drained from his shoulders as

her sensual lips quirked in a rueful smile. She shook her head and playfully punched him in the gut.

"You know what I mean. It's time for me to go back to being me. Trade my glass slippers in for a pair of Chuck Taylors."

He caught her wrist before she could walk away. Pulling her closer, he wrapped his arms around her and stared deep into those gorgeous brown eyes that had laid claim on him ever since he'd first gazed into them.

"Okay, Cinderella. If you insist that things go back to the way they were, there's not much I can do about that. But if you're mine until midnight, I won't be cheated. Let's forget the game, stay here and make love."

"But I've already got the tickets."

"I don't care." He slowly lowered his mouth toward hers. "I'll reimburse you."

"But they're on the fifty-yard line. At the stadium that's your absolute favorite place in the world."

"Not today it isn't." He feathered a gentle kiss along the edge of her mouth, then trailed his lips down her neck.

"Ryan, we can't just blow off the—" She dug her fingers into his bare back and a low moan escaped her lips as he kissed her collarbone. The sound drifted below his waist and made him painfully hard.

"We can do anything we damn well please." He pressed a kiss to her ear. One of the many erogenous zones he'd discovered on her body during their weekend together. Tessa's knees softened, and her head lolled slightly, giving him better access to her neck.

"But the article…they're expecting us to go to the game, and if we don't…well, everyone will think—"

"Doesn't matter what they think." He lifted her chin and studied her eyes, illuminated by the morning sunlight spilling through the windows. He dragged a thumb across her lower lip. "It only matters what you and I want."

He pressed another kiss to her lips, lingering for a moment before reluctantly pulling himself away again so he could meet her gaze. He waited for her to open her eyes again. "What do you want, Tess?"

She swallowed hard, her gaze on his lips. "I want both. To go to the game, as expected, and to spend the day in bed making love to you."

"Hmm...intriguing proposition." He kissed her again. Tess really was a woman after his own heart. "One that would require us to spend one more night here. Then we'll head back tomorrow. And if you still insist—"

"I will." There was no hesitation in her voice, only apology. She moved a hand to cradle his cheek, her gaze meeting his. "Because it's what's best for our friendship."

Ryan forced a smile and released an uneasy breath. Tried to pretend that his chest didn't feel like it was caving in. He gripped her tighter against him, lifting her as she wrapped her legs around him.

If he couldn't have her like this always, he'd take every opportunity to have her now. In the way he'd always imagined. Even if that meant they'd be a little late for the game.

Fourteen

They'd eaten breakfast, their first meal in the kitchen since they'd arrived, neither of them speaking much. The only part of their conversation that felt normal was their recap of some of the highlights during their team's win the day before. But then the conversation had returned to the stilted awkwardness they'd felt before then.

Ryan had loaded their luggage into the Maybach, and they were on the road, headed back to Royal, barely two words spoken between them before Tessa finally broke their silence.

"This is for the best, Rye. After all, you were afraid to tell my brother about that fake kiss we had on Valentine's Day in college." Tessa grinned, her voice teasing.

Ryan practically snorted, poking out his thumb and holding it up. "A... I am *not* afraid of your brother."

Not physically, at least. Ryan was a good head taller than Tripp and easily outweighed him by twenty-five pounds of what was mostly muscle. But, in all honesty, he *was* afraid of how the weekend with Tessa would affect his friendship with Tripp. It could disrupt the connection between their families.

The Batemans and Nobles were as thick as thieves now. Had been since their fathers were young boys. But in the decades prior, the families had feuded over land boundaries, water rights and countless other ugly disputes. Some of which made Ryan ashamed of his ancestors. But everything had changed the day Tessa's grandfather had saved Ryan's father's life when he'd fallen into a well.

That fateful day, the two families had bonded. A bond which had grown more intricate over the years, creating a delicate ecosystem he dared not disturb.

Ryan continued, adding his index finger for effect. "B… Yes, I think it might be damaging to our friendship if Tripp tries to beat my ass and I'm forced to defend myself." He added a third finger, hesitant to make his final point. An admission that made him feel more vulnerable than he was comfortable being, even with Tess. "And C…it wasn't a fake kiss. It was a little too real. Which is why I've tried hard to never repeat it."

Ryan's pulse raced, and his throat suddenly felt dry. He returned his other hand to the steering wheel and stared at the road ahead. He didn't need to turn his head to know Tessa was staring at him. The heat of her stare seared his skin and penetrated his chest.

"Are you saying that since that kiss—" Her voice was trembling, tentative.

"Since that kiss, I've recognized that the attraction between us went both ways." He rushed the words out, desperate to stop her from asking what he suspected she might.

Why hadn't he said anything all those years ago? Or in the years since that night?

He'd never allowed himself to entertain either question. Doing so was a recipe for disaster.

Why court disaster when they enjoyed an incomparable friendship? Shouldn't that be good enough?

"Oh." The disappointment in her voice stirred heaviness in his chest, rather than the ease and lightness he usually felt when they were together.

When Ryan finally glanced over at his friend, she was staring at him blankly, as if there was a question she was afraid to ask.

"Why haven't you ever said anything?"

Because he hadn't been ready to get serious about anyone back then. And Tessa Noble wasn't the kind of girl you passed the time with. She was the genuine deal. The kind of girl you took home to mama. And someone whose friendship meant everything to him.

"Bottom line? I promised your brother I'd treat you like an honorary little sister. That I'd never lay a hand on you." A knot tightened in his belly. "A promise I've obviously broken."

"Wait, you two just decided, without consulting me? Like I'm a little child and you two are my misfit parents? What kind of caveman behavior is that?"

Ryan winced. Tessa was angry, and he didn't blame her. "To be fair, we had this conversation when he and I were about fourteen. Long before you enlightened us on the error of our anti-feminist tendencies. Still, it's a promise I've always taken seriously. Especially since, at the time, I did see you as a little sister. Obviously, things have changed since then."

"When?" Her tone was soft, but demanding. As if she needed to know.

It wasn't a conversation he wanted to have, but if they were going to have it, she deserved his complete honesty.

"I first started to feel some attraction toward you when you were around sixteen." He cleared his throat, his eyes steadily on the road. "But when I left for college I realized how deep that attraction ran. I was miserable without you that first semester in college."

"You seemed to adapt pretty quickly by sleeping your way across campus," she huffed. She turned toward the window and sighed. "I shouldn't have said that. I'm sorry. I…" She didn't finish her statement.

"Forget it." Ryan released a long, slow breath. "This is uncharted territory for us. We'll learn to deal with it. Everything'll be fine."

But even as he said the words, he couldn't convince himself of their truth.

After Ryan's revelations, the ride home was awkward and unusually quiet, even as they both tried much too hard to behave as if everything was fine.

Everything most certainly was *not* fine.

Strained and uncomfortable? *Yes*. Their forced conversation, feeble smiles and weak laughter were proof they'd both prefer to be anywhere else.

And it confirmed they'd made the right decision by not pursuing a relationship. It would only destroy their friendship in the end once Ryan had tired of her and was ready to move on to someone polished and gorgeous, like his ex.

This was all her fault. She'd kissed Ryan. Tessa clenched her hands in her lap, willing them to stop trembling.

She only hoped their relationship could survive this phase of awkwardness, so things could go back to the way they were.

Tessa's phone buzzed, and she checked her text messages.

Tripp had sent a message to say that he'd landed a meeting with a prospect that had the potential to become one of their largest customers. His flight to Iowa would leave in a few days, and she would be in charge at the Noble Spur.

She scrolled to the next text and read Bo's message reminding her that she'd agreed to attend a showing of *A Christmas Carol* with him at the town's outdoor, holiday theater.

Tessa gripped her phone and turned it over in her lap, looking over guiltily at Ryan. After what had happened between them this weekend, the thought of going out with someone else turned her stomach, but she'd already promised Bo.

And even though she and Bo were going to a movie together, it could hardly be considered a date. Half the town of Royal would be there.

Would it be so wrong for them to go on a friendly outing to the movies?

Besides, maybe seeing other people was just the thing to alleviate the awkwardness between them and prompt them to forget about the past three days.

Tessa worried her lower lip with her teeth. Deep

down, she knew the truth. Things would never be the same between them.

Because she wanted Ryan now more than ever.

No matter how hard she tried, Tessa would never forget their weekend together and how he'd made her feel.

Fifteen

Gus sat in his favorite recliner and put his feet up to watch a little evening television. Reruns of some of his favorite old shows. Only he held the remote in his hand without ever actually turning the television on.

The house was quiet. Too quiet.

Alexis was in Houston on business, and her brother Justin was staying in Dallas overnight with a friend.

Normally, he appreciated the solitude. Enjoyed being able to watch whatever the hell he wanted on television without one of the kids scoffing about him watching an old black-and-white movie or an episode of one of his favorite shows that he'd seen half a dozen times before. But lately, it had been harder to cheerfully bear his solitude.

During the months he and Rose had worked together to split up Daniel and Alexis, he'd found himself en-

joying her company. So much so that he preferred it
mightily to being alone in this big old house.

Gus put down the remote and paced the floor. He
hadn't seen Rose since the night of the bachelor auction
at the Texas Cattleman's Club. They'd spoken by phone
twice, but just to confirm that their plan had worked.

As far as they could tell, Alexis and Daniel were no
longer seeing each other. And both of them seemed to
be in complete misery.

Gus had done everything he could to try and cheer
Alexis up. But the pain in her eyes persisted. As did the
evidence that she'd still been crying from time to time.

He'd tried to get his granddaughter to talk about it,
but she'd insisted that it wasn't anything she couldn't
handle. And she said he wouldn't understand anyway.

That probably hurt the most. Especially since he really did understand how she was feeling. And worse,
he and Rose had been the root cause of that pain.

The guilt gnawed at his gut and broke his heart.

Rose had reminded him of why they'd first hatched
the plan to break up Daniel and Alexis. Their families
had been mortal enemies for decades. Gus and Rose
had hated each other so much they were willing to
work together in order to prevent their grandchildren
from being involved with each other. Only, Gus hadn't
reckoned on coming to enjoy the time he spent with
Rose Clayton. And he most surely hadn't anticipated
that he'd find himself getting sweet on her again after
all these years.

He was still angry at Rose for how she'd treated
him all those years ago, when he'd been so very in love
with her. But now he understood that because of her

cruel father, holding the welfare of her ill mother over Rose's head, she'd felt she had no choice but to break it off with him and marry someone Jedediah Clayton had deemed worthy.

He regretted not recognizing the distress Rose was in back then. That her actions had been a cry for help. Signs he and his late wife, Sarah, who had once been Rose's best friend, had missed.

Gus heaved a sigh and glanced over his shoulder at the television. His reruns could wait.

Gus left the Lone Wolf Ranch and headed over to Rose's place, The Silver C, one last time to say goodbye. Maybe share a toast to the success of their plan to look out for Alexis and Daniel in the long run, even if the separation was hurting them both now.

The property had once been much vaster than his. But over the years, he'd bought quite a bit of it. Rose had begrudgingly sold it to him in order to pay off the gambling debts of her late husband, Ed.

Rose's father must be rolling over in his grave because the ranch hand he'd judged unworthy of his daughter was now in possession of much of the precious land the man had sought to keep out of his hands. Gus didn't normally think ill of the dead. But in Jedediah's case, he was willing to make an exception.

When Gus arrived at The Silver C, all decked out in its holiday finest, Rose seemed as thrilled to see him as he was to see her.

"Gus, what on earth are you doing here?" A smile lighting her eyes, she pulled the pretty red sweater she was wearing around her more tightly as cold air rushed in from outside.

"After all these months working together, I thought

it was only right that we had a proper goodbye." He held up a bottle of his favorite top-shelf whiskey.

Rose laughed, a joyful sound he still had fond memories of. "Well, by all means, come on in."

She stepped aside and let Gus inside. The place smelled of pine from the two fresh Christmas trees Rose had put up. One in the entry hall and another in the formal living room. And there was the unmistakable scent of fresh apple pie.

Rose directed Gus to have a seat on the sofa in the den where she'd been watching television. Then she brought two glasses and two slices of warm apple pie on a little silver tray.

"That homemade pie?" Gus inquired as she set the tray on the table.

"Wouldn't have it any other way." She grinned, handing him a slice and a fork. She opened the bottle of whiskey and poured each of them a glass, neat.

She sat beside him and watched him with interest as he took his first bite of pie.

"Hmm, hmm, hmm. Now that's a little slice of heaven right there." He grinned.

"I'm glad you like it. And since we're celebrating our successful plot to save the kids from a disastrous future, pie seems fitting." She smiled, but it seemed hollow. She took a sip of the whiskey and sighed. "Smooth."

"That's one of the reasons I like it so much." He nodded, shoveling another bite of pie into his mouth and chewing thoughtfully. He surveyed the space and leaned closer, lowering his voice. "Daniel around today?"

"No, he's gone to Austin to handle some ranch business." She raised an eyebrow, her head tilted. "Why?"

"No reason in particular." Gus shrugged, putting down his pie plate and sipping his whiskey. "Just wanted to ask how the boy is doing. He still as miserable as my Alexis?"

Pain and sadness were etched in Rose's face as she lowered her gaze and nodded. "I'm afraid so. He's trying not to show how hurt he is, but I honestly don't think I've ever seen him like this. He's already been through so much with his mother." She sighed, taking another sip of whiskey. Her hands were trembling slightly as she shook her head. "I hope we've done the right thing here. I guess I didn't realize how much they meant to each other." She sniffled and pulled a tissue out of her pocket, dabbing at her eyes.

Rose forced a laugh. "I'm sorry. You must think me so ridiculous sitting here all teary-eyed over having gotten the very thing we both wanted."

Gus put down his glass and took Rose's hand between his. It was delicate and much smaller than his own. Yet, they were the hands of a woman who had worked a ranch her entire life.

"I understand just what you're feeling." He stroked her wrist with his thumb. "Been feeling pretty guilty, too. And second-guessing our decision."

"Oh, Gus, we spent so many years heartbroken and angry. It changed us, and not for the better." Tears leaked from Rose's eyes, and her voice broke. "I just hope we haven't doomed Alexis and Daniel to the same pain and bitterness."

"It's going to be okay, Rose." He took her in his arms and hugged her to his chest. Tucked her head beneath his chin as he swayed slowly and stroked her hair.

"We won't allow that to happen to Alexis and Daniel. I promise."

"God, I hope you're right. They deserve so much more than that. Both of them." She held on to him. One arm wrapped around him and the other was pressed to his chest.

He should be focused on Daniel and Alexis and the dilemma that he and Rose had created. Gus realized that. Yet, an awareness of Rose slowly spread throughout his body. Sparks of electricity danced along his spine.

He rubbed her back and laid a kiss atop her head. All of the feelings he'd once experienced when he'd held Rose in his arms as a wet-behind-the-ears ranch hand came flooding back to him. Overwhelmed his senses, making his heart race in a way he'd forgotten that it could.

After all these years, he still had a thing for Rose Clayton. Still wanted her.

Neither of them had moved or spoken for a while. They just held each other in silence, enjoying each other's comfort and warmth.

Finally, Rose pulled away a little and tipped her head, her gaze meeting his. She leaned in closer, her mouth hovering just below his, her eyes drifting closed.

Gus closed the space between them, his lips meeting hers in a kiss that was soft and sweet. Almost chaste.

He slipped his hands on either side of her face, angling it to give him better access to her mouth. Ran his tongue along her lips that tasted of smooth whiskey and homemade apple pie.

Rose sighed with satisfaction, parting her lips. She

clutched at his shirt, pulling him as close as their position on the sofa would allow.

She murmured with pleasure when he slipped his tongue between her lips.

Time seemed to slow as they sat there, their mouths seeking each other's out in a kiss that grew hotter. Greedier. More intense.

There was a fire in his belly that he hadn't felt in ages. One that made him want things with Rose he hadn't wanted in so long.

Gus forced himself to pull away from Rose. He gripped her shoulders, his eyes searching hers for permission.

Rose stood up. She switched off the television with the remote, picked up their two empty whiskey glasses, then walked toward the stairs that led to the upper floor of The Silver C. Looking back at him, she flashed a wicked smile that did things to him.

"Are you coming or not?"

Gus nearly knocked over the silver tray on the table in front of him in his desperation to climb to his feet. He hurried toward her but was halted by her next words.

"Don't forget the bottle."

"Yes, ma'am." Grinning, he snatched it off the table before grabbing her hand and following her up the stairs.

Sixteen

When he heard his name called, Ryan looked up from where Andy, his farrier, was shoeing one of the horses.

It was Tripp.

The muscles in Ryan's back tensed. He hadn't talked to Tess or Tripp in the three days since they'd been back from their trip to Dallas. He could tell by his friend's expression that Tripp was concerned about something.

Maybe he had come to deliver a much-deserved ass-whipping. After all, Ryan had broken his promise by sleeping with Tess.

"What's up, Tripp?" Ryan walked over to his friend, still gauging the man's mood.

"I'm headed to the airport shortly, but I need to ask a favor."

"Sure. Anything."

"Keep an eye on Tess, will you?"

Ryan hadn't expected that. "Why, is something wrong?"

"Not exactly." Tripp removed his Stetson and adjusted it before placing it back on his head. "It's just that Mom and Dad are still gone, and I'm staying in Des Moines overnight. She'll be kicking around that big old house by herself mostly. We let a few hands off for the holidays. Plus... I don't like that Bo and Clem have been sniffing around the last few days. I'm beginning to think that letting Tessa participate in that bachelor auction was a mistake."

Ryan tugged his baseball cap down on his head, unsettled by the news of Bo and Clem coming around. He'd paid a hefty sum at the auction to ward those two off. Apparently, they hadn't gotten the hint.

"First, if you think you *let* your sister participate in that bachelor's auction, you don't know your sister very well. Tess has got a mind of her own. Always has. Always will."

"Guess you're right about that." Tripp rubbed the back of his neck. "And I'm not saying that Bo or Clem are bad guys. They're nice enough, I guess."

"Just not when they come calling on your sister." Ryan chuckled. He knew exactly how Tripp felt.

"Yeah, pretty much."

"Got a feeling the man you'll think is good enough for your little sister ain't been born yet."

"And probably never will be." Tripp chuckled. "But as her big brother, it's my job to give any guy who comes around a hard time. Make him prove he's worthy."

"Well, just hold your horses there, buddy. It's not like she's considering either of them." Ryan tried to appear nonchalant about the whole ordeal. Though on the inside he felt like David Banner in the midst of turning into the Incredible Hulk. He wanted to smash both Bo and Clem upside the head and tell them to go sniffing around someone else. "I think you're getting a little ahead of yourself."

"You haven't been around since you guys got back." The statement almost sounded accusatory. "Looks like the flower show threw up in our entry hall."

"Clem and Bo have been sending Tessa flowers?" Ryan tried to keep his tone and his facial expression neutral. He counted backward from ten in his head.

"Clem's apparently determined to empty out the local florist. Bo, on the other hand, has taken Tessa out to some play and this afternoon they're out riding."

Ryan hoped like hell that Tripp didn't notice the tick in his jaw or the way his fists clenched at his sides.

Tripp flipped his wrist, checking his watch. "Look, I'd better get going. I'll be back tomorrow afternoon, but call me if you need anything."

"Will do." Ryan tipped the brim of his baseball hat. "Safe travels."

He watched his friend climb back into his truck and head toward the airport in Dallas.

Jaw clenched, Ryan uncurled his fists and reminded himself to calm down. Then he saddled up Phantom, his black quarter horse stallion, and went for a ride.

For the past few days, he hadn't been able to stop thinking about his weekend with Tess. The moments they'd shared replayed again and again in his head. Distracted him from his work. Kept him up staring at the ceiling in the middle of the night.

He knew Tess well. Knew she'd been as affected by

their weekend together as he had. So how could she dismiss what they'd shared so easily and go out with Bo, or for God's sake, Clem?

Phantom's hooves thundered underneath him as the cold, brisk air slapped him in the face. He'd hoped that his ride would calm him down and help him arrive at the same conclusion Tess had. That it would be better for everyone if they remained friends.

But no matter how hard and fast he'd ridden, it didn't drive away his desire for Tess. Nor did it ease the fury that rose in his chest at the thought of another man touching her the way he had. The way he wanted to again.

He recognized the validity of Tessa's concerns that he wasn't serious and that he'd be chasing after some other skirt in a few months. He couldn't blame her for feeling that way. After all, as Helene was fond of saying, the proof was in the pudding.

He wouldn't apologize for his past. Because he'd never lied to or misled any of the women he'd dated. So he certainly wouldn't give his best friend any sense of false hope that he'd suddenly convert to the romantic suitor he'd been over the course of the weekend, for the sake of the Texas Cattleman's Club.

Ryan wasn't that guy any more than Tessa was the kind of woman who preferred a pair of expensive, red-bottomed heels to a hot new pair of sneakers.

So why couldn't he let go of the idea of the two of them being together?

He'd asked himself that question over and over the past few days, and the same answer kept rising above all the bullshit excuses he'd manufactured.

He craved the intimacy that they shared.

It was the thing that made his heart swell every time he thought of their weekend together. The thing that made it about so much more than just the sex.

He'd even enjoyed planning their weekend. And he'd derived a warm sense of satisfaction from seeing her reaction to each of his little surprises.

Ryan had always believed that people who made a big show of their relationships were desperate to make other people believe they were happy. But despite his romantic gestures being part of a ruse to keep the club from being mired in scandal, they had brought him and Tess closer. Shown her just how much he valued her.

Maybe he didn't believe that love was rainbows and sugarplums. Or that another person was the key to his happiness. But he knew unquestionably that he would be miserable if Tess got involved with someone else.

He couldn't promise her that he'd suddenly sweep her off her feet like some counterfeit Prince Charming. But he sure as hell wanted to try, before she walked into the arms of someone else.

Ryan and Phantom returned to the stables, and he handed him off to Andy. Then he hurried into the house to take a shower. He needed to see Tess right away.

Seventeen

Tessa checked her phone. The only messages were from Tripp, letting her know that his plane had landed safely, and from Clem asking if she'd received his flowers ahead of their casual dinner date later that night.

She tossed the phone on the counter. No messages from Ryan. They'd maintained radio silence since he'd set her luggage in the entry hall, said goodbye, and driven off.

Tessa realized that the blame wasn't all his. After all, the phone worked both ways. On a typical day, she would've called her best friend a couple of times by now. She was clearly avoiding him, as much as he was avoiding her.

She was still angry that Ryan and Tripp had made a pact about her. As if she were incapable of making her own decisions. Mostly, she was hurt that Ryan hadn't countered her accusation that he'd eventually tire of her and move on to someone else.

She wanted him to deny it. To fight for her. But Ryan hadn't raised the slightest objection. Which meant what he really wanted was a no-strings fuck buddy until something better came along.

For her, that would never be enough with Ryan. She was already in way too deep. But the truth was, she would probably never be enough for him. She was nothing like the lithe, glamorous women who usually caught Ryan's eye. Women like Sabrina Calhoun who was probably born wearing a pair of Louboutins and carrying an Hermès bag. Or women like Lana, the overly friendly barmaid. Women who exuded sex and femininity rather than looking like they shopped at Ranchers R Us.

Headlights shone in the kitchen window. Someone was in the driveway. As soon as the vehicle pulled up far enough, Tess could see it clearly.

It was Ryan's truck.

Her belly fluttered, and her muscles tensed. She waited for him to come to the kitchen door, but he didn't. Instead, he made a beeline for the stables.

Ryan had likely come to check on the stables at Tripp's request. He was obviously still avoiding her, and she was over it.

Nervousness coiled through her and knotted in her belly. They both needed to be mature about this whole thing. Starting right now.

She wouldn't allow the fissure between them to crack open any wider. If that meant she had to be the one to break the ice, she would.

Tessa's hair, piled on top of her head in a curly bun,

was still damp from the shower. She'd thrown on an old graphic T-shirt and a pair of jeans, so she could run out and double-check the stables.

Not her best look.

Tess slipped on a jacket and her boots and trudged out to the stables.

"Hey." She approached him quietly, her arms folded across her body.

"Hey." Ryan leaned against the wall. "Sorry, I haven't called. Been playing catch-up since we returned."

"I've been busy, too." She pulled the jacket tighter around her.

"I heard. Word is you've got a date tonight." The resentment in his voice was unmistakable. "You spent the weekend in my bed. A few days later and suddenly you and Bo are a thing and Clem is sending you a houseful of flowers?"

"Bo and I aren't *a thing*. We've just gone out a couple times. As friends." Her cheeks were hot. "And despite what happened this weekend, you and I *aren't* a thing. So you don't get a say in who I do or don't spend time with." The pitch of her voice was high, and the words were spilling out of her mouth. Tessa sucked in a deep breath, then continued. "Besides, are you going to tell me you've never done the same?"

Crimson spread across his cheeks. He stuffed his hands in his pockets. "That was different."

"Why? Because you're a guy?"

"Because it was casual, and neither of us had expectations for anything more."

"How is that different from what happened between us?"

Ryan was playing mind games with her, and she didn't appreciate it.

"Because I *do* expect more. That is, I want more. With you." He crept closer.

Tessa hadn't expected that. She shifted her weight from one foot to the other, her heart beating faster. "What are you saying?"

"I'm saying I want more of what we had this past weekend. That I want it to be me and you. No one else. And I'm willing to do whatever you need in order to make it happen."

"Whatever *I* need?" The joy that had been building in her chest suddenly slammed into a brick wall. "As in, you'd be doing it strictly for my benefit, not because it's what you want?"

"You make it sound as if I'm wrong for wanting you to be happy." His brows furrowed, and his mouth twisted in confusion. "How does that make me the bad guy?"

"It doesn't make you a bad person, Ryan. But I'm not looking for a fuck buddy. Not even one who happens to be my best friend." She pressed a hand to her forehead and sighed.

"I wouldn't refer to it that way, but if it makes us happy, why not?" Ryan's voice was low, his gaze sincere. He took her hand in his. "Who cares what anyone else thinks as long as it's what we want?"

"But it isn't what *I* want." Tears stung Tessa's eyes, and her voice wavered.

Ryan lifted her chin, his green eyes pinning her in place. "What *do* you want, Tess?"

"I want the entire package, Ryan. Marriage. Kids, eventually." She pulled away, her back turned to him for a moment before turning to face him again. "And I'll never get any of that if I settle for being friends with benefits."

"How can you be so sure it wouldn't work between us?" he demanded.

"Because you can't even be honest about what you want in bed with me." She huffed, her hands shaking.

There, she'd said it.

"What the hell are you talking about, Tess?"

Her face and chest were suddenly hot, and the vast barn seemed too small a space for the two of them. She slipped off her jacket and hung it on a hook.

Though the remaining ranch staff had left for the day and Tripp was gone, she still lowered her voice. As if the horses would spread gossip to the folks in town.

"I know you like it…rough. You weren't like that with me."

"Really? You're complaining about my performance?" He folded his arms, his jaw clenched.

"No, of course not. It was amazing. *You* were amazing. But I overheard Sabrina talking to a friend of hers on the phone when you two were still together. She was saying that she liked rough sex, and there was no one better at it than you."

Tessa's heart thumped. Her pulse, thundering in her ears, seemed to echo throughout the space.

"You overheard her say that on the phone?"

Tessa nodded.

"You know that wasn't an accident, right? She got a kick out of rattling your cage."

Tess suspected as much. Sabrina had never much liked her.

"You didn't answer my question." She looked in his

direction, but her eyes didn't quite meet his. "No judgment. I just want to know if it's true."

"Sometimes." He shrugged. "Depends on my mood, who I'm with. And we're not talking whips and chains, if that's what you're imagining." He was clearly uncomfortable having this discussion with her. Not that she was finding it to be a walk in the park either. "Why does it matter?"

"Because if that's what you like, but with me you were…"

"Not rough," he offered tersely. "And you're angry about that?"

"Not angry. Just realistic. If you can't be yourself with me in bed, you're not going to be happy. You'll get bored and you'll want out."

Ryan stared down at her, stepping closer. "I responded to you. Gave you what I thought you wanted."

"And you did." She took a step backward, her back hitting the wall. She swallowed hard. "But did it ever occur to you that I would've liked the chance to do the same for you?"

Sighing heavily, Ryan placed one hand on the wall behind her and cradled her cheek with the other. "It's not like that's the only way I like it, Tess. I don't regret anything about my weekend with you."

"But the point was you felt you *couldn't*. Because of our friendship or maybe because of your promise to Tripp. I don't know. All I know for sure is that pretending that everything will be okay is a fool's game." She forced herself to stand taller. Chin tipped, she met his gaze.

"So that's it? Just like that, you decide that's reason enough for us to not be together?" His face was red, and anger vibrated beneath his words, though his expression remained placid.

"Isn't that reason enough for you?"

"Sex isn't everything, Tess."

"For you, it always has been. Sex is just sex, right? It's not about love or a deeper connection." The knot in Tessa's stomach tightened when Ryan dropped his gaze and didn't respond. She sighed. "Tigers can't change their stripes, Ryan. No matter how hard they might try."

She turned to dip under his arm, but he lowered it, blocking her escape from the heated look in his eyes. His closeness. His scent. Leather. Cedar. Patchouli.

Damn that patchouli.

"Ryan, what else is there for us to say?"

"Nothing." He lowered his hands to her waist and stepped closer, his body pinning hers to the wall.

Time seemed to move in slow motion as Ryan dipped his head, his lips hovering just above hers. His gaze bored into hers. She didn't dare move an inch. Didn't dare blink.

When she didn't object, his lips crushed hers in a bruising, hungry kiss that made her heart race. He tasted of Helene's famous Irish stew—one of Ryan's favorite meals—and an Irish ale.

His hands were on her hips, pinning her in place against the wall behind her. Not with enough force to hurt her, but he'd asserted himself in such a way that it was crystal clear that he wanted her there, and that she shouldn't move.

She had no plans to.

As much as she'd enjoyed seeing a gentler side of Ryan during their weekend together, the commanding look in his eye and the assertiveness of his tone revved her up in a way she would never have imagined.

He trailed his hands up her sides so damned slowly she was sure she could count the milliseconds that passed. The backs of his hands grazed her hips, her waist, the undersides of her breasts.

The apex of her thighs pulsed and throbbed with such power she felt like he might bring her over the edge just from his kiss and his demanding touch.

Her knees quivered, and her breaths were quick and shallow. His kisses grew harder, hungrier as he placed his large hands around her throat. Not squeezing or applying pressure of any real measure. But conveying a heightened sense of control.

Ryan pulled back, his body still pinning hers, but his kiss gone. After a few seconds, her eyes shot open. He was staring at her with an intensity that she might have found scary in any other situation. But she knew Ryan. Knew that he'd never do anything to hurt her.

"You still with me, Tess?"

She couldn't pry her lips open to speak, so she did the only thing she could. Her impression of a bobble-head doll.

His eyes glinted, and he smirked. Ryan leaned in and sucked her bottom lip. Gently sank his teeth into it. Then he pushed his tongue between her lips and swept it inside the cavern of her mouth. Tipped her head back so that he could deepen the kiss. Claimed her mouth as if he owned every single inch of her body and could do with it as he pleased.

Her pebbled nipples throbbed in response, and she made a small gasp as his hard chest grazed the painfully hard peaks.

His scorching, spine-tingling kiss coaxed her body into doing his bidding, and his strong hands felt as if they were everywhere at once.

Tessa sucked in a deep breath when Ryan squeezed her bottom hard, ramping up the steady throb between her thighs.

When she'd gasped, he sucked her tongue into his mouth. He lifted her higher on the wall, pinning her there with his body as he settled between her thighs.

She whimpered as his rock-hard shaft pressed against the junction of her thighs. He seemed to enjoy eliciting her soft moans as she strained her hips forward, desperate for more of the delicious friction that made her belly flutter and sent a shudder up her spine.

"Shirt and bra off," he muttered against her lips, giving her barely enough room to comply with his urgent request. But she managed eagerly enough and dropped the garments to the floor.

He lifted her higher against the wall until her breasts were level with his lips. She locked her legs around his waist, anchoring herself to the wall.

Ryan took one heavy mound in his large hand. Squeezed it, then savagely sucked at her beaded tip, upping the pain/pleasure quotient. He gently grazed the pebbled tip with his teeth, then swirled his tongue around the flesh, soothing it.

Then he moved to the other breast and did the same. This time his green eyes were locked with hers. Gauging her reaction. A wicked grin curved the edge of his mouth as he tugged her down, so her lips crashed against his again.

Could he feel the pooling between her thighs through her soaked underwear and jeans? Her cheeks heated, momentarily, at the possibility. But her embarrassment was quickly forgotten as he nuzzled her ear and whispered his next command.

"When I set you down again I want you out of every single stitch of clothing you're wearing."

"Out here? In the stable? Where anyone could see us?" she stuttered, her heart thudding wildly in her chest.

"There's no one but us here," he said matter-of-factly. "But if you want me to stop…"

"No, don't." Tess was shocked by how quickly she'd objected to ending this little game. The equivalent of begging for more of him. For more of this.

At least he hadn't made her undress alone. Ryan tugged the beige plaid shirt over his head and on to the floor, giving her a prize view of his hard abdomen. She wanted to run the tip of her tongue along the chiseled lines that outlined the rippled muscles he'd earned by working as hard on the ranch as any of his hands. To kiss and suck her way along the deep V at his hips that disappeared below his waist. Trace the ridge on the underside of his shaft with her tongue.

Ryan toed off his work boots, unzipped his jeans and shoved them and his boxers down his muscular thighs, stepping out of them.

Tess bit into her lower lip, unable to tear her gaze from the gentle bob of his shaft as he stalked toward her and lifted her on to the edge of the adjustable, standing desk where she sometimes worked.

He raised the desk, which was in a seated position, until it was at just the right height.

"I knew this table would come in handy one day." She laughed nervously, her hands trembling slightly.

He didn't laugh, didn't smile. "Is this why you came out here, Tess? Why you couldn't be patient and wait until I came to your door?"

Before she could respond, he slid into her and they both groaned at the delicious sensation of him filling her. His back stiffened and he trembled slightly, his eyes squeezed shut.

Then he cursed under his breath and pulled out, retrieving a folded strip of foil packets from the back pocket of his jeans.

They'd both lost control momentarily. Given into the heat raging between them. But he'd come prepared. Maybe he hadn't expected to take her here in the stable or that he'd do so with such ferocity. But he had expected that at some point he'd be inside of her.

And she'd caved. Fallen under the hypnotic spell of those green eyes which negated every objection she'd posed up till then.

Sheathed now, Ryan slid inside her, his jaw tensed. He started to move slowly, but then he pulled out again.

"On your knees," he growled, before she could object.

Tessa shifted onto all fours, despite her self-consciousness about the view from behind as she arched her back and widened her stance, at his request.

Ryan adjusted the table again until it was at the perfect height. He grabbed his jeans and folded them, putting them under her knees to provide cushion.

Then suddenly he slammed into her, the sound of his skin slapping against hers filling the big, empty space. He pulled back slowly and rammed into her again. Then he slowly built a rhythm of rough and gentle strokes. Each time the head of his erection met the perfect spot deep inside her she whimpered at the pleasure building.

When he'd eased up on his movement, stopping just short of that spot, she'd slammed her hips back against him, desperate for the pleasure that the impact delivered.

Ryan reached up and slipped the tie from her hair, releasing the damp ringlets so that they fell to her shoulders and formed a curtain around her face.

He gathered her hair, winding it around his fist and tugging gently as he moved inside her. His rhythm was controlled and deliberate, even as his momentum slowly accelerated.

Suddenly, she was on her back again. Ryan had pulled out, leaned forward, and adjusted the table as high as it would go.

"Tell me what you want, Tess," he growled, his gaze locked with hers and his eyes glinted.

"I... I..." She couldn't fix her mouth to say the words, especially here under the harsh, bright lights in the stable. She averted her gaze from his.

He leaned in closer. His nostrils flared and a subtle smirk barely turned one corner of his mouth. "Would it help if I told you I already know *exactly* what you want. I just need to hear you say it. For you to beg for it."

His eyes didn't leave hers.

"I want..." Tessa swallowed hard, her entire body trembling slightly. "Your tongue."

He leaned in closer, the smirk deepening. "Where?"

God, he was really going to make her say it.

"Here." She spread her thighs and guided his free hand between her legs, shuddering at his touch. Tess hoped that show-and-tell would do, because she was teetering on the edge, nearly ready to explode. "Please."

"That wasn't so hard, now, was it?" He leaned down and lapped at her slick flesh with his tongue.

She quivered from the pleasure that rippled through her with each stroke. He gripped her hips, holding her in place to keep her bottom at the edge of the table, so she couldn't squirm away. Despite the pleasure building to a crescendo.

Tess slid her fingers in his hair and tugged him closer. Wanting more, even as she felt she couldn't possibly take another lash of his tongue against her sensitive flesh.

Ryan sucked on the little bundle of nerves and her body stiffened. She cursed and called his name, her inner walls pulsing.

Trailing kisses up her body, he kissed her neck. Then he guided her to her feet and turned her around, so her hands were pressed to the table and her bottom was nestled against his length.

He made another adjustment of the table, then lifted one of her knees on to it. He pressed her back down so her chest was against the table and her bottom was propped in the air.

He slid inside her with a groan of satisfaction, his hips moving against hers until finally he'd reached his own explosive release. As he gathered his breath, each pant whispered against her skin.

"Tess, I didn't mean to…" He sighed heavily. "Are you all right?"

She gave him a shaky nod, glancing back at him over her shoulder. "I'm fine."

He heaved a long sigh and placed a tender kiss on

her shoulder. "Don't give up on this so easily, Tess. Or do something we'll both regret."

Ryan excused himself to find a trash can where he could discreetly discard the condom.

Tessa still hadn't moved. Her limbs quivered, and her heart raced. Slowly, she gathered her bra, her jeans and her underwear. Her legs wobbled, as if she were slightly dazed.

She put on the clothing she'd managed to gather, despite her trembling hands.

When he returned, Ryan stooped to pick up her discarded shirt. Glaring, he handed it to her.

She muttered her thanks, slipping the shirt on. "You're upset. Why? Because I brought up your sex life with Sabrina?"

"Maybe it never occurred to you that the reason Sabrina and I tended to have rough, angry sex is because we spent so much of our relationship pissed off with each other.

He put his own shirt on and buttoned it, still staring her down.

Tessa felt about two inches tall. "I hadn't considered that."

She retrieved the hair tie from the standing desk, that she'd never be able to look at again without blushing. She pulled her hair into a low ponytail, stepped into her boots, and slipped her jacket back on.

"It can be fun. Maybe even adventurous. But in the moments when you're not actually having sex, it makes for a pretty fucked-up relationship. That's not what I want for you, Tess. For us." He shook his head, his jaw still clenched. "And there's something else you failed to take into account."

"What?"

"Rough sex is what got Sabrina off. It was her thing, not mine. What gets me off is getting you there. But I guess you were too busy making your little comparisons to notice." He stalked away, then turned back, pointing a finger at her for emphasis. "I want something more with you, Tess, because we're good together. We always have been. The sex is only a small component of what makes us fit so well together. I would think that our twenty plus years of friendship should be evidence enough of that."

Tessa wished she could take back everything she'd said. That she could turn back time and get a do-over.

"Rye, I'm sorry. I didn't mean to—"

"If you don't want to be with me, Tess, that's fine. But just be honest about it. Don't make up a bunch of bullshit excuses." He tucked his plaid shirt into his well-worn jeans, then pulled on his boots before heading toward the door. "Enjoy your date with Clem."

"It's not a date," she yelled after him, her eyes stinging with tears.

He didn't respond. Just left her standing there shaking. Feeling like a fool.

And she deserved it. Every angry stare. Every word uttered in resentment.

She'd been inventing reasons for them not to be together. Because she was terrified of the truth. That she wanted to be with Ryan more than anything. She honestly did want it all—marriage, a house of her own, kids. And she wanted them with her best friend. But she wouldn't settle for being in a relationship where she was the only one in love.

And she was in love with Ryan.

But as much as she loved him, she was terrified of the deafening silence she'd face if she confessed the truth to him. Because Ryan didn't believe in messy, emotional commitments.

He'd never admitted to being in love with a single one of his girlfriends. In fact, he'd never even said that he loved Sabrina. Just that there was a spark with her that kept things exciting between them. Something he hadn't felt with anyone else.

Tessa's sight blurred with tears and she sniffled, angrily swiping a finger beneath each eye. She'd done this, and she could fix it. Because she needed Ryan in her life. And he needed her, too. Even if all they'd ever be was friends.

Tessa's phone buzzed. She pulled it from her pocket. *Clem.*

She squeezed her eyes shut, her jaw clenched. Tess hated to bail on him, but after what had happened between her and Ryan, the thought of going out with someone else made her physically ill.

She answered the phone, her fingers pressed to her throbbing temple.

"Hey, Clem, I was just about to call you. Suddenly, I'm not feeling very well."

Eighteen

Ryan hopped into his truck and pulled out of the Noble Spur like a bat out of hell. He was furious with Tess and even madder that he'd been so turned on by her when she was being completely unreasonable.

He pulled into the drive of the Bateman Ranch and parked beside an unfamiliar car. A shiny red BMW.

As Ryan approached the big house, Helene hurried to the door to meet him. By the way she was wringing that dish towel in her hand, he wasn't going to like what she had to say one bit.

He glanced at the car again, studying the license plate. Texas plates, but it could be a rental car. And only one person he knew would insist on renting a red BMW.

Hell.

This was the last thing he needed.

"Ryan, I am so sorry. I told her that you weren't home, but she insisted on waiting for you. No matter how long you were gone." She folded her arms, frowning.

"It's okay, Helene." Ryan patted the woman's shoulder and forced a smile.

"Well, well, well. Look who finally decided to come home." His ex-fiancée, Sabrina Calhoun, sashayed to the front door. "Surprised to see me, baby?"

The expression on Helene's face let him know she was fit to be tied. Never a fan of the woman, his house manager would probably sooner quit than be forced to deal with his ex's condescending attitude again.

Ryan gave Helene a low hand signal, begging her to be civil and assuring her that everything would be all right.

Sabrina was the kind of mistake he wouldn't make twice. No matter how slick and polished she looked. Outrageously expensive clothes and purse. A haircut that cost more than most folks around here made in a week. A heavy French perfume that costed a small mint.

His former fiancée could be the dictionary illustration for high maintenance. He groaned internally, still kicking himself for ever thinking the two of them could make a life together.

Sabrina wasn't a villain. They just weren't right for each other. A reality that became apparent once she'd moved to Texas and they'd actually lived together.

Suddenly, her cute little quirks weren't so cute anymore.

"What brings you to Royal, Sabrina?" Ryan folded

his arms and reared back on his heels. He asked the question as politely as he could manage.

"I happened to be in Dallas visiting a friend, and I thought it would be rude not to come by and at least say hello." She slid her expensive sunglasses from her face and batted her eyelashes. "You think we can chat for a minute? Alone?"

She glanced briefly at Helene who looked as if she was ready to claw the woman's face off.

"Do you mind, Helene?" He squeezed her arm and gave her the same smile he'd been using to charm her out of an extra slice of pie since he was a kid.

She turned and hurried back into the house, her path littered with a string of not-so-complimentary Greek terms for Sabrina.

Ryan extended an arm toward the front door and followed Sabrina inside.

Whatever she was here for, it was better that he just let her get it out, so she could be on her merry way.

They sat down in the living room, a formal space she was well aware that his family rarely used. An indication that he didn't expect her visit to last long. And that he didn't consider her visit to be a friendly one.

"The place looks great." Sabrina glanced around.

He crossed his ankle over his knee and waited a beat before responding. "I don't mean to be rude, Brie, but we both know you're not the kind of person who'd drop by unannounced without a specific purpose in mind. I'm pressed for time today. So, it'd be great if we could just skip to the part where you ask whatever it is you came to ask."

"You know me well. Probably better than anyone."

Sabrina moved from the sofa where she was seated to the opposite end of the sofa where he was situated.

Ryan watched her movement with the same suspicion with which he'd regard a rattlesnake sidling up to him. Turning slightly in his seat, so that he was facing her, he pressed a finger to his temple and waited.

He knew from experience that his silence would drive Sabrina nuts. She'd spill her guts just to fill the empty void.

"I have a little confession to make. I visited my friend in Dallas because she emailed that article about you."

He'd nearly forgotten about that article on the bachelor's auction featuring him and Tess. Helene had picked up a few copies for his parents, but he hadn't gotten around to reading the piece. Between issues on the ranch and everything that had been going on with Tess, the article hadn't seemed important.

"And that prompted you to come to Royal because...?"

Sabrina stood, walking over to the fireplace, her back to him for a moment. She turned to face him again.

"It made me think about you. About us. I know we didn't always get along, but when we did, things were really great between us. I miss that." She tucked her blond hair behind her ears as she stepped closer. "I miss you. And I wondered if maybe you missed me, too."

Ryan sighed heavily. Today obviously wasn't his day. The woman he wanted insisted they should just be friends, and the woman he didn't want had traveled halfway across the country hoping to pick up where they'd left off.

He couldn't catch a break.

Ryan leaned forward, both feet firmly on the floor. "Sabrina, we've been through all this. You and I, we're just too different."

"You know what they say." She forced a smile after her initial frown in response to his rejection. "Opposites attract."

"True." He had been intrigued by their differences and because she'd been such a challenge. It had made the chase more exciting. "But in our case, it wasn't enough to maintain a relationship that made either of us happy. In fact, in the end, we were both miserable. Why would you want to go back to that?"

"I'm a different person now. More mature." She joined him on the sofa. "It seems you are, too. The time we've spent away from each other has made me realize what we threw away."

"Sabrina, you're a beautiful woman and there are many things about you that I admire." Ryan sighed. "But you just can't force a square peg into a round hole. This ranch is my life. Always has been, always will be. That hasn't changed. And I doubt that you've suddenly acquired a taste for country living."

"They do build ranches outside of Texas, you know." She flashed her million-dollar smile. "Like in Upstate New York."

"This ranch has been in my family for generations. I have no interest in leaving it behind and starting over in Upstate New York." He inhaled deeply, released his breath slowly, then turned to face her. "And I'm certainly not looking to get involved."

"With me, you mean." Sabrina pushed to her feet and crossed her arms, the phony smile gone. She peered up at him angrily. "You sure seemed eager to 'get in-volved' with your precious Tess. You went all out for her."

"It was a charity thing. Something we did on behalf of the Texas Cattleman's Club."

"And I suppose you two are still *just* friends?" The question was accusatory, but she didn't pause long enough for him to respond either way. "Suddenly you're a romantic who rents her fantasy car, knows exactly which flowers she likes, and which wine she drinks?" She laughed bitterly. "I always suspected you two were an item. She's the real reason our relation-ship died. Not because we're so different or that we want different things."

"Wait. What do you mean Tess is the reason we broke up?"

Sabrina flopped down on the sofa and sighed, shak-ing her head. "It became painfully obvious that I was the third wheel in the relationship. That I'd never mean as much to you as she does. I deserve better."

Ryan frowned, thinking of his time with Sabrina. Especially the year they'd lived together in Royal be-fore their planned wedding.

He hadn't considered how his relationship with Tessa might have contributed to Sabrina's feelings of isolation. At the time, he'd thought her jealousy of Tess was unwarranted. There certainly hadn't been any-thing going on between him and Tess back then. Still, in retrospect, he realized the validity of her feelings.

He sat beside Sabrina again. "Maybe I did allow my relationship with Tess to overshadow ours in some ways. For that, I'm sorry. But regardless of the reason for our breakup, the bottom line is, we're just not right for each other. In my book, finding that out before we got married is a good thing."

"What if I don't believe it. What if I believe…" She inhaled deeply, her stormy blue eyes rimmed with tears. "What if I think it was the biggest mistake I ever made, walking away from us?"

"We never could have made each other happy, Brie." He placed his hand over hers and squeezed it. "You would've been miserable living in Royal, even if we had been a perfect match. And God knows I'd be miserable anywhere else. Because this is where my family and friends are. Where my future lies."

"Your future with Tessa?" She pulled her hand from beneath his and used the back of her wrist to wipe away tears.

"My future with Tessa is the same now as it was back then." Regardless of what he wanted. "We're friends."

Sabrina's bitter laugh had turned caustic. She stalked across the floor again. "The sad thing is, I think you two actually believe that."

"What do you mean?"

"You've been in love with each other for as long as I've known you. From what I can tell, probably since the day you two met in diapers. What I don't understand is why, for the love of God, you two don't just admit it. If not to everyone else, at least to yourselves. Then maybe you'd stop hurting those of us insane enough to think we could ever be enough for either of you."

Ryan sat back against the sofa and dragged a hand across his forehead. He'd tried to curtail his feelings for Tess because of his promise to Tripp and because he hadn't wanted to ruin their friendship. But what lay at the root of his denial was his fear that he couldn't be the man Tess deserved. A man as strong as he was loving and unafraid to show his affection for the people he loved.

A man like her father.

In his family, affection was closely aligned with weakness and neediness. In hers, it was just the opposite. With their opposing philosophies on the matter, it was amazing that their parents had managed to become such good friends.

He'd been afraid that he could never measure up to her father and be the man she deserved. But what he hadn't realized was the time he'd spent with Tessa and her family had taught him little by little how to let go of his family's hang-ups and love a woman like Tess.

Sabrina was right. He *was* in love with Tess. Always had been. And he loved her as much more than just a friend. Tessa Noble was the one woman he couldn't imagine not having in his life. And now, he truly understood the depth of his feelings. He needed her to be his friend, his lover, his confidante. He wanted to make love to her every night and wake up to her gorgeous face every morning.

He'd asked Tess to give their relationship a chance, but he hadn't been honest with her or himself about *why* he wanted a relationship with her.

He loved and needed her. Without her in his life, he felt incomplete.

"It wasn't intentional, but I was unfair to you, Sabrina. Our relationship was doomed from the start, because I do love Tess that way. I'm sorry you've come all this way for nothing, but I need to thank you, too.

For helping me to realize what I guess I've known on some level all along. That I love Tess, and I want to be with her."

"As long as one of us is happy, right?" Her bangs fluttered when she blew out an exasperated breath.

Ryan stood, offering her an apologetic smile. "C'mon, it's getting late. I'll walk you to your car."

Ryan gave Sabrina a final hug, grateful to her. He'd ask Tess again to give them a chance.

This time, he wouldn't screw it up.

Nineteen

Tessa had been going crazy, pacing in that big old house all alone. She hadn't been able to stop thinking about Ryan. Not just what had happened in the stables, but she'd replayed everything he'd said to her.

She hadn't been fair to him, and she needed to apologize for her part in this whole mess. But first, she thought it best to let him cool off.

Tessa got into her truck and drove into town to have breakfast at the Royal Diner. It was a popular spot in town, so at least she wouldn't be alone.

She ordered coffee and a short stack of pancakes, intending to eat at the counter of the retro diner owned by Sheriff Battle's wife, Amanda. The quaint establishment was frozen in the 1950s with its red, faux-leather booths and black-and-white checkerboard flooring. But Amanda made sure that every surface in the space was gleaming.

"Tessa?"

She turned on her stool toward the booth where someone had called her name.

It was the makeup artist from PURE. Milan Valez.

"Milan. Hey, it's good to see you. How are you this morning?"

"Great. I always pass by this place. Today, I thought I'd stop in and give it a try." Milan's dark eyes shone, and her pecan brown skin was flawless at barely eight in the morning. "I just ordered breakfast. Why don't you join me?"

Tessa let the waitress know she'd be moving, then she slid across from Milan in the corner booth where the woman sat, sipping a glass of orange juice.

When the waitress brought Milan's plate, she indicated that she'd be paying for Tess's meal, too.

"That's kind of you, really, but you're the one who is new in town. I should be treating you," Tess objected.

"I insist." Milan waved a hand. "It's the least I can do after you've brought me so much business. I'm booked up for weeks, thanks to you and that article on the frenzy you caused at the charity auction. Good for you." Milan pointed a finger at her. "I told you that you were a beautiful woman."

"I'm glad everything worked out for at least one of us." Tess muttered the words under her breath, but they were loud enough for the other woman to hear.

"Speaking of which, how is it that you ended up going on this ultra-romantic weekend with your best friend?" Milan tilted her head and assessed Tessa. "And if you two are really 'just friends'—" she used air quotes "—why is it that you look like you are nursing a broken heart?"

Tessa's cheeks burned, and she stammered a bit before taking a long sip of her coffee.

"Don't worry, hon. I don't know enough folks in town to be part of the gossip chain." Milan smiled warmly. "But I've been doing this long enough to recognize a woman having some serious man troubles."

Tessa didn't bother denying it. She took another gulp of her coffee and set her cup on the table. She shook her head and sighed. "I really screwed up."

"By thinking you and your best friend could go on a romantic weekend and still remain just friends?" Milan asked before taking another sip of her orange juice.

"How did you—"

"I told you, been doing this a long time. Makeup artists are like bartenders or hairdressers. Folks sit there in that chair and use it as a confessional." Milan set her glass on the table and smiled. "Besides, I saw those pictures in the paper. That giddy look on your face? That's the look of a woman in love, if ever I've seen it."

"That obvious, huh?"

"Word around town is there's a pool on when you two finally get a clue." Milan laughed.

Tessa buried her face in her hands and moaned. "It's all my fault. He was being a perfect gentleman. I kissed him and then things kind of took off from there."

"And how do you feel about the shift in your relationship with…?"

"Ryan," Tess supplied. She thanked the waitress for her pancakes, poured a generous amount of maple syrup on the stack and cut into them. "I'm not quite sure how to feel about it."

"I'm pretty sure you are." Milan's voice was firm, but kind. "But whatever you're feeling right now, it scares the hell out of you. That's not necessarily a bad thing."

Milan was two for two.

"It's just that we've been best friends for so long. Now everything has changed, and yeah, it is scary. Part of me wants to explore what this could be. Another part of me is terrified of what will happen if everything falls apart. Besides, I'm worried that…" Tessa let the words die on her lips, taking a bite of her pancakes.

"You're worried that…what?" One of Milan's perfectly arched brows lifted.

"That he'll get bored with a Plain Jane like me. That eventually he'll want someone prettier or more glamorous than I could ever be." She shrugged.

"First, glammed up or not, you're nobody's Plain Jane," Milan said pointedly, then offered Tess a warm smile. "Second, that look of love that I saw…it wasn't just in your eyes. It was there in his, too."

Tessa paused momentarily, contemplating Milan's observation. She was a makeup artist, not a mind reader, for goodness' sake. So it was best not to put too much stock in the woman's words. Still, it made her hopeful. Besides, there was so much more to the friendship she and Rye had built over the years.

They'd supported one another. Confided in each other. Been there for each other through the best and worst of times. She recalled Ryan's words when he'd stormed out of the stables the previous night.

They *were* good together. Compatible in all the ways that mattered. And she couldn't imagine her life without him.

"Only you can determine whether it's worth the risk to lean into your feelings for your friend, or if you're better off running as fast as you can in the opposite direction." Milan's words broke into her thoughts. The woman took a bite of her scrambled eggs. "What's your gut telling you?"

"To go for the safest option. But that's always been my approach to my love life, which is why I haven't had much of one." Tessa chewed another bite of her pancakes. "In a perfect world, sure I'd take a chance. See where this relationship might lead. But—"

"There's no such thing as a perfect world, darlin'." A smile lit Milan's eyes. "As my mama always said, nothing ventured, nothing gained. You can either allow fear to prevent you from going for what you really want, or you can grow a set of lady *cojones*, throw caution to the wind, and confess your feelings to your friend. You might discover that he feels the same way about you. Maybe he's afraid of risking his heart, too."

Milan pointed her fork at Tessa. "The question you have to ask yourself is—is what you two could have together worth risking any embarrassment or hurt feelings?"

"Yes." The word burst from her lips without a second of thought. Still, its implication left her stunned, her hands shaking.

A wide smile lit the other woman's face. "Then why are you still sitting here with me? Girl, you need to go and get your man, before someone else does. Someone who isn't afraid."

Tess grabbed two pieces of bacon and climbed to her feet, adrenaline pumping through her veins. "I'm sorry, Milan. Rain check?"

"You know where to find me." She nodded toward the door. "Now go, before you lose your nerve."

Tessa gave the woman an awkward hug, then she hurried out of the diner, determined to tell Ryan the truth.

She was in love with him.

Ryan was evidently even angrier with Tessa than she'd thought. She'd called him repeatedly with no answer. She'd even gone over to the Bateman Ranch, but Helene said he'd left first thing in the morning and she didn't expect him until evening. Then she mentioned that his ex, Sabrina, had been at the house the day before.

Tess's heart sank. Had her rejection driven Ryan back into the arms of his ex?

She asked Helene to give her a call the second Ryan's truck pulled into the driveway, and she begged her not to let Ryan know.

The woman smiled and promised she would, giving Tess a huge hug before she left.

Tessa tried to go about her day as normally as possible. She started by calling Bo and Clem and apologizing for any misunderstanding. Both men were disappointed, but gracious about it.

When Tripp arrived back home from the airport, he brought her up to speed on the potential client. He'd landed the account. She hugged her brother and congratulated him, standing with him when he video conferenced their parents and told them the good news.

Tripp wanted to celebrate, but she wasn't in the mood to go out, and he couldn't get a hold of Ryan, either. So he called up Lana, since it was her day off.

Tessa had done every ranch chore she could think of

to keep her mind preoccupied, until finally Roy Jensen ran her off, tired of her being underfoot.

When Roy and the other stragglers had gone, she was left with nothing but her thoughts about what she'd say to Ryan once she saw him.

Finally, when she'd stepped out of the shower, Helene called, whispering into the phone that Ryan had just pulled into the drive of the Bateman Ranch.

Tessa hung up the phone, dug out her makeup bag and got ready for the scariest moment of her life.

Ryan hopped out of the shower, threw on a clean shirt and a pair of jeans. He picked up the gray box and stuck it in his pocket, not caring that his hair was still wet. He needed to see Tess.

He hurried downstairs. The entire first floor of the ranch smelled like the brisket Helene had been slow-cooking all day. But as tempted as he was by Helene's heavenly cooking, his stomach wasn't his priority. It would have to wait a bit longer.

"I was beginning to think you'd dozed off up there. And this brisket smells so good. It took every ounce of my willpower not to nab a piece." Tessa stood in the kitchen wearing a burgundy, cowl-neck sweater dress that hit her mid-thigh. "I mean, it would be pretty rude to start eating your dinner before you've had any."

"Tessa." He'd been desperate to see her, but now that she was here, standing in front of him, his pulse raced and his heart hammered against his ribs. "What are you doing here?"

She frowned, wringing her hands before forcing a smile. "I really needed to talk to you. Helene let me in before she left. Please don't be mad at her."

"No, of course I'm not mad at Helene."

"But you are still angry with me?" She stepped closer, peering up at him intensely.

"I'm not angry with you, Tess. I…" He sighed, running a hand through his wet hair.

He'd planned a perfect evening for them. Had gone over the words he wanted to say again and again. But seeing her now, none of that mattered. "But I do need to talk to you. And, despite the grand plans that I'd made, I just need to get this out."

"What is it, Rye?" Tessa worried her lower lip with her teeth. "What is it you need to tell me?" When he didn't answer right away, she added, "I know Sabrina was here yesterday. Did you two…are you back together?"

"Sabrina and me? God, no. What happened with us was for the best. She may not see it now, but one day she will."

Tessa heaved a sigh of relief. "Okay, so what do you need to tell me?"

Ryan reached for her hand and led her to the sofa in the family room just off the kitchen. Seated beside her, he turned his body toward hers and swallowed the huge lump in his throat.

"Tess, you've been my best friend since we were both knee-high to a grasshopper. The best moments of my life always involve you. You're always there with that big, bright smile and those warm, brown eyes, making me believe I can do anything. That I deserve everything. And I'm grateful that you've been my best friend all these years."

Tess cradled his cheek with her free hand. The corners of her eyes were wet with tears. She nodded. "Me, too. You've always been there for me, Ryan. I guess we've both been pretty lucky, huh?"

"We have been. But I've also been pretty foolish. Selfish even. Because I wanted you all to myself. Was jealous of any man who dared infringe on your time, or God forbid, command your attention. But I was afraid to step up and be the man you deserved."

"*Was* afraid?'" Now the tears flowed down her face more rapidly. She wiped them away with the hand that had cradled his face a moment ago. "As in past tense?"

"*Am* terrified would be more accurate." He forced a smile as he gently wiped the tears from her cheek with his thumb. "But just brave enough to tell you that I love you, Tessa Noble, and not just as a friend. I love you with all my heart. You're everything to me, and I couldn't imagine my life without you."

"I love you, too, Rye." Tessa beamed. "I mean, I'm in love with you. I have been for so long, I'm not really even sure when it shifted from you being my best friend to you being the guy I was head over heels in love with."

"Tess." He kissed her, then pulled her into his arms. "You have no idea how happy I am right now."

Relief flooded his chest and his heart felt full, as if it might burst. He loved this woman, who also happened to be his best friend. He loved her more than anything in the world. And he wanted to be with her.

Always.

For the first time in his life, the thought of spending the rest of his days with the same woman didn't give him a moment's pause. Because Tessa Noble had laid claim to his heart long ago. She was the one woman whose absence from his life would make him feel incomplete. Like a man functioning with only half of his heart.

"Tessa, would you…" He froze for a moment. His tongue sticking to the roof of his mouth. Not because he was afraid. Nor was he having second thoughts. There were a few things he needed to do first.

"What is it, Ryan?" She looked up at him, her warm, brown eyes full of love and light. The same eyes he'd been enamored with for as long as he could remember.

"I'd planned to take you out to dinner. Maybe catch a movie. But since Helene has already made such an amazing meal…"

"It'd be a shame to waste it." A wicked smile lit her beautiful face. "So why don't we eat dinner here, and then afterward…" She kissed him, her delicate hands framing his face. "Let's just say that dinner isn't the only thing I'm hungry for."

"That makes two of us." He pulled her into the kitchen and made them plates of Helene's delicious meal before they ended up naked and starving.

After their quick meal, Ryan swept Tessa into his arms and kissed her. Then he took her up to his bedroom where he made love to his best friend.

This time there was no uncertainty. No hesitation. No regrets. His heart and his body belonged to Tessa Noble. Now and always.

Ryan woke at nearly two in the morning and patted the space beside him. The space where Tess had lain, her bottom cuddled against his length. Her spot was still warm.

He raised up on his elbows and looked around. She

was in the corner of the room, wiggling back into her dress.

"Hey, beautiful." He scrubbed the sleep from his eye. "Where are you going?"

"Sorry, I didn't mean to wake you." She turned a lamp on beside the chair.

"You're leaving?" He sat up fully, drawing his knees up and resting his arms on them when she nodded in response. "Why?"

"Because until we talk to our families about this, I thought it best we be discreet."

"But it's not like you haven't spent the night here before," he groused, already missing the warmth of her soft body cuddled against his. It was something he'd missed every night since their return from Dallas.

"I know, but things are different now. I'm not just sleeping in the guest room." She gave him a knowing look.

"You've slept in here before, too."

"When we fell asleep binge-watching all the Marvel movies. And we both fell asleep fully dressed." She slipped on one of her boots and zipped it. "Not when I can't stop smiling because we had the most amazing night together. Tripp would see through that in two seconds."

He was as elated by her statement as he was disappointed by her leaving. What she was saying made sense. Of course, it did. But he wanted her in his bed, in his life. Full stop.

Tessa deserved better than the two of them sneaking around. Besides, with that came the implication that the two of them were doing something wrong. They weren't. And he honestly couldn't wait to tell everyone in town just how much he loved Tessa Noble.

"I'll miss you, too, babe." She sat on the edge of the bed beside him and planted a soft kiss on his lips.

Perhaps she'd only intended for the kiss to placate him. But he'd slipped his hands beneath her skirt and glided them up to the scrap of fabric covering her sex.

She murmured her objection, but Ryan had swallowed it with his hungry kiss. Lips searching and tongues clashing. His needy groans countered her small whimpers of pleasure.

"Rye… I really need to go." Tess pulled away momentarily.

He resumed their kiss as he led her hand to his growing length.

"Guess it would be a shame to waste something that impressive." A wicked smile flashed across Tess's beautiful face. She encircled his warm flesh in her soft hand as she glided it up and down his straining shaft. "Maybe I could stay a little longer. Just let me turn off the light."

"No," he whispered against the soft, sweet lips he found irresistible. "Leave it on. I want to see you. All of you."

He pulled the dress over her head and tossed it aside. Then he showed Tess just how much he appreciated her staying a little while longer.

Twenty

Ryan waved Tripp to the booth he'd secured at the back of the Daily Grind.

Tripp was an uncomplicated guy who always ordered the same thing. At the Royal Diner, a stack of pancakes, two eggs over easy, crispy bacon and black coffee. Here at the Daily Grind, a bear claw that rivaled the size of one's head and a cup of black coffee, two sugars.

Ryan had placed their order as soon as he'd arrived, wanting to get right down to their conversation.

His friend slid into the booth and looked at the plate on the table and his cup of coffee. "You already ordered for me?"

"Don't worry. It's still hot. I picked up our order two minutes ago."

Tripp sipped his coffee. "Why do I have the feeling that I'm about to get some really bad news?"

"Depends on your point of view, I guess." Ryan shoved the still warm cinnamon bun aside, his hands pressed to the table.

"It must be really bad. Did something happen to our parents on the cruise?"

"It's nothing like that." Ryan swallowed hard, tapping the table lightly. He looked up squarely at his friend. "I just... I need to tell you that I broke my promise to you...about Tess." Ryan sat back in the booth. "Tripp, I love her. I think I always have."

"I see." Tripp's gaze hardened. "Since you're coming to me with this, it's probably safe to assume you're already sleeping with my little sister."

Ryan didn't respond either way. He owed Tripp this, but the details of their relationship, that was between him and Tess. They didn't owe anyone else an explanation.

"Of course." Tripp nodded, his fists clenched on the table in front of him. "That damn auction. The gift that keeps on giving."

Ryan half expected his friend to try to slug him, as he had when they were teenagers and the kids at school had started a rumor that Ryan was Tess's boyfriend. It was the last time the two of them had an honest-to-goodness fight.

That was when Tripp had made him promise he'd never lay a hand on Tess.

"Look, Tripp, I know you didn't think I was good enough for your sister. Deep down, I think I believed that, too. But more than anything I was afraid to ruin my friendship with her or you. You and Tess...you're more than just friends to me. You're family."

"If you were so worried about wrecking our friendships, what's changed? Why are you suddenly willing to risk it?" Tripp folded his arms as he leaned on the table.

"I've changed. Or at least, my perspective has. I can't imagine watching your sister live a life with someone else. Marrying some other guy and raising their children. Wishing they were ours." Ryan shook his head. "That's a regret I can't take to my grave. And if it turns out I'm wrong, I honestly believe my friendship with you and Tess is strong enough to recover. But the thing is... I don't think I am wrong about us. I love her, Tripp, and I'm gonna ask her to marry me. But I wanted to come to you first and explain why I could no longer keep my promise."

"You're planning to propose? Already? God, what the hell happened with you guys in Dallas?" Tripp shut his eyes and shook his head. "Never mind. On second thought, don't *ever* tell me what happened in Dallas."

"Now that's a promise I'm pretty sure I can keep." Ryan chuckled.

"I guess it could be worse. She could be marrying some dude I hate instead of one of my best friends."

It was as close to a blessing as he was likely to get from Tripp. He'd gladly take it.

"Thanks, man. That means a lot. I promise, I won't let you or Tess down."

"You'd better not." Tripp picked up his bear claw and took a huge bite.

It was another promise he had every intention of keeping.

Ryan, Tessa, Tripp and both sets of their parents, had dinner at the Glass House restaurant at the exclusive five-star Bellamy resort to celebrate their parents' return and Tripp landing the Noble Spur's biggest customer account to date.

The restaurant was decked out in festive holiday decor. Two beautiful Douglas firs. Twinkling lights everywhere. Red velvet bows and poinsettias. Then there were gifts wrapped in shiny red, green, gold and silver foil wrapping paper.

Tessa couldn't be happier. She was surrounded by the people who meant the most to her. And both her parents and Ryan's had been thrilled that she and Ryan had finally acknowledged what both their mothers claimed to have known all along. That she and Ryan were hopelessly in love.

Ryan had surprised her with an early Christmas gift—the Maybach saddle she'd mused about on their drive to Dallas.

Even Tripp was impressed.

The food at the Glass House was amazing, as always. And a live act, consisting of a vocalist and an acoustic guitar player, set the mood by serenading the patrons with soft ballads.

When they started to play Christina Perri's "A Thousand Years," Ryan asked her to dance. Next, the duo performed Train's song, "Marry Me."

"I love that song. It's so perfect." Tessa swayed happily to the music as the vocalist sang the romantic lyrics.

"It is." He grinned. "And so are you. I'm so lucky that the woman I love is also my best friend. You, Tess, are the best Christmas gift I could ever hope for."

"That's so sweet of you to say, babe." Her cheeks

flushed and her eyes shone with tears. She smiled. "Who says you're not romantic?"

"You make me want to be. Because you deserve it all. Romance, passion, friendship. A home of our own, marriage, kids. You deserve all of that and more. And I want to be the man who gives that to you."

Tessa blinked back tears. "Ryan, it sounds a lot like you're asking me to marry you."

"Guess that means I ain't doing it quite right." Ryan winked and pulled a gray velvet box from his pocket. He opened it and Tessa gasped, covering her mouth with both hands as he got down on one knee and took her left hand in his.

"Tessa Marie Noble, you're my best friend, my lover, my confidante. You've always been there for me, Tess. And I always want to be there for you, making an incredible life together right here in the town we both love. Would you please do me the great honor of being my wife?"

"Yes." Tessa nodded, tears rolling down her cheeks. "Nothing would make me happier than marrying my best friend."

Ryan slipped on the ring and kissed her hand.

He'd known the moment he'd seen the ring that it was the one for Tess. As unique and beautiful as the woman he loved. A chocolate diamond solitaire set in a strawberry gold band of intertwined ribbons sprinkled with vanilla and chocolate diamonds.

Tessa extended her hand and studied the ring, a wide grin spreading across her gorgeous face. "It's my Neapolitan engagement ring!"

"Anything for you, babe." Ryan took her in his arms

and kissed her with their families and fellow diners cheering them on.

But for a few moments, everyone else disappeared, and there was only Tessa Noble. The woman who meant everything to him, and always would.

* * * * *

THE RIVAL'S HEIR

JOSS WOOD

This book is dedicated to anyone
who has struggled with infertility.
I get how hard it is.
You have my love and prayers.

Prologue

Callie Brogan looked around the lavish crowded function room at the Lockwood Country Club and edged her way to the side. She'd attended, and hosted, many parties in this very room and knew all the escape routes.

A few steps backward and her back was against the floor-to-ceiling glass doors. She fiddled behind her and yep, there was the handle. Callie pushed it down, felt the door swing open and as quickly as she could, ducked onto the small balcony that ran the length of the ballroom. She closed the door behind her, allowing her eyes to adjust to the darkness.

She didn't mind the dark, nor the cold—in fact she welcomed both. Anything was better than loud music, louder laughter and incessant chatter. Staring a new year in the face, she needed a few minutes of quiet, just to think.

Her beloved husband, Ray, was gone. He had been for many years.

It was time to let him go.

She couldn't hold on to him while she had an affair with the man she'd come here with tonight. It wasn't fair to either of them.

Callie looked down at the ring Ray had put on her finger over thirty years ago. She turned it around and around again. It was time to take it off, to put it away or at the very least, move it to her right hand. She wasn't Ray's anymore.

And while she might be sleeping with Mason—adventurous, inked and hot—she didn't belong to him either. She needed a new life, one that was hers alone. She wanted more. She no longer wanted to be the person she was, but she also didn't know who she wanted to be.

She had to reinvent herself.

But how?

Before she could finish the thought, a soft coat settled on her shoulders, broad hands on her hips.

"Are you okay?" Mason asked, his warm breath on her ear.

"Fine," Callie answered, wincing at her terse answer. She'd just wanted five minutes on her own, to figure things out.

But it was New Year's Eve, they were at a ball, and she had tomorrow to think about her life and why she was so discontented, in spite of having a fantastically sexy man sharing her sheets. The music was playing, the countdown would soon start and her issues could wait.

Callie looped her arms around Mason's neck, pushing a smile onto her face.

"Let's go inside, grab a drink and dance," Callie said, trying for gaiety.

Mason stepped back and shook his head. "I've been watching you for the last ten minutes. I saw you playing with your ring."

Callie frowned down at her hand and the big diamond winked back at her. "Okay?" she replied, confused.

Mason pinched the bridge of his nose. "Just once, Callie, I'd like to go somewhere, do something, that isn't tinged with the memories of your husband."

Before Callie could tell him that she hadn't been thinking about Ray, he continued, "Is it going to be like this for the next year, two years, ten? I'm asking so I know how long I'll be competing for your attention."

Callie felt the burn of shock, the heat of anger. "That's not fair."

"No, what's not fair is you mentally wandering off to join him while I am here. What's not fair is you wearing his ring while I bring you to orgasm, his picture facedown in the drawer next to your bed. Do you bring him out when we're done, Callie? Sneak him back into place when I leave?"

She did. God. And Mason knew.

Callie lifted her hands in protest. Because she felt embarrassed, she went on the attack. "Why are you hassling me? I thought this was just an affair. Why are you sounding all possessive and jealous?"

Mason opened his mouth to respond, then cursed before snapping it shut. His expression cooled, then turned inscrutable. "You're right. Forgive me." His deep voice was coated with frost.

From inside, the revelers started to count down to the New Year and when the crowd roared, Mason bent down and kissed her cheek, as remote as an Antarctic iceberg. "Happy New Year, Callie."

When Callie went back inside just a few minutes later, Mason was gone.

One

Darby Brogan listened with half an ear to the presentation but couldn't make herself concentrate. Unlike the other architects in the room who were listening intently, her thoughts were a million miles away from the project of a lifetime. Designing Boston's newest art museum was, suddenly and unexpectedly, the very last thing on her mind.

Darby crossed her legs, tapped her phone against her knee and mentally urged the speaker to hurry up. Modern, fresh, distinctive, ecologically friendly... Yes, she got it. This was all in the bid documents.

Her phone vibrated in her hand. Darby swiped her thumb across the screen and quickly read the messages posted in the group only she, her twin, Jules, and their best friend and business partner, DJ, had access to.

Where are you? Why aren't you back? How did your appointment with Dr. Mackenzie go?

Darby typed a quick reply to DJ's question.

At the museum bid presentation. Should be back in an hour or so.

Darby saw that Jules was typing and waited for her message to pop up on the screen. As she expected, it had nothing to do with work and everything to do with the appointment Darby had just come from.

Tell us!

Darby wished she hadn't recently pushed DJ to be more open and forthcoming. It made it difficult for Darby to keep her own secrets from her best friend and her twin.

It's not good. Basically, I'm running out of time. If I want a child, I should attempt IVF in the next six months.

She waited a beat before adding:

So that's a big decision I need to make. And quickly.

Judging by their lack of an immediate response, Darby knew her friends were absorbing her news, trying, like she was, to make sense of what she'd learned.

Darby wanted children. Being a mommy was her biggest wish. But despite knowing that she was going to have problems carrying a child, she'd always believed she'd need to face her infertility issues sometime in the future. She'd thought she had time, options, but...no. Her condition had been upgraded from serious to severe and she'd been told to expect a hysterectomy within the next few years.

And she had yet to hit thirty.

I thought I'd have a husband, at least a partner, when I needed to go there. I never imagined I'd have to do this—if I'm going to do this—alone.

You'll never be alone!!!

What Jules said, DJ added.

They were great, and she loved them, but Darby imagined strong arms, a broad chest, a male perspective. She'd been called beautiful, strong and smart, but she still went to bed alone every night.

Being an alpha female was hard enough for most men to accept. Being an alpha female with infertility issues seemed a step too far. The reality was that she couldn't afford to wait any longer to find a man who shared her dreams for a family; she had no more time to waste. If she wanted a child, she'd be doing it now, solo, albeit with the help of science. And a sperm donor.

DJ's name popped up again on her screen.

How can we help?

Darby smiled, so glad these women were in her life. Darby ignored her burning eyes and straightened her shoulders. It was bad news, sure, but she hadn't received a death sentence. Her dreams were in ICU, but she wasn't.

Keep it in perspective, Brogan. Humor, as she'd

learned, was always a good deterrent to negativity, so she thought a moment before typing again.

I'll expect you to help me select a sperm donor.

Any excuse to openly ogle guys! Jules's answer flashed on her screen. I'm there.

DJ repeated the sentiment, adding a couple of heart-eyed emoji to convey her excitement. Darby knew they were just being kind. They were both engaged to and head over heels in love with smart, successful, stupidly sexy men.

Darby was not jealous…

Well, maybe a little.

They all—including her mother!—had hot guys in their beds. Jules was engaged to her childhood friend; DJ and her long-term on-again, off-again lover had recently decided to be permanently on. As for Darby's mother, Callie? She was having an affair with a scorching hot man a decade younger.

Darby wouldn't mind a sexy tattooed man to have some fun with. Her life for the past year or so had been all work and very little play… Actually, that pretty much summed up her life in total. She didn't play much at all, she never had.

After a lifetime of school and college success, she'd recently been named one of the most exciting 40 Architects Under 40 in the latest edition of a well-known design publication. She was a partner in what was described as the most successful design house in Boston, possibly on all the East Coast. She was reasonably attractive, wealthy and healthy. Well, except for her annoying reproductive system.

And she was single…

So very, very single.

She felt panic tickle her throat. What if she were incapable of loving someone, of being in a have-it-all partnership? What if she was too independent, too strong willed, too competitive to build her life with a man?

As for a solo attempt at motherhood…could she do this?

Darby shifted in her seat. She refused to give negative thoughts space in her brain. She wanted a child and she could be a single mom. It was okay that she'd yet to meet her special someone. She was glad she hadn't wasted her valuable time on a he'll-do guy.

If she was going to settle down, she wanted someone who wanted what she did…everything. Kids, a kick-ass career, a stable, respectful relationship.

World peace, an end to famine…

Darby frowned when she realized that the organization's director was no longer speaking. She looked around the ballroom, seeing that the attendees had shifted their focus to the back of the room. Turning in her seat, her brows lifted when she saw the lone figure leaning against the wall, one ankle crossed over the other.

Oh…

Oh…*wow.*

Judah Huntley was better looking in person than the pictures she'd seen of him online. Taller, too. Being tall herself, she guesstimated he was six-two or six-three, and under his charcoal, obviously designer Italian suit, his body was tougher, harder, more muscular than she would have expected. Broad chest, long legs, thick arms and a masculine face. Stubble covered his cheeks and jaw, his nose looked like it had been broken once, maybe twice and his thick wavy espresso-colored hair looked like he routinely combed it with his fingers.

Sexy, built and the brightest architectural mind of his generation.

Darby swallowed, conscious that her mouth was dry and her heart was banging against her chest. There was an unfamiliar heat between her legs—welcome back, libido! Damn, she wouldn't mind taking Judah Huntley out for a spin.

Whoa, Brogan, not like you.

The men she dated and—very rarely—slept with had to work damn hard to get her to that point but Darby knew Judah Huntley would just have to crook his finger and she'd come running.

Maybe it was her kooky state of mind, yet here she was, panting over a man across the room.

Darby couldn't pull her eyes from Huntley's fallen-angel face. *Be sensible, Brogan.* This scorched-earth attraction was an aberration, nothing to be concerned about. She was only intrigued by Judah Huntley because he was such a phenomenal architect, because he'd designed that ecohouse in Denmark that was a brilliant piece of art, as was that ski lodge in Davos and the new headquarters for one of the world's leading software companies in Austin. He was creative and innovative, throwing together contrasting materials and techniques and making them work.

And he was sexy enough to make her soul ache.

Dark eyes—black? blue?—under strong brows met hers.

And Darby felt the world shift beneath her.

A small smile pulled the corners of his mouth upward

and she placed her hand to her heart. God, the way he looked at her, like he was imagining her naked...

He straightened, pushed his hands into the pockets of his suit pants and she saw that his stomach was flat. She remembered a photo of him running on a beach in Cyprus... That muscled, ridged stomach. Just looking at him was more pleasure than she'd had in a while.

Unbidden, the image of her eggs and his sperm colliding in a petri dish, creating a baby in the lab, jumped into her head. If she imagined them in bed together, practicing the art of making babies the old-fashioned way, her panties might explode.

Darby fought the temptation to get up, walk over to him, hold out her hand and lead him away. She didn't think he'd say no. Damn, she was tempted.

"Miss Brogan? *Miss! Brogan!*"

Darby turned her head at the irritated voice of the director at the front of the room. What was his problem? Frowning, she looked around and saw the amused faces of her colleagues.

"May I continue?"

Darby quickly nodded, her face flaming. She heard the muffled snickers. Dammit, the entire room had caught her looking at Judah Huntley. Since, as her family frequently told her, she had the most expressive face in the history of the world, they all knew she'd been imagining Huntley naked.

Darby slid down in her seat, only just resisting the urge to cover her face with her hands. Even if she found the guts to proposition him—a very big *if*—sleeping with Judah Huntley wasn't an option. Especially since she was now embarrassed beyond all belief.

Darby kept her eyes on the speaker while she fought

the urge to look back and take just one more peek. *Yeah, good plan, just embarrass yourself further, Brogan, add some fuel to the fire.*

It took all her willpower to keep her eyes forward and when the presentation finally ended—the longest ten minutes in the world—Darby stood up and oh-so casually looked across the room.

Judah Huntley was gone.

Six weeks later

Judah Huntley took a sip of overly sweet champagne from the glass in his hand and tried not to wince. God, he hated these functions. He strongly believed in the power of an old-fashioned email, quietly stating whether he'd been awarded the commission or not. Putting on a suit and noose and making small talk was his level of hell.

But Jonathan, his business manager, had RSVP'd on Judah's behalf, saying that he'd be glad to attend the foundation's cocktail party. He'd also promised that if Huntley and Associates was commissioned to design the new art museum, Judah would hire a local architect to be the firm's local liaison.

It made sense to hire someone local to do the grunt work of visiting the planning offices, research, smoothing the way. The Boston-based architect wouldn't do any drafting or design work; Judah had an experienced team back in New York to implement his ideas. They were the best and brightest of the bunch and routinely met his high standards.

As a winner of two of the world's most prestigious architecture awards, Judah knew his interest in designing the art museum was unexpected. It wasn't a big project or even a lucrative one. Since the project was being funded by a nonprofit, his design fees would be laughable. But thanks to international businessmen with very deep pockets who wanted his name attached to their buildings, Judah had a fat bank account and could afford to take on a project at cost.

He had buildings all over the world but had yet to design one in Boston, his hometown. He wanted to create something that was beautiful and functional, something Bostonians would enjoy. He was renowned for his innovative corporate buildings and envelope-pushing mansions but there was something special, something intoxicating, about designing a building to hold art and treasures. The box had to be as exciting, as electrifying as the contents...

And that was why he was standing in a stuffy ballroom waiting for someone to announce what everyone already knew: Judah would be awarded the project.

Upsides to being in Boston were a gorgeous site and an interesting project. Downside? Being in Boston. The smells, the air, the buildings all made him remember how his life used to be. Stifling. Demanding. Claustrophobic. Long on responsibility and short on fun.

Judah was grateful for the feminine hand on his arm that jerked him back to the present. An attractive woman stood in front of him, blond hair, red lips, bold eyes. He chatted with her politely, but she wasn't the woman who'd first come to mind.

The last time he'd stood in this room, he'd locked eyes with a younger, sexier blonde who'd made his stomach bungee jump. Initially, she'd reminded him of a storybook Cinderella, all flashing eyes and tiny frame, but then he'd caught the look in her eyes, on her face, and decided that she was more a duchess than a princess, more sophisticated than simple.

He wondered if she was here again tonight.

But, if she was, what did it matter? Though he'd been rocked by their instinctual attraction—when last had he felt such an instant physical reaction to anyone?—the thought of making small talk, doing the dating dance, felt like too much effort.

Chatting up a woman, taking her back to his hotel room and having sex was the mental equivalent of riding an immensely popular roller coaster. Patience was required to get on the ride, there was the brief sensation of pleasure, then the inevitable anticlimax when the cart rolled to a stop.

After Carla, he'd ridden as many roller coasters as he could. A year and too many women later, he'd realized that mindless sex with mindless women wasn't working for him and he went cold turkey. In the past eighteen months, he'd gone from being monogamous to being a player to being a monk.

Judah sighed. While no guy rapidly approaching his forties preferred having solo sex, he did like having a life that was drama-free.

But that blonde he'd seen here before—tall, slim, stunningly sexy—was the first woman in six months who'd caught his interest. She'd made his core temperature rise. She had the face of a naughty pixie, the body of a lingerie model and the eyes of a water nymph. When he'd looked at her, reality faded. All he could see was her, stretched out on a rug in front of a roaring fire, naked on the white sands of Tahiti or on the cool marble of a designer kitchen. Hell, up against the fabric-covered wall of an intensely uninteresting hotel ballroom.

He'd wanted her.

And because he'd been so damned tempted to walk over, take her hand and find the closest private space where he could put his hands on that body, he'd acted like the adult he professed to be and left. He didn't want mindless sex anymore, but the thought of anything more—becoming emotionally involved, making a connection—terrified him.

So he was in no-man's-land, dating himself. And, man, was he so tired of that...

Half concentrating on the conversation with the woman in front of him, Judah looked up to see the director of the foundation heading to the podium. Standing at the back of the room, Judah's height allowed him to see over the heads of most of the guests and he recognized some candidates from the meeting weeks ago.

He cursed himself when he realized he was looking for a bright blond head and exceptional legs.

"Ladies and gentlemen, on behalf of the Grantham-Ford Foundation..."

Judah pushed his hands into the pockets of his suit pants, tuned out the opening remarks of the chairman of the board and looked toward the door, his attention caught by an elder man in a suit, his tanned face scanning the crowd, obviously looking for someone. He looked vaguely familiar, like a worried version of someone from Judah's past.

Intrigued, Judah edged his way closer to the door. The man's dark eyes caught his movement and Judah saw relief cross his face. The man was looking for *him*. But why here at this hotel, in the middle of a function? Judah had an office, an assistant who managed his schedule.

Odd.

"We were all blown away by the designs submitted and it was difficult to make a choice…"

Judah ignored the droning voice and frowned as the man eased away from the doorway, gesturing for Judah to join him in the hallway. Judah tossed a look over his shoulder, guessing the director would ramble on for a few more minutes—the man seemed to like the sound of his own voice. Judah pulled the door to the room partially closed behind him. If he was needed, he had no doubt someone would find him.

"Mr. Huntley! I am so glad I managed to track you down."

Judah's heart sank when he heard the masculine version of Carla's heavy Italian accent. Judah scowled. His ex, the opera-singing heiress, had hit a new low if she was sending her minions to deliver her messages. Judah had nothing to say to her face or via her employees. She'd cheated on him—he was pretty sure it hadn't been the first time—but he'd caught her. She and her lover had been in *his* bed, in *his* apartment. Naked on his sheets.

Judah didn't share, ever. Infidelity was his hard limit. And he was still pissed that he'd felt compelled to buy a new bed and give those expensive sheets to a charity shop. He'd thought about selling his apartment, but that was going a step too far. Carla wasn't worth the sacrifice of his stunning views of Central Park.

Judah held up his hand. "Not interested."

"Wait, Mr. Huntley."

Judah lifted an eyebrow dismissively. "You have thirty seconds and I'm only giving you that much because this evening is sadly lacking in entertainment."

Thin shoulders pushed back and an elegant hand

smoothed a lock of silver hair off the man's forehead. "I am Maximo Rossi. I am Carla's personal lawyer."

Okay. And what did Carla's personal lawyer want from Judah? Thanks to being the sole beneficiary of her father's billions, Carla had more money than God, along with her luscious body and stunning face. She also had the voice of an angel. They hadn't had any contact for months, so why now? Judah felt his stomach twist itself into a Gordian knot. This couldn't be good.

He forced himself to remain calm. "Is Carla okay?"

"She's fine…mostly."

Oh, God. He recognized the weariness in the older man's eyes, the frustration that dealing with Carla Barlos incurred. The man probably had a stomach ulcer and high blood pressure. Judah could sympathize. Carla was hard work.

"What does that mean?" Judah demanded, hearing the apprehension in Rossi's voice.

"Bertolli has written a new opera, one just for her."

Bertolli's music sounded like screeching cats, but what did Judah know? But even he, philistine that he was, understood how a big a deal it was to have Bertolli, the most exciting composer in the world, build an opera around Carla.

"It's a morality tale. Carla's lead character is a crusader for moral reform."

While Judah appreciated the irony, he didn't understand why Rossi was here, telling him this. Why should Judah care what Carla was up to? He hadn't seen her for more than eighteen months.

Deciding he was done here, Judah was about to excuse himself when he heard the arrival of the elevator. The doors opened and a long leg, ending in a blush-colored pump, emerged from the box. A frothy peppermint-colored dress danced around slim thighs.

She was here, she was back.

Rossi forgotten, Judah's eyes wandered upward, taking in a thin belt around a tiny waist, skating up a narrow chest. Her breasts were fantastic, small but perky. Athletic but not overly so, fit but still oh-so feminine. And God, that face.

Judah felt his cold heart sputter as blood drained south. A wide mouth made for kissing, high cheekbones, eyes the color of zinc under arched brows. Blond hair pulled back into a sleek ponytail.

He'd last seen her across a crowded room weeks ago. He'd thought her sexy then. Now, he upgraded that assessment to heart-stoppingly hot.

He wanted her. Now, immediately, up against that wall, his hands on those tanned thighs, his tongue on her neck, her nipple, her naval. He could go back to being a monk tomorrow...

But she had yet to notice him. Her attention was taken by the other occupants of the elevator, a black-haired, dark-eyed baby held by a hard-faced, middle-aged woman. The woman held the kid like she would hold a test tube of poison, awkward and fearful. He didn't blame her; he wasn't a kid person either.

He used to be, but that was a long time ago. When he was young and stupid.

Rossi cleared his throat. "That is my assistant and the baby is Jacquetta Huntley. Carla needs you to take her for at least six months. She can't be responsible for her and prepare for the biggest performance of her career."

While Judah struggled to make sense of the man's

words, a booming voice from the front of the room rolled into the hallway.

"I am pleased and proud to announce that the architect designing the Grantham-Ford Art Museum will be Judah Huntley. Judah, please come forward and say a few words."

Judah's eyes darted between three faces: Rossi, the baby and the blonde.

It was official. He'd just fallen down Alice's rabbit hole.

Two

Three things occurred to Darby at the same time.

One, Judah Huntley was more gorgeous than she remembered.

Two, he had a kid he didn't know about.

Three, hers wasn't the only messed-up life.

Oh, he was good. On hearing he had a child, his expression barely changed, but his ink-blue eyes held disbelief and a heavy dose of *WTF*. The baby, stunningly gorgeous with rosy cheeks and hair the color of bitter chocolate, looked at them from the stiff arms of the woman carrying her.

Darby knew she should move away, she should give them some privacy but...

She wasn't that noble, and this was too good to miss. How would Judah Huntley juggle the announcement of the commission *and* the news that he had a child? Would he flip, freeze, flee?

Darby couldn't wait to find out.

The baby let out a soft cry, Judah was called to the front of the room again and the weary woman took a step toward Judah, holding the baby out like a parcel. Judah threw up his hands in a hell-no gesture and the baby responded by letting out a shriller cry.

Darby forgot about the drama playing out in front of her eyes and focused on that small face scrunched up and turning red. The wails grew louder and someone she recognized as one of the foundation's board members appeared at the door.

"Mr. Huntley, they are calling for you. You've been awarded the design contract."

No surprise there. Judah was an amazing architect.

But his ability to ignore a screaming baby annoyed her. Pushing past the lawyer, she reached for the little girl, ignoring the look of relief on the older woman's face. Tucking the baby into the crook of her arm, Darby placed her pinkie finger in the little girl's mouth and felt the tug of tiny lips.

Darby looked at Judah. "She's hungry."

He threw his hands up in the air and shook his head. "Not my problem."

"Apparently it is," Darby responded tartly.

"Um… Mr. Huntley. Really, you need to come back inside." The man tugged the sleeve of Judah's jacket.

Darby noticed, *again*, that the jacket covered a set of rather big arms and broad shoulders. Judah's easy dismissal of this beautiful baby was irritating, but her hormones had yet to receive the message that she shouldn't be imagining what Huntley's body looked like under that expensive suit.

Judah pushed his hand through his thick, expertly cut hair and she heard the barely audible swear he dropped. Yeah, Huntley wasn't having a good day.

He gripped the bridge of his nose. After a brief pause, he lifted his head and Darby saw the determination on his face, the assertiveness in his eyes. There was something superhot about an alpha male doing his thing...

Judah nodded to the closed door of the ballroom.

"I'm going to go back in there to accept this damn commission. Rossi, you are going to take the baby with you and you will call me and we will arrange a suitable time to meet and discuss Carla's insanity. Do not ambush me again." That dark blue gaze scraped over her and he shook his head. "You, I have no idea who you are but if you'd kindly give the kid back, we can all go on with our lives."

His tone suggested that he wasn't interested in hearing any arguments and when no one spoke, he turned around and walked back into the ballroom, the board member following closely behind. Darby heard the audience's roar of applause and looked down at the little girl in her arms.

She had Judah's nose and the shape of his eyes and Darby could see the hint of Judah's shallow dimple in the baby's left cheek. Like his, the baby's hair was dark, her sweet brows strong. She was utterly perfect and those deep dark eyes—brown, not blue—looked up at Darby's, content to suckle on her pinkie.

She was, possibly, the most beautiful baby Darby had ever seen and as she'd been obsessed by babies for longer than was healthy, she'd seen more than a lot. This little girl looked like what she was, the offspring of two boundlessly beautiful people.

Before his death, Darby's father had been a well-known Boston businessman and her parents had been, at one time, the heart of Boston society, so she'd had a taste of fame. But Huntley and his ex-girlfriend were famous on an entirely different level. Carla, an exciting, lushly beautiful, stunningly wealthy opera-singing heiress, had millions of social media followers and was tabloid gold. Thanks to his talent, his stupidly sexy body, and his penchant for dating models and actresses, Judah was also a media golden boy.

They might be famous, but Darby wasn't impressed by either of the little girl's parents right now.

How could Carla just shove her child out of her life, pass her on like she was an unwanted package? And why hadn't Judah stepped up? Didn't they realize that a child was a gift, indescribably precious? What was wrong with these people?

Had the world gone mad?

The baby burped and then her face scrunched up, her eyes closing. Darby had enough experience to know that the little girl was about to fill her diaper. The telltale smell wafted up and Darby half smiled. Yep, there it was.

Darby looked up and saw the two lawyers grimace in immediate expressions of distaste.

"She needs changing," Darby stated just in case they hadn't made the connection between the smell and the problem.

Identical looks of horror and two steps back. "No! No, no, no!"

The baby squirmed in Darby's arms and let out a

wail loud enough to be heard in Fenway Park. Okay, time to go.

The baby was stunningly cute and too adorable for words, but Darby had come here to work. It wasn't a surprise that Huntley had been awarded the project, but Darby knew there were lots of well-heeled socialites in that room with money to burn. Some of them might want a summer place designed or a house renovated.

Business had been a bit slow lately and she needed a new, lucrative project. She also needed to finish the renovations to two small apartment buildings she owned in Back Bay and get them on the market, but she knew it might take some time to sell them at the price she wanted.

Thank God she was due her quarterly dividend check from Winston and Brogan tomorrow; that was the money she'd allocated to her IVF fund. With that money and any she managed to save over the next four months, she could have the procedure in five months' time. At the thought, her stomach churned, then burned.

Unlike Huntley and his ex, she wanted a child.

Didn't she?

The two Europeans exchanged a long look as if they were silently arguing about who was going to do the honors of changing the little girl. They both looked horrified.

"I need to get going," Darby said.

A charming smile crossed the lawyer's face. "The nanny we hired to look after Jacquetta since we left Italy has been dismissed. Could you change her since neither of us knows how?"

"What makes you think I do?" Darby asked.

Mr. Slick just shrugged, and Darby knew she was

being played. It had been years since she'd changed a
diaper, but she'd looked after babies as a teenager. She
was sure it was like riding a bike; one didn't just forget.
And God, if she left little Jacquetta—goodness, what a
mouthful—in their hands, the kid would be more miserable than she was now. It was one diaper, Darby could
deal.

Darby held out her hand for the bag draped over the
lady's shoulder. Darby would change Jacquetta—*Jac*—
make up a bottle for the little girl and send them on their
way. There was no doubt she'd remember this encounter
for the rest of her life: hot guy, cute kid, drama…

"There's a baby room just around the corner." Darby
jerked her head at the woman. "You're coming with me."

"Perché?"

Why? Jeez, these people were seriously whacked.
"Because you don't just hand over a baby to a stranger,
that's why."

Mr. Slick smiled at her. "The corridor ends just beyond the restroom so there is nowhere to take little Jacquetta. If you wanted to steal her, you'd have to pass by
us. And we'll be here waiting."

Darby frowned, unease crawling across her skin.

"Besides, this is one of the best hotels in Boston, there
are cameras everywhere." Mr. Slick winced as Jacquetta's
cries escalated in volume.

Dammit. She was going to do this.

Darby started to walk down the hallway. Feeling eyes
on her, she looked back. Her gut was screaming at her
that their expressions were too bland, that she was being
played. How the hell had she ended up in this situation?

Then Jac released a high-pitched scream and Darby
looked down, her heart hurting over the little girl's dis-

tress. The baby, defenseless and innocent, had to come first. Darby would change her and make up a bottle, maybe give her a little cuddle and then Darby would hand her back.

Her life would go back to normal in ten minutes.

Darby walked down the corridor, her hand tapping Jac's little bottom, unable to resist dropping a kiss on the baby's curly head. In the baby changing room, Darby laid Jac on the soft changing table and looked down into the little girl's exquisite face.

"Should I have one just like you?"

Jac, being no more than nine months old, didn't have a clue.

Little Jac sucked her bottle as Darby walked back down the hallway, her shoulders aching from the unaccustomed weight of holding a baby and a seriously heavy baby bag. The baby was clean and happy, and Darby could hand her over and go back to her life.

Except that, when she turned the corner, there was nobody to hand the baby back to.

Hearing noise from the elevator, Darby spun around and saw the two lawyers standing in the elevator.

"Give the baby to Judah Huntley," Mr. Slick told her, his words sliding between the closing doors.

Darby couldn't believe what they'd done. They'd left Jac with a stranger! How did they know she wasn't a psycho, that she wouldn't just walk off with the baby?

Dumping the heavy bag into the stroller and leaving it in the hallway, Darby pushed open the door to the ballroom with her hip and scanned the audience. It wasn't difficult to find Huntley since he was taller than pretty much everyone. His dark head was bent to better hear the words of an olive-skinned brunette wearing a low top. Her expression brazenly suggested that she wouldn't say no if Huntley invited her to take a tour of his guest suite, or the nearest closet.

Irrationally annoyed, Darby focused on the photographs flashing onto the presentation screen on the far side of the room, each image stealing her breath. The first photo was of Huntley's proposed design for the Grantham-Ford museum and it was fantastic. The building looked curvy and feminine, sultry and almost, dare she say it, sexy. It was stunning and, dammit, so much better than her own design. The man deserved to win the commission. As images of his previous designs rolled across the wall, she stood there, blown away yet again by his talent.

Darby pulled her gaze away from the images and looked back to the creator of those magnificent buildings, surprised to find his eyes on her. God, he was a good-looking man. An intriguing combination of sexy and smart, tough and taciturn.

She jerked her head to summon him over and studied him as he made his way toward her, graceful despite his height and large frame.

Stepping back into the hall, Darby glanced down at the sleeping bundle in her arms, smiling at the very feminine version of that masculine man heading her way. She'd hand Jac over to her him and remind herself that this beautiful child was not her problem. She had her own baby issues to figure out.

As Judah reached the door, the chairman of the board, so in love with his own voice, tapped his glass with a spoon and the room fell quiet.

Puffed up with self-importance, he spoke into the

microphone. "Given this foundation's commitment to supporting Bostonian talent, I understand that some of our local professionals might be upset that the design has been awarded to a New York–based architect, but the winning design was simply outstanding. That said, it is my great pleasure to announce that Huntley and Associates is looking for a local architect to work with Judah Huntley on the art museum project."

The room erupted into clapping and cheers, and Darby looked at Judah, her eyebrows raised.

Judah shrugged before murmuring, "He's making it sound like more than it is. My new hire will be little more than a glorified intern, the liaison between the foundation and myself."

Darby felt the sharp nip of annoyance. "She or he won't get to work on the construction documentation?"

"I have a team back in New York for that. They are a well-oiled machine."

So the position was not something she was interested in. She was an architect, not an intern. "Do you intend to pay this person or are they expected to work for the honor of being able to put your name as a reference on their resume?"

He didn't react to her snippiness. "They'll be paid."

"How much?" Darby demanded. She wasn't interested in working as an intern but she was curious what world-renowned architects paid.

Judah named a figure and Darby's mouth fell open. That much? Seriously? Well, wow. At that rate, her interest rose. Pity he was a baby-rejecting jerk or she'd put her name in the hat.

Jac hiccuped in her sleep and Judah's eyes shifted to the living doll in Darby's arms. She looked into his face for any hint of acceptance or compassion and felt disappointed when she found none. She didn't like him, but she reluctantly conceded that his hard and brooding expression was as sexy as his debonair and urbane facade. The many faces of Judah Huntley, Darby mused.

This man, who is uninterested in his own child, is the opposite of what you are looking for in a man.

"Why do you still have the child?"

Darby narrowed her eyes at his clipped tone. "I have her because I changed her diaper for your friends. They said they'd be waiting for me in the hallway, but they left before I could hand her back."

Judah glared at her and in the dim light, she saw concern jump into his eyes. "What?"

He was a smart guy, why was this difficult to understand? "Do try to keep up, Huntley. I changed her diaper, made up some formula and when I got back, the two Italians were in the elevator. I thought about chasing them down, then figured the easier option was to hand Jac over to you."

"Jack? Her name is Jack?"

Darby heard the weird note in his voice and wondered why the name rocked his boat. "They called her Jacquetta but that's too much of a mouthful, so I shortened it to Jac," Darby replied. "Here you go."

Darby tried to hand Judah the child, but he stepped back, looking horrified.

Oh, no! She'd already done more than enough. "This is a child, Huntley! *Your* child, apparently. You don't just get to throw your hands up in the air and step back. She's a baby, not a package you can refuse."

Judah rubbed the back of his neck. "Damned Carla. What the hell is she playing at?"

"So, I take it Jac is a bit of a surprise? That you didn't know about her?"

"Of course I didn't know about her! She's not—" Judah snapped his mouth shut and gripped the bridge of his nose in frustration.

That he'd been about to say that the baby wasn't his was easy to work out. But Darby wasn't that much of an idiot. Judah might not want Jac to be his, but the little girl was a carbon copy of him, down to her nose and stubborn chin.

Judah glanced down at Jac and lifted his big shoulders. "I can't take her."

Oh, God, she was so done with this. Darby lifted her free hand, gripped Judah's lapel and stood up on her toes, annoyed to realize that she still needed more height to look him in the eye. "Listen to me, you spoiled, inconsiderate ass! This baby was brought to you by those useless fools and if I track them down, I will carve them up for leaving her with a stranger and then disappearing. I could've been a baby trafficker, a nut case, a psycho!"

Amusement jumped into Judah's eyes. "Are you?"

God, when he half smiled, that dimple deepened and her stomach quivered. It was like he just dialed his sexy factor up to lethal and—

Why was she thinking about that? She was supposed to be tearing him a new one! Sexy or not, he was going to get a very big piece of her mind. "You're an idiot if you can't see how much Jac looks like you! And even though I am the only one who seems to give a damn about this child, she is not my responsibility."

"You agreed to change her, you let them go. You could've handed her back."

Could he really be that unfeeling, that cold? This man

who created art in buildings with such verve, such emotion in every line. How could he be so devoid of warmth?

"You heartless bastard! Do you know how lucky you are to have a child? Do you know how many people would love to be you?" Darby winced when her voice rose. Then she decided that she didn't care. Somebody needed to stand up for Jac, to put her first, and it seemed Darby had been nominated. "She's the innocent party and if you can't see that, then you are a complete and utter waste of space."

Darby knew she was panting, knew she was on the edge of tears and knew she had to leave before she lost it. She also had to leave before she walked away with the baby nobody but her seemed to want.

Pulling Judah's arm from his side, she bundled Jac into his embrace, making sure he had a firm grip before letting the little girl go. Refusing to look at him, Darby dropped a quick kiss on Jac's smooth forehead.

Darby smacked Jac's empty bottle into Judah's other hand and sent him a hard, tight smile. "My friend DJ says that having kids should be heavily regulated and subject to licensing. I've never agreed more with that statement than right now." She stared up into his beautiful face, confusion replacing anger. "I don't understand how someone so talented, who can put so much emotion into a building, can be so hard. And so cold."

Judah dipped his head so she could feel his breath on her ear, so she inhaled his unique scent of lemons and detergent and something earthy and sexy that made her want to bury her face in his neck and breathe him in. For a moment—a small infinitesimal moment—she imagined that she and Judah were a couple, that he was standing guard over his family, but the words that left his mouth shattered that image.

"This baby isn't mine."

Of course he'd say that.

"No, you just don't want her to be yours," Darby muttered. "She should be good for about another half hour or so. After that, I hope she gives you hell. Bye now."

Judah's eyes hit hers and Darby felt their punch. All that gorgeous blue, that face and that body, wasted on a self-absorbed cretin.

Good luck, Jacquetta, you're going to need it, honey.

Three

Way to make friends and influence people. Judah watched the Duchess step toward the elevator, cursing when the doors closed on a froth of fabric. She was gone, and he should be glad.

Should being the operative word.

She'd just reamed him but instead of getting pissed he'd just been turned on... But, in his defense, she was smokin'.

She was also gone.

Judah shook his head. Well, that was that. Looking down at the little girl he held, he watched as her eyes fluttered closed and her mouth softened. She did look like him, Judah admitted. Then again, he and Jake both took after their dad and no one ever suspected that they were half siblings and not full blood brothers.

Judah thought he'd been the only casualty of Jake and

Carla's illicit weekend spent together in his apartment but no, they always went a step further than necessary. Why light a Roman candle when you could detonate a bomb?

Judah felt the back of his throat burn. A year and a half had passed; how could the double betrayal still hurt so damn much? He ran his knuckle over Jac's flower-soft cheek. His pain, the fiery anger, he realized, wasn't only for him but also for Jacquetta. This little human, this doll-faced child, deserved better than two dysfunctional cretins as parents.

Judah used his free hand to pull his phone from the inside pocket of his jacket and scroll through his contact list. He hadn't dialed this number in so long, he hoped it was still operational.

The phone buzzed, beeped and started to ring.

Keep your cool, keep your cool...

"Judah, baby."

Her growly, sexy voice raised nothing more than red-hot anger. "What the hell, Carla? A baby? Are you insane?"

"I know it's a bit of a surprise, but I need you to take her for a while so I can finish this project."

"Let me think about that..." Judah replied, trying his utmost to keep his voice low. "No. A thousand times no! This isn't happening."

"It is." Carla's voice turned hard. "Either you or your brother have to take her until I decide I want her back."

"Then call Jake, for God's sake! He's her father, not me! And don't you think one of you should've let me know I have a niece?"

"You made it very clear to both of us that you'd washed your hands of us."

"You talk as if I didn't find you naked in my bed,

in a position I still can't get out of my head. Then you spilled the ugly details of our breakup to distract the press from finding out you were cheating on me with my much younger brother while I dealt with the mess Jake created."

Why had he even mentioned the past? Carla didn't care then, and she didn't care now.

"Call Rossi back or get Jake to come get his daughter," he said. "She. Is. Not. My. Problem."

"Do you think it would be wise of me to leave Jac with Jake? He's an addict with a felony record, thanks to you. He's not daddy material."

"Carla, you can't just dump a baby on me like she's a UPS parcel!" Okay, he'd borrowed that from the Duchess, but it applied. God, what had he seen in Carla? Oh, yeah, the sex had been phenomenal but like Turkish delight, she was best taken in small doses. "Come and get her, Carla."

"No," Carla replied. "I need some time. Just hear me out, please?"

He shouldn't, he really shouldn't, but his silence gave her room to speak.

"I have a new job, Bertolli is composing an opera and I am the lead character."

"Yeah, I heard. You are being cast against type."

"You are not the first to notice that. There have been a lot of insinuations already, about my past, you, my relationship with Bertolli."

"Which is?"

Carla didn't answer, which meant there was a very good chance she was sleeping with Bertolli. She was playing with fire. If word got out that she was sleeping with one of Italy's most conservative, outwardly faithful men, the country's favorite composer—a national treasure!—she would be labeled a sinful temptress and the press would eat her alive.

Judah walked to the end of the hallway and placed his hand on the floor-to-ceiling window. He looked down at the bustling streets of downtown Boston below, resting his forehead on the cool glass.

"There was a story recently, suggesting you are not her father. I cannot take the chance of the world finding out that Jake is Jacquetta's father and not you. It was enough of a scandal that I had a baby out of wedlock but if they find out about my liaison with Jake—"

"Affair."

"If they find out about Jake, that he is your brother and a heroin addict, that I had his baby not yours, the story will be on the front page of every tabloid from here to China. It will be a scandal and my contract with the new production says I have to remain scandal-free."

His heart bled. None of this had anything to do with him. Jake and Carla had had sex in Judah's bed and now they had to deal with the consequences of their actions. He was in no way responsible for them or the fruit of their loins.

Judah glanced down at the little girl and ignored the tiny lump in his throat.

She could've been his...

No, he didn't want kids; he never had. He remembered having to change Jake's diapers, night after night rocking him to sleep because their parents were out on the town or simply out of town. For six years, he'd been Jake's primary caregiver, the adult in the house. He'd bought Jake clothes, made him meals, packed his school lunches. As a twelve-year-old child himself, Judah had stepped up to the plate and taken on responsibility for another human being—because his father and stepmother were useless—and Judah had promised himself that he would never again put himself in that position.

After a pregnancy scare in his early twenties, he'd wanted a vasectomy, to take the issue off the table permanently. But the doctor refused, telling Judah he was too young, he might still change his mind. Furious, Judah had vowed to find another doctor, but then his career took off and he'd never found the time to go back.

But he would. When he stopped being a monk, he'd find another doctor. He was thirty-five, he hadn't changed his mind in ten years and he wouldn't be refused again. As a child, he'd raised his baby brother and he didn't want to raise another child.

A scholarship to college had been his exit out of that life and he still felt guilty for leaving six-year-old Jake behind. Despite Judah's attempts to keep tabs on his brother from afar, Jake was smoking weed by thirteen, fully addicted and boosting cars to feed his habit by sixteen. By eighteen, he was in juvie.

Never again would Judah put himself in the position of having to choose between his future and his obligations. So, no kids. And after a few relationships that went nowhere and Car Crash Carla, no commitment.

To anyone.

Ever.

Judah sucked in a calming breath. "I'm at the Sheraton, downtown Boston. Presidential suite. Get Rossi back here."

Carla pulled in a deep, ragged breath. "I tried to call him just before you called but his phone is off."

Judah gripped the bridge of his nose and cursed. "Make a plan, Carla."

Carla thought for a minute. "I'll call an agency, hire a nanny. They can send someone."

God, she was going to ask a stranger to pick up Jac? Now that was exactly the type of dick move his father and stepmother would've pulled. Judah felt the burn of intense anger. "No, Carla. You will come and get her. Yourself. Personally."

"I can't. It's just not possible." Carla spluttered her reply, making it sound like he'd asked her to become a nun.

"Jacquetta is your daughter, so you come and get her. It's not up for negotiation"

Carla finally ran out of expletives. "I'll come but I need some time."

"You've got a day. Be here in twenty-four hours or I'm going to be the one calling the tabloids, Carla."

"Judah, no! I am in Como, it will take more time than that."

"You should've thought about that when you played pass-the-parcel with your daughter," Judah said, not bothering to hide his annoyance. "Hurry up, Carla. The clock is ticking."

Judah disconnected the call and banged the face of his phone against his forehead. He released his own series of curses and looked down to see Jac sending him a wide-eyed look. "Your mom is something else, kid."

Jac blinked once, then again and then she smiled, revealing a gorgeous dimple and pink gums. Man, she was cute. And despite being passed from person to person, remarkably sanguine.

"So, I guess it's you and me for the next twenty-four hours."

Jac waved her pudgy arms in the air and kicked her legs.

"Glad you are on board with that program. It's been a while since I made bottles or changed diapers so if you can try not to be hungry or need a change in the next day or so, I'd be grateful."

Jac sent him what he was sure was a get-real look.

Judah walked her back to where the stroller stood, dropped her bag into the storage compartment and strapped her in. It had been years and years since he'd been in charge of anyone under two feet tall but he still instinctively knew what he was doing.

He could look after this child for a day. A day wasn't so long. Not when he compared it to looking after his brother day in and day out for six or so years.

This time around he was an adult and he had a voice. And he'd damn well use it.

After work the next afternoon, Darby sat down on the deep purple sofa in the showroom of Winston and Brogan and tucked a bright yellow cushion behind her back. While she loved color, and frequently approved of Jules's interior design choices, she simply did not like the industry's current obsession with eggplant. But Winston and Brogan were cutting-edge designers and they always reflected what was hot.

DJ squeezed Darby's shoulder before sitting down next to her, the diamond on the ring finger of her left hand so big Darby was sure she could see it from space. Jules's emerald was just as large, as valuable, as impressive. Darby's future brothers-in-law—one by law and both by love—were crazy about Jules and DJ respectively. Darby was happy they'd found their soul mates.

Hers was probably stuck up a tree or had been run over by an out-of-control bus. Or maybe there wasn't a man who would put up with a determined, driven, stubborn, type-A personality with fertility issues.

Jules placed a cup of tea on the white coffee table between them before taking the seat to DJ's left. DJ squeezed Darby's hand. "Sorry you didn't get the Grantham-Ford project, Darbs."

Darby forced a shrug. She hated to lose, even if it was to a Pritzker Prize winner. "It wasn't a surprise that Huntley got it. They'd be fools to pass up his design. It was magnificent."

So was Huntley, for a cold, hard jerk bucket.

Jules linked her hands around her knee. "And have they announced who will be his liaison between Huntley and Associates and the Grantham-Ford Foundation?"

Every architect in the city wanted a shot to work with Huntley, to be at his beck and call. Everybody but Darby. She'd seen the measure of the man last night and she was less than impressed.

"Don't care. It's an intern position and I'm not interested." She took the stack of paper DJ handed her and smiled. Financials. A discussion, then her dividend check. Yay.

DJ tapped the end of her pen against the stack of papers in her lap and cleared her throat. "Let's go through the financials first. Let's ignore page one and two and go straight to page three."

Darby flipped to the right page and saw the column detailing income and expenses. Compared to Jules's interior design income for the past six months, the architectural side of the business—Darby's side of the business—was trailing Jules's contribution by half. Up until this year, they'd been equal contributors, with DJ running the finances. It had been the perfect triangle, but now it looked like Darby's side was collapsing.

She took the check DJ handed her and looked at the total. Then she looked at DJ, wondering if she'd left off a zero.

"This is it?"

"Yes."

Well, hell.

DJ leaned forward, her eyes sober. "It wasn't a great quarter, it's tough out there. The interior design had a boost in income thanks to Noah employing Jules to do yacht interiors, and you had small jobs but nothing that brought in big money."

Darby stared at her check, her mind spinning. This check didn't come close to what she needed to pay for IVF. She'd have to put her buildings up for sale immediately, take what she could get for them. She might not even clear her costs, but it would free up the money. Any way she looked at it, she was moving backward, not forward. *Dammit.*

"There are other factors that contributed to a less than stellar year, Darby."

"Like?" Darby demanded.

"The rent on this building went up significantly—"

"We agreed we needed to be here, that this was the best place for us to be," Darby countered. "And that was only a ten percent increase." She skimmed the lines, looking for other anomalies. "The real reason we aren't growing is because I didn't bring in enough income."

The proof was there, in black and white. She hadn't been an equal contributor. She'd failed.

Darby didn't like to fail.

"I'll make it up to you. This next quarter, you'll see."

She felt the need to apologize again. "I'm so sorry. You guys have worked so hard and I didn't pull my weight."

"Oh, for God's sake!" Jules muttered before sending her twin a hard look. "Can I hand you a hair shirt? Would that make you feel better?"

"But—"

"Who bankrolled this business, Darby?" Jules demanded, not giving Darby a chance to answer. "You did. You bought and fixed up that cottage and the profit you made paid our expenses for the first six months. Thanks to you, we didn't have to borrow money from Mom or Levi or a bank."

"The cost of renting the warehouse, the additional staff we've had to take on because we've expanded have all contributed to the drop in profits," DJ explained. "It's normal, Darby."

Darby looked at the profit-loss line and winced. "It's shocking."

DJ rolled her eyes. "You are such an overachiever, Darby. We can afford one less than stellar quarter. We still made a small profit."

But not enough, not nearly enough. From now on, Darby would be all over every project she could find. She'd work longer hours, take in as much work as she could. She had to make up the shortfall, and that meant doubling her income. She needed work, and lots of it.

"Oh, God, she's got that crazy look in her eye," Jules said. "You just flicked her competitive switch." She leaned forward, blue eyes pinning Darby to the seat. "We're in this together, Darby, so stop thinking this is your problem to solve. This is not a competition."

It was a refrain she'd heard all her life: you're too

competitive, Darby. You can't treat anything as fun, Darby. You don't have to win at everything, Darby.

What no one understood was that being competitive was the way she was made. She couldn't remember a time when winning wasn't her goal.

One of her earliest memories was being on the playground, wanting to be the girl who could run the fastest, jump the longest, swing the highest. She excelled at all sports, was one of the most popular girls in school. She could remember dreading the results of tests, needing to achieve better grades than, well, everyone. Her report cards were all As and when she got her first C, in college, she'd been devastated.

Yes, she was competitive. Yes, she was driven. But, dammit, being both got results. She just had to refocus, redefine her goals. Do better, be better. Determination, her old friend, flowed through her, energizing her.

Darby Brynn Brogan had always produced the results and she would this time, too. Options, scenarios and plans buzzed through her brain.

DJ leaned her shoulder into Darby's. "Business is about troughs and highs, Darby, everything balances out in the end. I promise that Winston and Brogan is okay. The next cycle will be a lot better."

What if it wasn't? What if the economy worsened? She didn't deal in what-ifs, in maybes. She needed a plan to boost her side of the business. She needed work, a lucrative contract, and she knew one place where she could get one.

Judah Huntley had found his Boston-based architect. He just needed to be notified of the decision.

Four

After twenty-four hours of looking after Jac, Judah was hanging on to the end of his rope with his teeth. He was exhausted. He needed a shower and to sleep for a week.

Jac, he was certain, was as shattered as he was. She constantly needed to be reassured. She did this incredibly effectively, by crying incessantly. He'd changed her, fed her, held her, paced the room with her but the kid just cried.

And then she cried some more.

How had he done this as a child, a teenager? He must've had a guardian angel, some celestial being giving him guidance, because, God knew, the adults in the house hadn't been interested.

Judah pushed his hand into his hair and wondered, again, where Carla was. He hadn't managed to reach her the past twelve hours. For the first ten of those hours, he hadn't been worried. She was in the air. But her flight landed two hours ago and she should have rocked up an hour ago. Judah tensed and reminded himself that Carla had the attention span of a three-week-old puppy. She was easily distracted and being an hour late was nothing.

She could be stuck in a traffic jam or held up at customs. There were lots of reasonable explanations for her tardiness. She would get here eventually. Late but begging him to forgive her, flashing that big smile and batting those enormous, expressive brown eyes.

He would forgive her anything if she would just take Jac and let him get some sleep.

Judah moved Jac up onto his shoulder, patted her little bottom and sighed when she let out another high-pitched wail. Why wasn't she asleep yet?

Hearing the buzz of the hotel room phone, Judah walked across the presidential suite and lunged for the phone before remembering he was holding a baby. Cursing, he tightened his hold on Jac, shook his head when her volume control went up and barked a greeting into the phone.

"Mr. Huntley you have a visitor—"

"Send her up," Judah muttered, banging the receiver down. He rubbed Jac's back. "Your mommy is here, Jac. Think she can save us both?"

Jac's wail was his answer and he nodded. "I understand your worry. But if I know your mom, she will have brought a nanny with her and you'll be in safe hands."

Sleep was within his grasp. He looked across the room to the open door of the bedroom, sighing at the California king-size bed made up with fine Egyptian sheets and an expensive comforter. Ten minutes, maybe fifteen and he would be facedown in blessed quiet.

He liked quiet. He liked calm. Most of all, he liked sleep.

Judah went to stand by the front door. He would stay calm, he told himself. He would just hand Jac over, not engage with his volatile ex-lover—screaming and throwing stuff was Carla's favorite way to negotiate an argument—and then he'd lock the door behind him and strip off as he headed to his bedroom. He smelled like regurgitated milk since Jac had shown her disgust for the situation by vomiting all over his shirt. He should shower but he probably wouldn't; his need for sleep was too strong.

At thirty-five, he was too old to go for days without sleep. He was too old for drama, full stop.

Judah yanked open the door. All thoughts about keeping his cool disappeared. "I always thought you were unbelievably self-absorbed, but this behavior is beyond where I thought you would ever go. She's a little girl, Carla, not a doll— *Jesus.*"

Judah blinked once, then again before lifting his free hand to rub his bleary eyes. But when he opened his eyes again, the Duchess still stood in the doorway, her silver-gray eyes dominating her face.

Hoping against hope, Judah pulled her to the side and stuck his head into the corridor. Nope, no feisty Italian opera singer in sight. He looked down at his watch. She was now an hour and a half late.

Judah was, not to put too fine a point on it, starting to worry. He needed to start making some calls. Something about this entire situation felt wrong.

"This isn't a good time, Duchess."

The use of the nickname didn't impress her, but Judah didn't care. He was too tired to deal with an uptight blonde.

She stepped into the hallway, carefully shut the door behind her and looked at the still-crying Jac. "How long has she been upset?"

"Forever," Judah replied wearily. "I don't think she's stopped crying."

"When did you last change her?" Darby demanded in that crisp, no-nonsense, answer-me-dammit voice. It turned him on. Why he had no idea. Maybe he was nuts or maybe it was the fact that she was wearing tight black trousers that showed off her long, lean body to perfection. The button-down shirt was a shade of blue that reminded him of the sea around Corfu and it nipped in at the waist, flashing a hint of a bra the same color. He'd bet his fortune—a considerable amount—that her panties matched her bra. The Duchess seemed the type.

Which reminded him, he couldn't keep calling her by that nickname. "Who are you?"

"Darby Brogan, architect. I'm a partner at Winston and Brogan," she replied. "Well, when?"

She was also waiting for a response and Judah used all his processing power to remember what she'd asked him. Right, changing a diaper. "A half hour ago."

Darby's perfectly arched eyebrows flew up toward her hairline. "Her last bottle?"

This was like the Spanish Inquisition. "Around the same time."

"Mmm."

What did that mean? Was that good or bad? Then he stopped caring because Darby, God bless her, reached for the baby. Relieved, Judah walked back into the living room, dropped his six-foot-three frame onto the closest sofa and stretched out.

Yeah, *this*. He fought to keep his eyes open. Rolling his head, he watched Darby take a small blanket from Jac's bag. He wasn't too tired to appreciate her long-legged and sexy-as-hell stride as she walked toward him. Using one hand, she spread the blanket on the chair and the little blood left in his brain ran south at the vision of that perfect ass bending over in front of him. He could easily imagine her naked, her blond hair touching the floor as she bent at the waist. High heels, a naughty smile—she was the girl in the posters he had on his bedroom wall as a teenager.

Okay, maybe he wasn't that tired.

Unaware that his mind was playing in the gutter, Darby placed Jac in the middle of the fabric square and quickly and efficiently bundled her up. Then she placed Jac against her chest and rhythmically patted the baby's back. Within twenty seconds, Jac's volume button was on low and then it was on mute.

Darby turned her back to him so he could see Jac's now peaceful face. "Is she asleep?"

She was, thank God. Thank Darby. "If I wasn't so damn grateful, I might be swearing at you right now. I've been trying to get her to go to sleep for, God, three hundred years."

"Babies are barometers, they need to know the adults in the room know what they are doing. You obviously don't." He was too tired to take any offense at her sarcasm. If only she knew…

Darby sat down on the chair, leaned back and eyed Judah. He felt like a bug under the microscope. Suddenly self-conscious, he wished he'd had the time to take a shower, to wash his face, to brush his hair. While Darby looked fresh and sexy and clean, dammit, he felt like he'd been dragged through a pigsty backward.

She didn't look impressed, and why should she? But why did he care whether he impressed her or not? And why was he so damn pleased to see her again?

Pushing aside his fall-at-her-feet gratitude for getting little Jac to stop crying, he admitted those silver-tinged thundercloud eyes enthralled him, and her take-control attitude made his mouth water. He was a driven guy, someone who instantly took control in tense situations and he generally didn't appreciate anyone muscling in on his turf. Yet Darby's take-charge attitude was not only refreshing, it was sexy as hell. She was the very last person he expected to knock at his door...

Which raised a point in his overtired brain. "Why are you here?"

Darby didn't waver, she didn't look away. "I want to work with you, for you."

Judah rubbed a hand over his face. "What the hell are you talking about?"

"You need a local architect to work with you on the Grantham-Ford project. I want to be that architect. Well?"

Huh. Darby was not only driven and direct, she was impatient, too. In between Jac's crying sessions, he'd lobbed a hundred and one things at his business manager, Jonathan, today. Jonno tossed as many back and the local liaison for Boston was way down their list of priorities. They'd get to it, they'd decided, in a day or two. But Darby had beaten them to it.

He couldn't employ her. He wanted her, naked and doing very unprofessional and non-architect-related things.

Man, what a mess. He didn't play where he worked. Ever.

Darby lifted her pretty nose. "I want the job."

He didn't like being bossed around, even if it was by a gorgeous blonde with the face of an angel. "In the past two days, I've had a maximum of four hours of sleep and I spent the whole of today and the best part of last night dealing with Jac. I'll tell you the same thing I told my business manager, I'll get to it when I get to it."

She looked both maternal and fierce, a perfect modern woman as she held a baby and kicked ass. "If you'd take the time to look at the designs I submitted, you will notice that my concept was more innovative than those of my competitors. I used modern building techniques, interesting materials, made it eco-friendly. I need—" Judah heard her voice hitch, heard the desperate note as she hesitated. "I deserve that job."

Interesting.

Something told him that Darby Brogan was here because she needed to be, not because she wanted to be. Oh, she probably thought he was a good architect, even a great one, but working with him, having his name on her résumé, wasn't why she was here...or it wasn't her primary reason for barging into his hotel room and throwing her demands at his head.

Somehow, she needed his help. Her desperation seemed more immediate than his name opening doors in a few months or years. Judah wondered if she needed the money the job commanded. Judah skimmed her outfit: designer pants, expensive top, stylish shoes. Discreet but tasteful jewelry. Darby didn't look like she needed cash.

"Don't bother interviewing the other competitors, Judah, just hire me. I'll work harder for a lot longer, I'll give you my all."

The *all* he wanted from her involved her hair flowing

down her back as he slid into her from behind, holding her breasts in his hands, his big body enveloping hers.

Judah ran a hand over his face and ordered his body to stand down. He was beyond tired; how could he possibly feel horny?

And his reaction to her was a very good reason *not* to hire her.

Darby shifted to the edge of the seat, her eyes never leaving his face. "I'm not married or involved so I'd be at your beck and call." *Oh, God, don't say that.* "I can give you references, show you other designs—"

A headache threatened to cleave his brain in two so Judah held up his hand and Darby, thank God, stopped talking. But five seconds later, she opened her mouth to talk again and he shook his head. He wasn't in a place to make any decisions about any projects or to think about hiring her. He was wickedly attracted to her and that fact complicated everything.

Before he made any decisions about bringing her into his life and company, he needed at least ten hours of sleep. He had to shut down this conversation before Darby hustled him into giving her a job.

Under normal circumstances *he* did the hustling, but nothing about the past thirty-six hours had been normal. Where the hell was Carla?

"I have a flash drive containing my portfolio—"

"Shut up, Darby."

Darby stopped talking and frowned.

Judah wanted to smile. He was pretty sure few people spoke to her in an obey-me-now tone of voice. Hell, he was impressed that she'd listened. But he absolutely knew she wouldn't remain silent for long.

Right, priority list: hand Jac over, make an appointment to meet with the very sexy—*stop thinking of her in those terms, Huntley!*—very smart and very determined Darby Brogan. And then sleep.

Picking up his phone, he dialed Carla's number. Instead of going straight to voice mail, her phone rang, and relief coursed through his body.

"Judah?"

He recognized that voice. Judah frowned, wondering why Carla's manager was answering her phone. "Luca? Why do you have Carla's phone? And where the hell is Carla, she should've been here already!"

Judah's voice rose, and he winced when he saw Darby's frantic gestures telling him to keep it down so he didn't wake Jac. Right, waking Jac would be a very bad thing.

"Are you telling me she's still in Italy?" Judah swore and gripped the back of his neck. "Okay, I will bring Jac to her."

"You can't, Judah. She can't care for Jac."

Of course, she couldn't, Carla had the mothering skills of a grasshopper. "She'll hire a nanny, do what she always does, pass her responsibilities on to someone else," Judah bitterly replied.

He shouldn't have trusted Carla, he should've just taken Jac back to Italy in the first place. The best predictor of future behavior? Past behavior.

"She's in the hospital, Judah. Her appendix burst and she collapsed."

What? No, she was about to storm through that door, and she'd throw a temper tantrum about how much he'd inconvenienced her. He stared at little Jac, frantically praying that he was mishearing Luca's words.

"She was rushed straight into surgery and she's now in ICU. We are waiting for her to come around."

"She's that ill?"

"No, it's just a precaution and also because ICU has better security than the general wards. She's expected to make a full recovery."

Judah felt adrenaline surge through his system. "I'll catch the next plane. Hell, I'll hire a private jet. We'll be there by morning." Judah scrambled to his feet and headed to the bedroom. He was about to pull open the door to the closet to start packing when Luca spoke again.

"Please don't, Judah."

Judah frowned, tightening his grip of the door to the closet. "And why not?"

"Judging by the press, you'd think she had a heart attack, not an appendectomy," Luca grumbled. "Do you think your entrance into the country, with the baby, will go unnoticed? There is so much speculation, so much gossip... We don't need more." Luca's sigh was deep and heavy.

Crap. Luca was right, the situation was volatile enough without Judah's presence.

"I need you to keep Jacquetta for two weeks, maybe three. Just until the press attention dies down. Before Rossi left with her, we made Carla sign a document stating that she was happy for you to have temporary custody of Jacquetta." Luca's next words were another shock. "And you need to keep your brother away, as well!"

"I haven't spoken to Jake for eighteen months, Luca, you know that. I don't know where he is," Judah retorted.

"The press is reporting that he is in the area and that

he's been in contact with Carla, but that could just be rumormongering. The last person I need here is her drug-addicted ex-lover."

Definitely rumormongering. "Don't you think you are overreacting? They spent *one* weekend together, Luca."

"Judah, it wasn't one weekend. Carla was doing an eight-week stint at the Met and you said she could stay at your place while she was in New York. Your brother moved in three days after she did, the week after you left for Sydney. They lived together for three months."

It was a blow, but just a sideswipe, not a full-on punch. Did the duration of their affair matter? One weekend? Three months? Judah didn't think so. Betrayal was betrayal.

When Judah didn't speak, Luca spoke again. "I'm asking you to keep Jacquetta, Judah. Please?"

"Why should I, Luca? Why should I flip my world upside down for her?" Judah demanded.

"Because you loved Carla once? Because Jac has nowhere else to go for the next two weeks? Because I need to keep that baby out of the limelight and I need you, as her uncle, to help me do that."

Crap. "Dammit, Luca. I thought I was done with the drama."

Luca managed a small snort. "As long as Carla is in your life, you never will be, my friend."

And wasn't that a solid-gold truth.

Mason, tallying receipts in his head because that was more fun than using a calculator, looked up as the door chime jangled.

It was four o'clock on a snowy winter's afternoon and he hadn't had a customer in over two hours. He'd let his staff go home an hour ago and Mason considered telling the bundle consisting of a heavy coat and a thousand scarves that he was closing but figured he could give out a cup of coffee before he sent the person back into the snow.

Mason watched as the cap came off first, revealing bright blond hair—hair he'd buried his face in. Blue eyes, pink cheeks, that luscious mouth he'd been—was still—addicted to.

Callie.

Mason gripped the edge of the counter, fighting the twin waves of fury and desire. He hadn't seen or heard from her since New Year's Eve, nine weeks and two days ago. She hadn't stepped into his coffee shop. He hadn't seen her car driving around. He'd noticed that her house was shut up tight.

He'd been annoyed that evening—competing with a ghost wasn't any fun—and he'd expected her to run over to his house and apologize. She'd run but in a direction he never expected.

"Had fun wherever the hell you went?"

Callie kept her coat on as she walked over to the register, her eyes locked on his. "I did, actually. I went to Thailand, then Bali."

"Good for you." Mason pushed the words out between gritted teeth. "A postcard would've been nice. Or, you know, an explanation."

"You left that party without a word, you didn't call. When you didn't bother to connect with me, I assumed we were done."

He'd been angry and annoyed and jealous, but done? Oh, hell, no.

When he heard that she'd left for Southeast Asia, he'd been on the point of caving, going after her. Furious with her, and himself, he'd gone on one or two dates but, because he was an idiot for this woman in front of him, he couldn't take up even one of the many offers of sex that he'd received.

He'd been celibate but... He took a closer look at Callie's eyes and knew something had changed within her. She looked relaxed, confident, assured...

And Mason somehow knew she'd crossed off another item on her bucket list: sex in the sun. Mason ground his teeth together. He wasn't going to ask.

He was not going to ask...

"Who was he?" he asked.

"Who was who?"

He wanted to know what happened in Southeast Asia. Because, God, any fool could see that something had.

Mason opened his mouth, then shut it. He had no claims on her, had no right to be jealous. There was nothing more between them than hot sex, a raging attraction. He had no hold on Callie. They didn't owe each other exclusivity. Neither of them wanted commitment.

They'd made the rules and now he had to play by them.

Callie placed her hands over his fingers, which were flat on the counter, and Mason felt like she'd plugged him into a power source. God, he'd missed her.

Callie peered past his shoulder, trying to look into the tiny kitchen behind him. "Who else is here, Mace?" she asked.

He looked over his shoulder, not quite understanding the question. "Uh...no one?" Why was she asking? What did that have to do with anything?

"Good." Callie smiled, lifted her hands to her coat and started to undo the buttons. "So, want to pick up where we left off?"

Mason barely heard her words because, instead of a sweater and jeans, Callie's slow striptease revealed a black lacy bra and an equally lacy triangle at the juncture of her thighs. Surely, this could not be happening.

Mason ground his teeth together again and watched as Callie's designer coat fell to the floor.

Black lace lingerie and thigh-high boots.

Holy, holy crap.

Mason knew his eyes were bugging out. He could not believe that straitlaced, slightly prudish Callie Brogan was nearly naked in his coffee shop while the snow pelted down outside. Somebody could arrive, somebody might drive past...

He really didn't care.

Mason boosted himself up and over the counter, grabbing Callie's hand and marching her to the door. He flipped the lock, gave the deserted landscape a quick once-over. The chance of discovery, thanks to the snow, was minimal.

He wouldn't make love to her out here but if someone drove past and saw a nearly naked Callie Brogan, in black lace and boots, being kissed within an inch of her life, then it was her own damn fault.

She should never have left him; she should've come back sooner. He wanted to yell at her, kiss her, take her up against the door...

He never wanted to miss her as much as he had missed her ever again. A life without Callie Brogan in it was a colorless place...

Callie wound her arms around his neck and brushed her mouth against his. "Kiss me, Mace. I've missed you."

Five

Darby placed Jac in her stroller before walking across the penthouse suite to the open door of Judah's bedroom. Judah stood by the closet, his shoulder pressed into the door, looking utterly played out. Yes, she wanted the job as his local architect and she'd had no intention of leaving until she had his assurance that the job was hers, but right now, he looked shattered.

Her heart swelled with sympathy. Judah, she suspected, didn't like surprises and he liked to steer his own ship. Discovering that he had a child he hadn't known about was a complication that would be totally out of his comfort zone.

Despite the discussion held in rapid Italian, Darby sensed Jac was staying with him. He was either feeling utterly out of his depth or frustrated beyond belief. Possibly both. With no warning and little thought, Judah's ex had backed him into a corner. A guy like Judah—strong, alpha, confident—didn't do corners.

"Hey."

Judah's head shot up and she saw emotion dancing through his eyes. Fear, sadness, worry. Yep, that conversation had rocked his world. Those eyes, all that ink blue, held confusion and anger and, though he would never admit it, pain.

His body was drool worthy, and she was in awe of his talent. But her attraction to his mind was what made her earth tilt. This visceral, intense, knee-shaking need to know what drove him, what scared him, what motivated him—it terrified her and made her take a few mental steps back.

She had a business to bolster, money to earn, a baby to breed. She couldn't afford to be distracted by a tired hot luscious man whose depths ran deeper than the Mariana Trench.

"I was expecting Carla to collect Jac but she's in the hospital," Judah explained, sounding tired beyond belief. "I've got to look after her, take care of her for two weeks."

Well, he was Jac's father. That was what dads did.

A part of Darby, a big part, hoped that when Judah got over his shock at having a daughter he'd fight to be part of Jac's life on an ongoing basis, that the little girl would have at least one parent who cared about her. But Judah was a man always on the go, his work had him living from city to city, job to job. She doubted Jac would find any stability with him.

Darby shook her head, confused. Here she was, someone who would be a good mom and unable to have kids. Yet Carla and Judah didn't want the beautiful baby they had.

It was so unfair…

Familiar with this negative thought process, Darby knew she needed to leave, to find some distance and perspective. Being around Jac made her sad about what she couldn't have. It didn't help that she wanted Jac's dad, too.

"Okay, well, if you can let me know a suitable time for me to be interviewed…"

Judah straightened and walked over to her. Darby couldn't yank her eyes from his. He stopped in front of her, so close she could feel his heat, smell his deodorant, see that he had a tiny scar on the corner of his left eye and another on his chin. His fingers gripped her hips and a tremor skittered through her. If she lifted herself onto her toes, just a little, her mouth would be aligned with his, she would know his taste.

Don't do it, Darby. Bad, bad, dreadful *idea.*

Judah's other hand snaked around her back, splaying across the top of her butt as he gently pulled her toward him. Her breasts scraped his chest, her nipples puckering against the lace of her bra. She wanted his mouth there, she realized, shocked. She wanted him tugging on her, trailing his lips across her naval and down to where she was wet and throbbing.

Potential boss alert! Unprofessional! Ding! Ding! Ding!

Darby ignored her brain's loud screech and kept her eyes locked on his, seeing images of what could be in his eyes.

While he would never force her to do anything she was uncomfortable with, he wouldn't be a gentle lover. He'd demand everything from her, make her experience every last drop of pleasure. She wanted that, wanted to be intensely, absolutely in the moment with him, experiencing the mind-stealing, heart-shattering bliss she suspected he could give her.

Judah covered her mouth with his, and as she expected, colorful fireworks exploded behind her eyes.

For the first time ever she felt, God help her, like she'd stepped into an alternate reality where nothing could touch her, where this man and his mouth and his broad hands moving over her body, felt good and...right.

Under her hands, his pecs were hard and his stomach flat, the ridges suggesting an impressive six pack. His hips were narrow but his erection, pushing into her stomach, was hard and long and thick. His mouth never lefts hers, that tongue doing wicked things to her. He fed her kisses in a way that each stroke, each slide left her hungry for more.

Their behavior was so far beyond unprofessional it wasn't even funny...

Darby pulled back, pulled her bottom lip between her teeth and dragged her reluctant hands off his body. "That was, uh... Dammit."

Judah lifted a strand of her hair that was stuck to the corner of her mouth. Instead of pushing it behind her ear, he wrapped the strand around his index finger.

Leave, Brogan.

But Darby stayed where she was, an inch from him, fighting the urge to go in for more, knowing that it would be deeper, harder, more intense. She also knew that if she did, the chances of them making use of that very big and comfortable-looking bed were sky-high.

Avoid the bed, Brogan.

"I really should go," Darby said. This time her feet cooperated, and she managed to put a good half foot between them and her hair slipped from his finger.

Judah didn't say anything, he just stood there and looked at her, his eyes conveying exactly where she should go and what she should do when she got there. His bed and naked.

His message wasn't that difficult to decipher.

Ignore it, ignore him. Be an adult, Darby.

Sex was easy but the chance of working with a world-famous architect who paid higher than normal rates didn't come along daily. Or even every year.

Darby walked back into the sitting room, feeling Judah's eyes on her back. In the hallway, she picked up her bag, pulled it over her shoulder, and lifted her hair up and off her neck, allowing it to fall down her back. Taking a deep breath, she turned to face him, hoping her smile was polite rather than please-take-me-now.

Judah's expression remained inscrutable and she wished she had a small idea of what he was thinking. "So, I really hope to hear from you soon. I'd just like to reassure you that you'd never regret giving me the job."

"I know I won't."

Darby blinked, frowned and tipped her head to the side. "Sorry… What?"

"You've got the job."

Before her brain could assimilate that thought, Judah spoke again. "And just so we are clear about what just happened, I kissed you before I made the offer. I don't mess with my colleagues or employees." Judah's voice was all controlled determination.

"I see," Darby replied. It was all she could say since she was still fighting the urge to slap her mouth against his and take up where they left off.

She knew they couldn't sleep together or have any sort of affair. There were too many risks—how would she know if he was impressed with her work or her rusty mattress skills? It was always awkward when it ended and ending it with her *boss* would be even more so.

So why did she still feel like a hot, fast orgasm or two would be worth the fallout? That mouth. That strong tanned neck. Those very broad muscled shoulders...

Focus, Brogan.

"Thank you," Darby said when her overstimulated brain finally kicked into gear.

She had the job, but she still craved the man.

"There is one proviso," Judah muttered, rubbing the black stubble on his jaw.

Oh, God, what now?

"I want help with the baby. Due to the press interest around Carla and by association Jac, I need to lie low, keep out of the limelight. I'll give you the job if you help me out with the kid. I'll stay here, in Boston, for the next two weeks. You can work with me on the new art museum and together we look after Jac. And if you agree to do that, I'll give you another five percent."

Darby made a swift calculation in her head. If he did that, she'd boost Winston and Brogan's bottom line. She would be working with someone she respected as well as looking after a baby, two of her favorite things. How could she refuse?

Except her competitive nature never would allow her to accept without pushing the envelope a little further.

"Okay," Darby said, keeping her tone cool. "And to compensate for the extra hours, I want a flat daily fee for looking after Jac." She named a figure, saw Judah's eyes widen and expected him to bargain her down to half that amount. Even at the bargain price, she'd be adding a significant amount to her IVF fund.

To her astonishment, and delight, Judah nodded and waved his hand. "Fine."

He whirled around, stomped back into the living room and Darby followed him. At the door to his bedroom, he turned. "But that means you start now, you're on kid duty tonight. Do not wake me unless Jac has arterial bleeding and is about to spontaneously combust from a high temperature. 'Night."

Darby watched, openmouthed, as he slipped inside his bedroom. The door slammed in her face.

Well, okay then. At what he was paying her, she couldn't refuse. Besides, she could deal with Jac, she'd had tons of experience with babies.

Three hours later, when Jac was still crying, Darby wasn't so sure.

The next morning, in the coffee shop attached to the hotel, Darby took her first sip of her third cup of coffee and glanced at Jac, who was finally sound asleep in her stroller.

It had been a hell of a night.

The door to the shop opened and Darby looked up to see Jules and DJ walking into the too-early-to-be-busy shop. They stopped at the counter and ordered their beverages before sauntering her way. Darby was relieved to see her large leather tote bag over Jules's shoulder. Darby was still in yesterday's clothes and desperately needed a shower and a change.

The unwelcome image of Judah sharing her shower, his big body slick with soapsuds, flashed behind her eyes and she frowned.

Damn him for kissing her last night. Now that she knew how his lips felt on hers, how talented that mouth was, how his big hands felt skating over her hips, down her spine, she'd been bombarded with X-rated images all night. It was like she'd fallen into an erotic novel.

It had been a night short on sleep and long on frustration.

"I need sex," Darby muttered, blushing when she realized that she had not only said the words out loud, but DJ and Jules had also heard her.

Jules grinned. "We can highly recommend sex."

"Shaddup." Darby yawned, covering her mouth with her hand. "I got the job as Huntley's local liaison."

DJ pointed at beautiful Jac. "It looks like you got more than that." DJ shook her head. "I should be shocked that you went to snag a job but ended up with a baby, but I'm not."

"How on earth did you end up looking after a baby, Darby?" Jules asked.

Darby couldn't resist running her hand over Jac's sweet soft curls. "Judah and I struck a deal. I get the job, as long as I help him with little Jac here."

She could see the concern in their eyes, but it was DJ who lobbied the first question. "He doesn't have enough money to hire a nanny?"

Darby leaned forward and told them, quietly and quickly, what she could about Jac's arrival in Judah's life.

"I went online last night. Carla is stable, but the press is looking for any angle. They're already reporting on Judah being here in Boston. Judah wants to keep Jac out of the public eye. He's paying me extra, both as his architect and as his nanny, to help him out with her. It's a good deal."

Jules narrowed her eyes. "It's an *unusual* deal."

Darby felt a wave of exhaustion sweep over her. "It's just business, Jules."

Well, apart from that kiss last night.

That was far and away the best kiss she'd ever had, both sweet and sexy, hot enough to blister but tender enough to soothe. If he was that good a kisser, he'd be a dynamite lover.

DJ snapped her fingers in front of Darby's nose. "Hey, you! Where did you go?"

Oh, don't mind me, I was just sliding all over a big and bold Judah, exploring that fantastic body with my teeth and tongue.

Yeah, if she said that out loud they'd have a field day.

DJ released a half snort, half laugh. "Oh, God, though it's been years, I recognize that foggy look in your eyes."

Darby fussed with Jac's blanket so she didn't have to meet DJ's eyes. "I have no idea what you are talking about."

"Like hell you don't. You've had a crush on him for months."

Darby felt like the roots of her hair were on fire. "I have not," she spluttered, glaring at her best friend. "There's a distinct difference between admiring his work and crushing on him." She'd been crushing on his buildings for years; her attraction to the man was a recent development. Again, not something they needed to know. "Why are we using that word? How old are we, thirteen?"

DJ's smile turned wicked. "Then would you care to explain why you showed me a photo of him running shirtless on some beach?"

Trust DJ to remember that. Darby scowled. "You are so annoying."

DJ laughed. "I try." She picked up Darby's phone and swiped her thumb across the screen. "Jules, let me see if I can find the picture she showed me."

Dammit, why had she never put a code on her phone? Darby snatched her phone back and tossed it into her tote bag. She glanced at her watch, saw it was later than she thought. Although she'd left a note for Judah telling him where she was, along with her phone number, she thought it was time she returned to his hotel suite. They had much to discuss and she really wanted that shower.

"Thanks for bringing me my stuff," Darby said, standing up. She dropped a kiss on Jules's cheek and was about to do the same to DJ when she saw Judah step into the coffee shop.

All the moisture in her mouth dried up as his eyes slammed into hers. Darby immediately forgot about Jules and DJ, even little Jac, as she fell into that vat of dark blue. In his eyes, she saw everything she wanted him to do to her...

From a place far away, she heard DJ mention something about the air fizzing with electricity and that she needed a fan.

Darby gave herself a mental slap and dropped back into her seat, keeping her eyes on Judah as he flashed a smile at the barista behind the counter. She'd expected a bleary-eyed, rough-looking, moody architect. But the man paying for his coffee was bright eyed, clean shaven and impeccably dressed. He'd tucked a white shirt into a pair of caramel-colored chinos, topped the shirt with a sage-colored cashmere sweater, sleeves pushed back to reveal a very expensive watch and muscled forearms.

Judah walked over to where they were sitting, stopped next to the stroller and looked down. The tip of his finger glided across Jac's downy head. For a guy who didn't want kids, he was very comfortable with the baby.

"Morning. How was your night?" Judah asked her,

placing his hand on the back of the empty chair next to hers.

Because she couldn't kiss him or feel that small smile against her lips, she glared at him. "Sleepless."

"You have to suffer to earn the ridiculous fees you charge," Judah murmured, taking the seat next to hers. Not waiting to be introduced, he held out his hand to Jules and then to DJ.

They had their men and were both stupidly in love, so it was very annoying to watch her smart, confident, kick-ass partners melt at his feet. He wasn't that good-looking.

Okay, he was, but really? She expected better from them.

Darby bent down and pulled her laptop from the stor-age area under the stroller and placed it on the table in front of her. She lifted the lid and sent Jules and DJ a pointed look. "I'm sure you want to get to the shop."

DJ shook her head. "Actually, we don't. Since we hired Maribeth as office manager, we are a lot more flexible. We can sit here for a bit."

Darby glared at her friend, who just smiled back. Oh, yeah, they'd have words later. Ignoring her, Darby turned her attention back to Judah. "We should go back upstairs. We have a lot to discuss."

"Not before I finish my coffee," Judah replied.

Why was no one listening to her? Irritated, Darby pulled up a document on her computer and angled the laptop so Judah could see the screen.

He squinted at her, shook his head, still damp from the shower, and gestured to the colorful screen. "What the hell is that?"

"A plan of action," Darby replied, ignoring the groans coming Jules and DJ.

Jules leaned forward, looked at the screen and sent Judah a commiserating look. "That's a hell of a list. Sympathies."

Really, whose side was Jules on? Not Darby's, obviously.

Before Darby could utter a scathing retort, DJ changed the subject. "Judah, I understand that you know my fiancé? Matt Edwards?"

Judah smiled, and Darby's internal organs started to fizz. Man, he was seriously delicious. His smile should be registered as a weapon. Unfortunately, or maybe fortunately, it wasn't directed at her.

"Human rights lawyer? I met him in Amsterdam. How is he?"

"Good." Excitement crossed DJ's face. "I'll be staying with him in The Hague. He can't get away right now so I'm going there."

"Send him my regards."

Mischief danced in DJ's eyes. "If you are planning on staying in Boston for a while and you want a more private place to stay, you're welcome to use my apartment."

What? No! Darby widened her eyes at DJ, silently begging her to rescind her offer.

"DJ has the apartment over the garage at our childhood home, the house Darby still shares with our older brother, Levi," Jules explained to Judah. "We all live in the Lockwood Country Club gated community. I'm surprised Darby hasn't mentioned it to you since you are trying to keep a low profile."

I didn't mention it because I need distance from the sexy architect, my new boss. I don't *need to live within shouting distance of him.*

"I don't think that would work for Judah," Darby protested. Of course, it would but it sure as hell wouldn't work for her!

"It makes sense, Darby. You can use the study in the house as your office base and nobody will mind if you bring that gorgeous creature—" DJ nodded to Jac, still asleep in her stroller "—to work."

Was DJ matchmaking? If so, Darby was going to kill her, best friend or not. The attraction between her and Judah was crazy enough without forcing them to be in super close proximity.

"Through my fiancé, Noah Lockwood, I'll arrange for you to become a temporary member of the Lockwood Country Club, Judah. There's golf, obviously, but also a state-of-the-art gym, an Olympic-size swimming pool, and if you get swamped and need help with Jac, there are experienced nannies on call that you can hire by the hour, or day," Jules offered.

Oh, God, two against one.

Before Darby could think of another reason why Judah shouldn't move next door to her—why wasn't her brain working?—Judah spoke. "That's a very kind offer, which I'll gratefully accept."

Oh, damn. Oh, hell.

Darby closed her eyes and shook her head. She knew Judah was intelligent, but this wasn't a smart plan. Levi rarely spent any time at home. She and Judah would mostly have the big house to themselves. Because it was inside a sprawling neighborhood, with acres of greenery between the houses, they could go for days, weeks, without anyone seeing them.

They could have a roaring red-hot affair and nobody would know about it.

As one, DJ and Jules stood up. Darby glared at them. *Yeah, mess with my life and plans and then go. Nice.*

Jules just grinned at her, but DJ walked around the table and bent down to give Darby a hug. "I'll see you in a few months. Love you."

Darby hugged her friend back. Turning her mouth, she whispered in DJ's ear, "You are so dead."

Darby felt DJ's smile. Her whisper brushed her ear. "You are so going to get laid. Let me know what you decide about the IVF. In the meantime, have some fun with Mr. Sexy. After all, it might be the last sex you get before becoming a single mom."

Callie sat in the corner of her big sofa, her legs tucked up under her, and wondered when the nor'easter would wind down.

She'd been back in the States for forty-eight hours yet she was already tired of the cold heavy damp snow. It was a minor miracle that she hadn't frozen to death as she'd run from her car to Mason's coffee shop yesterday. And thank the Lord she hadn't crashed her car or spun out; she would be the talk of Boston if the emergency services team found her dressed in just a coat and sexy underwear.

It had been a stupid thing to do, and she'd kill her daughters if she found out they'd braved an ice storm to seduce a man, but Callie had been unable to wait. She'd needed to know whether Mason still wanted her, whether her time away had killed his desire for her.

Judging by his passionate response, not even a little bit.

For her part, from the moment she'd touched down in the States, she'd been unable to think of much else except seeing Mason, touching him, re-exploring that powerful body, inhaling his scent, having his words and voice and hands and mouth touching her skin.

Callie couldn't even blame her impatience on sexual frustration since she'd seen a little action while she was away. She smiled. Callie Brogan, society doyenne, Ray Brogan's wealthy, once-proper widow using *seeing* and *action* in the same sentence.

Callie picked up her phone and scrolled through her pictures of Thailand, stopping on the photo of a blond man holding a beer in his big hand. That hand had cradled her face, caressed her body and, for one night, she'd enjoyed his touch. She'd met him on the beach in Ko Tao and had slept with him two nights later.

It had been nice sex, fun sex...

Callie scrolled on and stopped at the image of a black-haired man, younger than her but not by much. She'd been in Candidasa and she and Greg had spent the week together before she'd allowed him to kiss her, to indulge in some heavy petting under a full moon.

She was fifty-five years old and she'd now slept with three and a half men. Two and half in the last two months. Callie was both proud and flabbergasted but not ashamed.

Maybe she should be, but she sure as hell wasn't.

Her heart had been in hibernation for so long, her libido for even longer, and Mason had yanked her out of her cave. She hadn't realized it when she impulsively booked a flight to Southeast Asia but she needed to go away to meet herself, to find out who she was and what she wanted.

She missed her husband, she probably always would, but in Thailand, she'd finally accepted that Ray was gone, that her actions didn't—couldn't—affect him. Her life was her own.

As was her body. She could sleep with whomever she pleased.

It took a little time, a lot of honesty and facing the best and worst of herself before she came to the profound acceptance of the fact that she was allowed to question her life and her beliefs. That she could not only explore herself, her sexuality and her future but she *owed* it to herself to do exactly that. She was the only one she had to consult, the only person to please.

She also owed it to herself to find out who she was and what she wanted.

She had money, lots of it, and she wanted to use her wealth in ways that mattered, ways that would honor Ray and the businessman he'd been. She had thoughts about providing seed money to fund micro-businesses in developing countries; her business degree and being Ray's right-hand person reassured her that she could spot a good idea when she saw one. There were lots of options, many places and people who needed her help. She'd never be bored again.

But how did she really feel about that big demanding rebellious tattooed math geek who—what was the expression Darby used?—set Callie's panties on fire?

Was Mason just a fling, a bridge from her old life to her new one, or was he simply someone or something different? Was he her rebellion? Was he just good sex? Or maybe just a total contrast to Ray, who'd been so safe, so stable?

Yesterday had been anything but safe and stable; her actions had been outright madness. Okay, the coat and the sexy lingerie hadn't been necessary, or even clever, in a snowstorm, but seeing the shock on Mason's face had been worth the risk of hypothermia.

After slapping her bare butt against the glass door of his coffee shop and kissing her brainless, he'd hoisted her over his shoulder and jogged back to his cramped office, where he'd taken her on top of his keyboard, papers, pens and receipts.

It had been wild and sexy and the very opposite of nice.

After her two Thailand encounters, she now suspected Mason was the only man who could turn her core molten, who could whip her up to a point where she begged, who could turn her into a wild, crazy, on-fire-for-him woman.

Callie sighed. She no longer wanted the sex she'd had in Thailand: gentle, considerate…nice sex. She wanted the heart-pumping, soul-destroying, clothes-tearing sex she'd had with Mason yesterday.

She'd always love Ray, would always hold on to the memories of him, but now the only person she could imagine in her bed, in her life, was that surly annoying man down the road.

But how could she have Mason and the new life she needed? She wanted her freedom, but dammit, she wanted Mason, too.

Something was going to have to give. She'd have to compromise. But what would she have to lose?

Her freedom and her future or Mason?

Six

"Interesting friends."

Darby turned back to Judah and nodded. They *were* interesting—and very damn annoying. "Don't feel obligated to take DJ up on her offer of the apartment."

Judah leaned back and laced his fingers over his hard belly. "I never feel obligated to do anything. But I think it's a practical solution to my tabloid press problem." He tipped his head to the side. "But you don't think so and I'm curious as to why not."

He hadn't asked a question, so Darby didn't respond, choosing to look at her laptop screen instead.

"Could it be because you are worried you won't be able to keep your hands off me?"

Heat rocketed into Darby's cheeks, across her forehead, down her neck. But embarrassment—and him putting his finger on that solid-gold truth—wasn't a good enough reason to let his statement remain unchallenged. "I could kill myself jumping off your ego."

Darby liked the way his face remained inscrutable while laughter sparked in those ink-blue eyes. Her eyes dropped to his lips and she remembered the taste of him, his assured way of holding her, his confidence in what he was doing and how to do it. He would take control in bed and the thought excited her. A lot.

Of course, she was worried about being able to keep her hands off him. He was spectacular.

She was not going to get hot and bothered. *Not, not, not.* She could not afford to bring that much drama into her life.

Jac snuffled and Darby sent her a fond, if exasperated, look. The baby had kept Darby awake for most of the night and now, when it was time to wake up, she was dead to the world.

Judah, in contrast, looked refreshed, smelled like an orchard of something citrusy and was firing on all cylinders. She was...

Not.

Darby pushed her shoulders back and straightened her spine. There was nothing she could do about her appearance right now. It was more important to get her life—their lives—on track. Throughout the night, whenever Jac settled down enough to allow Darby a couple of minutes to work, she started listing the steps they'd need to take to make the next couple of weeks a success.

Or at the very least, avoid neglecting Jac, failing the art museum project or killing each other.

Darby turned her attention back to her laptop screen and the spreadsheet she'd compiled during the night.

She immediately felt calmer. With her lists, she could achieve world domination if she wanted.

Right now, her main aim was to bring a certain famous architect over to her way of thinking.

Darby turned the laptop and moved her chair so they both had a good view of the screen. His wonderful scent and the warmth from his body flipped her switch. Shaking her head, she forced herself to ignore the lust river coursing through her body. This was about work, not play.

Judah gestured to her monitor with his coffee cup. "What's this?"

"A plan of action."

Judah leaned forward, frowning. "It's all color coded."

"It's pretty but functional. Pink is Jac related, green is the color I allocated to the art museum project, aqua is your personal business, purple is mine—"

Judah looked at the screen again. "Why have you booked a day off next week?"

Darby flushed, heat coursing through her. Whether she decided to try IVF now or later, she'd need eggs, and thinking that her dividend check would be bigger, she'd made an appointment and paid the deposit to have her eggs harvested.

The urge to tell Judah that she was infertile, that there was a strong possibility she'd never be able to hold her own child, was both strong and strange. She rarely shared her gynecological history with anyone. It wasn't anyone's business but her own.

Darby looked at his profile and for the first time in a long time—years and years and years—she wanted to tell someone—*him*—that she felt inadequate. Crazy. Why him and why now? All she knew about Judah Huntley was that he was a supremely talented architect, that he wasn't a pushover and that he kissed like a dream.

She was simply tired and not thinking straight. Once she got a few hours' sleep, she would feel normal again.

She hoped.

"You didn't answer my question."

And she had no intention of doing so. Darby tapped the touch screen and another list came up. "This is everything I could think of that needs to be accomplished. If you think of anything, you can add it here. I've set up an account so we can share these and I've emailed you the authorization codes."

Judah looked from the screen to her and back to the screen. "When did you do this?" he demanded.

"Last night. In between Jac's bouts of misery." Darby saw his puzzled look and lifted her hands. "What?"

"You are a spreadsheet freak. I have never seen anything like it in my life."

Darby wasn't sure if his statement was a mockery or a compliment. "I like lists. They keep me organized."

Judah leaned back in his chair and cocked his head. "Oh, I think you like them because they make you feel like you are in control."

She *was* in control. There was no "feeling" involved. Darby dismissed his observation with a wave of her hand. She'd always known what she wanted and how to get it. One just needed to be prepared and to persevere. Most situations could be solved by making lists and breaking a big project down into manageable tasks.

Unfortunately, no matter how many lists she made, she couldn't get her body to cooperate with creating a child. And it was just as impossible to convince potential life partners to stick around after explaining that effort and money would be needed for her to start a family and that failure was a very real possibility.

Enough now, Darby. You're on a solo journey. Get used to it.

Darby forced her attention back to her list. "We need to make a couple of decisions about Jac. The first is that I would like to get her checked out by a doctor. I think she might have an ear infection and that's why she's not sleeping."

"She could also be feeling unsettled because she's in a strange place with strange people and she has no clue what's going on," Judah suggested, and Darby heard the annoyance in his voice.

"Sure, that's a possibility, but she also thumped her fist against her ear and I remember one of the babies I looked after doing that and it turned out she had an ear infection." Darby, unable to sit this close to him and not touch him, shifted to put some distance between them.

"You looked after babies when you were a kid?"

Darby nodded. After she'd been given the news that she might never have her own children, she'd sought out babies, needing to be around what she thought she couldn't have. Being told no, that she couldn't do something, was like waving a red rag at a bull. Her stubborn, determined nature immediately kicked into higher gear.

Thank God she hadn't had a boyfriend in her teens; she might have had unprotected sex with him just to prove to herself that she could get pregnant.

Was that why she was strongly considering IVF? Because someone had told her no?

Uncomfortable with the direction of her thoughts, she moved back to the list. "I've made an appointment for ten thirty with a pediatrician working out of the same practice as my doctor and I gave him your billing information," Darby told him. "I'd like to go home first to shower and change. While I'm doing that, you can look over DJ's apartment and see if it will suit you."

Judah placed his coffee cup on the table in front of him and scanned her list again. "Are you always this obsessively detailed?"

She wanted to lie, to play it down, but he'd find out the truth sooner rather than later. "Yes."

Judah grinned. "God help me." Turning to face her, he lifted his hand to brush her hair back from her forehead. His eyes slammed into hers and Darby saw amusement mixed with concern in all that blue. "Take a breath, Brogan, don't worry so much."

She wasn't worried, she was organized. Being organized stopped her from being worried. It kept her on track to reach her goals, made sure she achieved what she set out to do. Why couldn't people understand that?

"I'm not worried. I just want to do my job." Darby's body stiffened with tension.

The corners of Judah's mouth lifted. "And that job would be world domination?"

Oh, now he was just mocking her.

Darby felt her spine snap straight and she cursed the blush she could feel in her cheeks. "Are you prepared to consider what I said or not?"

Judah played with a strand of her hair, rubbing it between his fingers. "Yeah, we'll take Jac to the doctor, and fair warning, I've pretty much already decided to take DJ up on her offer to loan me her apartment. I'm just hoping that you cook."

Nice try, mister. "I'll cook every second night. And

you'll share the responsibilities of looking after Jac, I'm not doing it by myself. I'll draw up a schedule."

"Of course, you will," Judah said, his thumb gliding over her full bottom lip. "Tell me, do you schedule sex?"

Darby jerked back, shocked. "What?"

Judah flashed her what she was coming to recognize as his pirate grin. It was cheeky and cocky and so damn in-your-face confident. He lifted one broad shoulder in an insouciant shrug. "I just thought that a woman intent on taking over the world should have a measure of stress relief."

"Not with you!" Darby said, annoyed beyond belief.

The pirate morphed back into the professional and his eyes cooled. "Obviously, not with me. We can't possibly confuse this situation with something sexual."

Her brain knew that was the sensible course of action. But her long-neglected libido vehemently disagreed.

And when she looked in Judah's blue eyes and saw the deep regret in all that blue, she suspected his libido disagreed, too.

After another shower—the quick one she had in Judah's hotel room didn't really count—Darby walked into the massive family kitchen in her house and headed straight for the coffee machine.

Needing a break, she reached for her favorite cup and shoved it under the spout of Levi's fancy coffee machine. She hit the correct button, then gripped the counter and straightened her arms, looking down at the black-and-white tiled floor beneath her flat-soled leather boots.

She needed five minutes, ten, enough time for caffeine to jolt her awake.

After returning from the doctor—her suspicions about

Jac having an ear infection turned out to be correct—
she and Judah hit the mall. When she suggested they stop
to pick up a couple of items for Jac—more diapers and
formula, clothes better suited for Boston in a blizzard—
instead of hitting a discount supermarket, Judah steered
his luxury SUV into the parking lot of an exclusive mall
housing one of the city's most famous boutique baby
stores.

By the time they left, they had not only a car seat,
but also a six-foot-tall brown bear and everything in
between, including baby monitors and a cot that turned
into a bed suitable for a toddler. The total at the checkout had been staggering, but Judah just handed over a
black credit card and didn't blink.

Judah would probably have all this stuff shipped to
his apartment in New York when he was done in Boston... Did that mean he planned on seeing more of Jac?

Darby really hoped she wasn't in lust with a guy
who'd only pay attention to his daughter if and when
it suited him.

Darby heard the kitchen door open and close and then
the familiar sound of Levi kicking off his boots. Turning around, she watched her big brawny brother walk
into the kitchen, a scowl on his face. Darby had given
up trying to work out whether he was pissed at her or
not; it could go either way with Levi.

They'd never been close, even though they still shared
the same house, and she knew she would never have the
same kind of relationship Levi shared with Jules or with
DJ. He adored them. Her? Not so much.

"Hi," Darby said, her tone wary. "You're home early."

Levi pushed a hand through his dark brown hair,

tinged with red. A blonde, a brunette and a redhead—none of the Brogan siblings looked alike.

"I'm heading out of town," Levi curtly replied. "I got a message from DJ saying she's loaned her apartment to Judah Huntley?"

"Yeah. He's there now." Darby pulled her cup from under the spout and automatically handed it over to her brother. She placed another cup under the spout for herself. "He's got his daughter with him, she's nine months old. I'm working with him, helping him with a project here in Boston. I've also agreed to help him look after Jac."

As she expected, disapproval settled on Levi's masculine features. He rubbed his hand over his face. "God, you and babies."

"What is *that* supposed to mean?"

Levi sipped his coffee and raised one powerful shoulder. "Why do I have to hear about your latest IVF news from Mom?"

Dammit. Darby wrinkled her nose, silently admitting that she should've told him. But she'd been trying to avoid an argument, trying to avoid being told what to do. Levi loved telling all of them what to do. Darby hadn't listened since she was seven years old.

"Is this a good idea, Darby? Have you thought it through?" Levi demanded.

For God's sake! She hadn't done anything but think.

Darby, because sarcasm was her default setting around Levi, rolled her eyes. "I'm not going to spend tens of thousands of dollars on something I'm not sure of, Levi! For God's sake, give me some credit!"

"Darby—"

Tired and stressed, Darby tapped her stomach. "My

body, my decision, my life. I haven't, nor will I, ask you for cash or to help me look after my baby, if and when I decide to have one. You don't have a say."

Darby thought she saw hurt flash in his eyes.

Then Levi surprised her by rubbing his hands over his face. "And maybe that hurts, too, Darby, that you can't ask me. You'll ask Mom or Jules or DJ for help, but me? Not a damn word."

Oh, God. He was hurting. She had no idea what to say so she just stared at him. She and Levi sniped at each other, traded insults, stuck to neutral topics. They didn't discuss anything deep; they never had.

Levi banged his coffee cup onto the kitchen table and his gaze slammed into hers. "Where did we go so wrong, Darby? Why does every conversation have to end in a fight? I just want you to be happy, to protect you! Is that so hard to understand?"

Yeah, it really was, because since she was seven years old, she'd always felt like the spare sister, the one who really didn't matter.

She opened her mouth to say…what? She had no idea.

Levi didn't give her the chance to respond. He did what he always did when they argued. He simply walked away.

In the apartment over the four-car garage, Judah stood back and looked around the room, the once perfectly decorated loft apartment now covered in bags holding baby stuff. Lots and lots of clothes and diapers and equipment and toys and…

God, babies needed a lot of things.

But he might, as Darby had suggested a few times, have gotten a bit carried away… Shoving his hands into his pockets, Judah looked down at the little girl asleep in her bouncy chair, her long lashes smudges on her cheeks, that perfect rosebud mouth slightly pursed. His heart stuttered.

Judah reminded himself that while this was a Kodak moment, he knew better than to be affected by the pretty picture she made. This was one of those moments life gave you to lure you into thinking raising kids wasn't that tough, that it wasn't as demanding as everyone said.

It was. No question about it.

Jac was a novelty, a cute distraction, but Judah knew that after a week or two of doing the same mind-numbing, repetitive tasks, boredom would kick in. Make bottles of formula, change the diaper, pray the kid went to sleep, rinse, repeat—for weeks on end. Interrupted sleep got old very quickly and being at the beck and call of a tiny infant and then a demanding toddler who couldn't regulate her emotions or behavior was soul-numbingly, brain-meltingly boring.

He'd done it and was still convinced that having kids wasn't an option for him. Being childless left a million doors open to him: it allowed him to live out of his suitcase doing projects all over the world. If he didn't want to return to New York City, he didn't have to. He could take a holiday in Prague or Patagonia if he felt the urge. Being childless meant eating out every night, watching midnight movies, attending the opening of new art galleries, clubs and restaurants.

Having kids meant saying goodbye to fun and freedom.

He'd had neither as a teenager, and he was damned if he'd lose out as an adult. Loving and raising a child—and committing himself to a relationship—meant sacrificing his career and his freedom. He couldn't do that. He wouldn't.

He'd give his niece, and by extension Carla, two weeks. But not a minute more.

The door to the apartment opened and Darby slipped inside, quickly closing the door to keep out the winter wind.

The slick expensive business clothes and subtle makeup were gone. Dressed up, she looked like what he knew she was, a strong independent woman in control of her life. But wearing just jeans and a simple shirt, well-worn boots on her feet and her hair pulled back into a rough ponytail, she looked younger, softer, incredibly feminine. Flat stomach, long legs, an ass that was a perfect fit for his hands. His new employee was hotter than Abu Dhabi on a scorching summer's day.

He wanted her.

He really didn't want to want her. He didn't need that much trouble in his life.

So Judah pulled his brain out of the bedroom and noticed the emotion in her eyes that hadn't been there earlier. A little pain, some confusion, too much stress. He shouldn't be curious, but he was... She was that intriguing, that compelling.

"Everything okay?" he asked.

Her smile came too quickly, was a shade too bright. "Sure, just tired."

She lied really well but he wasn't fooled. She was more than just tired. Judah watched as Darby covered Jac's new crib mattress with a sheet and stood back. Judah smiled when she picked up the teddy bear and moved it a fraction to the right. Obsessive but so damn efficient.

Jac let out a little squeak and they both whipped

around, expecting to see the little girl awake. Jac's eyes fluttered open, the lips of her rosebud mouth lifted into a tiny smile before she turned her head and slid back to sleep.

"She's been asleep for a while now, do you think she's okay?" he said. "Do you think they gave her too much pain medication?"

He heard the worry in his voice and knew Darby wouldn't miss it. She lifted her hand and rubbed his shoulder. "She's fine, Judah. She didn't sleep well last night, and now that she's pain-free, she's catching up." Darby looked at her watch. "I'm going to leave her to sleep for as long as possible, but we do have to wake her up in a few hours to give her antibiotics."

"And she should be fine in a day or two?"

"She'll be fine in a couple of hours," Darby told him. "Babies usually respond quickly to medicine. Stop worrying, Daddy."

Daddy? Judah frowned, turning the word over in his mind.

He sent her a hard stare and Darby responded by lifting one thin, arched brow. "Problem?"

Well, if she still thought Jac was his, then they did have a very big problem.

Judah held up his hand. "Just give me a second."

Darby shrugged, reached for another packet and pulled out warm winter vests and leggings. Removing the tags, she placed the clothes in a laundry basket that held the soft towels and blankets they'd purchased.

Darby still believed he was Jac's dad? How was that even possible? Judah thought back over the past thirty-six hours and suddenly realized that he'd allowed Darby's original assumption to stand.

After rubbing his hands over his face, he placed his hands on his hips and stared at the floor. He'd been super reluctant to care for Jac, unwilling to play Carla's games because he wasn't the baby's father, but when he looked at the situation through Darby's eyes, he came across as an asshat of the highest order.

He lifted his head and stared at her stunning profile. "Darby."

Darby looked at him, a tiny frown creasing her smooth forehead. She had the most gorgeous skin, soft and smooth.

"Darby, I've just realized that you have the wrong end of a very large stick."

"I do?"

"Yeah. Jac isn't my daughter," Judah told her and waited for the words to penetrate.

Darby looked from him to Jac and back again. "I know you would like her not to be, but she looks just like you," she quietly responded.

Judah allowed himself a small smile at her diplomacy. "She looks just like my half brother, who looks just like me."

Darby opened her mouth, snapped it closed and opened it again. Swallowing, she held up her finger. This time it was her asking for a minute. Judah was happy to give it to her, God knew he wasn't eager to discuss the details of his brother's affair with Judah's girlfriend.

"Well, that explains a hell of a lot."

Was that really relief he heard in her voice, a little more respect? He met her eyes and saw those emotions crossing her face. He had to force his wobbly knees to lock.

Why, on such short acquaintance, did her opinion matter so much? But the relief he felt at having that faint veil of censure removed was more than he'd expected, deeper than he'd imagined.

Now for the inquisition, the long list of questions. He owed her some answers since he'd been an idiot not to realize she was acting on bad information.

Darby surprised him by placing the back of her fingers on Jac's forehead, then her cheeks. "She hasn't developed a temperature, so I think we caught the infection before it got out of control."

They were talking about Jac and her ear infection again. Thank God. He'd take the change of subject.

Judah rubbed the back of his neck. "I feel sick wondering how long she's been in pain." He sat down on the couch and placed his ankle on his knee. "Carla isn't the most attentive mother, I doubt she would've noticed, but you did, straightaway. Thank you."

"Years of babysitting." Darby rolled a tiny pair of socks together.

He shuddered. "By choice?"

She smiled at his horror. "Well, no one held a gun to my head and made me do it."

No guns had been involved in his house, but coercion, expectation and bullying had been powerful weapons. "Didn't you want to do what normal teenagers did? Dating, partying, sports?"

"Why do you assume that I didn't do those things, too? I did, I just looked after babies in between."

Oh, *balance*. Not a concept his father and stepmom were familiar with.

Darby sat down in the chair across from him and faced him. "I'm not going to pepper you with questions about Carla and your brother, so relax. But I do just want to say one thing—"

Judah braced himself for her words, told himself not to react.

"In light of what you've just told me, I deeply respect you taking Jac and looking after her."

Okay... Not what he'd been expecting. But he couldn't accept her praise.

"What else could I do, Darby? Her mom is in the hospital, my brother is God-knows-where, Jake's parents—" they'd disowned Judah, so he wouldn't call them his parents "—are useless and I couldn't let her go into foster care." He raked his fingers through his hair. "Yeah, having a baby is disrupting but she's nine months old, none of this is her fault. I will do what I need to do for a couple of weeks. It's not a life sentence."

A small smile touched Darby's sexy mouth. "And you aren't planning to become emotionally attached to her?"

He wasn't prepared to become emotionally attached to anyone. Besides, how attached could you become to someone in a few short weeks? "That's the plan."

Her amazing smile reached her eyes. "Let me know how that works out for you."

"I don't allow attachments, Darby." He wasn't sure whom he was reminding, her or himself. "It's not what I do."

She didn't break eye contact, didn't squirm or fidget. She just looked at him with eyes the color of soft rain clouds. She opened her mouth to speak, closed her eyes and shook her head. When she looked at him again, she wore a back-to-business expression.

"Jac's asleep and should sleep for a little while yet. We have the baby monitors working. Would you like to look at the study, see where we'll work?"

"No. I want to take you to bed. Any thoughts on that?"

The words flew out of his mouth before he could stop them and while he wanted to regret them, he couldn't.

Darby stared at him, a little shocked, a lot turned on.

She had thoughts. Lots and lots of thoughts. Some scary. But most were variations of the phrases *yes, please* and *take me now*.

Darby watched as Judah walked over to her and placed his hands on the arms of her chair, bending his head so she could taste his sweet breath, watch desire flicker in his eyes.

He had a small scar on the underside of his chin and his tanned neck was a perfect contrast to his white shirt. Smooth warm skin to explore, thick hair to shove her fingers into, a mouth to lose herself in.

He could be her last act of madness before she headed toward single motherhood. Before she put herself on this journey that was all hope, potential heartbreak and hormones. Before she became someone's mother, she could be Darby.

Judah could be her last chance to experience desire, to lose herself in lust.

It had been so long, and she was so out of practice but since she was a woman who didn't club or barhop, didn't socialize that much outside of time with her family, she hadn't had many chances to meet a guy she felt attracted to and comfortable enough to give her body to. Judah might be her last hope for good sex for a long, long time.

Despite not knowing him for very long, she knew she'd be safe with him. Judging by that kiss, he'd be a considerate lover. She'd be safe in his hands. She was almost thirty, a strong, empowered woman who wasn't afraid to express her sexuality. She could do this; she *should* do this.

Yeah...*nope*.

He was too much. It was too soon. The attraction between them was too intense, too out of control. He would be like riding a wild horse, exciting but uncontrollable.

Darby forced herself to stand up, to brush nonexistent lint off her jeans. "My only thoughts are that we should get to work. We've got a lot to do."

Judah's smile was both gentle and determined. "We're going to have to deal with this chemistry at some point, Darby."

Probably. But only when she felt like she could contain the resulting explosion.

Seven

After two days of dealing with urgent business in New York, Judah ran up the stairs to the Georgian-inspired house in Boston. Before he could reach the top step, Darby opened the door and Judah allowed his eyes to skim over her, his excited heart settling and sighing. He was...

God, he'd almost said *home*.

He was back. That would do.

Jac, from her seat on Darby's hip, handed him a gummy drooling smile and waved her arms in the air. She leaned toward him and Judah felt a rush of unexpected pleasure at her gesture, idly wishing that Darby would fall into his arms as easily.

"Hey, mouse," Judah murmured, taking Jac and brushing his chin across her downy head. He'd missed her and that surprised him. He'd been reluctant to leave

Jac, but Darby assured him that she could handle two nights on her own with the baby, that Darby's mother would help if Darby needed her to. He'd left, thinking he'd be so swamped in New York that he wouldn't have time to think about Jac or Darby. He'd also thought he'd welcome being diaper- and drool-free.

The opposite had happened.

He'd been in the middle of a presentation and seen a pigeon fly past the conference room's window. He'd thought of Jac and her laughter every time she saw a bird. Or a dog. A cat. A butterfly.

He'd been talking about floor space and eco-efficiency when the image of Darby bent over a desk, her nose wrinkling in concentration, flashed on the big screen of his mind. Long legs, blond hair, sexy as hell.

His concentration had taken a beating.

"I was about to take Jac for a run, she loves it." Darby gestured to the three-wheeled stroller. "How was New York?"

"Good. Busy."

Darby lifted her arms, gathered all that silky hair and pulled it into a rough ponytail, raking the strands back with her fingers. She pulled a band from her wrist and Judah watched her chest rise, her small nipples puckering in the cold wind blowing through the open door. He felt the movement in his pants and sighed.

He'd had a proposal for no-strings sex in New York, but he'd declined. He wanted sex, but the only person he could imagine in his bed was Darby.

And she was the one person he absolutely couldn't have. Because if something went wrong, he'd not only lose the services of a fantastic architect who was anything but an intern, but also the person sharing the looking-after-Jac load.

Sleeping with Darby would be a stupid thing to do, but the more he tried not to think about it, the more he *did*. Now wanting her was becoming pretty much all consuming...

Great.

"Blow off your run and let's go for breakfast. It's Saturday, the sun is finally shining and we are on schedule, so we can take the day," Judah suggested.

He'd just got home, and he hadn't seen her for days. If she went for a run, he might not see her again for hours.

Darby walked onto the porch and headed for the enclosed back corner. The sun was weak there, but in this corner they were out of the wind and it was almost pleasant. She shook her head. "Why don't you phone the club, hire a sitter for an hour to look after Jac and come with me?" Humor danced in her eyes. "If you can keep up..."

Judah sat down on the porch swing and placed Jac on his knee. He sent Darby a steady look. "Put that competitive streak away, Brogan. Besides, we both know that in any race I'd whip your ass."

The I-can-take-you spark in her eyes morphed into ten-foot-high flames. "Want to test that theory? I bet you'd spend the whole time eating my dust."

"The only reason I'd be behind you was to watch your spectacular ass."

Desire jumped into her eyes, softened her mouth, made her nipples tighten. He was about to stand, to pull her in for a kiss, when the door behind them opened.

Cursing, Judah watched Levi Brogan step onto the porch. He frowned at Judah and darted an enigmatic glance at Darby. "Judah, this is my brother, Levi. Levi,

Judah Huntley. I'm working with him on the Grantham-Ford commission."

Judah shook Levi's hand and did an internal eye roll when Levi squeezed his hand harder than necessary. It was a mess-with-my-sister-and-I'll-mess-you-up squeeze.

Yeah, he got it.

Then Levi surprised Judah by dropping to his haunches in front of Jac. He slowly smiled and Jac waved her hands in the air, her little body quivering with excitement. Little Jac was a flirt, Judah conceded with a wry smile.

"Hey there, cutie." Levi rumbled the words, poking the tip of a gentle finger into her thigh. Jac leaned toward him and Judah allowed Levi to pick her up. Levi put Jac on his hip and picked up Jac's hand and pretended to eat her fingers. Jac howled with laughter.

Levi turned to Darby and placed his free hand on his hip. "I'm going away for a few days. Are you going to be okay?"

"I always am, Levi."

"I'm just checking, Darby," Levi snapped, and Judah heard the frustration in his voice.

"I'm a big girl, Levi," Darby replied, steel in hers.

Levi handed Jac back to Judah and he thought he saw a flash of hurt and disappointment cross Levi's face, but it was gone so quickly he might've imagined it. The tension between the siblings was palpable and Judah suspected they'd spent most of their lives butting heads.

After a quick goodbye, Levi jogged toward and then down the stairs. Judah watched him walk over to his muscle car parked next to the detached garage. Within minutes, the low roar and hard rumble split the morning air and Judah sighed. He needed to get himself one of those...

But he didn't have a garage to house a car or time to enjoy one. His primary modes of transport were planes and hired cars and, when he needed a vehicle of his own, rentals. Judah looked at Darby and her eyes were on her brother's disappearing back.

"Complicated relationship?" he asked.

"Very." Darby sat down on the bench swing and pulled her knees up to her chest.

He shouldn't ask but he was curious, and she looked like she could do with a friend. "What happened?"

Darby was suddenly fascinated by the multicolored laces on her sneakers.

He needed to know what was going on behind that distant expression. Jac, he noticed, had fallen asleep on his shoulder. He thought about moving her to her stroller or taking her inside but shrugged the thought away. He knew to let sleeping babies lie.

"Tell me what happened, Darby."

"Why?" Darby demanded.

Always challenging, always demanding. God, she was hard work, but Judah was coming to think he might like sparring with her. Up until this point, the women in his life had been, with the exception of Carla, undemanding and acquiescent.

Darby was anything but.

"Because I asked you," Judah replied, patient. The sun was shining, Jac was asleep and he had nowhere urgent he needed to be except here, getting to know what made this fascinating, and exasperating, woman tick.

"It's not a big deal, Judah."

"Then you shouldn't have any problem telling me."

"God, you're annoying."

"So I've heard. Now stop stalling and spill."

"It's an open secret in our family that Jules is Levi's favorite sister, followed by DJ. I come a distant third."

"Why do you feel that way?"

Darby tucked her leg under her bottom and rested the side of her head against the back cushion of the swing. She played with the edge of her long-sleeved shirt, rubbing the fabric between her thumb and index finger.

"I was seven and it was Christmas. We were opening presents under the tree. Levi gave Jules a music box. When you opened it, a ballerina started dancing and music played. It was beautiful. I loved that damn box."

"What did he give you?"

"A baseball card. It was secondhand, he didn't even bother to wrap it. He had a stack of them. I bet he just grabbed the oldest, yuckiest one and handed it over."

Judah remembered having a stack of baseball cards himself and knew that sometimes the oldest cards were the most valuable. "Who was the player?"

"It was over twenty years ago, Judah, I have no idea. I just remember throwing the card in the fire, screaming that he didn't love me, that Jules was his favorite, that he'd ruined Christmas for me. I refused to come down for Christmas lunch and cried for the rest of the day. I pretty much spoiled Christmas for everyone that year," Darby said, subdued. "Since then there's been this barrier between us. Levi and Jules have always been closer, and I've always felt like I am on the outside looking in, that he loves her far more than he does me."

"I'm sure that's not true."

"I've always been competitive, Judah, but that Christmas was a turning point for me. From then on, every time I came in second, I've felt unloved, shortchanged, inadequate."

Judah placed his hand on Darby's slim thigh and squeezed, astounded that this remarkable, talented and intelligent woman could feel this way. She had everything going for her except the belief that she was perfectly acceptable just the way she was. Would she ever learn that she didn't need to compete with anyone?

Probably not, he conceded. And it was not—repeat, not—his job to tell her that, to show her that.

Darby sighed, and her hand dropped to rest on his. Her fingers slid between his and pleasure rocketed up his arm and down his spine, lodging in his balls.

Yep, he was hard. Though, really, when wasn't he when he was around her?

Darby dropped her head to rest her temple against his shoulder and he felt her sigh. He could imagine her soft breath on his skin, her warm lips branding him, those elegant hands skimming his skin.

God, he wanted her.

He wanted to know her, slide into her, make her his. Because she wasn't the type of girl he could have sex with and then leave, he'd have to settle for her head on his shoulder.

And that, in this moment, was almost enough.

"I just feel like Levi can't be bothered with me. But that could be my fault because my default reaction is to push him away, to tell him I don't need him." Darby sat up and linked her hands between her knees. "I need him to be my brother, not my bossy protector."

As a big brother, Judah knew what it was like trying to protect someone who didn't want his protection, who refused to listen. Darby, he suspected, was as hard-headed as Jake. Because Judah was a take-charge-and-fix-things type of guy, as he suspected Levi was, the inability to fix what was broken drove him nuts. That was why, when he reached the end of his rope with Jake, he'd had to cut his brother out of his life.

He didn't think Darby and Levi were there yet. He doubted they ever would be.

"His emotional distance hurts, Judah," Darby quietly admitted.

"Then tell him that, Darby," Judah suggested. "Men are simple creatures, we need clear direction. We don't do subtlety."

"As a species, you men are pains in the ass."

He couldn't argue with that. "Talk to your brother, Darby. You're not seven anymore, have an adult conversation with him. Tell him that you are disappointed in him, that you don't feel supported."

"Wouldn't that make me look weak?"

God, so vulnerable but so damn feisty. "He's your brother, Brogan! You're allowed to look weak with him."

Darby turned to face Judah. Looking into her spectacular eyes, his breath caught in his throat.

He had to touch her. He couldn't wait a moment longer.

Judah stood up and walked over to the stroller, placed Jac on her side and pulled a blanket up and over her shoulders. Opening the front door, he pushed Jac into the hall, hoping that the connection, the band of attraction that arced between him and Darby, would make her follow him inside.

When she closed the door behind her, he looked from her to the imposing staircase that dominated the hall and back to her flushed face.

He could see it. She wanted him as much as he wanted her.

Thank God.

Judah didn't hesitate. He took a couple of quick strides and pressed his mouth against hers.

He felt her fingertips dig into his chest. He thought she might push him away, in spite of what he'd seen in her eyes, but then her amazing lips softened beneath his and her tongue darted past his teeth, wanting to play.

Judah placed his hands on Darby's hips and lifted her up and into him, pressing his hardness into her tight stomach. Her hands snaked up his chest and then her fingers were in his hair and her tongue was tangling with his and Judah felt like he was walking on an electrified tightrope.

Time stopped, the earth stopped turning and gravity disappeared...

All because Darby was kissing him, making desperate sounds in the back of her throat. Because her hand was on his jaw, on his neck, burrowing into the collar of his shirt...

Because she wanted him.

Judah pushed his hand under her thermal exercise top and pulled it up her torso. He wanted to look down and see her creamy skin but couldn't bear the thought of pulling his mouth off hers, not yet. Maybe not ever. Pushing the fabric up, his hands passed over her breasts and his erection hardened in response to the pointy little buds.

He needed her naked, now.

Judah had to break contact with Darby's lips to pull her shirt over her head and he took the opportunity to look down.

She was as beautiful as he'd imagined. Soft skin,

strong shoulders, slim but powerful. He ran a finger over her collarbone, down that creamy skin to where her nipples hardened beneath the cotton of her sports bra. That serviceable garment had to go. He wanted the gorgeousness underneath, the fury and fire, her heat.

"Judah…"

His name was a whisper and a plea. He pulled his gaze to her face. He saw trepidation, masking the desire.

Hell, no, he wanted her mindless with pleasure, squirming and panting his name, no doubt allowed.

Judah held her jaw with his hand, keeping his touch gentle. "This has nothing to do with anyone or anything but us. It's not about Jac, the commission, our work. It's just us. Only us. Only this. Tell me you understand that, Darby," he added, hearing the desperation in his voice.

Darby nodded. He said a quick prayer of thanks, ran his hand up her rib cage and his thumb swiped her nipple. He heard her intake of breath, watched her eyes cloud over. She'd stepped out of her head. Her body—her wants and needs—were calling the shots. It made him feel powerful, masculine, that he could make her agile brain stop thinking, stop running scenarios, counting the odds.

He felt like Atlas and Bogart and Clooney rolled into one. She made him weak, but he'd never felt stronger in his life.

Judah lifted her sports bra up and over her breasts and ducked his head to tug a pretty raspberry-hued nipple into his mouth. Like the juiciest fruit, her taste was a tiny burst of flavor on his tongue. Needing more, his other hand pushed between the fabric of her exercise pants to cup her butt, pushing his fingers deeper until he could feel her heat, her wet warmth.

He needed more. He needed all of her and now, immediately. He needed skin on skin, heat on heat.

But a part of him hesitated, also needing to keep checking. There was too much at stake to make a wrong move, to regret this later.

Judah pulled back and looked into Darby's passion-filled eyes. "Are we stopping or are we continuing?"

Darby's hand drifted over his stomach, moving down. Her palm stroking the long length of him was an answer of sorts, but he needed her to say the words. They couldn't afford any misunderstandings.

He held her hand against him, forcing himself to concentrate. "Darby…"

"Mmm?" Her thumb rubbed his tip and he thought he'd lose it, there and then.

"Are we doing this?"

She smiled, and he felt his heart bungee jump out of his chest to grovel at her feet. Stupid thing. Her thumbnail drifted across the edge of his head and his eyes smacked the back of his skull.

He felt her fingers on his belt buckle, felt the first button of his jeans pop open, then another. He couldn't hold on much longer; if she didn't speak soon, he was going to explode, in more ways than one.

Then her hand was circling him, pumping him, priming him. "I don't know what you are doing," Darby murmured in her sun-and-sex voice, "but I'm going to play with this."

"Good enough," Judah muttered.

Before his brain completely closed down, he pulled his wallet from the back pocket of his jeans, dug out a strip of two condoms and placed them on the hall table. Trying to ignore, as best he could, her hand on his shaft, he pushed her exercise pants down her legs. Stepping away from her, he stood out of her reach, taking in the sight of her, looking flushed and pretty and totally turned on.

Kicking off his shoes and socks, he pushed his jeans and boxers down his legs, watching her eyes widen as she first caught sight of him. She licked her lips, her mouth a perfect O and he hardened further, a feat he didn't think was possible.

She stood next to a painting of a Brogan ancestor, a severe-looking lady dressed in ruffles and a long skirt, dark hair pulled back in a bun. Next to Darby, a hall table held photographs of her family, her mom and dad and siblings, friends and cousins. This was her family home and Judah knew, from this day onward, she'd never look at this room the same way.

Good.

He had no problem with her thinking about him every time she walked through that front door.

Judah, his hand touching her shoulder, trailed his fingers down her arm to link his palm with hers. He rested his forehead on hers, the hair on his chest brushing against her nipples. "I want you right now."

Darby found his lips, her mouth telling him the words he so badly needed to hear. He heard "yes," he heard "more," he heard her beg him to touch her, so he did.

His mouth found her jawline, tracked kisses down her neck and nibbled his way across her collarbone. He flicked a glance upward, saw her watching him, her mouth open, her eyes wild. She knew what she wanted, but to test her, he kissed the top of her breast, sucking her soft skin just hard enough to leave the faintest red mark.

Darby whimpered, need and pleasure combining to make the sweetest sound he'd ever heard.

He sucked one nipple while teasing the other with his fingers. He moved his hands down, flirting with that small patch of carefully groomed hair, lightly playing with her.

He smiled when he felt her legs fall apart, a silent gesture begging him for more. Judah obliged by rubbing his finger over her clit and Darby shot off the wall.

Liked that, did she? Well, there was more... A lot, lot more.

Judah dropped to his knees and lifted her right thigh so that her leg draped over his shoulder. Nuzzling into her, he inhaled her, his head swimming. Going down on a woman was a curiously intimate act for their first time together but he wanted to know every inch of her and this was a good place to start. Judging by her satisfied murmurs, Darby was as into it as he was.

He licked, he tugged, he pushed in, retreated and generally drove her crazy. When he felt she was close, he edged one finger, then two, into her slick channel, curled his fingers and tapped her inside walls, his tongue working her clit.

Heat—hers, his—surrounded them and Judah knew she was on the edge, so close. He wanted their first time to be like this. He wanted her to come on his tongue, for her to fall apart in his arms.

Darby arched her back and slapped her hands against the wall behind her. He felt her clench around him, milking his fingers.

So responsive, he thought, as another orgasm hit her, this one bigger than the first. He kept working her until he was sure she was done, only lifting his head when he felt her body slump, when her supporting knee buckled.

Holding her hips to keep her steady—she looked like a feather might knock her over—he stood and held her face in his hands. So pretty, so damn sweet.

Judah covered her mouth with his, allowed her to taste herself, and sighed when one hand went down to cup his balls and the other encircled him in a hot grip. He patted the table next to them, picked up the condoms and removed the latex from its cover. Darby took the latex from him and rolled it down his shaft, so slowly he thought he might come if she didn't hurry the hell up.

"Wall or floor?" she whispered.

Judah smiled. "Neither. Stairs." Judah walked backward, sat down on the third step. "Straddle me," he ordered.

Darby didn't hesitate. She lowered herself on him, stroking her hot and still-wet core against him, sending a firestorm sprinting from his balls up his spine.

"Take me inside you," Judah said, lifting his hands to push her hair off her face. He needed to see her, wanted to look in her eyes as he made her come again.

His tip slid inside her, just a half inch, and he gritted his teeth, reminding himself that he was a big guy and that she probably needed time to adjust.

"You okay?" he asked, keeping perfectly still.

"Fine. Just not sure if I'm doing this right."

She might be teasing but he couldn't think straight so he pushed the thought aside. "There is no wrong way for me to be inside you. Take as much time as you need… just hurry up, okay?" Okay, he hadn't meant to say that out loud.

Darby laughed and slid down him, only stopping when he was balls deep and mindless.

"Holy, holy, holy…"

He couldn't complete the sentence; he was so close to the edge. Reaching between them, he found her sensitive bud and rolled his fingers across her. He needed her to come, now, before he lost his mind.

Darby released a surprised mewl, closed her eyes and rocked hard. The chandelier above their head was a fire burst of stars, the hard staircase a feather bed, the hallway a boudoir. Darby was perfection and he pumped his hips once, maybe twice, and she shattered, allowing him to snap the cord of his control and follow her into that pleasure-drenched paradise.

When he could string a coherent thought together, he realized Darby was sprawled on top of him and her hair was in his mouth. A wooden step was trying to saw his back in half and his right thigh was cramping. His butt had, he was sure, carpet burns from the stair runner.

Yet he'd never felt better because he'd just had the best sex of his life in the hallway of Darby's childhood home. He couldn't, wouldn't regret a damn thing.

Maybe when his leg fell off from lack of blood, he'd feel a bit pissed, but other than that? He'd stay where he was as long as he could.

Eight

Judah sprinted around the corner leading to the Brogan house, enjoying the feeling of the bitingly cold air burning his lungs. Darby had left earlier that morning to do whatever she intended to do on her "personal" day and he'd given up trying to look after Jac and get some work done around half past three.

Desperate to exercise, he'd called the country club and within ten minutes he had a highly recommended babysitter on his doorstep. As he was about to leave the residence, Jac cooperated and fell asleep in the sitter's arms and Judah knew he had ninety minutes, two hours if he was lucky, to exercise. He'd immediately headed for the state-of-the-art gym at the club and followed that session with a punishing run.

Now, Judah approached Darby and Levi's house and frowned when he saw a luxury car pulling into the driveway. Slowing down, he watched as a slim blonde woman exited the car and walked around to the passenger door. Frowning, he watched Darby slowly climb out. The older blonde, who could only be Darby's mom, placed her arm around Darby's waist as they slowly walked up the steps to the front door.

Judah released a low curse and accelerated, reaching them as they hit the top of the steps. "What's the matter? What happened?"

Mother and daughter both turned, and Judah frowned at Darby's pale, pale face. "Are you okay? Where's your car?"

Callie placed a hand on his arm. She quickly introduced herself and then said, "Darby's fine, Judah. She's had a minor procedure. She's sore. I'm driving because she isn't allowed to drive for twenty-four hours."

"Where's Jac?" Darby demanded, her mouth tight with worry.

Judah jerked his head toward the front door. "I hired a sitter from the club. She was sleeping when I left."

Callie smiled at Darby before giving her a gentle hug. "I'm going to leave you in Judah's capable hands, darling. Take it easy, okay? I'll call you in the morning."

"Wait, Mom…what?" Darby frowned as Callie all but jogged down the steps. Looking from her to Judah, Darby threw her hands up in the air. "She was going to look after me, be at my beck and call, help me with Jac."

"I'm here, so is the sitter." Judah opened the door and gestured for her to step inside the warm house. He saw her wince and her hand went to her side. Concerned by her dull eyes and pinched mouth, he didn't hesitate. He bent down and scooped her up, holding her against his chest.

"Dammit, Huntley, I can walk," Darby hissed, thumping his chest.

"It'll be quicker if I carry you."

Judah swiftly carried her down the hallway to the study, kicked the door open with his foot and gently placed her on the large sofa in front of the enormous flat-screen TV that dominated one wall. Sitting down on the coffee table in front of her, he allowed his hands to dangle between his legs, reminding himself that he couldn't interrogate her. He didn't have that right.

"Where the hell have you been and what happened?"

Not a good start. But he needed to know she was okay, that she wasn't ill or injured. He placed his hand on his heart and tried to rub away the burn. He hated to see her injured, hurt, a diluted version of the vibrant woman he knew.

Darby couldn't meet his eyes, so Judah gripped her chin to lift her face. In her eyes, he saw traces of embarrassment, a truckload of defiance and underneath it all, fear. He gentled his touch, gave her a small smile. "Darby, a million things are running through my mind right now, none of them good."

Darby sucked in air, then grimaced. "I had my eggs harvested today. It turned out to be a bit more painful than I expected."

Judah frowned. What? What on earth was she talking about? "I'm sorry, I don't understand."

Darby drew patterns on her leggings with the tip of her index finger. "I have severe fertility problems. I will never be able to conceive a child naturally and it's been recommended that if I want children, I undergo IVF within the next few months. The first step is having my eggs harvested and then frozen."

Judah opened his mouth to say something sympathetic, then abruptly pulled the words back. She didn't need sympathy, she needed understanding and he didn't know where to start with that. "And I'm presuming you want kids?"

Darby touched her top lip with the tip of her tongue. "Yes. I can't afford to wait so I'm doing this solo."

Brave, brave woman. And so Darby: there was something she wanted so she went out and grabbed it.

Judah heard the knock on the door and the sitter poked her head around. "I heard you come in. Jac's in her playpen. I gave her a bottle and a banana for a snack. I hope that's okay?"

Judah nodded. "Do you have anywhere you need to be?" he asked. "Can you hang around for another two hours?"

She nodded. "Sure."

The door closed behind her and Judah looked at Darby, worried. She looked so pale, so tired. "Can I get you something? Coffee? Cocoa? Pain pills?"

"I took some meds earlier," Darby replied. She picked up her legs to lie down on the couch. She tucked a pillow under her head. "Thanks for not making an inane comment about my wonky womb."

He knew she was trying to sound brave, but she just sounded defeated. Judah lifted his hands and spread them apart. "Honestly, Darby, I have no idea what you are feeling. I am exactly the opposite. I really don't want kids and am very happy with the idea of being childless."

"Really?"

Judah nodded. "Yeah."

"Can you tell me why?"

They were wading into uncharted territory, into

deeper waters. This conversation would take them from colleagues who were sleeping together to…something deeper, undefinable. He didn't like deep or undefined, but she'd been honest with him and he needed to— wanted to—reciprocate.

Judah couldn't think of a decent reason not to tell her the truth. "My brother is twelve years younger than me and when he was born, I, somehow, ended up being his primary caregiver," Judah stated, his tone flat. "My father and stepmom's contribution to raising Jake was to make him and birth him. Up until I left for college, I all but raised him."

Darby shook her head, as if she didn't believe what he was saying. "You mean you looked after him after school, you helped him with his homework, that kind of stuff, right?"

This is why he never spoke about his childhood. People—Darby type of people—never wanted to believe what he was telling them. "No, I looked after him. He was born at the beginning of the summer holidays when I was twelve, and my stepmom had very bad postpartum depression. She literally could not take care of him and my dad had to work. When I had to go back to school, she roused herself enough to look after him until I got home but then I was on duty while she slept or went out. Somehow, God knows how, the responsibility of raising Jake was passed on to me."

"Oh, God, Judah, that's horrible."

He shrugged and noticed the empathy in her eyes. Thank God there was no pity. Pity made his skin crawl. "I didn't have time to do sports or date or do anything at all. My job was to take care of my brother. When my father started making noises about me attending a local college, I knew I had to do something to escape so I studied and got a full-ride scholarship. I abandoned Jake to save myself."

God, he hadn't meant to say that last part. There was something about Darby that made him want to open up, and that scared the crap out of him.

Darby linked her hands around her knees, her eyes focused on his face. "And the guilt nearly killed you."

Judah lifted one shoulder in acknowledgment of her statement. "I tried to come home as often as I could but every time I came home, I felt Jake slipping further and further away from me. He was so mad at me for leaving so he did whatever he could to piss me off. Joyriding, boosting cars, alcohol, weed, stronger drugs."

"You had a right to live your life, Judah, to have a life."

He knew that, he *did*. Intellectually. "Jake's never stopped being pissed at me."

"And that's why he had an affair with your girlfriend."

Judah winced. "Yep. I loaned her my apartment in Manhattan. She had a gig at The Met and I was in Australia on a project. Jake, somehow, hooked up with her and moved in. I caught them in bed together and gave them the rest of the day to clear out. Jake took my meaning literally, he stripped my apartment. Anything that he could sell for drugs, he did."

Darby lifted her fist to her mouth, seeming shocked and pissed on his behalf. "I hope you had him arrested."

She got it, thank God. Choices and consequences... "My father insisted I drop the charges or I'd be kicked out of the family."

"You chose the latter," Darby said, her voice holding no trace of judgment.

"He served a year. I'm blamed for his criminal record. My family and I have no contact."

Darby shook her head in disbelief. "After all you did for Jake? Unbelievable."

After so long, it felt both strange and wonderful to have someone get it, to have someone smart and together and thoughtful be on his side, agreeing with his choices. The hand squeezing his lungs eased and the guilt, for the first time in years, retreated. Judah felt like he could breathe. "So that's why I don't want kids. I've been a dad, it wasn't that great."

Darby touched his hand with the tips of her fingertips. "And you've never had second thoughts?"

Judah shook his head. "No, in fact, I even came really close to having a vasectomy about a decade ago."

Darby's smile was both humorous and self-deprecating. At his lifted eyebrow, she shrugged. "I was just thinking that we are a badly matched pair. You don't want kids, I do. Thank God there's nothing more between us than great sex. We'd be disastrous together."

Apart from them disagreeing about what they wanted from life—that little thing!—they were damn good together. Sexually and mentally compatible, equally strong, equally independent. She was the only woman he'd ever encountered whom he could see in his life five or ten years down the track. That had never happened before, and he wasn't sure how to deal with her, what to think.

Judah noticed her heavy eyes, so he leaned forward and placed his lips to her forehead, keeping them there for longer than he intended. "Sleep, sweetheart. I'll be here when you wake up."

* * *

Mason rolled off Callie and stalked naked to her en suite bathroom. After cleaning up, he gripped the edges of one of the freestanding basins and stared at his reflection in the mirror above his head. He looked the same, he noted. Blue eyes, a three-day beard. Same mouth, nose, body...

So then why did he feel like he was a stranger inside his skin?

Flipping on the tap, he bent down to drink water from his hand before splashing it on his face. Four months ago, five, he was living a perfectly normal life as a single father, having discreet affairs when time and circumstances allowed. He'd been reasonably content running his coffee shop, running herd on his boys. Coasting.

Then Hurricane Callie blew into his life.

He'd thought it so damn simple: he liked her, they'd have sex, they'd keep having sex for as long as it was fun. Then they'd drift apart, no harm, no foul.

But here he was, two and a half months into the year, and he was floundering. His business was successful, but it was boring; his kids were growing more independent by the day, and living in this community was like living in a goldfish bowl. Mason was so damn jealous of Callie's trip to Thailand, of her freedom to pick up and go.

Actually, every time he thought about Thailand his brain wanted to explode.

"Let's talk, Mace."

Mason turned to see Callie standing in the doorway, her lush body covered with a white robe, holding two glasses of red wine. Walking over to her massive square cedar-clad bathtub, she sat down on the edge and crossed her legs.

She nodded to a towel and Mason grabbed it, wrapping it around his hips before taking a glass from her. He gulped and leaned his shoulder into the wall.

"It's not the same, is it?" Callie asked, her eyes wide and blue.

He wanted to lie, but he didn't. "No." But that didn't mean it was bad, just different.

"Is it because I've come out of my shell…sexually?"

Mason nearly choked on his wine. "God, no." Her sexual confidence was amazing and such a turn-on. The sex was the only thing going right at the moment.

"Then what's the problem, Mace?"

How to put this into words? He was a numbers guy; they made sense. His annoying, undefinable feelings were harder to explain.

He raked his hand through his hair. "I can't put my finger on it, but I feel like I am looking at a math problem and I know the formula is wrong, but I don't know why."

Callie nodded. "With me or with your life?"

Mason shrugged. Feeling like he was frying in the spotlight, he decided to swing it onto her. "You're different, too, Callie."

Callie tipped her head and waited for him to continue.

"You're calmer, more centered. Less nervous, more confident."

"And that's a problem?"

No…but it was different.

"Are you tired of the chase, Mason?" Callie asked in a bland tone.

Her eyes were shadowed, and he couldn't read how she was feeling, couldn't discern what she was thinking. Before the New Year, before her Southeast Asia travels, he'd been able to read her. Now she seemed like a closed book.

Then her words sank in and he felt impossibly, undeniably angry. "*What* did you ask me?"

Callie swirled her wine in her glass and refused to meet his eyes. "Months ago, I was lost, quite naive, lacking in confidence sexually. Then I ran into you, all big and bold, demanding that I face life again, that I enjoy you and sex and kissing and touching. I listened, and I took a chance on you." Callie raised her eyes to him and grimaced. "We had a marvelous week between Christmas and New Year's. The night of the party, I stepped back from you, just for a moment, and you used my actions as an excuse to run."

Her words lodged in his skin and exploded as little bubbles of truth. Not able to deal with how much he enjoyed being with her, how wonderful he'd felt having her in his life, he'd used Ray as an excuse.

Mason's feelings for her scared him and he'd run. *Ouch.*

But because he was in the wrong, he did what guys do and went on the attack. "I didn't run as far as you."

"Fair point. But I took my ring off, put Ray's photo away and, crucially, I came back. We've been together twice since the coffee shop encounter, we have had what I thought was miraculous sex but...but I feel like something is off. The only conclusion I can come to is you are tired of the chase."

He couldn't let her think that. "It's not that, Cal. I'm not tired of you."

"Well, I'm not going to sit here and play guessing games with you, Mace." Callie stood up and folded her arms across her chest, her wineglass resting against her upper arm. "I'm going to be the adult and tell you what I am feeling, dealing with. I'm not ready to slide into retirement, to live the rest of my life as a wealthy widow. I want to do something, Mason, be someone. I've always been Ray's wife or the kids' mom, supporting their dreams, their goals, their interests. I want to *contribute*."

He loved her fire, her determination to keep growing as a person and carve out her place in the sun.

Oh, God, he thought he might love her.

"I've been looking into some projects I can contribute to, but you should know that I'm not going to be living here on an ongoing basis. I loved traveling, Mason, I want to do more of it. I loved Bali and Thailand and there are so many more places I want to see, experience." Callie pulled in a deep breath and tried to smile. "I'm crazy about you, Mace, but if I stay here, content to coast, to wait for visits from you, I'll find myself drifting again and then I'll be lost. I don't want to be lost again."

Mason, touched beyond belief, had no words. He feared losing her, but he was even more terrified of asking her to stay, asking her to sacrifice herself to be with him. He valued freedom—his own and others'—too much do that to someone he adored.

Instead of talking, he pulled her into his arms and tucked her head under his chin. He understood her need to fly, he just needed to find a way to hand her a set of wings.

Or to find a set of his own.

Darby walked into the games room at the Brogan house and quickly scanned the area.

Judah, Noah, Matt and Levi were playing a game of pool on the table first bought by a Brogan ancestor at the turn of the century. A barrage of insults flew across the green fabric and Darby winced; four alpha men, it was bound to get competitive. Good thing she wasn't playing.

She walked over to the table and saw that Judah had a difficult shot to make.

"You're a decent player, Judah. You should play Darby sometime. She likes to play, and we don't like playing with her."

Judah fell into Noah's trap. "She's that bad, huh?" he said, looking up from his bent position over the table.

Darby forced a scowl onto her face. "Hey! I'm not *that* bad."

"We hate playing you, Darby," Matt said, whistling as Judah made the trick shot.

Huh, Judah might be worth her time. She could challenge him to a game of strip pool. It would be fun to see how quickly she got him of his clothes.

Judah walked around the table, patted her butt and dropped a sexy "yes" in her ear.

Darby rolled her eyes. "Yes to what?"

"Yes, to whatever you're cooking up regarding you and me and pool," Judah whispered, pulling her hair away from her neck to place his lips beneath her ear. Unconcerned by their amused audience, he pressed his big body against her back, his hand on her stomach, and he felt so warm, smelled so amazing. And that mouth on her sensitive skin…dynamite.

"And why," Judah growled, his voice back to its normal level, "do I have this sneaky suspicion these guys are trying to hustle me? I think you might be good at pool. Good as in exceptional."

Darby tried to keep her face innocent as she turned around. "Why would you think that?"

Darby melted under his sexy grin, aware that the game was over and that her friends had moved on to discussing a new yacht Matt was designing. "Their very careful choice of words. They do hate playing with you because you are good. That's not a surprise because there isn't a damn thing you aren't good at and you're competitive. And I'm not an idiot."

Dammit. Judah had a hell of brain to go with that gorgeous face and brawny body.

"And yes, strip pool would be fun," he quietly added.

Darby threw up her hands, laughed at his smirking expression and turned her back on their game. Needing to get some distance before she embarrassed herself by throwing her arms around Judah and kissing him comatose, Darby walked over to the fireplace. DJ and Jules sat on the squishy couch and Callie sat opposite them, totally absorbed by the baby sitting in her lap.

Mason wasn't here at this family dinner and that was a surprise.

DJ looked up and smiled. "Oh, Lordy, Darby, you have to hear the latest nonsense Mrs. Jenkins has come up with. I swear the old lady is losing her mind."

Mrs. Jenkins had been ancient when they were kids. For as long as they could remember, in rain or snow or hailstorms, every afternoon she hopped on her motorized scooter and did a tour of the grounds. She was the community's primary source of news and gossip.

"She said she saw a half-naked woman in the window of Mason's coffee shop last Wednesday. She was plastered up against the glass door and a man was kissing her."

Yeah, the sweet old thing was losing it. Mason would never let something like that happen at his place. Darby thought back. "Last Wednesday was the height of the blizzard, no one was out."

"I think she's getting a little more senile," Callie said, her hands over her face as she played peekaboo with Jac, who thought it was a brilliant game.

"Has Mason said anything about the rumor, Mom?" Jules asked.

"Mason doesn't listen to rumors. But I'm sure he'll find the story amusing," Callie said. Holding on to Jac, she stood up, her cheeks tinged with pink. "Uh, it's getting a bit hot this close to the fire."

Darby, who was standing closer, hadn't noticed the heat. "I think it's you, Mom."

Callie flushed a deeper red. "Me? What's me?"

Why was her mom acting so weird? "Are you getting sick? Do you have a temperature? There's a lot of flu going around."

Callie nodded. "I'm fine, don't fuss. Come on, Jac, let's go change you."

Darby looked at Callie's departing back. She'd changed Jac not a half hour ago but...okay. Since returning from Bali, her mom had been acting a little weird.

Turning back to her twin and best friend, Darby remembered something she'd been wanting to ask. "Listen, have either of you two borrowed my thigh-high black boots, the sexy ones I bought for that Halloween party? I can't find them anywhere."

Jules and DJ said they didn't think so, but they would check—their closets were a mess of borrowed items—and the conversation moved on. Darby, curled up in the opposite sofa, tuned out and just watched her family.

In all her dreams growing up, this is what she'd imagined. Her sisters, one by blood, the other by heart, were happy and in love with good men, her mom was seeing a man who wasn't her dad and she was okay with that. And there was a man across the room who made her feel amazing every single day. Jac was as sweet as sugar and wonderfully easy to look after.

Her business was going well. She was a professional success and she should be happy.

Except that she wasn't. It was all a lie, a sham, an illusion. Oh, not her sisters, they were, as far as she knew, as happy as they looked, and her mom seemed reasonably content, but as for the rest? The baby, the man?

Darby and Judah weren't what they looked like.

Darby closed her eyes against the familiar wave of pain and embraced it, allowing the barbs and the spurs to pick at her skin. She welcomed the way it scratched and burned because pain was better than fooling herself, imagining there was a chance this was what the rest of her life would look like. There was no possible way it could.

No matter how she looked at it, a happy-ever-after was not possible for her and Judah.

Their relationship was tied into this short-term project and into looking after Jac. The little pretend family they'd so swiftly become had an imminent expiration date. The news from Italy was good, Carla was recovering nicely and was interviewing nannies. They were expecting the call that would whip Jac out of their lives.

Darby, as the local liaison for Huntley and Associates, had everything for the museum project under control, and she knew Judah had a bid on a project in Kuala Lumpur and he'd been approached to design an eco-friendly lodge in Costa Rica.

He'd hand Jac back to Carla, kiss the baby goodbye and move on with his life. And Darby should look to move on with hers. She had to make a definite decision about whether to try IVF.

No matter what happened in the future, she was glad she'd had this time with Jac; it had given her a realistic idea of what caring for a baby day in and day out meant. She had a better idea of the work involved, how much energy it took. If she had to do it on her own, she could but...

But it would be so much easier with a partner, with Judah.

But Judah didn't want kids.

Ever.

And she'd, foolishly, fallen in love with him. Dammit. Her heart was convinced he was her forever man, but her brain couldn't fathom how she could love someone who didn't want what she wanted. How could he be so fabulous with Jac—patient, kind, calm—but not want to experience having a child himself? How had that happened? Why had it happened? How could life be this cruel?

Darby rested her head against the cool column, reluctantly respecting his decision not to procreate but also not understanding it. Judah was warm, funny, loving... In her opinion, he should have kids. He needed a partner, a home, children.

Over the past week they'd discussed her desire to have a child, his desire to remain childless, and she knew there was no hope of a future with him that looked anything like the future she wanted, of a house filled with noisy boys and feisty girls.

Even if she and Judah agreed to keep seeing each

other after Jac left—the distance between Boston and New York wasn't that far—Darby knew nothing would come out of it but some sexy times. Judah would never love her like Noah loved Jules, like Matt loved DJ.

Darby was competitive, she admitted it, and knowing that her lover didn't love her the same way her sister's and friend's men loved them—with everything they had—would kill her. It would be a slap in the face at every family gathering. She'd be reminded that Judah might love her body, appreciate her skill as an architect, but he still chose to stand apart from her and from everything that a family meant.

It would be better, cleaner, if they all moved on now. Jac needed to go back to Carla, Darby needed to try IVF, Judah needed to do whatever Judah wanted to do.

Darby bit her bottom lip, her eyes on Judah. He wore chinos and a loose white button-down shirt with the sleeves rolled up. He hadn't shaved for a couple of days and his stubble gave him a rakish air. He looked hot and amazing. Her life and her bed were going to be lonely, lonely places without him in it.

As if he felt her eyes on him, Judah snapped his head up and looked for her. Finally finding her, he frowned. Heading toward her, he laid his arms on the back of the sofa and touched his knuckle to her cheekbone.

"Hey, you okay?"

Darby forced a smile onto her face. "Sure. I was just about to go and find Jac. Callie took her, saying she needed to be changed."

At that moment, Callie appeared in the doorway to the living room, Jac in her arms. "Supper is almost ready. Can I have some help in the kitchen?"

Judah's hand on Darby's shoulder kept her in place while the others obeyed Callie's cheerful request. When they were gone, Judah rested his hip on the back of the sofa. He placed his big hand on her bent knee. "What's going on, Darby? You look a little lost."

Whether it was to her work or to her body, Judah paid attention. "I just wanted a minute to think."

"I expected you to be at the pool table, telling Noah and Levi how to sink their shots," Judah teased.

"I'm not that bad."

Darby met his eyes and saw the speculation in them, knew she wasn't hitting the light tone she was aiming for. Trying to distract him, she reached for the bottle of beer in his hand. She took a long sip and rested the bottle against her cheek. "I have a slight headache."

"When are you going to realize you can't lie to me, Brogan? Something else is going on inside that big brain of yours."

"I'm fine, Judah."

"No, you're not. I've been watching you for a while and you're anything but fine," Judah persisted. He squeezed her knee. "Talk to me, Darby."

She couldn't. She couldn't tell him that she loved him, that she wanted the dream, the full house, the family dinners with kids they'd raised together.

Feeling like her skin was too tight for her body, Darby stood up. "Have you spoken to Carla lately?"

"Yeah."

"Any word on when Jac is going back?"

Judah's mouth compressed to a thin line. "Soon. Within the next few days."

Darby nodded, telling herself she would not cry. "I'm going to miss her."

"I know." Judah raked his hair back, his eyes miserable. "If I had known you wanted children so badly, I would never have asked you to look after her."

"You didn't ask, you offered me a deal. I took it."

"Still, it wasn't fair to you."

He made it sound like he'd forced her into looking after Jac. That simply wouldn't do. "I'm an adult, Judah, I make my own decisions. Looking after Jac has been fun but…" She hesitated.

"But?" Judah pressed.

Darby gathered the scattered bits of her courage. "But I'm sort of glad she's going soon. I'm getting attached and the longer she stays, the harder it's going to be to say goodbye," Darby said, keeping her voice low.

Judah didn't say anything for a long, long time. "That bad, huh?"

Yeah, it was that bad.

But she didn't want only the little girl, she wanted the man and her dream and the house and… No, enough. She had to stop thinking about what she didn't have and look forward to what she could have. Being a single mom, raising a child on her own.

She tasted panic, fought to find air. She could do it; she *would* do it.

And really, she had to let Judah go, to do his own thing. She refused to live her life hoping he'd change, that he'd come to love her enough to give her something she wanted but he didn't. Sleeping with him, staying with him, playing happy families with him was too difficult; she couldn't do it for much longer.

She loved him and every time she made love with him, she fell a little harder, a little deeper. Every time they argued about architecture, discussed books, art, sports, politics, she found herself rolling around in his mind, enjoying his sharp intellect and his dry humor.

She loved him and loving him was starting to feel a little like torture.

"What do you want, Darby?" Judah quietly asked, his expression as serious as she'd ever seen it.

He'd said that nobody could become attached in two weeks, but he'd been so wrong.

"Unfortunately, I want everything, Judah. I want it all."

Nine

Having abandoned DJ's apartment to move in to the big house the day after he and Darby first made love, Judah opened the back door to the mudroom, kicked off his boots and shrugged out of his coat. Outside, the wind was picking up and the clouds were low in the sky. The weather reporters were talking about another massive nor'easter hitting Boston sometime during the night and they would wake up to many inches of snow.

The house was quiet, and Judah frowned. For the past fifteen years, he'd treasured quiet but now it seemed oppressive, almost strange. After just two weeks, he was used to music, Jac's squeals, Darby singing off-key, a radio or television playing in the background.

The sounds of home.

Wondering where his girls were, Judah pulled out his phone to call Darby, but before he could pull up her number, his phone rang. He stared at the phone like it was an annoyed snake ready to strike, knowing the call would flip his life back to normal.

He didn't want his life to go back to how it had been. He loved his life with Darby, with Jac.

He shouldn't. But he did.

The call died, but two seconds later, the same number popped up on his screen. He couldn't avoid her. He had to have this conversation.

"Carla."

"Hello, Judah." Carla's voice sounded thin and thready. Nothing like the sultry tones he remembered so well. "How's my girl? How is Jacquetta?"

Happy. Content. Full of smiles. Judah swallowed those words and opted for a simple reply. "She's fine. Are you out of the hospital?"

"I am back at my home in Como. With a full-time nurse. Luca has hired a nanny for Jac, an American who has a degree in early childhood development."

Jac didn't need a teacher, she needed a mom.

"I need peace and quiet to recover, to build my strength. The nanny and Jac will live in the cottage until I am recovered enough to have them in the house."

Jac wasn't the noisy equivalent of a construction site. Carla had undergone an appendectomy, not a heart transplant. *God.*

"She's not an untrained puppy, Carla, she's your daughter!" Judah said. He ground his teeth together so hard he was sure he felt enamel pepper his tongue.

"Nevertheless, it's imperative that I focus on myself, in doing whatever I can to recover quickly. I will send the nanny to come and get Jacquetta. She will be there on Friday. Please have her packed and ready to go."

Over my cold, dead body.

Judah gripped the bridge of his nose so hard that a sharp pain ricocheted into his sinuses. "I am not handing Jac over to some stranger."

Carla waited a beat before speaking again. "Then the only other alternative is for you to bring her to me."

"If that's what I have to do," Judah ground out.

Carla's husky voice drifted into his ear. "Don't worry so much, Judah. The nanny is good, and I will try to be a better mother to Jacquetta."

If wishes were horses and all that crap. And her name was Jac...

"I want normality, Judah, a simple life. A man, my baby, sun on my face, fresh air and good food. Just a simple life."

Carla wouldn't know simple if it bit her on the butt. Judah raised his eyes to the ceiling and pushed his shoulder into the wall. As soon as she was better, this conversation would be forgotten, and she'd be fighting her way back into the limelight. She was the moth that needed the flame of attention and she'd burn herself, and everyone around her, before she stepped out of the fire.

Poor Jac.

Thinking about Jac constantly looking for Carla's attention lit the detonation cord attached to his explosive temper. "Try to remember that Jac is not a damned book you can loan out, have returned and loan out again, Carla. She's a little girl and she needs stability. Can you give her that?"

"Stability is overrated. I never had any as a child but I'm okay."

Okay was a nebulous term. Her okay was his very messed up.

"Bring Jacquetta home, Judah. You'll never have to be bothered with her again."

Judah heard the phone disconnect and shook his head, lifting the phone to bang it against his forehead.

Jesus, how was he going to tell Darby that Jac was leaving? How was he going to find the strength to take her back? But he had to...

Jacquetta wasn't Darby's and she sure wasn't his. He didn't want kids, remember?

He needed to go back to his old life, back to freedom, to long nights working at his desk, early morning walks through whatever city he happened to be in, or sleeping the morning away, waking up and finding a small local restaurant for a late lunch. Working through the next night...

No one to report to, no one to worry about, no one to worry about him.

So, if that was what he wanted, why did he feel hollow inside?

Annoyed with himself, Judah walked into the kitchen, tossed his phone onto the marble-topped island and padded into the hall. At the bottom of the stairs, he finally heard girly laughter. He was too far away to hear individual words, but he allowed the soft feminine sounds to wash over him. As he climbed the stairs, the words became more distinct and Darby's off-tune voice became stronger.

Judah walked down the long hallway of the first floor and wondered how he could go back to silence. How was he supposed to embrace freedom when freedom didn't include Darby's singing and Jac's bold smile and naughty laughter?

Judah pushed open the door to Darby's bedroom,

sighed at the mess—an unmade bed, a lilac bra on the floor, a trail of her clothes leading to the bathroom. Judah nudged open the door to the bathroom with his shoe and looked toward the massive claw-foot bathtub in the corner.

Woman and baby were a study in contrasts, light and dark, equally compelling, stunningly beautiful. The bath was filled to the brim with both water and bubbles and Darby leaned back, knees poking out. Jac was sitting on her stomach, scooping bubbles out of the water and trying to eat them.

Darby's eyes were on the little girl, and through her smiles, he saw, possibly for the first time, her need to have her own child, the depth of her longing.

Yeah, he knew she feared the responsibility, that she was questioning whether she was on the right path, but he saw her desire to be a mommy, how much she wanted to be the center of a child's universe. He'd understood, on an intellectual basis, why she'd had her eggs harvested, but only in this minute did he understand her soul-deep need for someone to call her Mom.

It utterly terrified him.

Yet, he wanted to give her a child, his child.

Not because he wanted to be a dad or because children were what he wanted, but because, for the first time in a long time, he valued someone else's happiness above his own. Darby wanted children, her *own* children, and he would do anything in his power to give them to her.

The thought made beads of sweat break out on his forehead. Making a baby, making babies, with Darby was a hell of a big deal. It would be the biggest project of his life.

Judah wiped the moisture from his forehead, wishing he could fully embrace the life she craved, but he couldn't imagine being fully responsible for another human or being invested in their welfare. He'd done that with Jake and looked how it had ended: Jake was a drug-addicted ex-con and Judah had no idea where his brother even was.

How he wished Darby didn't have this need to procreate, that they could be a family of two. She was a talented architect, they worked well together, and he could see them traveling the world, designing buildings in foreign and exciting places. For the first time in his life, he could imagine settling down. He could imagine them buying a plot of land—maybe here in this community—and designing their perfect house. Jules would decorate it and they'd spend some of their time in Boston, the rest somewhere else, anywhere else.

They could be free, unencumbered.

But Darby wanted a baby and he wanted to be the guy who gave it to her.

But he knew if he did that, she would also insist he be a dad, be *the* dad. She wouldn't allow him to half-ass anything. He would have to step up to the plate.

Could he do that, be that person, for her? To make her happy?

Hell, he would do anything to make her happy… He was in love with her…maybe.

God, he didn't know what love felt like, but he thought about her all the time. He couldn't get enough of her luscious body. Making her smile and laugh was his priority. He enjoyed talking to her. She was the only person who knew about his past and the impact it had on him. Over the course of two weeks, he'd found his best friend and his lover, had met the one person who was able to crack open his withered soul, climb inside and warm it up.

He didn't want kids, but he'd have them.

For her.

With her.

Jac's delighted squeal refocused his attention on the very pretty scene in the bathtub. Jac waved her hands in welcome and Darby tipped her head back to look at him, a sexy smile on her face.

"Hey." She sat up, half turned and smiled slowly. "You look cold. And miserable."

She had no idea. He needed to tell her that Jac was leaving, that he had to take her back. When Darby reconciled herself to Jac leaving, he'd tell her that he wanted to keep seeing her, that he was prepared to father her child, her children. That he'd do this, for her.

Darby frowned, looking to the window, and Judah followed her gaze. Snow was starting to fall and if he didn't have the weight of his news on his shoulders, it would be a lovely scene. A naked Darby, snow, a big bath...

Judah glanced at his watch and realized it was Jac's bedtime. Maybe he could put off the news until tomorrow. They could heat up the water in that bath and he could draw pictures on Darby's skin with bubbles.

Darby snapped her fingers, pulling his gaze from her lovely breasts to her even lovelier face. "What's going on, Judah?"

Judah walked over to the heated towel rack, pulled off a warm fluffy towel and reached for Jac. After nuzzling her cheek, inhaling her precious baby smell, he wrapped her in the towel and cradled her against his chest.

He looked down at Darby and smiled. "I'll dress her and put her to bed."

A small frown pulled Darby's eyebrows together. "I left her bottle in a warmer on my bedside table. She should go down fast, she's exhausted."

Judah didn't reply, he just bent down to place his lips against Darby's. Through his touch, he tried to warn her, to comfort her, to reassure her that they would be okay, that he had a plan. He felt her hesitancy, her fear, and sighed against her lips.

He'd do anything not to hurt her. He'd do anything at all.

But, as much as he wanted to, he couldn't give her Jac.

Judah half closed the door of Jules's old room, allowing the light from the hallway to spill into the space where Jac was sleeping. Opening the door to Darby's bedroom, the place where they'd loved and laughed, he sat on the edge of her bed and waited for her to come out of the bathroom.

This wasn't a conversation he could have when she was naked.

Resting his forearms on his thighs, he stared down at the hardwood floor beneath his feet, conscious of a pounding headache behind his eyes. Emotional connections—this was why he'd avoided them.

"She's going back, isn't she?"

Judah looked up. Darby stood in the doorway, his sweatshirt hanging down to her thighs, her hair in a messy knot on top of her head. He immediately noticed the haunted look in her eyes, the wobbly lower lip.

He nodded. "Yeah."

Darby's arms wrapped around herself and her face paled. "When?"

"As soon as possible. I'll charter a jet in the morning

and we'll leave as soon as we can." Judah flexed his fist. Apart from walking away from Jake, this was going to be the hardest thing he'd ever done.

Why had he agreed to look after her, why hadn't he insisted that Luca make another plan? Oh, because she was Judah's niece, her father was a drug-addicted loser and there had been no one else. Darby had warned him, but he hadn't thought he could become this attached, this soon. Sending Jac back was turning out to be insanely horrible for him and he knew Darby was as deeply affected.

Had he known how much she wanted children, he would never have asked her to become involved in Jac's life. But by the time he found out, he couldn't let Darby go.

He would never be able to let her go.

Judah stood up, walked over to her and skimmed his knuckle over her still-damp cheek. From her bath or from tears? He couldn't tell.

"Are you okay?"

Darby lifted one shoulder. "It's not as if we didn't know this was going to happen."

That wasn't an answer. "Carla's her mother, Darby, we can't keep her."

Darby sent him a sharp look. "I know that, Judah. I never expected to keep her, I'm not that much of a delusional idiot."

She's hurt, she's upset, be gentle. "I don't think you're an idiot. I just know you've bonded with Jac and it has to hurt to let her go." He kept his voice low and even. This situation was tough enough. He didn't want to argue.

Darby pushed past him and walked around the bed to stand at her window, moving aside the drapes to look at the swiftly falling snow. "You are acting like this is all about me, like I'm the only one who'll be affected by her leaving. You're going to miss her, too, Judah."

Sure. But there was no point in dwelling on that.

Darby whirled around, her eyes enormous in her colorless face. "I know you watch her when she sleeps, Judah. I see how affectionate you are with her, the love you have for her."

Judah rubbed the back of his neck. "She's a cute kid and she is my niece, Darby."

"She's more than that and you know it! Why won't you fight for her?" Darby demanded. "She has a useless mother, who is going to hand her off to a nanny as soon as you land. She'll have everything she'll ever want but she won't have one damn thing she needs! She won't have a parent to raise her, to teach her, to guide her."

"So, you think I should just demand that Carla hand over custody to me?" Judah raised his voice. Was she nuts? That wasn't how this worked.

"Yes," Darby said, her voice fierce. "That's exactly what I think you should do!"

Okay, she was upset, he'd known she would be. He gestured to the door. "Let's go downstairs, light a fire, order pizza, have a glass of wine."

"You want to eat?" Darby asked, incredulous.

Well, yeah. It had been a long, tough day. "Come downstairs, Darby."

Darby turned back to the window. "I need some time alone, Judah."

Judah walked over to her and wrapped his arm around her waist, pulling her into him. "I know this hurts, Darby. I know you love her. But this is the way it must be. We always knew this was going to happen."

"And us? Is this the end of us, too?"

"I don't want it to be," Judah admitted. "We're good together, Darby. We enjoy each other's company, we have great sex, this...works."

It worked? God, what was the point of his very expensive education if he couldn't get the words out? It wasn't difficult: *I want you in my life. I need you. I love you.*

They were just words, but the emotions behind them felt as big as a Montana sky, as deep as a Norwegian fjord.

What if she said no? What if she wasn't feeling the same way? She loved Jac, he knew that, but did she love him? He didn't know, couldn't guess.

So he picked his way through this minefield of a conversation, wary to advance until he was sure of his position.

"We're going to miss Jac, but in a week or two, when we start adjusting to life without her—" the pain would recede, they'd be okay "—we can start anew. One of my oldest clients has bought a plot of land in Arizona, deep in the heart of the desert, and he wants me to design a house that complements its surroundings. I'd like you to come with me."

If nothing else, working, being creative, might distract them from the brown-eyed, rosy-cheeked smiler who would no longer be part of their lives.

"I have a business here, Judah. I can't just leave on a whim."

It would be a business trip, for both of them. He valued her opinion as a professional, he'd pay her as he would pay any other consultant. But now wasn't the time to go into that, he'd broach the subject again when they weren't feeling so raw.

"Let's go downstairs, Darby. Curl up by the fire,

have some wine." And hopefully, that pizza. His stomach didn't care that his heart was bleeding and his brain felt like it was about to explode.

Darby shook her head, lifting her hand to place it on the cold windowpane. Judah could feel her slipping further and further away from him, retreating behind that shield she erected to protect herself. He tightened his arms around her, trying to keep her anchored to him.

He wished she'd cry, scream, fight… She felt like a particularly brittle pane of glass in his arms.

"Darby, stay with me," he implored.

She didn't reply, and he buried his face in her neck, inhaling her scent. He hated to see her this hurt, couldn't bear to watch this brave, strong independent woman's heart breaking before his eyes. He'd do anything for her…

Even this.

"Darby, you can't have Jac, but if you want a baby, I'll give you one."

Shock rippled through her, a mini-earthquake. Her laugh, when it came, was forced and her words laced with disbelief. "Sorry. I thought you said that you'd give me a baby."

"I will." He turned her around, cupped her face in his hands and bent his knees so he could look directly into her eyes. "Instead of choosing a sperm donor, take me. Let's make a baby, together."

Darby bit the inside of her lip, her eyes troubled. "Why?"

Judah placed a kiss on her forehead, then dropped his lips to her mouth. So sweet, so sexy. His.

He pulled back, resting his forehead against hers. "Because you want one, sweetheart. If you wanted the moon, I'd try to get it for you."

* * *

It was such a huge offer, unbelievably generous and gut-wrenchingly sincere.

On top of hearing that Jac was leaving, this was too much. Darby felt too exposed, like she was a piece of faulty wiring, sparking intermittently. She wanted to say yes, she wanted to scream no, she wanted to run, to hide, to roll her life back six weeks to when she was just faced with the reasonably easy choice of becoming a single mother or not.

Judah, Jac—they'd complicated her life beyond measure. Saying no was impossible, saying yes was too easy. He'd offered her everything she wanted but nothing she needed.

She was beyond confused and maybe it was better that words had deserted her. She had no idea what to say, how to act.

So Darby did the only thing that came naturally, took the only action she could. Lifting herself to her toes, she touched her mouth against his, gently skimming her lips across his, imprinting the feel of his mouth on her brain. Hooking her arm around his neck, she plastered her body to his, sighing when his hand skimmed up and under her sweatshirt and finding the bare skin of her hip, banding his arm under her butt cheeks to jerk her into his body. She was off her feet now, her breasts pushed into his chest as his tongue slid into her mouth, setting her world ablaze.

This. This was what she understood. Judah touching her, loving her. This made sense.

This she could do.

Darby wrapped her legs around his waist, trusting him to hold her while she pulled the sweatshirt up and over her head, so that she was fully naked in his arms. Dropping the garment to the floor, she looked into his eyes, watching as the color went from dark blue to a shade of black. It was the color of midnight seas and dark nights full of sin and sex.

Their gazes clashed and held and beneath the lust and the desire, she saw a deeper emotion, something that scared her, beckoning her to surrender, to fall under his spell. Tempted but terrified, Darby dropped her gaze to his sexy mouth and touched her lips to the shallow dimple at the side of his cheek, feeling his stubble on her tender skin. He smelled like snow and cologne, temptation and terror. She could give this man her heart, hand it over, it would be so easy to do...

Take it, take me. Love me as I love you.

The words hovered on her tongue but she swallowed them down, knowing that once they were out they couldn't be retrieved. No, she would speak with her mouth and hands, with her aching-for-his-touch body.

This she could have; this she could do.

Darby dropped her feet to the floor and stepped back, filling her fists with black cashmere and the fine white cotton of his collared shirt. She pulled the garments up his chest and Judah helped her by reaching back with one hand and tugging the shirt and sweater over his head in one fluid move.

Darby immediately put her hands on his chest, feelings his flat nipples under her palms. "You are so hot, Judah. I want you so much."

Judah sucked in a breath, standing stock-still as she trailed her fingers over his ribs, across his ridged stomach, ruffling the hair of his happy trail. Darby looked down and saw that his erection was tenting his pants, straining the fabric.

As if reading her mind, Judah lifted his hands to his belt buckle, but Darby shook her head, needing to do this, to love him right. Pushing his hands away, she put her fingers between the smooth skin of his abdomen and the band of his black pants, small, slight touches that brushed the tip of his cock, causing his breath to turn choppy.

She ignored, as best she could, his hand running down her hip and thigh, scooting closer and closer to her happy place. When his hand brushed her strip of hair, she pushed it away, not wanting to get distracted, to lose herself to pleasure.

Judah clenched his hands into fists but kept them at his sides, seeming to sense that this was the one area where she knew the right moves to make. She was angry and sad about Jac leaving, blown away by his offer to father her children, confused by what it all meant—but loving Judah, touching him, this she knew how to do.

Darby flicked open the snap on his pants, pushed her hands inside and pulled the fabric over his butt, down his hips. She looked down and there he was, straining upward, desperate for her touch.

Judah toed off his shoes and socks, kicked the garments away and just stood there, his eyes narrowed, his mouth taut.

Darby ran the tip of her finger down his shaft. "You are so damned beautiful, Judah. Everywhere."

"Darby."

Her name was a small word but he saturated it with need. Darby felt the moisture pool between her legs, stunned that she could be this turned on by just looking at Judah, from the briefest of touches.

She wrapped her hand around him, her other hand cupping his balls. She lifted her face. "Kiss me."

Her demand was rough and insistent, and Judah didn't hesitate. His mouth plundered hers, seeking and demanding everything she had. This was unlike any kiss they'd shared before, there was no finesse, no sophistication, just raw need. It was out of control, wild, perfectly passionate, hot, hungry.

Darby felt Judah lift her and when he lowered her to the bed she knew she was no longer in control...but, then again, neither was he.

He left her mouth to pull her nipple between his lips and she whimpered, arching her back so he could take more of her, to increase the pressure. He pulled away to lavish attention on her other breast but before he could, she wiggled down so that her tongue swiped across his nipple, a small smile blooming when that tiny bead contracted. Moving down his body, she rubbed her nose over the ridges of his stomach, allowing her lips to make brief contact with his tip...

Darby squawked when Judah released a muted roar and then she was on her back, his knee pushing her legs apart, the head of his erection probing her entrance.

His hands flat on the bed on either side of her head, he held himself still, his eyes blazing when he looked down into her. "Darby! Do you want this?"

"Yes." She gasped, lifting her hips, so close and needing completion.

Judah balanced on one hand and his other gently cradled her jaw. "Open your eyes."

Darby forced her eyelids up, trying to widen her legs, to make him come inside.

Didn't he understand she needed him? *Now.*

Judah shook his head. "Sweetheart, I need to know if this is okay, me without a condom?"

God, she hadn't even noticed, and she didn't care. Condom, no condom, she just wanted to shatter, to not think, just feel.

"Yes, dammit. I need you, Judah." Darby heard the sob that followed her words, but she didn't care. She'd sob, beg, plead, cry…anything to have him completing her. Judah, in her, loving her, taking her up and up, was the only thing in her life that made sense, the only thing she could trust.

He wanted her, she wanted him. Pure, simple truth.

Judah surged inside her and her sobs turned to pants. Darby locked her legs around his hips, skin on skin, heat on heat, unaware that tears rolled down her cheeks. She'd never imagined that he'd feel so perfect, so right.

Judah rocked into her and lifted her higher, rocked again and boosted her up a level. She couldn't take much more. It was too much, the pleasure so intense. Then Judah rotated his hips, hit a spot and she hurtled into that bright light that was both fire and ice, blissful and shockingly intense. From what felt like a galaxy away, she heard Judah's hoarse cry, felt him come and she shattered again.

Perfection. Pleasure. Judah.

Darby wrapped her arms around his head and held on, tears rolling down her cheeks and onto his face as they tumbled back to earth.

And reality.

Ten

Judah sent an email confirming that he and Jac would meet the private jet he'd hired to fly Jac back to Italy later that afternoon.

He leaned back in his chair and glanced over to the playpen where Jac sat, babbling nonsense to the soft yellow duck she adored. He'd be packing the yellow duck and her favorite blanket, but he'd leave everything else he'd purchased for Jac here in Boston.

Carla, ridiculously wealthy, had everything she needed, and maybe, sometime in the future, he and Darby could use all the baby equipment. It was, after all, brand-new.

Judah glanced across the room to where Darby sat on the couch, pretzel-style, her laptop in her lap. He'd woken up in an empty bed and went hunting for her and Jac. He found them in the spare room, curled up on the window seat, Jac lying on Darby's chest, fast asleep.

Darby's eyes had been closed but he knew her too well to believe she was sleeping. But when she didn't open her eyes, he respected her silent appeal for some time alone with Jac, for some space.

Not wanting to push, they'd exchanged polite conversation throughout the morning. They'd addressed the subjects of work and the renovations on the buildings she wanted to sell, talking about the next steps needed regarding the art museum, that he was heading for New York after Italy to sign some contracts and to meet with a client.

On the surface, they were both acting like their world hadn't shifted, as if he hadn't offered to give her a child, both so very aware that she'd yet to give him an answer to his extraordinary proposal. He was savvy enough, mature enough to know that she'd ducked answering him by making love to him.

She'd handed over her body to him but not her biggest dream.

Knowing that Darby didn't like to be pushed, he'd given her most of the morning to broach the subject, but they were running out of time. Judah rubbed the back of his neck and steeled himself. This needed to be settled. It might as well be now.

"Darby, we need to talk."

Tension ran through her, as tangible as the snow still falling outside. "Can you manage on your own with her?" Darby asked, not looking up from her computer. "Should I come with you?"

He wanted to say yes, to give her more time with Jac, but he knew that would just delay the inevitable. Whether they said goodbye to Jac today or tomorrow morning in Como, it would still hurt the same.

"I'll be fine."

Darby jerked her head in acknowledgment but didn't meet his eyes.

Sighing, Judah pushed his chair back, walking around the desk to where she sat. When she didn't look up, he sat down on the sturdy coffee table and pulled her laptop out of her hands, firmly closing the lid. Darby scowled at him and folded her arms across her chest.

She brushed her hair off her forehead. "Don't forget to pack her duck and her pink blanket. What do you want me to do with the rest of her stuff? Have it shipped to Italy?" she asked, her voice brittle.

Judah leaned forward and allowed his hands to dangle between his thighs. "I'm hoping you'll keep it, that we'll eventually use it."

Darby stared at a point past his shoulder, pulling her bottom lip between her teeth, gray eyes darkening. She didn't speak, and Judah sighed.

"Are we seriously going to pretend that I didn't ask you to have my child?"

Darby's eyes flew back to his face and she shook her head. "You don't know what you are asking, Judah. It's not that simple."

"Okay, then explain it to me."

"IVF is an expensive process and the chances of it being successful the first time around are low. It's emotionally draining and mentally demanding. It's more than just offering me your sperm."

He wasn't an idiot, he understood that. Why did she make it sound like his boys were all that he was offering?

"Darby, I understand that. I didn't make the offer lightly. I want to do this for you."

Darby stared at him for a long time before shaking

her head and pointing her finger at him. "There, that's the problem in a nutshell."

Judah rubbed his forehead, confused. "I really don't understand. Explain, for the love of God."

Darby pulled her feet up onto the couch and wrapped her arms around her shins. She rested her chin on one knee, her eyes locked on his. "In a perfect world, would you be making this offer?"

He couldn't lie to her. "No. I'd be asking you to travel with me, to explore the world, help me design spectacular buildings. Having kids is not my first choice."

Darby shot Jac a glance. "Even after the fun we've had, knowing how wonderful she is, how can you not want to have kids?"

Because having Jac was a fairy tale. They were playing house. It was a novelty, a step out of time. "It's not always this good, Darby. I know how tough raising a child can be."

Darby vehemently shook her head. "You know how tough it can be raising a kid when you are barely more than a kid yourself. You're still looking at that time with Jake through the lens of an exploited teenager. You're an adult, Judah, and we'd do it together."

Her words rocked him, and he felt off-kilter.

She was wrong, she had to be.

"Darby, I did this for six years and it's not like this, not all the time." He ran agitated fingers across his forehead, tapped his foot. And why was she fighting him, he was offering what she most wanted! "But you're missing the point, I said that I *would* do it, I would go through that again because you want a child. When I get back from New York, we'll see your specialist together, work out what we need to do next."

"You're missing *my* point, Judah," Darby said, her voice infinitely sad. "I'd rather do this alone than have you becoming a father as a favor to me."

What?

No, wait, *what*?

Judah stared at her, unable to comprehend what she was telling him. Was that a no? Seriously? "I don't understand."

He loved her. Fully, completely, utterly. For as long as he lived, whatever he had was hers. He wanted to give her this thing she most wanted but she was saying no? If she didn't want to have a baby with him, how could he persuade her to accept his heart?

"You're just saying all this because you don't want to let me go."

Of course, he didn't want to let her slip away. What man in his right mind would?

Darby looked, if that was at all possible, paler than she did last night. "Do you know how tempting your offer is? You're smart and funny and gorgeous and I am so in love with you—"

He opened his mouth to tell her that he loved her, too, but she held up her hand, asking for his silence. "If I take you up on your offer, there's so much that could go wrong. I don't want to live with this niggling reminder that having a baby wasn't your first choice, that you are going through this horrible process for me. That you'll question whether the time and energy and money is worth it."

He tried to talk again but she spoke over him. "I heard about this couple, she wanted kids, he didn't. They had a baby and she felt resentful because he wasn't involved in raising their child. He said that he never wanted children, so why should he change a diaper or make a bottle?"

"That's not a fair comparison to make. I'm not like that."

"I don't know, Judah, we've only known each other a short time! Can you understand that your offer is too big, too encompassing, too quickly made?" Darby quietly asked. "This isn't a building, Judah, the shape of a roof, the placement of windows, something that can be redrawn, rebuilt if we make the wrong choice. We will be creating life. Do you understand that? It will be a life we will both be responsible for until the day we die, whether we want to be or not. My child, *our* child, deserves the very best we both have to offer, Judah, the best you have to offer. Saying you will *give* me a child is far from your best and I won't accept less than full involvement from you, or from any other man." Darby stood up. "I'd rather do this solo."

Judah stared at her, shocked. Feeling as if she'd ripped out his heart and ground it under the heel of one of her designer shoes. He felt both sick and supremely...pissed.

Hurt. Frustrated. Soul deep angry.

Did she not understand how hard it was for him to make that offer, how much he loved her to even consider *having* a child? He was prepared to give up his freedom, a considerable amount of cash, his time to do this with her...but she was refusing.

Stubborn, contrary woman.

Because anger was easier to deal with than pain, he lashed out. "Are you sure your motives about having a child are that pure, Darby?"

Darby frowned at him, caught off guard. "What are you talking about?"

"You have all the answers—" damn good answers but he would die before he admitted that to her "—but maybe a part of you only wants a child because it's the only thing you've ever failed at."

Darby looked like he'd plunged a knife into her chest. He should get up and walk away, but the words flew off his tongue. "Maybe this need to have a child is all about having control, about proving it to yourself that you can and less about your mothering instinct. You're prepared to toss us away, an exciting dynamic life, to change diapers and make bottles and be restricted and confined. Do you know how stupid that is?"

When fire flashed in her eyes, he knew that *stupid* had been the wrong word to use. Hell, all his words were asinine; he knew it even as he said them.

"You're on thin ice, Huntley."

Yet he still couldn't stop, the anger, the loss, was too much. "I offered you the one thing I never wanted in order to make you happy, but you tossed it in my face."

"Then you went on to question my motive for wanting a child. Don't forget that!" Darby leaped to her feet, her expression wild.

"If you were so sure you wanted kids, you would've made the decision to have IVF months ago and not thought twice about it!"

Judging by her shaking hands and wobbly bottom lip, Judah knew that he'd pushed a very big button.

"That's not fair, Judah," Darby whispered, in a voice so broken it caused his throat to close.

"So much about life isn't, Darby," Judah muttered.

A small wail pulled their attention away from their argument and back to Jac. They both stepped toward the playpen, but Darby reached the red-faced and sobbing child first. She picked her up, cuddled the baby to her chest and swayed from side to side.

At that moment, seeing her instinctive urge to comfort, Judah realized that in his anger, he'd made a very big error. She was smart, talented, so very driven, but yes, she was born to have it all. The career, the success, the child…the children.

"Shhh, baby," Darby murmured and Jac's sobs lessened. Then Jac tucked her face into Darby's neck, wrapped her little hand around a lock of her hair and pulled it to her cheek. Her eyes closed, and she was instantly fast asleep.

Darby kissed her little face, hugged her once more and placed her back on the mattress in the playpen. Pulling Jac's pink blanket over her tiny body, she touched her fingers to her lips before placing them back on Jac's little head. "I love you, baby girl. I hope you find your happy."

Darby's eyes skittered over Judah before she looked away. "She's all yours."

Judah watched, his heart breaking, as Darby walked out the door and, he presumed, out of his life.

Radio silence from Mason. Again.

Callie, pulling her earbuds out of her ears, stopped outside the front door to Mason's coffee shop and squinted at the glass doorway. Four days had passed since Mason walked out of her life, since she'd seen him, spoken to him.

She'd said what she needed to, told him where she stood. But the man had yet to tell her what he needed, what he was thinking or what he wanted.

Callie rested her back against the wall and lifted her foot, placing her sneaker on the wall behind her. The neighborhood was quiet this time of the morning. Few people chose to rise this early, but since she was awake anyway, she thought she might as well get some exercise.

Callie looked around with fresh eyes. While she and Ray had traveled extensively, she hadn't lived anywhere else but here. She'd miss this place, of course she would. She'd miss her children more. But she needed to leave, to be someone other than her kids' mom, Ray's widow.

Mason would have to stay here, for a year or two at least, until his youngest son completed school.

Callie looked up at the bright bold blue of the winter sky and sighed. She wanted to keep Mason in her life, but she didn't want a long-distance relationship. That wasn't fair to either of them. She could ask him to join her when he could but who knew where she'd be, what she'd be doing, whom she might meet between then and now?

There was only today. She couldn't make plans that far into the future. She needed to go, he needed to stay, so…maybe it was time to let Mason go.

Callie heard the rumble of Mason's Jeep and turned her head to the right, watching as he steered the black SUV into his customary parking spot. Switching off the engine, he stepped out and slammed the door closed. He leaned back against his vehicle and looked at her, those deep eyes serious.

"I'm in love with you."

Callie pushed her sunglasses up into her hair, wishing he hadn't said the words. Knowing he felt the same way she did would make leaving so much harder.

"I didn't want to fall in love with you, it wasn't the plan." Mason rolled his big shoulders. "You were supposed to be another diversion." His eyes moved from her to the windows of his shop, his expression a mixture of exasperation and amusement. "This worked for me, for a few years. After the stress of my previous job, making cappuccinos and lattes felt like heaven. I had time for my kids, time to work out, to chill. It felt right. It *was* right."

Callie placed her palms against the wall and her breathing turned shallow. Where was he going with this?

"Fair warning, if we do this, you'll be the one making coffee. All the time. I'm done with coffee shops."

Callie bit the inside of her lip as her throat closed. With fear or anticipation. A little bit of both. "What are we going to do, Mason?"

Mason folded his arms across his chest and Callie noticed the lines around his mouth were deeper, his eyes worried. For the first time ever, Mason seemed to be feeling a little out of his depth. Seeing that, strangely, relaxed her. She wasn't the only one, as Levi would say, with skin in the game, and that was reassuring.

"My kids were my greatest worry, my biggest challenge. I've had custody of them since I got divorced, although my ex is very involved in their lives. I've spent a lot of time thinking about how I can have them and you. How can I make this work?"

"Your kids come first, Mace. That's not up for discussion," Callie said, her tone fierce. She would not be the person who came between Mason and his sons.

"Emmet will be off to college in a few months and Teag has another eighteen months before he goes, too. The boys like their stepdad, they all get along well. I might have custody, but my boys spend as much time with Karen and Doug as they do with me." He pulled in a breath. "So, my ex and her husband are happy for the boys to come and live with them, in fact they are all damn excited." A small smile touched Mason's lips. "When I am in the country, the boys will stay with me, obviously."

In the country? What? "I don't understand."

Mason folded his arms against his chest. "I want to come traveling with you, Cal. Provided we don't go mad, I earn enough from my investments to cover my obligations to the boys and to live comfortably. If I need more money, or get bored, there are university departments all over the world who'd be interested in having me as a guest lecturer, organizations that would hire me to solve some of their trickier problems."

"You and your big brain," Callie murmured, feeling the need to tease him. It was either that or cry. She felt overwhelmed, terrified, so happy she wanted to burst out of her skin.

"The point is, I could travel with you, I *want* to travel with you." Mason rubbed the back of his neck. "If that's something you might be interested in."

Something she *might* be interested in? Really?

It was only a dream come true.

"I know you want to find yourself, carve out your own identity, be Callie. I don't want to stop you from doing that, from doing whatever you want to do." Mason's voice held a hint of panic. "I just want to watch you while you do it. But I understand if it's something you need to do alone. I won't like it, but I'll understand."

This man…this amazing, supersmart, hot man. He just got her.

Mason didn't want to change her. He wanted to love her while she explored the next phase of her life. It was an enormous gift, a marvelous realization. She could do anything, be anything and Mason would be there, standing behind her.

Callie wanted to go to him but there were still words to be said, conditions to be discussed. "I would love for you to come traveling with me, Mace, to be with me, more than anything in the world. But I think you should know, now, that I'm never going to marry you. I'm going to love you, probably until I die, but I'm not going to marry you."

"I'm good with that." Mason nodded, his eyes filled with amusement. "That way I'll always know you're with me because you want to be and not because a piece of paper says you have to be. I'm especially happy about the you-loving-me part." He pretended to wipe a bead of sweat off his forehead. "That's a bit of a relief."

"I think I fell in love with you when you first offered to help me out with my bucket list," Callie admitted.

Mason's eyes were steady on her face, his expression all sincere tenderness. "You are the adventure I've been waiting for, Cal."

There was nothing she wanted more than to step into his arms, to embrace her future, but she still had words to say. She held up her hand. "Wait. I'm not done."

"Make it sharp, Brogan, I need to kiss you." Mason rolled his index finger in a gesture that told her to hurry up.

"No matter where we are, what we are doing, we come back to Boston every year for three months in the summer. And for two weeks over Christmas. That's family time, yours and mine. We spend that time with our kids, either together or apart. But we see our kids, twice a year. That's not negotiable."

Mason's expression turned back to tender. "I'm so behind that. Anything else?"

"No." Callie allowed her smile to bloom, feeling like the luckiest woman in the world. She'd had a husband who loved her, and now she had a lover and a partner to spend the rest of her life with. How lucky was she to be loved by two amazing men?

As Mason put his hands on her hips to pull her to him—God, he felt so good—she slapped her hands on his chest, laughter bubbling. "Apparently, Mrs. Jenkins saw my impromptu striptease the other day. Half the neighborhood is wondering what kind of hanky-panky was happening in your coffee shop. The other half is convinced she's nuts."

"Nobody suspects you?" Mason murmured.

"I don't do public displays of affection, everyone knows that." Callie made her voice deliberately prim. "It's not what good girls do."

"Such a liar." Mason, deliberately, cupped her breast and swiped her nipple, his mouth an inch from hers. "The real Callie Brogan isn't a good girl, she's a hot wild strong woman. And I'm nuts about her."

Mason's thumb moved up her neck, across her jaw. "There's a group of joggers at the top of the street. Behind them is Mrs. Jenkins on her scooter. Want to give them something new to talk about?"

Laughter skittered through Callie. She lifted her face up, brushed her lips against Mason's mouth. "Oh, yes, please. PDA the hell out of me, Mace."

Eleven

Darby forced herself to work, to tie up all the loose
ends outstanding for Huntley and Associates, pushing
from minute to minute, hour to hour.

Even so, her thoughts kept drifting to Jac, wondering if the little girl knew that her little life was about to
take another detour, wondering if she was old enough
to miss Darby or Judah. But then thoughts of Jac took
Darby to thoughts of Judah—as if she could *not* think
about him!—and she wondered how he was holding up.

Despite their fight, his ridiculous belief that he didn't
want children, she knew that handing over Jac would rip
his heart in two. It was the right course of action—that
fantastic ray of human sunshine had only been on loan
to them—but no matter how stoic Judah acted, Darby
knew that taking Jac back to Carla would be difficult.

He'd insist on interviewing Jac's new nanny and

Darby was pretty sure he'd offer the woman some additional cash to keep him informed about Jac's progress, to let him know if she needed anything, to send him photographs. To call him if Carla went off the rails again.

Jac might be his niece but she was also the child of his heart.

Curled up in the corner of the sofa in her mother's house, Darby looked up when Jules walked into the room, dark hair glistening with moisture. Callie had called to check up on Darby and immediately knew that one of her chicks was in pain. She then called in reinforcements. There was a laptop on the coffee table and Darby knew DJ would be calling in soon from the Netherlands. When a crisis struck, the Brogan women didn't let a little thing like distance come between them and much-needed support.

Callie walked into the room carrying mugs of cocoa. Darby took her cup, looked down at the little marshmallows bobbing in the creamy richness and felt her throat gag. Her life, everything that mattered, was on a plane heading to Europe and her throat was tight, her stomach cramping. Darby placed her mug on the table and rested her head on the back of the sofa, closing her eyes.

She heard the incoming Skype call, DJ's voice, but didn't open her eyes. She didn't want to face this moment, this life that didn't have Judah or Jac in it. Her two Js, the loves of her life.

Callie sat down next to Darby, placed her hand on her thigh and Darby opened her eyes to look into Callie's bright blue eyes.

"I'm okay, Mom," she said, because she felt she had to. She was a strong independent woman...

Who felt like her heart had been ripped in two.

"Has Jac gone back?" DJ asked.

Darby looked at the laptop screen and nodded. "Carla is at home and she's hired a nanny."

"You knew this day would come," Jules softly said.

Darby couldn't argue with that. "I did, and I thought I could handle it." She shrugged. "Turns out I can't."

They all turned at the sound of footsteps in the hallway and Darby was surprised to see Levi walking into the living room and not Mason. Running a hand through his damp hair, he looked at Darby with worry on his face. "Mom called, said that Jac and Judah had left." He shuffled from foot to foot. "I wanted to see if you were okay."

Darby was touched by his concern. She'd managed to contain her tears with Callie and Jules but knowing that her big brother had left work early to check up on her flipped the switch to make the waterworks flow.

"Oh, crap." Levi held up his hands. "Sorry. I'll go."

Darby shook her head and held out her hand to him, frantically wiping her face with her other hand. Levi walked across the room and sat down on the arm of the sofa and Darby leaned into him, needing his strength.

She felt his hand on her head and forced the words over her tongue. "He offered to give me a baby."

DJ was the first to respond with a loud "woo-hoo!"

Callie grinned and Jules wiped an imaginary bead of sweat off her brow. "Yay, no sperm donors. He's hot and smart and yeah, we like him."

Darby looked up to see Levi's reaction. Of the three of them who knew her so well, it was her brother who immediately understood that Judah's offer wasn't welcome.

"You want a baby, Judah has said that he'll give you one. What's the problem?" Levi asked, frowning.

Darby lifted one shoulder and played with the ring on her middle finger. "Judah doesn't want a child and is only offering because he wants me to be happy."

Jules's face softened. "Oh, that's so romantic. He loves you."

Maybe he did. She understood their confusion: a gorgeous man was offering her a relationship and a child. Her perfect, much-dreamed-about life was a yes away and she was crying. It shouldn't make sense, but it did, to her.

Darby shook her head. "He cares for me, I admit that. But you know me, I'm not prepared to settle."

Jules and Callie exchanged a confused look. "How would you be settling?" Callie asked before lifting her mug to her mouth.

"His idea of a perfect relationship is different than mine. He wants us to travel, to design buildings, to be childless and free. My idea of a perfect relationship is a house we've both designed together, having a career while raising a passel of kids. A husband that is fully committed to our life, to me, to his kids."

"You're worried that if you have children together, he might feel resentful, that he will put his career, and not you and your children, first," Levi stated.

Darby nodded. "I could, almost, maybe, play second fiddle to his career—"

"Oh, you could not!" Jules interrupted.

"Maybe not," Darby admitted. "But I know myself, if we had children and he wasn't the type of dad to them I know he can be, if he didn't give them his all, I'd lose respect for him. And that wouldn't be fair because I knew how he felt going in."

She continued, "I also think that if we go through this

process, this difficult and expensive process, to have children and we didn't give them everything we had as parents, that would be—" Darby searched for the word "—I don't know the exact word I'm looking for… *immoral*? *Unfair*? No, I think I'd prefer to do it on my own."

When none of her family responded, Darby wondered if she was overthinking this, whether she'd been too analytical, too hard. She hoped they wouldn't try to change her mind because she would be easily tempted to take a chance, to try it Judah's way.

She loved him that much. She didn't want to be without him.

But a voice deep in her soul, that part of her connected with the earth and the universe and whatever life force that created her, insisted she shouldn't. It was better to find another way to have the babies she so desperately wanted.

If she actually wanted babies and not control.

She couldn't get Judah's words out of her head, had turned them over and over again. Examined them from every angle. Darby ran her hands down her thighs, wrinkled her nose and looked up at Levi. He'd tell her straight; he wouldn't try to cushion his words. Levi was unflinchingly honest.

"Judah said I want children because I like control, because I haven't failed at anything else and that I don't want to fail at this either."

Levi lifted his eyebrows and fury darkened his eyes.

She held up her hand, not needing his protection but his honesty. "Do you think he's right?"

Callie opened her mouth to speak but Darby kept her hand up and her eyes on Levi. She wanted his opinion.

Levi opened his mouth, closed it and rubbed the back of his neck. "I think it's a factor."

Darby ignored the protests from her female backup team and slowly nodded. She placed the balls of her hands into her eye sockets and tried to push the pain away. She dropped her hands, opened her eyes and watched as Callie and her sisters argued with Levi, who didn't try to defend himself. He just sat there, absorbing their ire, his eyes on her face.

When she couldn't take any more, Darby lifted her hand. "He's right."

It took a long moment for her words to sink in. When silence dropped into the room like a heavy wet blanket, she looked at her mom, then Jules, then DJ, making eye contact with each of them before leaning into Levi's thigh.

"He's right, so is Judah. Not a hundred percent, but a little bit right."

Callie frowned. "I don't understand, Darby."

"I didn't either, until Judah had the balls to say it. It's something I've been battling with over the past few months, but I wouldn't put my fears into words, so I couldn't identify it." Darby stood up and walked to the fireplace, picking up a photograph of her, Levi and Jules, taken when they were toddlers. Jules sat in Levi's lap, her arms around her middle and Darby stood next to them, a small gap between her and Levi.

"I've always been competitive, it's a part of my nature. You are our father's son, Levi, but I am his daughter." She turned and looked at her brother, holding the frame of the photo. "You and Jules always had this special bond. My earliest memories of you are of me, wanting that bond with you."

Levi nodded, a small gesture, but Darby took it as encouragement. It was time to lance the wound, to allow all the poison to escape.

"When I was seven, you gave Jules a music box for Christmas. You gave me, God, a ratty baseball card."

"You threw a hissy fit and wouldn't come out of your room for the rest of the day. I couldn't understand what I did wrong. You'd just started to play baseball and that was my favorite card."

It had been mangled and torn and, yeah, ugly. What had she been supposed to think? But he'd thought he was doing something nice, she'd been insulted. Darby shook her head. Boys. She'd never understand them.

"I saw the disparity in the gifts as you loving Jules more, something I'd long suspected. That Christmas Day I vowed that I would never be second-best, that I would always, always be first and maybe, someday, you would love me as much as you loved her."

"God, Darby," Levi muttered, standing up. He walked over to her and pulled her into his chest, holding her against his big body.

Darby sucked in his strength, wanting to stand there forever, but she pushed him away, determined to get this done. She knew her mom and sisters were crying and she couldn't look at them because then she'd totally lose it. "So, my competitive streak was born. Recently, when I heard that my time was running out to have IVF, I suddenly got cold feet. This was my goal, why couldn't I pull the trigger? What if I failed? What if it didn't work? What if I only wanted to become a mom because I didn't want to fail?"

Levi dropped to the rug and pulled Darby down so she was sitting opposite him, mirroring his crossed legs.

He placed his big hands on her knees and looked into her eyes, the green of his brilliant in the soft light.

When he spoke, his voice was a low soothing rumble. "Even as a little girl, you were so damn fierce, so very independent." His mouth quirked at the corners. "So damn opinionated. Jules allowed me to protect her, to play the older brother, you refused to. I couldn't help you over puddles, you'd plow through them. I'd tell Jules that a tree was too dangerous to climb. She'd listen. You? You climbed higher. You were fearless, determined, God, so annoying. I couldn't protect you because you wouldn't let me protect you and it drove me nuts, it *still* drives me nuts."

He took a breath and continued, "For any pain I caused you, I'm sorry. I should've found another way to deal with you, to make you feel as special as Jules, but that doesn't mean I love you less than Jules. Frankly, all three of you are pains in my ass."

Muted laughter dissolved some of the tension.

"But to come back to your question about whether you are having kids because you're competitive…"

Darby held her breath, worried that he would confirm her worst fears about herself.

"Is your competitive streak a factor in wanting to have kids? Sure it is. But it's not your driving force. Beneath your bossy ways, you're a nurturer, but because you are strong and independent, people don't see it."

Levi carried on. "You'd be a fearless mom, Darby, because you are fearless. You'd be the mom climbing trees, playing in the sand, learning to surf. Because you are independent and strong, you'll raise strong and independent girls and you'll raise your sons to respect strong and independent women. You want kids because you have something to give them, Darby, don't doubt that. And yeah, I agree with you. You can't settle with Judah. You'd resent him for it and he'd resent himself for doing it. You're the type of people who don't ever settle, and love, well, love shouldn't ever involve settling for less than the very best."

Darby nodded, knowing he was right. She bit her bottom lip, knowing her tears were about to fall. "It hurts, Levi."

Levi hauled her into his arms, rocking her gently. "I know, honey, I really do. Love—having it and losing it—hurts like hell."

In Carla's luxurious lakeside villa, Judah held Jac in his arms, unable to hand her over, to let her go.

Carla, as he'd expected, showed little interest in Jac and had languidly introduced him to Jac's new nanny. While Carla lay on a sofa bed, flicking through a magazine, looking pale and disinterested, Judah, keeping a firm hold on Jac, interrogated Joa, Jac's new nanny.

The woman, in her mid to late twenties, was tougher than she looked and held up well to his barrage of questions. Her credentials were solid and she'd passed the background check with flying colors. She seemed warm, capable and organized, and Jac liked her. Hell, if he had permanent custody of Jac, Joa was exactly the type of nanny he would've hired to look after his little girl.

He liked Joa, he did. It was Carla he had the problem with.

Judah looked at his ex and while he felt sorry for her, he had to wonder what he'd ever seen in her. She was stunning, sure, but self-absorbed and selfish. He'd stuck around, he suddenly realized, because he knew

Carla was no threat to his single status, because he knew that, with her, he'd never be faced with the question of whether he should settle down, whether he loved her enough to commit to her, to plan a life with her.

That gray-eyed feisty blonde back home was the only one who'd ever managed to make him change his way of thinking.

Home, he'd used that word to refer to Boston. Was that where his home was now? Judah thought about that for a minute. Home was wherever Darby was. He loved her.

How the hell was he going to live his life without her?

He didn't think he could let Jac go either, not now or ever. She was his, as was Darby.

They were his girls and he needed to fight for them, fight for this life he'd never expected to want. The house filled with naughty boys and girls; their smart, hot mom who would not only help Judah create buildings but more important, create his life. A life filled with kids, and pets, and love and arguments and fantastic sex—

"I think it's time, Mr. Huntley," Joa said.

It was. It had been time for the last half hour.

Judah tightened his grip on Jac and lifted his free hand to grip the bridge of his nose. Handing Jac over was the legal thing to do but it wasn't the right thing to do.

Jac was his. And Darby's...

God, how could he make this work? What could he say that would allow him to leave with Jac? What argument would work with Carla?

Judah heard the door to the sunroom open and he saw Luca, Carla's manager, walk into the room, followed by a young man who looked like... Jesus, was that Jake?

Judah, keeping a firm hold on Jac, leaped to his feet, his eyes sweeping over his younger brother. Jake looked nothing like the thin, haggard, addicted man he'd last seen eighteen months ago. His dark hair was longer than Judah's and his eyes were a lighter shade of blue but, thank God, clear of drugs. His face had filled out, as had his body. He looked strong and healthy.

Relief swept through Judah, then anger. "Where the hell have you been? I heard you left rehab, that you disappeared."

He expected Jake to lash back but he just walked toward Judah, his hand held out to shake. "It wasn't working for me, so I decided to try something else."

Jake looked disappointed that Judah didn't shake his hand but he didn't say anything, just dropped his hand, then bent at the knees to look at Jac. "So, this is Jacquetta. She's beautiful."

He and Carla were pretty people, what the hell did he expect?

"What are you doing here, Jake?" Judah demanded. He glanced at Carla, who didn't look remotely surprised to see Jake. "Will someone tell me what the hell is going on?"

Luca lifted his eyebrows. "So, those rumors that your brother was in the area weren't wrong. Apparently—" Luca frowned at Carla "—Carla thought it would be a good idea to let the world think she was having an affair with Bertolli while sneaking off to see Jake."

Judah rolled his eyes at Luca and was rewarded with a small smile. His ex and his brother fed off drama.

"Then my appendix burst, and Jake spent the last two weeks sneaking into my hospital room late at night to see me," Carla said, sending Jake a grateful look that appeared, holy crap, full of love.

Oh, God, were these two back together?

Judah looked inside himself and realized he didn't care. He only cared about Jac. He glanced down and saw that Jac had fallen asleep in his arms. He couldn't give her up; he wouldn't.

Jake was an addict and while he might be clean now, the chances of him slipping back into addiction were high. As much as Judah liked Joa, he couldn't put Jac back into a house inhabited by two highly unstable and volatile people.

He was about to tell them that he was taking Jac, that they could fight him for custody, when Jake surprised Judah by walking over to Carla and dropping to his knees in front of her. She looked at him, defiance in her eyes.

"Carla. You need to make this decision, babe."

Judah looked at Joa, who lifted her eyebrows, seeming to be as confused as he was. He turned to Luca, who just shook his head, silently asking him to wait. Okay, he would wait, but not for long. In five minutes, he would be walking out with Jac—maybe with Joa, too—and to hell with the consequences. Though a spell in an Italian jail for kidnapping didn't appeal, it was a risk he was willing to take.

"Honey, we've spoken about this," Jake quietly stated. "When you told me that you spoke to Judah, I thought you discussed the possibility of leaving her with him, not him bringing her back."

What. The. Hell? Judah didn't understand any of this. It sounded like they were talking about letting him leave with Jac. Letting him *have* Jac…

Carla bit her lip. "But people will think I am terrible, that I gave up my daughter."

"They'll think you handed your daughter over to

her father and I'm sure Judah will allow you visitation rights."

"But you're her father!" Carla wailed. "You and I made her!"

Jake stood up and looked down at her, love and regret on his face. "Honey, you and I, we're not good for her. We're not what she needs. We're too broken, too damaged... That's why we understand each other so well. If Jacquetta stays with us, we'll just raise another broken soul and I've caused enough damage to enough people. I don't want to do that anymore."

Jake turned to Judah and in his brother's eyes, he saw the child who'd adored him, the boy he remembered. "You were a better father, a better man as a twelve-year-old than both Dad and me put together. You were incredible and still are today... I both love and hate you. I love you for looking after me, I hate you for leaving, although I understand why you did it."

Judah swallowed down the emotion. "You do?"

Jake's eyes radiated understanding. "You needed a life, Judah. The one you were living, looking after me, was killing you. I made my own choices, I knew better, even at thirteen, to not do the things I did, but I did them anyway. Possibly to force you to come back."

"Jake." His brother's name on his lips was a plea for forgiveness.

"It's okay, Judah, it really is. You weren't my father, you were not responsible for me. When I'm sober and clearheaded, I understand that. I don't understand it when I'm using." Jake sighed. "I've been clean for a few months, but the temptation is always there, and I can't guarantee that I won't slide again. Carla is addicted to attention, to her career, to herself."

Carla shrugged. "He's right."

"Neither of us are remotely adult enough, responsible enough, to raise a child. We won't ever be," Jake quietly stated. He nodded at Luca, who walked over to the desk. "Luca has papers, signing over full custody of Jacquetta to you. Will you take her? Will you raise her, as you did me?"

Judah felt his heart slam into his chest. He wanted to say yes, to grab what they were offering and run.

"What if you change your mind? What if you want her back? What then?"

Luca spoke. "It's ironclad, I made sure of it. If you sign, they relinquish all rights to her. You can refuse visitation rights. You can bar them from having any contact with her until she's an adult. I don't expect you to take my word for it. We can send the documents to your attorney and have him examine the legalese if you are in doubt."

Judah looked down at Jac's downy head, her red cheeks and perfect mouth, and suddenly realized that without her, without more kids, he would become as self-absorbed as his brother, as Carla, as addicted to his work and lifestyle as they were to drugs and attention. He'd designed and built fantastic buildings all over the world, but they were bricks and mortar, cold steel. They had no soul.

He'd made the choice earlier to live his life differently, but this conversation with his brother cemented his resolution to do exactly that.

Of course, he'd take Jac. He'd love her and any other kids he and Darby were lucky enough to have. He would be a good dad. Even his messed-up, currently sober brother thought so.

It was now time to be a *great* dad—the dad, the man, Darby needed him to be.

Judah stepped over to the desk, pulled the document toward him, grateful it was written in English and contained the minimal amount of legal speak. It was as Luca said, a full-custody agreement, signing over Jac to him.

Not hesitating, Judah grabbed the nearest pen and dashed his signature across the page. He stared down at his scrawl, the thought hitting him that he now had a daughter.

He loved her. With all his heart.

He had his child, all he needed now to make his life complete was his woman.

Meet me at the northeast corner of the neighborhood in an hour. I'll bring coffee.

Why?

Don't be late, Judah's next text stated.

Darby accepted that she and Judah were unconventional, that their entire relationship was odd, but she didn't understand why Judah insisted on seeing her before breakfast on Monday morning. Why they had to meet at this deserted, undeveloped part of the neighborhood was beyond her. Darby pulled her car up next to Judah's SUV and shook her head.

Snow covered the ground and the windchill factor dropped the temperature to just above freezing, but Judah stood on top of the slope to her right, hatless, his hands shoved into the pockets of his heavy jacket.

Why was he here? Why was he standing there looking cold but determined? Why wasn't he in New York, as he said he'd be?

Despite hot air blowing from her heater, Darby shivered. There was little point in talking—to be together, one of them had to make a major life-changing sacrifice for the other—so wasn't it better just to go their separate ways?

Talking wouldn't find a solution... There was no solution.

Darby saw Judah pull his phone out of his pocket and seconds later, hers rang. Darby stared down at her phone, shaking her head. If she got out of the car, she'd run up that hill and throw herself into his arms and tell him she didn't want to lose him. She loved him. She'd do anything—have his babies, not have his babies—to have him in her life. They'd be happy, for a year, two, maybe four. Then the doubts would creep in, then resentment and regret. They'd end up hating each other.

No, it was better to walk away now, while there was still love and respect.

Darby took one last glance at Judah and told herself to put the car into Drive, to leave. Her phone dinged with an incoming text and she looked down at the lit screen.

Five minutes. Please?

Not giving herself any more time to think, Darby switched off the engine and opened the door. The cold slapped her in the face, but she forced herself to leave the car, instantly burying her face in her cashmere scarf.

This was ridiculous. If Judah wanted to talk, why couldn't they have a conversation back at the house or in her office over coffee? She was already miserable, she didn't need to be cold, as well.

Darby walked up the hill, glad she was wearing flat boots with a decent grip. If she fell on her butt, she would be even more unhappy than she already was. And she was plenty unhappy…

When she reached Judah, he held out his bare hand, which Darby ignored. She stared out over the incredible view of rolling land. It had been years since she'd been up to this remote area. The architect in her noted that the plot of land had a helluva view. She knew Noah had plans to develop this area at some point. She remembered him saying something about retaining this land for very exclusive high-end buyers. Hopefully, she might, with her connection to the developer, be asked to design one or two of the houses.

But that was for the future, the future without Judah.

"Care to tell me why I am freezing my butt off?" Darby demanded, her tone as cold as the air swirling around them.

God, he looked so big and warm and wonderful. How was she going to stand watching him walk out of her life again?

"Noah is prepared to sell this land."

So?

"To me. I made him an offer and he accepted," Judah quietly stated, his voice low and slow. "I know exactly what I'd build here."

He had a client, someone Noah had recommended no doubt. Maybe Judah wanted to consult with her again. She could be his point person while he took on bigger and better projects all over the world.

No.

He'd have to find another local architect. In order to survive him leaving her life, he needed to leave her life. Utterly. Completely.

Darby had zero interest in the property or any of Judah's plans. Thinking of a future free of Judah felt like a red-hot dagger rhythmically plunging into her gut. "I can't work with you, Judah. Yes, being associated with you is wonderful for my career, but it hurts too much knowing there's no way for us to be together." Darby gestured to her car. "Can I go now? I'm freezing."

Judah's hand on her shoulder stopped her from walking away. "I'd build something long, something with glass and wood and steel."

Judah turned her so she faced the snow-covered fields and the woods at the end of the property. Darby knew that, on a clear day, they could see the sea.

"We'd wake up to this view every morning, but I'd give it not much more than a passing glance because all my attention would be on a gray-eyed blonde with messy hair, thanking God that she's in my life."

Darby stepped away from him, tipping her head back to look into his blazing eyes, blue fire in his pale face.

"What did you say?" she quietly asked, her heart slamming against her rib cage.

"I'd try to cop a feel, get you half-naked, but I'm pretty sure one of our kids would demand our attention before I got to the fun stuff. We'd argue about whose turn it is to get up and deal with our brood, but I'd go just because you smiled at me. Just because I'd be so damn happy to have you, to have our kids, to have our life."

Darby heard the sincerity in his voice, could see her dreams in his eyes, but she held up her hands, yanking herself out of the spell he'd put her under. "Judah, don't. Please don't."

"Please don't what?" Judah asked, still not touching her, his eyes still connected with hers.

"Don't show me the dream I so desperately want but can't have," Darby whispered.

Darby felt Judah's hand on her cheek, his thumb stroking her jaw. "I'm offering it to you, Darby, all you have to do is take it. We can build our dream house here, fill it with kids. Don't walk out of my life, Darby. Stay and live your dream."

He still didn't get it. "I don't want it to be my dream, Judah, I want it to be ours. I want you to want that, too, but you don't!"

Judah looked at her for a long moment before a tiny smile lifted the corner of his lips. He pointed to a huge oak, its thick branches now devoid of leaves. "I want to hang a tire swing from those branches for Jac, take her tadpole hunting in the creek behind the house. I see her catching lightning bugs in that field."

He spoke as if Jac would be a permanent part of his life. "What are you trying to tell me, Judah?"

Judah rubbed the back of his neck, looking frustrated. "Okay, I'm obviously not explaining properly. I want to build a house here, on this land, with you. For us and Jac. And any other children we might have. I'll still have to travel but you and our kids can come with me. If you stay behind, I'll make damn sure I'm back within a week, ten days. I want you to carry on working, with me or by yourself, I don't care."

Darby looked at him, poleaxed.

"I want your dream, Darby. The house, the kids… you. It all starts and ends with you."

Darby ignored the white-hot bolt of joy hurtling through her and focused on Judah's eyes. There was no hesitation there, no fear. He was telling the truth. He wanted the life he'd described. He genuinely wanted what she did.

But before she could fall into the happiness he promised, Darby still felt the need to warn him about what he was getting into. "Judah, my fertility issues... It's not going to be easy."

Judah clasped the back of her neck and rested his forehead on hers. "Sweetheart, it might take some time, and cash, for us to have kids but I'm a hundred percent committed to the process. I will do whatever it takes for you to carry your own baby. This is a journey we are now on together. I promise you we'll find a way."

He'd mentioned Jac. Did that mean he wanted to fight for her? How? Was that even possible?

Before she could ask, Judah spoke again. "Until we manage to get you pregnant, I have another little girl who desperately needs a mom."

Darby stepped backward, slapping her hands to her cheeks. He'd hinted at having Jac, but she hadn't wanted to believe that was a possibility. Losing Jac had hurt almost as much as losing Judah.

"You have Jac? You can get her back? When? What's the plan?"

Judah smiled, his face full of love. "The plan is that I tell you that I love you, ask you to marry me and after you say yes, we'll head back to the house, where I strip you naked and have my way with you. Or you can have your way with me, I'm not picky."

Darby grinned.

"After a couple of hours of loving you, we'll head

over to Callie's and drag our daughter out of her sticky fingers."

Wait…what? By the name of all things holy, what? He'd said so much, she couldn't take it all in. One thing at a time.

"Jac is at my mom's? You *have* her?"

Judah nodded. "It's a long, complicated story but the condensed version is that my brother and Carla, who are back together, signed over full custody to me. I'd like us to formally adopt Jac as ours. Do you want to do that with me?"

She needed about two seconds to think about that. "Um…*yes*." Darby couldn't help doing a happy dance in the snow. Her baby was back. Her little girl…

The urge to run down the hill to her car, to drive immediately to where she could hug her daughter was strong. But she and Judah still had some issues to deal with.

Darby tipped her head to one side. "You love me? You want to marry me and build a house for us?"

Judah shook his head. "Not only a house, a *life*. I want a life with you at the center of it, sweetheart."

"Judah, you're anti-marriage, anticommitment, anti-kids. You love your freedom," Darby stated, suddenly scared. What if he changed his mind? What if he gave her this dream life for a couple of years and then started feeling hemmed in, constrained?

"I love you more," Judah said, his voice cracking with emotion. "Darby, I'm not going to change my mind. I'm not going to leave you with a house and kids, go off on my own. I've had my freedom, seventeen years of it, and I'm done being alone. I want you and Jac and however many more kids come our way. I want you. I want us."

Darby, needing to touch him, threw her arms around him and stood on her toes to bury her face in his neck. Ignoring her tears, she held on tight, trying to make sense of the last ten minutes. As Judah's arms banded around her—as he pulled her into his warmth, into his heart, into the life he'd created for them—she abandoned understanding and allowed herself to feel.

She loved him.

Darby pulled herself off him, taking a step back. When Judah reached for her again, she held up her hands. "If you touch me, I won't be able to talk, and I need to, Judah... I need to speak."

Judah nodded, his beautiful eyes tender.

Darby pulled in a deep breath, blinked away her tears. "I love—" Her voice cracked, and she cleared her throat. She lifted one shoulder and tried to smile. "I love you. I could've lived without you, just as you could've lived without me—we are strong enough people to do that but, God, it would've hurt. I would've been miserable because having you in my life... You *make* my life." Trying to smile, she looked at him, her breath catching in her throat. "I want you, too. And yes, please, I'd love to be your wife. I want the life I see in your eyes."

Judah's smile was slow to come but when it did, it warmed her, on that freezing morning, from the inside out. He reached for her, lifting her off her toes, his laughter a low rumble. One arm held her under her butt, his other hand held the back of her head, their mouths aligned. "Fair warning, I'm going to kiss the hell out of you now."

Darby grinned. "Strangely, I'm okay with that."

"Then we'll get out of this freezing wind and we'll pick up our daughter and take her home."

Darby kissed Judah before pulling her mouth away. "We don't want to upset my mom by picking her up too soon. Maybe we can wait a couple of hours before we head over."

Judah's eyes deepened with laughter and passion. "I can't think what we might do to fill the time," he teased.

Darby pretended to think. "I'm sure it will come to us. We are, after all, reasonably intelligent."

Judah brushed her hair off her face. "You and I, Darby? Smartest decision ever made."

Darby absolutely agreed.

* * * * *

'With this ring, I accept you as my husband.'

Gwendolyn had neglected to put the ring on her finger, so she moved to rectify that, but Vidar stopped her by covering her hand with his. Gently, he took the ring from her and slid it on her finger. He didn't say anything, but it felt as if he'd claimed her. Just as his ring claimed her finger, he had claimed her as his.

He moved away, only to turn back with the sword his Jarl Eirik had given him. It was ornate, with two rubies set into the gilded hilt. He held it out to her, lying flat on both of his palms. 'I am entrusting this into your care, to be given to our firstborn son. May you bear me many.'

She nodded and took the sword from him, handing it off to Rodor. 'I accept,' she said, her voice low enough that only Vidar and Rodor were likely to hear her. 'But we never agreed to children.'

Now that the ceremony was finished he'd relaxed, and he even smiled at her when she said that. 'I'm looking forward to the challenge, my lady.'

They were well and truly wed now.

Author Note

Vidar's story brings to a close the books I've planned in the Viking Warriors series. I've had so much fun exploring the world of Jarl Hegard's sons, and their journeys to find love in the unforgiving Viking Age. Each book has meant so much to me, but I am especially happy to bring Vidar's story to you.

We first met Vidar in *Enslaved by the Viking*, when he was a young teenager working on his older brother's ship. We saw him again when he played reluctant nurse to his ailing and grumpy half-brother in *One Night with the Viking*. Now, Vidar has shrugged off the weight of his overbearing brothers and has come into his own with his very own love story.

However, his journey is anything but what he wants it to be. He's been saddled yet again with another responsibility that he doesn't want: a wife. No longer free to roam the seas, he must take up the responsibility of his wife and her ancestral estate whether he wants them or not. He's in for a surprise—because Gwendolyn isn't in the market for a husband any more than Vidar is for a wife. When these two clash, no one is safe!

I hope you enjoy Gwendolyn and Vidar's story. Please find me on Facebook if you'd like to chat about it (Facebook.com/harperstgeorge). Thank you so much for reading.